Birds in a Gilded Cage

Birds in a Gilded Cage

Judith Glover

Hodder & Stoughton

LONDON SYDNEY AUCKLAND TORONTO

British Library Cataloguing in Publication Data

Glover, Judith
    Birds in a gilded cage.
    I. Title
    823'.914[F]   PR6057.L64
    ISBN 0 340 38783 5

33-34 Alfred Place, London WC1E 7DP. Printed in Great Britain for Hodder &
Stoughton Limited, Mill Road, Dunton Green, Sevenoaks, Kent by Biddles
Ltd.,
Guildford and Kings Lynn. Photoset by Chippendale Type, Otley, West
Yorkshire.
Hodder & Stoughton Editorial Office: 47 Bedford Square, London WC1B 3DP.

She's only a bird in a gilded cage,
A beautiful sight to see;
You may think she's happy and free from care,
She's not, tho' she seems to be. . .

A Bird in a Gilded Cage,
words by Arthur J. Lamb,
music by Harry von Tilzer.

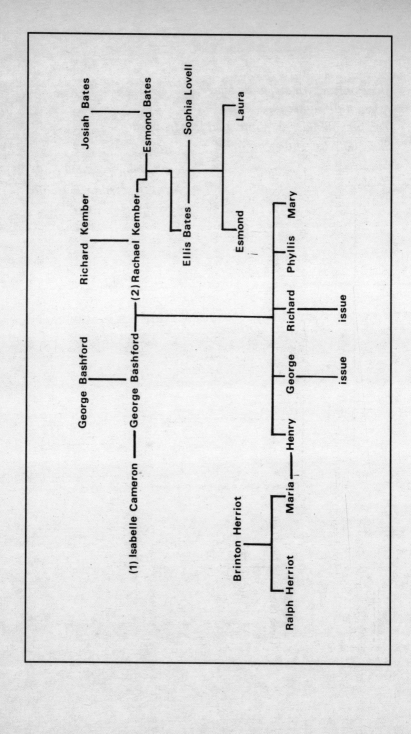

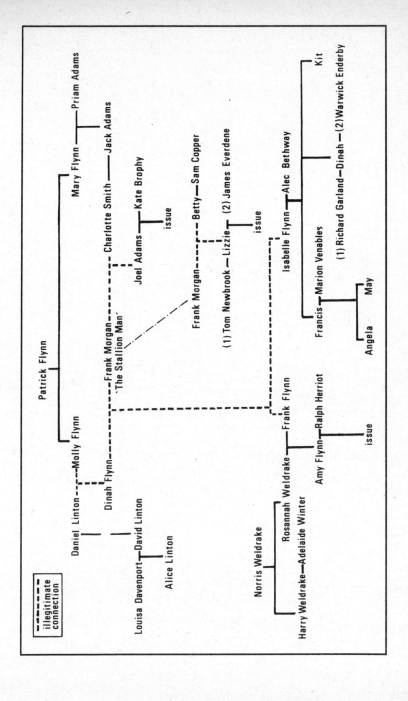

1

"If I have to play the Dead March from Saul many more times, I can't help it, I shall scream aloud," Dinah Garland declared, allowing the lid of the theatre piano to drop with a decisively loud bang.

She pushed back her stool and got up.

"I mean, it's been twice a night for a week now. Every performance the same. And matinées, too. There's a limit to the novelty of watching motion pictures of a funeral, surely."

"Not *a* funeral," her companion reminded her, putting away his violin into its case. "Not just any old funeral. Consider who we have for star turn. None less than King Edward the Seventh himself – and you can't go better than that. *And* supported by a cast of hundreds."

"Oh, hardly hundreds, Algie. They'd never have got them all on to the news-reel."

The young man returned her smile. "Well, dozens, then. But what dozens! All of 'em hand-picked for quality performance. Kaisers, kings, archdukes, peers, princes of the realm, prelates, politicians . . . and one small dog. Jolly nice touch that, don't you think, getting in the dog?"

"Our patrons seem to like it."

"Not half they do! No sooner does the sub-title appear on the screen than the whole house falls a-sighing."

Turning himself in a dramatic manner, Algie Langton-Smythe threw out an arm and in solemn tones announced to the emptied auditorium of the Electric Picture Theatre – "His late Majesty's faithful terrier Caesar, grieving for his master as he follows behind the gun carriage."

"Was there really a dog in the procession?" Casting her fellow player a look, Dinah leaned across to pick up her hat from the top of the piano.

"Must have been. Else what was it doing on the news-reel

9

film?" He moved round to face her again. "The camera can hardly record what wasn't there in the first place, can it?"

She gave a doubting little shake of the head, and glanced past him up at the blank square of the muslin screen. The lights had been doused now, and in the dimness its taut flat surface, powdered over with a coating of aluminium dust, shone with a ghostly luminescence in the black-lined alcove above the stage. The Electric Picture Theatre had been opened here in Lewes only two years ago, in 1908, and prided itself greatly on the innovation of American-made kinematographic equipment and concealed projection. The fixed red-plush seating was all new, too; and only the arrangement of stalls, dress circle and upper gallery betrayed the building's origins as a former Sussex music hall.

Algie folded his music stand and propped it behind the piano. Then, taking his blazer jacket from the back of his chair, draped it casually about his shoulders before moving the chair out of the way against the wall. Though grown to a man's full height, his round, snub-nosed features gave him very much the look of a boy still, his skin peppered with freckles and his gingery-fair hair slicked flat except where it sprang up in a defiant tuft from the crown of his head.

He had been employed here as a music accompanist for just over three months now, since the end of February, playing violin to Dinah Garland's piano, and despite the ten-year difference of age, already there had developed between the couple an easy, friendly relationship which yet respected the other's privacy. All that Dinah knew of Algie Langton-Smythe was that he was an Oxford college graduate of good family background, lodging in straitened circumstances away from home; and all that he knew of her was that she was a widow, her husband killed in the Boer War, and that she lived alone at Southwood Place, the house until recently shared with her now-deceased mother-in-law.

She was also, Algie had not been slow to acknowledge to himself, a deuced fine figure of a woman, the type on whom maturity bestows an assured loveliness; and it had not surprised him in the least to discover that she'd attracted a number of gentlemen admirers from among those who regularly patronised the picture theatre.

"Am I allowed to walk you home this evening?" he offered nonchalantly, watching while she secured her fashionably large hat, embellished with tulle and plumy feathers, on top of her upswept auburn hair.

Dinah gave him a quick smile from beneath the wide brim. Then, removing the pearl-headed hat pin gripped in her teeth, answered, "No, that's all right, Algie. I've already got company."

"No need to ask who, I suppose?"

She smiled again, and shook her head.

It had been just a few months before young Algie appeared on the scene to eke out an impecunious livelihood as violin accompanist, that Dinah Garland had first made the acquaintance of the Enderby brothers. To be more precise, that of Warwick Enderby, the oldest of the three.

In common with many such houses, the Electric Picture Theatre was equipped with 'morality lights', whose diffused amber or rose-tinted illumination during performances prohibited members of the audience from using the darkness as a cover for activity. Without detracting from the clarity of the motion pictures showing on the projection screen, this low lighting was sufficient for the management to keep a watchful eye upon its patrons: not only amorous couples, but also petty thieves and those who might become so roused by the reality of a good dramatic story that they vented their feelings upon the villain by pelting the screen with whatever lay to hand.

From her vantage point at the piano in what had formerly been the old theatre pit, Dinah had a good view of those in the first few rows of seats; and when not watching the subtitles for the cue to play, was inclined to let her gaze wander to the audience. So it was that she could not help noticing one evening a stranger sitting almost at the end of the first row, whose attention seemed clearly far more taken by the theatre's pianist than by the black-and-white celluloid charms of the actress above on the screen. In the dull glow of the wall lights, Dinah had difficulty in distinguishing the man's features, but there was no mistaking his interest in

11

her: even the manager had remarked upon it during the short interval while the film reels were being changed.

"He'll know you again when he sees you, won't he?" he'd said with a jerk of the head. "What's the betting he'll be back tomorrow night?"

The guess was right. The same stranger was in the same seat the following evening. And the evening after that; though for all the notice he took of the flickering images overhead, he might just as well have saved himself the trouble of spending sixpence to come in, Dinah thought.

On the fourth evening, however, his place was empty, and she had felt a curious sense of anti-climax at the absence; so much so that when he re-appeared again on the next night she permitted herself a little smile in response to his cheery wave of greeting.

It had been after the matinée performance the following Wednesday afternoon that the pair of them had first spoken. Dinah was putting away her music when a current of air from the open fire escape door beside the stage had blown the top sheet of paper across into the aisle, and before she could move from behind the piano to retrieve it, her admirer had come quickly forward to catch it up and bring it back.

At this close distance it was impossible not to be aware how good-looking he was, and she had experienced a momentary frisson of pleasure as his fingers – whether by accident or purpose – brushed against hers as he handed her the sheet.

"My name is Warwick Enderby," he said without preamble. "I know yours already. It's Dinah, isn't it."

Taken aback by such a bold approach, she had felt the colour rush to her cheeks.

"I took the liberty of asking the doorman," he went on, sparing her the need to question. His tone of voice held a hint of drollery in it, reflected by the expression of humour in the dark blue eyes. "I hope you don't mind?"

She shrugged and looked about her, not knowing quite how to respond but thinking to herself that his behaviour was, to say the least, unmannerly. "You're free to ask if you wish, I suppose."

Then, turning away and pretending to busy herself putting

12

the sheets into her music case, she'd forced herself after a moment to go on in a matter-of-fact way, "And what else have you been finding out about me?"

The answer came without any hesitation. "That you're a widow."

She made no reply to that; and after a pause, he added, "I wouldn't have presumed to make your acquaintance otherwise, Mrs Garland."

"Indeed?" She'd given a little laugh, astonished at such breath-takingly frank directness and the self-assured manner in which it was delivered.

"Indeed." Warwick Enderby smiled, disclosing good firm teeth beneath the neatly-clipped moustache.

"And anything more?"

"Only that you are unattached. As a gentleman, I felt it my duty to ascertain the fact before making myself known to you."

"Well – really!" Sudden sharp indignation replaced the astonishment. This was going too far. Turning abruptly away from him, Dinah had made to move out into the aisle.

His hand on her arm detained her.

"I'm sorry. That was clumsily said. Don't be angry with me."

She brushed the hand aside.

Chaffing her a little, he went on, "I should have guessed you'd have a temper with that wonderful fiery hair of yours. I can almost see the sparks flying. Look – let me make amends, won't you? Let me invite you to have tea with me this afternoon? There's a place in Station Road where they serve the most superb cream cakes. What's it called, can you remind me? Something exotic, like Scarlatti's."

"Desatti's," she corrected him coolly.

"Of course. Desatti's. Good! You don't need to be back again till seven for the evening performance. That leaves us plenty of time to get to know one another better."

"And what if I say no, Mr Enderby?"

"But you won't, will you?"

"I've a very good mind to."

13

"Then I must warn you, Mrs Garland – I'm not the sort of fellow who takes no for an answer."

Why had she accepted his invitation that day last winter? Dinah couldn't possibly say for sure. She might just as easily have refused; and probably never seen him again. It was really quite ridiculous, the way he had made his attraction so blatantly obvious from the start, marching boldly up without any encouragement beyond a smile, expecting her to be swept off her feet by his charm, his debonair good looks, his smoothly self-confident attitude towards life and the world in general.

Yet swept off her feet she had been, right from the very beginning.

Oh, it was easy for others to criticise and say she was acting like a silly young girl, that she ought to know better at her age than go letting herself become infatuated with some stranger. Yes, it was so easy for them to warn her to be careful, warn her that she could find herself in the kind of situation where she'd be hurt, that she'd been too long without Richard to remember . . . remember what? The happiness of knowing herself cherished and wanted by the man she loved? The joy of feeling every fibre of her being alive again?

Much of this well-meant criticism had come from one source: her friends the Moores. Dinah had known Stephen and his sister Jessie since the time of her marriage, when she'd left the childhood sanctuary of her parents' vicarage at Eastbourne to come to live here in Lewes as Lieutenant Richard Garland's wife. And it had been to Stephen and Jessie that she'd turned in her grief when Richard died of typhoid in the epidemic which had ravaged Bloemfontein in 1900.

They had been married so briefly, no more than five months; and in that short time had lived together as man and wife for only three weeks before his regiment had embarked for the war in South Africa.

She had never seen him again, not even had the solace of a grave, for the strong young body which she'd loved so much had been buried far away in foreign earth, not brought back

14

as she'd wanted for interment in the family vault at All Souls Church in Lewes. He had been the last of the Garlands, and it was her mother-in-law's one complaint against Dinah that she had failed to conceive a child before Richard went away.

Stephen and Jessie Moore had been wonderful, the truest and kindest of friends; but they had no right now to try to turn her against Warwick Enderby with their well-intentioned dagger-thrust comments and cautious moralising. It was unfair, and unworthy: there had been no other man in her life since Richard's death. Friends, acquaintances, yes; but no close companion, certainly no lover. Not since the first sharp grief of loss had faded, leaving an emptiness in her heart where she had learned to live with sadness, not once had Dinah felt the inclination to think of re-marriage – even had there been opportunity, which there never was, for the senior Mrs Garland's failing health had required constant nursing during the final years the two widows shared alone together at the family house in Lewes.

When in the winter of 1907 her mother-in-law died, Dinah had found herself the sole beneficiary of the estate: at the age of thirty-one regarded by society as set up for life with her own property and a handsome annuity to supplement her Army widow's pension. It had, therefore, surprised and even alarmed her circle of acquaintances when she'd applied the following year for the vacant position of piano accompanist at the newly-opened Electric Picture Theatre in the high street.

What on earth did she think she was doing, they'd cried, to take it into her head to go out and earn a living – and what a living! – when she had no need to do any such thing?

Dinah's answer had given no comfort at all. She hated idleness, she told them candidly; hated having nothing to do, no occupation or distraction but to sit about sipping tea in drawing rooms, seeing the same faces, the same places, making the same small-town talk day after dreary day. Moreover, she was a good pianist – no concert performer, perhaps, but competent enough – and there was something about the novelty of moving-picture entertainment which quite fascinated her. That 'job vacant' advertisement in the

Sussex Express represented freedom, adventure, an opportunity to combine talent with interest and give her a practical diversion from the tedium of the endless inactivity of middle-class widowhood.

"But your family – how do they regard your working in a picture house?" Warwick had asked her early in their relationship, one day in January when they'd come as usual for afternoon tea at Desatti's. "It somehow doesn't quite fit the usual image of the parson's daughter, does it?"

"What image? There's no such thing any more, surely?" Dinah demanded of him in return, laughing. She was in a vivacious mood, wearing the new hat bought after their first meeting, a stylish 'Merry Widow' model with mauve plumes whose colour matched the amethyst brooch at the throat of her high-necked cream lace blouse. "Let me remind you, this is the era of the female suffrage movement."

"Dear me, that sounds suspiciously as though you're a sympathiser."

"Indeed I am! I mean, take my own case. Is it fair that I should own property, employ servants, pay rates and taxes – yet simply because I'm a woman be denied the right to decide who shall represent my interests in Parliament?"

"Haven't you enough already?" There was a flicker of something in her companion's tone, too quick to be registered, before the humour reasserted itself. "The next thing we'd know, by jove, you'd be clamouring for women to stand as politicians. No, Dinah, no – you ladies are quite dangerous enough without being given the vote."

"We'll see. The fight's only just started."

She glanced back at him, smiling, aware of the look of absorption in the handsome face opposite and warming herself in the apparent fondness she believed she could read there; and she remembered later being conscious of a sudden sense of release, as though she were no longer walking hand in hand with a ghost from the past.

"But to answer your question, about my family – no, they've raised no objection to the way I earn a living. Ours is a slightly unusual household in that respect. My mother is an artist, you see – her work is exhibited at one of the London galleries. And my younger brother Kit paints too, though only as a hobby – "

"Kit, he's the one you told me is serving with the Army?" Warwick interrupted to ask.

"No, th<u>a</u>t's my other brother, Francis. Kit has followed in Father's footsteps and entered the ministry. He's curate of a parish at Tunbridge Wells, where there's an enclave of amateur artists to indulge his daubing."

"And Francis?"

"Oh, Francis . . . well . . . " Dinah made an off-hand little gesture and looked about the busy, low-ceilinged tea room. "Every family has its black sheep, I suppose. Francis is ours. I'm the only one who ever sees much of him, and I dare say that's only because his regiment's quartered so near."

"The barracks at Southover."

She nodded. "The Sussex Artillery. My husband's regiment."

There had been no awkwardness when she said that: it was becoming easier to speak of Richard now without feeling the old sadness overwhelm her.

"My brother introduced us, you know," she went on. "Richard was a lieutenant in his company."

"Is that so? They served together in South Africa?"

"Yes. Would you – " she indicated the empty cups – "would you care for more tea? There's still some in the pot."

While it was poured, Warwick lit himself a cigarette from the monogrammed silver case he carried. Then, almost carelessly, he asked, "Why is your brother Francis viewed as such a scapegrace?"

"I suppose . . . well, I suppose it's because he doesn't see eye to eye with Father and Kit about some things. Different lives, different ways . . . you know how it is."

Natural reticence had kept her from telling the truth: that Captain Francis Bethway had severed himself from his family's affection by the flagrancy of his conduct towards his wife, whose quiet forbearance in the face of his numerous adulteries was something to be marvelled at.

Deflecting the subject, she said lightly, "Tell me, are there no black sheep among the Enderbys?"

"Grey ones, perhaps. In wolf's clothing."

17

"Oh?"

A shrugged smile. "What titled family doesn't have its share?"

But again there had been that momentary change of tone, as though the lightness of his words masked something deeper.

Dinah put down her cup and pushed it aside. The tea room's violinist had just started playing, a melancholy-faced Italian youth who was one of the proprietor's sons. As the muted strains of Puccini filtered across through the buzz of voices at the crowded tables, she turned to listen for a moment or two before looking again at her companion.

"You know, you've told me nothing about your family."

"That sounds like an accusation."

"Well, it's the truth. A few hints here and there, that's all. You've mentioned your brothers Guy and Neville, but for all else I know about you, you might be Warwick Buckland the actor, masquerading under an assumed name."

"Do I look like Warwick Buckland?" he asked, amused.

Dinah put her head to one side and pretended to examine him critically. Mr Buckland was one of the leading stars of the Cecil Hepworth acting company, and a much-idolised performer in romantic picture films. There *was* some slight resemblance: the same broad-shouldered build and thick dark hair, with a slim moustache on the upper lip to complete the well-groomed appearance. In fact, when Dinah had first learned Warwick Enderby's name she had remarked to herself on the similarity.

"A little," she agreed at last, with a smile. "Though I think Mr Buckland is rather more handsome."

She'd been about to add something further to this raillery when her attention was distracted by the sight of a couple who had just at that moment come into the tea room; and starting up, she exclaimed, "Oh, look – there are the Moores! You remember I spoke of them? I must introduce you, they've been simply dying to meet you." Then, with a teasing laugh – "Though I should warn you , Stephen's your greatest rival."

Half-rising to her feet, she waved across to the pair and after a few moments succeeded in catching the eye of Jessie

18

Moore, a young woman in a dark green tailored costume and smart veiled hat. With a responsive wave of recognition, Jessie indicated Dinah's table to her brother and the two at once began making their way between the chairs and brass-potted palms towards them.

As they approached, Warwick Enderby stubbed his cigarette into the ash-tray, and with noticeable deliberation took out his pocket watch and consulted it before getting slowly up from the table.

"Unfortunately I'm just about to leave," he apologised when the introductions had been made. "Frightfully sorry and all that."

"But you don't need to dash away so soon, surely?" Dinah objected.

He blew her a kiss, and by way of reply said, "See you Sunday afternoon."

"I thought you'd arranged to see *us* on Sunday afternoon, my dear?" Stephen Moore put in, a frown of surprise wiping the pleasure from his affable features. "We were taking a ride in the carriage to the alms cottages at Chailey Mill."

"I'm afraid not, sir," Warwick answered for her, smoothly. "Mrs Garland has already agreed to join *me*, for a spin out in my motor car. To Brighton, as it happens."

There was a short pause. Stephen looked down at Dinah. "Is this true?"

Again, it was Warwick who took it upon himself to answer; but hardly had he got out a word before there came a terse interruption.

"I trust, sir, you will be courteous enough to permit Mrs Garland to speak for herself. After all, it was with her that our plans were made." The other's tone was now noticeably cool. "Dinah – ?"

She glanced up with a quick, awkward smile. "I'm sorry, Stephen. How ill-mannered it must seem . . . but the temptation to accept Warwick's invitation was simply too much. I've never been out before in a motor car, so it was quite impossible to say no. *Would* you mind so very greatly, you and Jessie, if we were to postpone Chailey until another time? The Sunday after, perhaps?"

The response was a pained shake of the head.

"The arrangements have already been made. The old folk are expecting us, Dinah. Surely it can't have slipped your memory that the three of us were especially invited to a celebration afternoon tea with them all in the dining hall? We can't disappoint them – "

"My brother takes a great interest in the welfare of the aged poor, Mr Enderby," Jessie Moore came in assertively, as though defying argument. "The alms cottages at Chailey are among his concerns."

There was a slight raising of one eyebrow as Warwick considered this information; then, giving one of his most charming smiles, he responded blandly, "But surely, ma'am, Mr Moore is capable of pursuing his philanthropic hobbies without requiring Mrs Garland's presence to witness them? I would have thought the dear lady had already made herself sufficiently clear on the matter. Quite simply, she has declined the pleasure of your brother's company in favour of mine. And to be honest, who can wonder at it, given the choice?"

"May I know what choice is that, sir?" Stephen Moore's expression was set like stone.

"Why, sir, the choice between dull duty and a bit of jolly excitement. I ask you, what young lady of any spirit would prefer to suffer the meagre fare of a charity house at Chailey when she might be enjoying champagne and oysters at Brighton?"

2

"Honestly, Dinah, what can you be thinking of? You've scarcely known the fellow above five minutes, yet here you are as besotted with him as some naive convent schoolgirl."

Throwing up her hands in exasperation, Jessie Moore turned to look towards her brother, who had moved away across the lawn at Southwood Place to admire the colourful display of midsummer blooms against the far wall.

"Stephen!" she called out, vexed by this apparent lack of interest in the ever-pressing matter of Dinah's relationship with Warwick Enderby. "Stephen, do come back here and sit down and stop wandering off among the flowers. I need your support."

"You seem to be doing rather well without it," Dinah observed idly, lying back among the cushions of the garden hammock, eyes half-closed against the glitter of sunlight through the shifting leaves of willow forming a green canopy overhead. "Besides, perhaps Stephen is not quite so vehemently preoccupied with poor Warwick as you."

"Well, he jolly well should be," Jessie retorted crossly. "If he'd had any sense, he'd have asked you to marry him years ago, instead of letting things drift on in such an aimless fashion."

She picked up her glass of barley water from the circular wooden table beside her chair and took a sip from it.

"I mean, it's so ridiculous, the whole affair. Stephen *wants* to marry you."

"Do you, Stephen?" Dinah shifted her head on the cushions as he came strolling slowly back across the lawn. "Do you really want to marry me?"

"My sister has this obsessional interest in the hatchings, matchings and dispatchings of all around her," Stephen observed lightly, a smile in his warm brown eyes. "One

21

would have thought the fact that she's so soon to be married herself might've blunted her appetite. But, alas, not."

He leaned down to refill his own glass from the jug of barley water.

"If anything, imminent wedlock has whetted her zeal even more. I see I shall be forced to have a word with Esmond."

This was a reference to Esmond Bates, a fellow solicitor, to whom Jessie had become engaged the previous spring. Though both men worked for the same legal firm, Esmond's office was some distance from Lewes, in the Wealden market town of Weatherfield: it had been Dinah who'd effected the social introduction between them all, her family having been connected with the Bateses for many years.

"If anyone is to have a word with Esmond, it shall be I," Jessie declared roundly, "to see whether *he* cannot persuade Dinah of the folly of this absurd dalliance."

"Dinah's friendships are her own affair – even if this may not be the wisest one she has ever had."

"But the man's a perfect stranger!"

"Most people may be counted strangers to begin with until one gets to know them as friends," her brother said patiently.

"Agreed, but there is no need to fall in love with them."

"Are you in love with Mr Enderby, Dinah?" Stephen replaced his glass on the table, glancing down at her over his shoulder, the shadow of leaves hiding any expression on his face.

She hesitated a few moments before making her answer; then turned her head away to look across the sun-filled garden and said quietly, "I hardly know. But . . . yes, I suppose it must be love."

"There, you see!" Jessie exclaimed. "What did I tell you? She's behaving like some silly schoolgirl. Really, Dinah, how can you? The fellow's not even a gentleman."

"Nonsense, of course Warwick's a gentleman." The other raised herself on one elbow. "You're only saying that because he took the liberty of introducing himself. His family background is impeccable, as you very well know. His uncle is Lord Claverley – "

"Do we have a copy of Burke's to hand?"

The jibe was ignored. "And the family seat is at Whitmore Reans in Staffordshire – where Warwick and his brothers would have been raised were it not for the fact that their mother married against the late Earl's wishes."

"Ah, yes." Jessie uttered a laugh of disbelief. "What was the story? That the father was a classical actor whose Romeo was played to such perfection that the young lady was persuaded to elope with him and live for ever after as his Juliet in drearest Middlesex?"

"The facts are very likely. It's happened before, you know."

"Oh, indeed it has. And now the noble son is reduced to living on his uppers in a locality like Star Street."

"Warwick is not on his uppers! Why are you so spiteful towards him? His appearance is immaculate – "

"He has moth-holes in the lapels of his jacket," Jessie interrupted tartly, "his shoes are scuffed at the heel and his nails are badly manicured." Always beautifully turned out herself, she had a sharp eye for these little details. "If you want my opinion, my dear, the fellow is nothing but a fortune-hunter, and you are being a very gullible bait."

Dinah threw herself back again among the hammock cushions and cast Stephen Moore a look of troubled exasperation. Much as she liked his sister, this present abrasive attitude was becoming very wearing. They were so unalike, these two Moores: Jessie out-spoken and demonstrative, inclined at times to be somewhat insensitive of the feelings of those close to her, yet always warmly protective on their behalf; her brother quieter, gentler, altogether a more discreet individual who said little but observed much. Only in appearance did the pair share any similarity, having the well-shaped features and robust colouring which marked them as being of good Sussex gentry stock.

Returning Dinah's look, Stephen sketched a shrug of sympathy and said, "You mustn't mind my sister too much. She speaks from fond concern of you, that's all. As I do. We've been your friends for so long, it's natural we should both be suspicious of any outsider who seems to be casting a sudden influence."

"Not so very sudden, surely. I've known Warwick quite

23

six months now. And see him almost every day, except at weekends when he's out of town."

"Yes, where does he go to spend his weekends?" Jessie came in again.

"I don't know. I don't enquire."

"And he never says?"

A pause. "Not really, no."

"Odd, don't you think? He's usually so remarkably forthcoming about his business."

"All the more reason to be entitled to his occasional privacy. Anyway, there's no great mystery involved. I've an idea he visits his widowed father. Does that satisfy you?"

Jessie made a face. "You're only saying that. You don't know for sure. Why is it he never invites you to go visiting with him?"

"Why should he?"

"Well, if he's about to propose marriage, as you seem to hope – "

"Oh . . . this is becoming quite ridiculous!" Dinah sat up again and swinging herself from the hammock, got to her feet, her face colouring.

"Well?" the other challenged, and there was an undernote of something like anger in her tone. "It's true, isn't it? It is what you hope? You'd marry Warwick Enderby like a shot, and he knows it. That's why he's biding his time, I'll swear. He's positively enjoying playing you in like a fish on a line."

Warwick threw back his head and gave a shout of laughter. "And what did you have to say to that?"

"What could I say?"

Dinah looked up at him. To judge by his expression, Jessie Moore's forthright opinion had caused him no end of amusement.

She turned away again, vastly relieved by this humorous reaction, letting her eyes wander across the green and gold counterpane pattern of the fields below them on the slope of the Downs. All last night she'd lain awake wrestling with the decision whether to repeat yesterday's conversation or not, so unsure of herself was she still in this relationship, and so

24

anxious to avoid anything which might put at risk Warwick's interest in her.

She had been so long a widow that she'd all but forgotten the intricate *pas de deux* of romantic involvement; and being a gentleman born and bred, he was no doubt waiting for some positive sign of encouragement before venturing to deepen the bonds of amity between them. Well, Jessie's acid comment seemed as good a test as any. Surely, Dinah had argued with herself in the light of this morning's dawn, surely she knew him sufficiently well after all these months to judge the time now ripe for their relationship to advance beyond mere amity into something warmer, for they had gone as far as two people might before they crossed from friendship into courtship.

The division was a fine one, and rigidly adhered to in the social circles in which they both moved. A lady might allow a gentleman to touch her waist, for instance, but only in public, in order to guide or assist her; he was permitted to kiss her hand if she were wearing gloves, though not otherwise, for then the gesture was open to a more intimate interpretation; and he might visit her at her house in company, but never alone, and certainly never without invitation.

Only once had Warwick Enderby transgressed this unwritten code of conduct, when he called upon Dinah one day at Southwood Place quite unexpectedly, and not wishing to appear distant by turning him away, she had asked him inside and even shown him over the downstairs reception rooms before entertaining him to tea in the summer house. He had not committed the error a second time.

"What could I say?" she repeated, laughing with him. "It was quite awful of Jessie, to come out with a thing like that. I wonder sometimes whether she isn't just a little jealous of you, for stealing my company as much as you do."

Warwick pushed aside the wicker hamper and stretched himself out on the travelling rug, hands clasped behind his head, eyes squinting against the smoke from the cigarette between his lips. He had promised a picnic expedition in his motor car for this afternoon; but at the last moment the 'Torpedo' had apparently refused to start, and he'd

25

suggested instead that they take an omnibus to Alciston and walk from there a short way up into the Downs.

"My dear, it may well be you she's jealous of," he observed, removing the cigarette and lazily exhaling a blue cloud as he spoke. "I've been too neglectful, perhaps. I mean, an extraordinarily handsome chap like me . . . she's head over heels in love, and I've never even noticed." There was an exaggerated sigh, and then a smile. "Poor Jessie."

"What nonsense you do talk." Leaning back to rest herself on one elbow, her yellow silk parasol shading her face from the glare of the sun, Dinah looked fondly across at her companion.

"Nonsense, did you say? Are you suggesting, ma'am, that my good looks are not irresistibly attractive to you ladies?"

"Don't tease so. That wasn't at all what I meant. You know very well I was referring to Jessie's attitude towards – "

"Damn it, must we talk so much of the Moores all the time?"

Suddenly the humorous mood was gone. Sitting up, Warwick threw aside the half-smoked cigarette. The abrupt alteration in his manner was matched by a shift of expression on his face, giving those same good looks a boyish scowl.

There was a moment or two's silence, and when he spoke again his voice sounded flat and strained.

"The truth is, they resent me, the pair of them. No, don't try denying it, please. They've made it perfectly plain from the start that they regard me as some kind of cuckoo in their nest. Good lord, anyone would think they actually owned you, the way they've closed ranks against me."

"Now you *are* talking nonsense!"

"Am I? Oh, I admire your loyalty, Dinah my dear. But I wish you'd give a little of it to me, instead of defending your precious friends as you do. It makes me feel – well, such an outsider still, as though I were really nothing more to you than a temporary amusement."

The accusation stung her. "Believe me, you are very much more than that."

"Am I?" he asked again, turning his head away so that the words were muffled; and there was something so dejected in the gesture that it touched her.

26

"How am I to convince you?"

He glanced round at her again; then, leaning forward to clasp his arms about his bent knees, shrugged and said a little awkwardly, "We've never discussed how we feel towards each other, have we? People of our class are expected not to do that sort of thing . . . not expected to have emotions, far less show them. Frightfully infra dig. and all that. Smacks of a lack of self-control. Rather lets the side down."

"I'd have thought that's a view that's going out of fashion these days," Dinah answered quietly.

"You really think so?"

She nodded. "We're all human, whatever rank of society we happen to be born into. It's only breeding and background that sets us apart. But when all's said and done, we each of us share precisely the same needs, and hopes, and response to one another, the same ability to feel love, or pain, or pleasure. A silver spoon in the mouth is no guarantee of happiness. You know, I've always felt there's something a little to be envied in the manner in which two young shop-workers, for instance, can walk hand-in-hand on the street together – even embrace – for everyone to see, yet no one thinks it in the least extraordinary. But if you or I or any other of our class were to express our affections as openly and honestly – why, such behaviour would be attacked as nothing short of indecency!"

She paused; then, warming to her argument, began again, "Society is so reactionary still. Here we are in 1910, at the beginning of the twentieth century, yet people cling on to outworn Victorian attitudes. They deliberately blind themselves to the fact that with George the Fifth we're not only at the start of a new reign, but a new era, a new period of advancement. Suddenly so much seems possible! You know the slogan that everyone's repeating just now – 'every day, in every way, I'm growing better and better' – well, that's absolutely true. Every day, in every way, *everything's* growing better and better – our standard of living, our children's health, the prospects for women's achievement – "

She stopped abruptly in mid-sentence. Warwick had begun laughing again.

27

Rolling over on the rug so that he was resting beside her, supporting himself on one elbow, he put out a hand and brushed the back of his fingers lightly down the smooth bare skin of her forearm. It was the first time he'd touched her so intimately, and Dinah felt her heart give a sudden thump and its beat start to quicken.

"Dearest Dinah," he said, the smile warming his dark blue eyes in a way she'd always found so very attractive. "Dearest, dearest Dinah. You are a constant delight to me, did you know that? A delight and an amazement."

She returned the smile hesitantly, but kept silent, looking down at the strong, square hand which was now covering hers so that their fingers intertwined.

There was a pause; then, his voice quietly serious again, Warwick went on, "You have quite utterly bewitched me. My life has hardly been my own since that first moment I set eyes on you. I thought then what a deuced attractive woman you were . . . and I think so still, only more . . . that you are quite the most beautiful creature and there is not another to match you anywhere. You mustn't blame me, my sweet, if I'm a little in love with you. Tell me, please . . . you don't mind?"

Not knowing how to answer this, she shook her head and continued looking down, afraid that her expression might betray the confusion of her own feelings.

He kneeled up again, releasing her hand, and sat back on his heels; and for a little while remained like that, saying nothing, merely gazing intently at her downcast profile.

This was the kind of moment, Dinah told herself, that memories are made of: this delicious expectancy. She closed her eyes, and the waiting seconds seemed filled with the infinite peace of the Downs all around, their stillness broken only by the soft bleat of sheep in distant folds and the sough of a light breeze carried inland from the Channel, bringing a tang of salt to the fragrance of thyme and wild ling.

"Would you – " Warwick began, the words hardly more than a whisper so close against her cheek that she could feel his breath warm her skin, "would you be awfully offended if I were to kiss you?"

Again she made no response, only raised her mouth to his

in slow acceptance; and for the first time since her husband's farewell embrace so long ago, knew the persuasive tenderness of a lover's lips.

Had the years between so faded remembrance, she wondered when finally he drew away from her – had they so dulled her senses with their widow's chastity that she'd forgotten the responses of her own body? She could not recall Richard's kisses ever leaving her feeling quite as wonderfully weak as she did at this moment, nor the touch of his mouth ever sending such a sweet throb of pleasure singing through every nerve. But Richard, poor Richard – may God forgive her – for all that he was her husband, had been so young, so inexperienced, scarcely more than a boy still; whereas Warwick Enderby . . .

She opened her eyes again and smiled, longing for him to take her once more in his arms, prevented only by modesty from being the first to invite further intimacy.

The smile faded slowly from the generous mouth. As though some second thought were now causing him to regret the warmth of his behaviour, Warwick turned away instead of responding to her invitation and began rummaging in his blazer jacket pocket for his cigarettes, all his lover's boldness changed of a sudden to awkwardness.

This abrupt transition made Dinah too feel rather awkward; and it was as much to cover her slight embarrassment as for the sake of something to say that she indicated the yellow Turkish Abdulla packet he'd just opened and asked lightly, "What's become of your silver case? You've not mislaid it, have you?"

He made no immediate answer, seeming more occupied in searching for his matches; and having found the box, took one out and struck it, cupping it in his palm to light his cigarette.

Then, in a casual manner and still looking away, he replied, "No, I haven't mislaid it."

He blew out the match; and after another deliberate pause, added, "To tell the truth, my dear, I've had to pop it."

Unfamiliar with this expression, she repeated it after him, blankly.

"You know, run it along to the pop-shop." As Warwick said this, there was a quick glance over his shoulder to gauge her reaction. "Pop goes the weasel? Remember the old rhyme about pawnbrokers?"

"Pawn – ? Heavens above – you need *their* services? Why?"

"Why do you think, my darling? They provide a chap with ready money."

Dinah's expression revealed her perplexity. She had been led to understand that the three Enderby brothers had ample means of support, each receiving a sizeable income in the form of a monthly allowance from their late mother's estate.

Cautiously she asked, "And why should you require money . . . or is that being impertinent?"

He drew heavily on the cigarette, then threw back his head and forcibly blew the pungently-scented smoke out again. "Oh, it's all rather boring. You don't want to hear about it."

"Oh, but I do." Her tone grew more insistent. "You're not in trouble of any kind, are you?"

"Good lord, no! Let's not talk about it, there's a good girl."

"But why not?" This show of reluctance was now causing her real concern and she rushed on, "Only a while ago, Warwick, you were saying you loved me – surely you must trust me, too?"

"Of course I trust you, you little goose. It's just that the whole business is such a frightful bore." He brushed a fleck of grey ash from the knee of his flannel trousers; and after a moment continued, "If you really must know, a friend has rather gone and got himself into a tight corner and asked me to stand surety for him. I did the decent thing and agreed. Honour of the school at stake, and all that."

Now that he'd started talking about it, he grew more forthcoming. Shifting Dinah's parasol aside, he moved himself back close to her again and after a moment draped his arm about her waist.

"Well, dash it all, I could hardly do any less, could I? We were at Winchester together. And he's a first-rate chap. You'd like him no end. Name's Duncan Milne. Officer in the

30

Seaforth Highlanders. Brilliant future. Or did have, before he went and chucked it all away."

The information was produced in curious piecemeal fashion, as though the facts rather embarrassed him.

"I can't go into details of the case – all a bit hush-hush – but I stood him bail for quite a tidy amount. And now the fellow's gone and done a bunk, left the country or something. And I'm out of pocket – I mean, rather seriously out of pocket. Hence my cigarette case and other Enderby heirlooms finding their way to the pop-shop." There was a heavy sigh, followed by a shrug. "The Torpedo will have to go, too. Deuced nuisance, but there we are. It can't be helped."

"Why on earth haven't you told me any of this before?" Dinah's tone all too clearly betrayed how she felt. "Oh, Warwick, why? You know I'd have been only too ready to lend a hand in any way I could."

"The damsel rescuing the knight?" He gave a lopsided smile. "It's hardly the done thing, not when the pickle's of a fellow's own making."

"That depends upon circumstances. I don't see it's so terribly irregular that I should offer to make you a loan until you're able to repay me. Is the sum of money very great?"

"Three hundred pounds," he admitted candidly.

"As much as that?"

A nod. "Afraid so. It was a pretty serious business Duncan was involved in."

Now that her mind was made up, Dinah's resolve quickly took root. Not only was she eager to show herself able and willing to assist the man she was in love with, but also – and this pleased her quite as much – the very fact that she was in a position to offer such assistance would be a personal gesture for the cause of women's equality.

"I'll make an appointment with the bank first thing tomorrow," she said decisively. "If I were to authorise a draft on my account for the full amount, you could have it there and then in cash if you wished."

Warwick shook his head.

"You will!" she insisted, gripping the hand at her waist and pressing it warmly.

"Really, my darling, I'd much prefer you didn't go to such trouble. I can just about scrape along until next month, though I'm afraid it'll mean I shan't be able to entertain you very grandly."

"Now you're being stubborn. If it's a matter of pride – why, who's to know for heaven's sake whether I make you this loan or not?"

"I'd know." He cast her a look of doubt. "Besides, wouldn't it leave you . . . well, how shall I put it . . . stretched, yourself?"

She laughed at that. "I'm what is referred to as a woman of substance, don't you know. I'm perfectly sure I can afford to miss three hundred pounds for a while."

There was a pause. Then Warwick tossed away his cigarette.

"I'll say it again, Dinah – " his arm tightened about her – "you are a delight. An amazement. And I can't think what I've done to deserve you."

The old smile was back once more in his eyes as he leaned over and gently took her chin in his hand; and when he kissed her, the faintly exotic taste of smoke on his parted lips somehow added to the fresh sensation of pleasure she felt at the caress.

3

Captain Francis Alexander Henry Bethway, M.C., commanding officer no. 2 Battery, 1st Home Counties Brigade, formerly 1st Sussex Royal Garrison Artillery, squared his broad shoulders in front of the cheval-glass and looked back in admiration of the image presented in its surface.

Not bad, not bad at all, he thought, turning sideways to examine himself in profile, heels together, back straight, thumbs in line with the red trouser stripe of the dark blue Territorial Army uniform.

He swung back again to face the glass, straightening his leather Sam Browne belt so that its buckle was directly in line with the brass buttons on his single-breasted tunic.

"No, not bad at all," he remarked aloud to the handsome reflection opposite. The years might be marching on – he'd be thirty-eight in a few more months – but one would have to go a long way to find another who could hold a candle to him when it came to appearance. What matter that the thick dark hair, glossy with macassar oil, was flecked a little with grey at the temples: the body was still as lean, the shoulders as muscular, the stomach as flat, as those of any fellow full fifteen years his junior. And there wasn't an officer anywhere in the southern counties who could better him in performance on foot or on horseback – or in the bed of a willing woman.

These thoughts were interrupted by a sudden loud knock at the dressing-room door; and at the Captain's word of command it opened to admit the spare-framed figure of his batman, Corporal Walter Jackson, carrying a pair of boots whose gleaming leather bore testament to innumerable hours of elbow grease and dubbin.

"What d'you think, Jackson?" came the affable greeting in response to the other's smartly executed salute. "Damn' good fit, eh? Just look at the cut of those trousers."

"Yes, sir. Top-hole, sir."

The boots were conveyed across the small room to a panelled mahogany wardrobe which occupied almost the entire length of one wall and whose mirrored doors stood open to reveal in neatly serried rows the habiliments of officer and gentleman, from full dress, undress and mess kit to lounge suits, blazer jackets and flannels.

"Beggin' your pardon, though, sir – " the young batman straightened up from placing the pair of boots down on the floor rack. He had known his commanding officer long enough to risk expressing a personal opinion. "I don't care what anybody says, sir, the new T.A. uniform ain't a patch on the one we used to wear before."

He cast an eye towards the darkened recess of the wardrobe where there hung in solitary confinement among the usurping blue of the "Terriers" a single military outfit of grey Oxford cloth picked out in black on collar and cuff and trouser seam. This had been the uniform of the old volunteer militia, the Sussex Royal Garrison Artillery, which two years previously in 1908 had been absorbed with all other home territory volunteer units into the newly-created Territorial Army.

It was this one-time volunteer force which Captain Francis Bethway had entered as an officer-cadet in 1890, serving the regiment with distinction during the South African Campaign and being promoted to his present rank after the action at Itala in Zululand, in which his conspicuous bravery in getting through supplies of fresh ammunition to a position under heavy enemy fire had earned him the Military Cross.

Corporal Jackson had served under him during that action: a raw young soldier-boy thrust abruptly into the bloody conflict of war from the quiet Kentish fields of his father's farm, the cold metal of a Lee Enfield rifle obscenely alien to hands used to the smooth warm wood of a plough handle. He would remember all his life with gratitude how the Captain, recognising his fear without ever once referring to it, had taught the young recruit by his own example how to overcome the terror of those fire-edged nights of slaughter among the kopjes.

"I'd sort o' got used always to seein' you kitted out in the

34

old grey, sir," he went on somewhat mournfully, closing the wardrobe doors. "I suppose that's what it is, sir."

"A matter of adjusting to change, Jackson, that's all."

Francis Bethway viewed himself one last time in sidelong reflection; then moved away from the cheval-glass and began undoing the buckle of his belt to change out of uniform.

"Thank God we've been assigned a decent tailor."

"Not half, sir! That other chap didn't know a seam from a sow's elbow – mucked up no end o' good cloth."

"I'll say he did." Handing over the discarded belt, the Captain started on the buttons of his tunic. "What's the weather doing outside now? I wouldn't mind taking a ride on the Downs before dinner."

His batman directed a glance through the narrow sash window. The regimental officers' quarters were housed in what had formerly been a Sussex squire's imposing Georgian mansion set in countryside to the south of Lewes, but the charming rural aspect once to be had from its terraces was now obliterated by blocks of barrack buildings, reducing the outlook to a series of serrated roof-lines with here and there a glimpse of green Downland beyond.

"It was warm still when I came across the parade ground, sir." Jackson came forward to help him off with the tunic. "Wind's freshenin' a bit, though. We'll mebbe have a storm blow up afore nightfall."

The other dragged his collarless khaki shirt up over his head, revealing the naked strength of chest and torso, matted with dark hair. He made no further reference to the weather, but said instead, "Mrs Bethway received my message, did she? She's not expecting me at Southover tonight?"

"Yes, sir. She did, sir." The tunic was removed to a wooden hanger for brushing. "And no, sir. She's not." The shirt was put aside to be laundered.

"No point in leaving the camp so late. I'm on duty till ten."

"As you say, sir. Oh – Mrs Bethway asked you be told, sir, the little girls send their love to their father and hope he'll visit tomorrow."

"Yes. Yes, thank you, Jackson."

There was a long pause, as though the Captain were considering this request from his family; then he turned away and began unbuttoning his trousers, the sudden silence in the room in an odd way emphasising his lack of response.

It was not that he felt at all guilty towards Marion and their two daughters, he told himself irritably. They were not neglected: he saw them as often as his duties as an officer allowed, and provided them so far as he was able with every material comfort. They lived in a very nice privately rented house in the Southover district of Lewes – unlike the wives and children of other ranks who were accommodated in married quarters on the camp among the noise and roughness of barrack life – and Marion had expressed herself perfectly content, despite the loneliness, pursuing her various hobbies, caring for May and Angela, occasionally visiting her sister-in-law Dinah Garland at Southwood Place.

She never complained; never. That was her trouble. That was what her husband found so hard to understand about her.

They had been married when she was eighteen, a pretty little thing, the cherished only child of a colonel of The Gloucestershire Regiment. Francis himself was ten years older, and already very much a man of the world: perhaps it was this experienced knowledge of women which first attracted him to Marion, for she'd been such an utterly innocent young creature, her artless naivety arousing novel feelings of protectiveness in him and her freshness – even more than her exquisite figure – whetting an appetite jaded by an excess of baggage whores, shop walkers, and other men's wives.

He had been faithful to her for six whole months before succumbing to the temptation of adultery. And though he still cared for her as the mother of his children, there had been a number of other women since, but none of them ever important: means of gratification and nothing more. Francis never kept count. A fellow officer had once remarked in the company of the Mess that he was living proof of the old French saying "all cats are grey at night", and he'd laughed along with the rest of them, relishing the truth of those words.

For quite some time he'd managed to keep his illicit amours from Marion; but one of the other wives in the cruelly caring way of gossips had made it her business to see that she learned the truth at last. And Marion, broken-hearted at his unfaithfulness, had blurted out everything to his parents when next she went down on a visit to the parsonage at Eastbourne.

Francis had never been his father's favourite son. That honour was reserved for Kit – milk-and-water brother Kit who could seldom put a foot wrong in the pater's eyes, certainly not now that he was following the ecclesiastical tradition of the Bethways and sporting a curate's collar about his plumply respectable neck.

The news that marriage had proved no obstacle to the moral incontinence of their elder son had hardly come as a surprise to the Reverend and Mrs Alec Bethway, merely being the final straw upon the back of an already much strained relationship. From thenceforth Francis found himself banished completely from the family circle.

The only member to keep up any regular contact nowadays was his sister Dinah. He suspected this was rather more out of loyal sentiment for the memory of her dead husband Richard than for any other reason, for Richard and he had been close comrades in the good old days, before South Africa – although from what he'd heard from Marion, Dinah was beginning to emerge at last from purdah to enjoy something of a merry widowhood in the company of a member of the minor aristocracy.

About time, too, in Francis's opinion: electric picture theatres were all very well, with their celluloid make-believe heroes and lovers, but they were no substitute for reality, and it was a darned sight more fun for Dinah if she came down to earth for a bit and let some flesh-and-blood chap liven things up with a little real pleasure.

"I think you're right about the storm, Jackson," he said, breaking the lengthening silence and handing the batman his trousers to be folded. "The air's starting to feel rather close."

37

He was about to add that instead of riding he might take himself across to the Officers' Mess for a drink; but on quick reflection changed his mind back again, and aloud remarked, "No, damn it, I *will* go. I feel like the exercise. Lay me out a pair of breeches and a clean shirt, will you, then go and tell one of the grooms to saddle up Trojan."

Already Marion and the children had slipped entirely from his thoughts.

It was cooler up here on the Downs, the heaviness of the July afternoon relieved by a breeze from off the sea. Overhead, fat white clouds drifted across the softening blue of the sky, trailing shadows in their wake over the smooth bare flanks of the Sussex hills; but towards the western horizon they were darker and more thickly massed, and the sky had taken on a sultry gold appearance.

Slowing his horse from a long exhilarating gallop, Francis Bethway let the animal proceed at its own pace across the springy turf. He loved the silence up here, the sense of freedom, the vast empty spaces and the distant vistas. To his left, beyond the coastal smudge of Newhaven, stretched the open waters of the Channel, little choppy waves glittering like fish-scales in the rays of sunlight. To his right, hidden now by a massive shoulder of the Downs, Lewes lay with its clutter of narrow streets rising steeply from river bank to castle ruin, with here and there a spire or tower to punctuate the huddled townscape.

Much closer at hand, perhaps less than half a mile away, the solitude of the hills was interrupted by a scatter of buildings belonging to one of the isolated farmsteads which crouched among the hollows, the weatherworn red of its rooftiles showing clearly against the pale green setting of a ripening barley field. Checking the horse to a slow walk as they drew near, the rider fell into idle contemplation of this scene, half-lost in reverie as he watched the flowing pattern of wind-ripples moving in waves across the surface of the grain.

For some time he remained thus preoccupied, until his attention was of a sudden caught by the swathe of ripples deepening as the barley set up a thrashing motion in the

38

freshening breeze; and calling to mind how far he'd ridden, he turned his steed's head and chucked the reins to urge the animal back into a canter along the ridge above the farm.

At almost the same moment there came the first distant rumble of thunder from out to sea, like muffled cannonfire, and a glance across his shoulder showed Francis a black cloud, anvil-shaped, which had detached itself from the sulphurous ranks on the horizon and was now approaching at an unexpected rate, gathering considerably in size as it came.

He uttered a sharp curse of annoyance and pressed the horse to increase its speed, intending to reach a lower level of the Downs before the gathering storm should break. But he had misjudged his distance on the outward gallop and ridden rather further into the hills than he'd realised: the way down was still a good three or four miles away. Unless he wanted to be caught out here in the open and take the full brunt of the weather, he'd best make directly across to the farm and find shelter there.

Barely had this decision been made than there was a sudden vivid flash from the darkening sky, followed moments later by a second growl of thunder; and just as Francis gained the edge of the barley field the rain came on in single heavy drops which patched his shirt with splashes.

By the time he'd reached the barn further down the slope, these drops had multiplied into a continuous steady pour, so that it was with some relief that he jumped from the saddle in the lee of the building and hurried his horse round to where one of the double wooden doors stood slightly ajar.

Inside, the gloomy light revealed outlines of machinery and implements: a high-backed farm wagon, sheep hurdles stacked in a row to one side, the curved yoke of an ox team hung upon pegs on the stone wall, reaping hooks and scythe blades glinting dully against piles of sacking; and everywhere a warm, close smell of oil and hay and leather.

The noise of rain on the roof slope had by now turned to a sullen drumming which was almost lost in the reverberating rolls of thunder, each cannon-clap following immediately upon the brilliant lightning flash and causing the horse to start nervously and show the whites of its eyes.

Francis drew the animal further back inside the barn, away from the open door. It was as well that he did so, for no sooner had he made the reins secure than there was a crack from without as though the world had split apart, and a sparkling blue charge of electricity came dancing in at the door to earth itself in an iron plough-share not a foot from where he'd just been standing. At the same instant there was a sound – a cry of alarm – from somewhere at the back of the barn, and swinging sharply round he was in time to glimpse a figure darting from behind a stack of crates towards a ladder leading to the store loft.

"Hey there!" he shouted, in no mood for niceties. "Hey – you there!"

The figure paused among the shadows, one foot already on the ladder, looking back over its shoulder. Then quickly and in silence began to clamber upward with the nimble agility of a little monkey.

"You there – !" Francis tried again; but it was a wasted effort, since his voice was drowned completely by the barrage of thunder directly overhead. Seeing no point in continuing to shout, he made instead towards the rear of the barn, dodging round the crates which had concealed his elusive companion.

Reaching the far wall, he peered up. Whoever it was, they had now disappeared out of sight over the lip of the loft.

"Hello?" he called out again.

No answer.

"Hello?"

After waiting there several moments more without result, he gave a dismissive shrug and turned away. As he did so, his riding boot kicked against something; and on looking down to see what, he found it was a shoe – a woman's shoe – lying beside the ladder.

He bent to pick it up. Despite the soft suede leather being sodden and caked with mud, it was a dainty little thing and obviously belonged to a very small foot. Francis smiled to himself: this evidence that his reluctant fellow refugee was a female – quite probably a young female – lent a rather more interesting aspect to the situation.

Raising his voice once more above the noise of the storm,

he said loudly, "Don't be alarmed. I don't mean you any harm." And waited.

When there was still no response, he decided on more direct action and took a few steps up the ladder; but barely had he climbed three rungs when something flew past his head and landed with a thud on the earthen floor below. At the same time, a face appeared overhead, and a pair of hands gripped the uprights of the ladder and began to shove it sideways.

The Captain beat a hasty retreat down again.

"I'm not going to hurt you," he cried, rather amused by this show of spirit and not a little intrigued by its perpetrator. "I merely wondered whether you were frightened by the storm, that's all."

After a moment or two the face appeared again. In the gloom it was difficult to pick out any of its features, except that it was small and pale and framed by an extraordinary amount of thick dark hair.

"Won't you come down?" he cried again in his most beguiling tone.

"No!"

"Then you mean to stay up there?"

"Yes!"

The answers were made in a sharply angry voice.

He tried another tack. "I suppose you think I'm trespassing. I only came in here for shelter, you know. Your father won't object, I hope?"

"Why should he?"

"Well, the barn's his property, isn't it?"

"No."

"Oh." Plainly this line of conversation was getting nowhere, but Francis Bethway was nothing if not persistent with contrary females, and this one was proving a delightful possibility. "Then I take it you don't actually live here?"

"No."

"In that case, where *do* you come from?"

"That's my business."

"You won't tell me?"

"No."

41

This could go on all afternoon, and he had to get back to camp. It would seem another change of tack was called for.

"Perhaps I ought to introduce myself. My name is Francis Bethway. Captain Francis Bethway. Territorial Army."

There was no response to this.

"May I not know who you are?"

"Why should you?"

"It would be – well, more sociable, don't you think. We might be cooped here together another hour yet."

The young woman above appeared to give this possibility her consideration, for there was a long pause; then, sullenly, the answer, "Well, I might tell you my name. But there's one condition."

Things were looking brighter. "Any condition you care to make," Francis responded cheerfully.

Another hesitation. "You won't say you met me, will you? It'd mean trouble for me if anyone found out I'd been here."

"I swear upon my honour as a gentleman and officer," he assured her solemnly, placing a hand upon his left breast, "not a soul shall ever learn of it from me. Now won't you come down?"

"Only if you move away. I don't want you looking up my skirt."

"My dear young lady, as if I would." There was a dry note of humour in the rebuke as he did as he was asked and retreated a yard or so towards the crates.

With quite as much agility as she'd earlier demonstrated going up, his companion descended the ladder and turned around at the bottom to face him. Francis had a rather better view of her now, for the storm was lessening as it moved away inland over the Downs and the clearing sky lightened much of the dimness here inside the barn. She was about eighteen years old; and never in his life, he thought, had he come across such a proudly insolent-looking creature – the rounded chin lifted in defiance, full red lips set into a pout, gipsy-dark eyes staring back at him in a way that was both sulky and yet fearlessly self-assured.

Where on earth had she come from? And why had he never seen her before?

42

He smiled, and held out the suede leather shoe in a placatory gesture.

"Yours, I believe?"

"Yes."

She leaned casually against the ladder and thrust out a stockinged foot, clearly intending that he should put it on for her. Then, in a tone of total disinterest, asked, "What did you say your name was?"

"Francis." He made no move to obey but stayed where he was, the shoe swinging from his hand.

"Do they call you Frank?"

"No. Never."

"I shall." There was a sudden wicked smile, showing sharp white teeth between the parted lips, and she raised her foot still higher, causing the hem of her red skirt to fall back and disclose a slender line of ankle and calf.

"Put my shoe on, Frank."

Her impudence attracted him enormously, but he gave no sign, merely saying instead, "Only if you first ask properly. And give me your name."

She shrugged. "*Please*, Frank, will you put on my shoe."

"And – ?"

There was a proud lift of the head. "And – I am Cecilia Desatti."

The surname had a strangely familiar ring.

"But you may call me Sissy if you like. Everyone does."

"Thank you for the invitation." He knelt down and took the small, chilled foot in his hand. "Desatti . . . where have I heard that before?"

"In Lewes, of course. My father is Emilio Desatti."

Her accent was mundanely native with that slight broadening of the vowels which marked her as having been raised and educated here in Sussex, and there was not the slightest trace of Italian in the way in which she pronounced her father's name.

"Ah, yes. Desatti. Now I know where I've come across it."

Francis finished fastening the shoe; then straightened to his full height and leaned forward, grasping the ladder on either side so that he had her trapped there.

43

"You run the tea rooms in Station Road," he said baldly.

"They are not tea rooms!" Sissy's eyes flashed instant fire. Ducking smartly beneath the barrier of his arms, she sprang away and rounded upon him, hands set in fists on her slim hips.

"Tea rooms, indeed! My family own a proper restaurant, I'll have you know. Set courses – specialities – the best quality selection of dishes you'll find anywhere outside London. Is it our fault if our patrons prefer to feed their ignorant faces with cakes and cream buns like monkeys at the zoo?"

"Oh, I do beg your pardon." The other's lips twitched in amusement at this little spat of temper.

"I should think so!" She glared back at him for some moments; then the dark lashes drooped and the mouth fell again into a sullen pout. "It's my brother Giacomo's fault. He thinks we should be running the place like some fancy ice-cream parlour."

"I see," said Francis, not terribly interested in the problem of Giacomo. What was exercising his curiosity far more was how on earth this exotic little wild-cat had come to be sheltering out on the Downs miles from anywhere, unaccompanied and with no apparent means of transport.

Never one to let reticence stand in the way of progress, he changed the conversation to put this question, feigning indifference to the answer by walking a short way off towards his tethered horse.

Sissy tossed her head, flinging the heavy waves of jet-black hair back from her shoulders. Pettishly she said, "What's it to you how I got here?"

"A slight interest, that's all."

"Plain nosiness, if you ask me."

"As you like." He turned again to look at her, and smiled; then went on casually, "You can't expect me to believe you walked all the way from Station Road, surely."

There was a shrug.

"Is that all the answer I'm getting?"

"You're a persistent devil, aren't you, Captain Frank whatever-your-name-is."

44

"Francis Alexander Henry Bethway." He made her a mock bow.

The bow was ignored. "I'll satisfy your curiosity on one more condition."

"And what is it this time?"

"That you give me a ride back on your horse – just as far as Cliffe. I can walk it from there."

"Very well, agreed. But I was going to offer, anyway."

"You're a bold one, I'll say that for you!" She laughed suddenly, arching her long white throat and looking at him sideways through half-closed eyes. "Though not so bold as the other one, I hope."

"Which other one?"

"Him, out there – " She gave a jerk of the head. "Nursing his cheek where I left him in some tumbledown sheep hut. He brought me all the way up here to get a bit of fresh air, he said – though what he meant was getting fresh, more like, and forget about the air. Called himself a gentleman. Gentleman, my eye! He didn't fool me, for all his swank and fancy clothes and lah-di-dah talk about healthy exercise. You can take plenty of exercise and still keep your breeches on, as I very soon pointed out."

She laughed again and moved closer, swaying her hips provocatively. "I'll know him again all right next time I see him, walking out with his wife. He'll be the one man on the street who doesn't turn his head to stare in my direction."

The brazen manner in which all this was delivered had the effect of rousing Francis considerably. Before he could stop, he heard himself saying, "If I promised to treat you better than that, would you let me meet you again somewhere?"

And was as eagerly gratified as if he'd been some callow youth on the brink of his first liaison when Sissy Desatti answered "No" – but said it with the kind of smile which experience told him could only mean yes.

4

"A registry office?"

Kit Bethway's voice was resonant with disbelief.

"A *registry* office?"

Hardly able to credit the words of his own mouth, he looked from his father to his mother, and back again, utterly stunned by what he had just been told.

"Read Dinah's letter for yourself – " The Reverend Alec Bethway leaned forward to hand his son the folded pages. From the open parlour window across the room drifted the sound of band music being played in The Grove, a pleasant little park at the centre of Tunbridge Wells, whose trees in the full green leaf of high summer formed an almost rural outlook from Christ Church vicarage.

"She does not say much, but it's plain enough who put her up to this," the older clergyman continued bitterly. "Warwick Enderby, of course. Our new son-in-law. Heaven help us, I suppose we are obliged to acknowledge him as such, for all that he's crept his way into the family by the back door."

Kit glanced again towards his mother. Her face was pale and wore a tight, strained look; but she managed a small smile for him as she echoed her husband's words, saying quietly, "Yes, dear, read Dinah's letter for yourself. Perhaps it may help you to understand."

Taking up his spectacles from the table at his elbow, the young curate unfolded the closely-written pages and scanned through them with an almost urgent impatience. Then went back to the beginning to read them once more, and with greater concentration this time, in an effort to make some sense of his sister's pell-mell sentences.

Her letter opened with the bald statement that she and Warwick Enderby had been married by special licence at Caxton Hall, Westminster, on Saturday the sixth of August, and had spent two nights at the Strand Palace Hotel before returning home to Lewes.

There then followed what struck Kit as being an almost aggressive defence of her action. She and Warwick were two mature and fully independent adults, she wrote, and as such, accountable to no one but themselves. They had wanted a private, very quiet, very simple ceremony without fuss or expense; and having made their decision to marry, had wished to do so as soon as possible. All that had been required was that Warwick should be resident in the district of Westminster for a period of fifteen days before the wedding, a condition he'd been able to comply with at once since his London club was conveniently within a few streets of Caxton Hall.

At this point in the reading, a sudden and rather alarming thought presented itself to the curate. Laying the letter on his knee, he removed his spectacles to look across at his parents, and in a tone full of suspicion asked, "Dinah hasn't been guilty of an indiscretion, I hope. I mean – well, she hasn't gone and done something silly, has she? She's not *having* to marry?"

"May the Lord forgive us, but indeed, we have wondered whether that might not be the case," his father answered gloomily. "So much secrecy and haste . . . " He made a vague gesture and fell back into silence, shaking his bowed head.

"Though I'm sure there's not an ounce of truth in it," Isabelle Bethway came in, springing loyally to her daughter's defence. "I know there can't be – Dinah would have told me of it, else. Oh, she likes to be thought a 'modern woman' with all her talk about equality and such nonsense, but she's never been one to behave in an underhand fashion, you know she hasn't, Kit. Why, there've been times when she was almost too open and honest – "

"But this evidently is not one of them, Mother." He took up letter and spectacles again and continued his careful perusal.

After a further few minutes the frown between his thick, straight brows deepened and he looked up once more.

"What's this – " indicating a paragraph – "'I hope that you are not hurt or offended, but there was so little time to let you know my plans'? I find that very hard to swallow! And see what she puts here – 'It was not discourtesy which

47

kept me from inviting you all to the service, but fear of a refusal, knowing how very low is Papa's opinion of civil marriages'. To quote a hackneyed phrase, the lady doth protest too much, methinks . . . throwing up a lot of dust as a blind, when quite obviously she'd determined to set her heart upon something which she knew might not meet with the family's approval."

"Just so. Her choice of Mr Enderby. You have hit the nail exactly, my boy." Alec Bethway shook his head a second time, and passed a hand across his thinning grey hair. "As for registry weddings – it is true that I regard them as a most inferior procedure, indeed, little better than a public convenience for divorcees and the like, and I am ashamed to think that my own daughter should have gone behind my back to marry in one. Most certainly, neither your dear mother nor I would have attended the ceremony, even had we been invited – "

"That is not quite so, Alec," his wife interrupted gently. "*I* would have gone. And Dinah knew that. By keeping us in ignorance, I believe she intended only to spare us the disagreement of having to make any such choice."

"I see she has written," Kit Bethway came in again, turning to the final page of the letter, "that she and her husband hope we may agree to a service of thanksgiving and blessing here at Christ Church. But what a curious suggestion! Why Christ Church, in heavens name? What's wrong with St Mark's at Eastbourne? That's the family's own parish, after all."

"Now, Kit, don't work yourself up so." Mrs Bethway's voice was quietly composed in contrast to her son's rising tone. "It was at St Mark's that Dinah married poor Richard, remember. We must appreciate that she might not want to have her new marriage blessed in the same church as her previous one was solemnised. There would be too many sad reminders of the past. You know how devoted she's been to Richard's memory all these years."

"Not so devoted that she must needs betray that memory by rushing off to some registry office in unseemly haste to wed a man with whom she's barely acquainted."

"Now you're being unfair, as well as unkind." A little note

of impatience crept into the voice. "Dinah has known Mr Enderby since last autumn, and ten months is quite sufficient time in which to form a good judgement of someone. Speaking for myself, I gained a very favourable impression of him from those few occasions she brought him to visit us at Eastbourne."

"But then you have a tender nature, my dear," Alec Bethway came in, complementing his remark with a smile and a glance of affection. "And if I may say so, like most members of the weaker sex you are easily to be swayed by a handsome face and attentive manners – "

"A fault for which you should be grateful, Alec, for otherwise I might not have accepted you as husband," his wife reminded him sweetly.

He acknowledged this piece of humour with a courteous inclination of the head; then continued, "As for my own opinion of Mr Enderby, doubtless it would be rather more charitable if I were to know more of the gentleman himself."

"My own sentiments entirely, sir." Kit Bethway folded the letter away into a neat square and put it aside with his spectacles on the table. "I completely agree. We know everything of his background, yet nothing at all of him."

He could remember as though it were yesterday the first time Warwick Enderby had been introduced into the family vicarage at Eastbourne. Dinah had brought the fellow down for the day (or rather, he had brought her, in his motor car) and within ten minutes of their meeting Kit had found himself disliking him heartily.

It was not so much the slight air of condescension which led one to suspect that Enderby considered his aristocratic lineage infinitely superior to that of a brace of provincial clerics, as the urbane suavity with which he addressed himself to the females: a self-studied performance of raising an eyebrow a fraction and smiling in a half-asleep manner, lolling back at his ease, one leg crossed upon the knee of the other, elbow over the arm-rest of his chair, cigarette dangling from between his fingers.

To Kit's censorious eyes, it was a portrait of cocksure patronising swagger.

Having been treated throughout high tea to a monologue

49

of Mr Enderby's exalted pedigree, the young curate had
vented his irritation by repaying the compliment in similar
vein – a somewhat lacklustre effort, alas, since the few drops
of blue sap in the Bethway family tree made feeble
comparison with the other's ancient bloodline.

Clergymen and county clerks being dull fodder, he had
found himself by way of a defiant end-of-tea flourish
speaking of his mother's niece, Amy Herriot, who had
married very well to a Dorsetshire landowner and become
something of a protégée of the celebrated author Mr
Thomas Hardy. But not even Amy and her literary lion had
made much impression upon the noble guest, who promptly
launched into an account of his own father's distinguished
years in the English classic theatre.

It had all been very galling.

Not so much as a word, of course, had been mentioned of
the other side of the maternal family blanket. A pity, in
retrospect, thought Kit savagely, for that surely would have
sent Warwick Enderby haring off in a cloud of motor smoke
to escape such low contagion, and spared them all the bother
of further acquaintance. However, there were some things
one simply did not allude to, not even within the privacy of
the home, one of those awful cupboard-skeleton secrets
which no amount of time or distance could ever quite bury
but was always lurking somewhere in the background ready
to rattle its grim bones: that Isabelle Bethway had been born
the illegitimate child of a gipsy stallion leader and an
alehouse-keeper's daughter, and that her brother Frank had
killed himself in Maidstone Gaol while serving a life
sentence for manslaughter.

Kit was ashamed of his own shame; but there it was, and
there was no escaping from it. Trace his mother's pedigree
and you found a badness in the blood which seemed to
bubble up somewhere in every generation. In this present
one, brother Francis was the rotten apple in the barrel –
brave, bold Francis, a fine soldier but with the morals of a
tom-cat, an adulterer whose promiscuous womanizing would
be a scandal and embarrassment in any decent family, but
especially in one which was a noted pillar of the Church.

Even their sister Dinah, Kit suspected, was not quite free

50

of the old taint: one had only to look at her questionable decision to work in a picture house, for instance, and now this registry-office marriage, as though God and the Establishment were so much dreary old hat to her new-fangled suffragist notions.

"Kit?" Isabelle Bethway had to repeat her son's name, louder this time. "Didn't you hear what I said? You were miles away for a moment! I asked whether you'd like more tea if I were to ring for some."

"Tea?" He pulled himself back to the present. "Oh – only if you'd like some yourself, Mother."

"I think we can manage another pot between us, can't we, Alec? We don't have to catch the train home to Eastbourne for an hour yet."

The curate's eyes followed his mother as she rose gracefully from her seat to go across to the bell-pull beside the carved oak fireplace. Despite its lines of middle age, her face even now retained the loveliness which first had captivated his father all those years ago, and the pepper-grey hair still held a faint, warm echo of the copper-red which, like her beauty, she had passed on to Dinah. No one could possibly ever guess, he thought dully, that such a respected and respectable woman might be the fruit of bastardy and bloodshed, part-gipsy, part-Irish, part mystery. He himself, thank God, had inherited from that background nothing worse than his auburn colouring and his talent as artist; the rest of his character had been moulded by his father's side of the family, good sound English stock with not a bad 'un amongst them.

It had never occurred to Kit Bethway that along with his better traits, he was also inclined to be rather pompous, occasionally supercilious, and generally a little dull.

"But what are we to do about this business?" he wondered aloud, changing the course of his thoughts to address himself once more to the subject of his sister's marriage. "Ought we to acknowledge Dinah's husband, do you suppose? She'll want to bring him visiting, I dare say. What do you think? Should we behave as though the manner in which this wedding was arranged is really of no consequence?"

And before either father or mother had chance to reply,

51

he found himself hurrying on in a peevish, angry tone, "I must say, I do feel very strongly about the affair. And to be frank, I'm not altogether sure I welcome Mr Enderby as brother-in-law. So I hope Dinah's not expecting my congratulations, because as far as I'm concerned, she's put herself in the same boat as Francis – rather beyond the family pale."

Dinah had been prepared for the fact that her marriage might not meet with universal approval; but far from prompting her to reconsider her decision, the possibility of interference and criticism had served only to fuel her determination. In the manner of those who rush to meet trouble long before it presents itself, she'd already thrashed out in her mind all the arguments there might be against her acceptance of Warwick's proposal; and resolving to let no obstacle stand in the way of their happiness together, she'd therefore agreed with him upon a simple, private ceremony in London.

The idea of Caxton Hall as the venue had been entirely Warwick's own: it would be almost like eloping, he'd declared, *much* more romantic and fun than all the fuss and palaver and long-winded pother of a full-dress church performance. Dinah had had no second thought about accepting his suggestion, so much in love that there was nothing else in all the world that mattered more than pleasing him in every way she could.

As events turned out, far from being quiet and colourless, their marriage had proved quite a merry affair, for at the last moment they'd been joined at the registry office by Warwick's brothers, Guy and Neville, together with two young lady friends, a jolly pair of girls in brightly ornamented attire who'd enlivened the proceedings considerably with jokes and sallies and little snatches of West End chorus lines.

Following the ceremony, the bridal party had adjourned to a café near St James's Park for a champagne breakfast during which Mabel and Vera had become decidedly frisky, sitting on their partners' knees and tickling their ears with their feather boas, while the French proprietor, entering into the spirit of the occasion, brought out an old squeeze-box to serenade the group with sentimental songs of his native land.

Champagne and happiness together had soon combined to have a most heady effect upon Dinah. She had not realised how tense these past few weeks had been for her, and relaxation now produced a golden glow of euphoria which seemed to touch everyone and everything around with an extraordinary magic, even to the dusty London sparrows hopping in the sunlight at the open doorway in search of pastry crumbs. This delightful feeling was intensified by the sheer exhilaration of being the new Mrs Warwick Enderby, wife of the most handsome, charming and romantic man in the whole wide world; and before long she'd found herself leaning back against her husband's shoulder openly exchanging kisses, so drunk with love and joy and excitement that she thought she must surely die before he came to take her in his arms tonight and make her truly his own.

Bottles of champagne continued to appear beside the table at regular intervals, to be emptied almost as fast as the plates of appetising little *bonnes bouches* which Madame herself came out to serve. After a time the giggles and muffled shrieks of Vera and Mabel had grown louder, and the corresponding laughter from their male companions taken on a deeper note of intimate cajolery; until, as if at some given signal, all four of them together rose somewhat unsteadily to their feet.

"Well . . . we're off," Guy had said thickly, an arm around Vera's plump pink-satin waist. "Mustn't hold up the proceedings, eh?" He had his brother's strong build, but the face was slightly thinner, giving him an almost foxy look.

Neville, by way of contrast, was inclined towards stoutness, with moony features and a good-natured smile permanently tipping the corners of his mouth. The smile just now threatened to reach his ears as he echoed Guy's words with a genial wave, turning away towards the door, Mabel clinging at his elbow – "Yes, must be off. Toodle-oo, m'dears. Enjoy yourselves." A wish which caused the two young women to break into stifled titters of tipsy mirth as they were shepherded off the premises.

"But we haven't said goodbye!" Dinah cried, watching

them leave, half-amused, half-vexed by this sudden swift conclusion to her wedding celebrations.

"What d'you expect, my darling?" Warwick hugged her to him. "There's no more champagne left to drink, and that's as good as farewell. We'll see them again, no need to worry. They're bound to invite themselves down to stay with us."

"What – all together? Mabel and Vera too?"

"Lord, no! What odd little notions you do get in that lovely head of yours." Another hug, this time accompanied by a smile and a light kiss on the tip of the nose. "Mabels and Veras are ten-a-penny in Town, my sweet. We shan't be meeting that pair again, I don't suppose. It was my brothers I was thinking of. You *will* have them to stay at Southwood Place, won't you?"

Dinah nodded. "Yes . . . but – "

"No buts. Buts butter no bread." Warwick leaned forward to stub out his cigarette.

"Now – " pushing himself up from the table – "what would the new and very beautiful Mrs Enderby like to do next? We could walk across the park to the Guards Chapel at Wellington Barracks and inspect the ancestral roll of names. Or Downing Street's close by, if you'd care to enquire whether Mr Asquith's at home to newly-weds. Or, of course, there's Buck House in the opposite direction. On the other hand – " a teasing pause, and again, that warm, tender smile in the dark blue eyes – "our caravanserai awaits us in the Strand, with a double room, bath, breakfast, lunch and dinner, all for the princely sum of a guinea for two whole nights and days. What d'you think? It might be cosier, wouldn't you say, than traipsing about to view the city sights?"

Dinah had felt a flush of pleasurably nervous anticipation flood her cheeks with colour.

"Do you honestly need me to answer that question?" she'd said softly.

Her husband put out both hands to help her to her feet; and pulling her up against him, had kissed her full upon the lips in a possessive, unhurried embrace for everyone to witness.

"I've already ordered total privacy . . . meals served in

our room . . . champagne on ice," he whispered against her cheek. Then, taking her by the waist, suddenly swung away, head thrown back, laughing out loud in a wildly exuberant fashion.

"D'you know what else I've done this morning? D'you know what it was? You'll never guess . . . I sent off a telegram!"

"A telegram – ? Who to?"

"To a friend of yours, my darling. To Stephen Moore. 'Awfully sorry, old chap. Dinah now Mrs Warwick Enderby. Better luck next time'."

The laughter rang out again on a note of exultation.

"Oh, what I wouldn't just give to see his face when he reads it!"

5

"Algie? It is Algie, isn't it? Algie Langton-Smythe?"

The young man checked himself as he was about to step from the kerb and turned to look back to see who it was had called out his name.

A well-dressed woman in a Russian-style jacket and straight, narrow skirt was advancing across the pavement towards him, the uncertain smile on her handsome features broadening as she saw she had not been mistaken.

"You remember me, surely?" She put out a gloved hand. "Jessie Moore? We met earlier this year, at Dinah Garland's."

"Yes, of course." Algie returned the smile and shook the proffered hand. "Miss Moore. I'm sorry, I didn't notice you there. How are you?"

"Never mind that. Tell me – is it true? I hear Dinah's gone back to playing the piano at the Picture Theatre."

The eager, forceful manner of his questioner took Algie aback, and for a moment he could only stand looking at her.

"Well?" she demanded impatiently. "Yes or no?"

"Er – yes. Yes, she started again last Monday evening."

"I knew it! And married no more than a month. Oh, do come and have a bite or something with us, Algie. My fiancé and his sister are here in Desatti's – " Jessie waved towards the tea rooms just behind her. "We saw you passing from the window, and I couldn't resist running out to catch you. Do join us, won't you? We're dying to know what's going on."

Embarrassment coloured the young man's face, staining the tan of his freckled cheeks a dull red as she seized hold of his elbow and began pulling him with her across the pavement.

"Miss Moore – " he began awkwardly, aware that passers-by were turning to look. "Miss Moore, really, I haven't time – "

"Nonsense! A cup of tea won't take three minutes."

She had him at the open doorway now, the bands of the gaily-coloured awning overhead striping her face with shadow and lending it a wickedly catty expression as she smiled up.

"See – there are Esmond and Laura. Now you can't escape without seeming utterly boorish."

Easing himself from her grasp, Algie looked reluctantly to where she was pointing. A few yards away at a window table were seated a young couple, the man of professional appearance in a navy serge suit with single-breasted waist-coat and spotted bow-tie, the girl more sensibly dressed for the warm September afternoon in a peach-pink linen blouse and skirt.

Algie's glance passed over her; then, rapidly, back again, concentrating itself suddenly into an outright stare.

"Just one cup of tea?" Jessie was saying in her most cajoling tones as she steered him firmly towards the table.

"Oh . . . er, yes – rather! Thank you." The other's manner appeared to undergo an instant and dramatic change as he continued to look at Laura Bates. Introductions were made, though he scarcely had more than a quick nod and side-smile for Esmond, being far more intent upon the sister, whose shy hesitancy as she returned his handshake appealed to him quite as much as the demure prettiness of her appearance.

Thrusting his fingers in a self-conscious way through his gingery-fair hair so that it sprang up in a quiff from his forehead, he seated himself opposite.

"There – didn't I tell you? It *is* true," Jessie exclaimed triumphantly, signalling to the waitress for attention as she resumed her own seat next to her fiancé. "Algie's just confirmed the news, haven't you, Algie? Dinah's gone back to her 'Hearts and Flowers' in the orchestra pit."

Esmond Bates looked up at the ceiling in gravely thoughtful fashion; Laura bowed her head and cast Algie a quick sideways glance. Neither seemed to have any comment to make on this information.

"I don't suppose she told you why, did she?" Jessie went on to enquire in her usual point-blank way. "I mean, it's all so very peculiar, the whole thing. Oh, yes, dear – " this to

57

the waitress, a sulky-looking dark-eyed girl in starched lace cap and apron. "Another pot of tea, and an extra place. And would you bring a little more milk." Then, turning back to Algie – "Well? *Did* she say why?"

It occurred to him to suggest that the reasons, whatever they were, were surely Dinah's own affair, and if Miss Moore wished to learn them, why could she not ask for herself since she was such a close acquaintance. But three pairs of eyes were now turned upon him in expectation of an answer; and he heard himself saying awkwardly, "I believe it had something to do with her husband's brothers."

"The brothers?" Jessie swooped upon this titbit like a hawk. "How do you mean? In what way?"

"Well . . . they're always there at the house, I suppose . . . and . . ."

His voice trailed away into a mumble, and he looked at Laura Bates in an embarrassed, apologetic manner. She gave him a little smile as though understanding his predicament; and encouraged by this, he went on again rather more firmly, "Look here, I'm sorry but I really don't think it's any of our business."

"No, of course it isn't," Jessie came back, "but that doesn't stop us wondering what on earth's going on. Do you know, Algie, Dinah and I used to be as close as that – " crossing two fingers and holding them up – "but not now, not any more, it seems. Not since she allowed herself to fall completely under the influence of that odious Warwick Enderby. Oh, I tried to make her open her eyes, see him for what he really is, but whatever I said, she refused to see sense. She can be stubborn as a mule at times, can Dinah. Not even my brother Stephen could persuade her to change her mind. No, it was quite made up. She was in love with the fellow, and that was that. In the end we did nothing but quarrel, so I'm not in the least surprised we weren't informed she was getting married again. Not even her own parents knew, apparently. I had that information from her father himself, poor man, in reply to a letter I wrote to them at Eastbourne after we'd received that horridly cruel telegram."

Algie wondered what telegram this could be, but thought

58

it best not to ask while Miss Moore was in full flow or they might all be sitting here for the rest of the afternoon.

"I decided to call at Southwood Place a fortnight afterwards, and do you know, the maid made me wait upon the doorstep – *me*, whom she's known as a visitor ever since the start of her employment – while she informed 'the Master' I was there, even though I'd twice insisted it was Mrs Enderby I'd come to see."

There was the briefest pause to raise her cup and take a sip of tea; and then she was off again.

"Well, there I was left out upon the step like some unwanted parcel, when 'the Master' himself appeared. He didn't mince his words, I can tell you. In the space of ten seconds or less I learned that my brother and I were not welcome there, that Dinah had no longer any wish to continue our friendship, and that it was very much hoped I'd have the courtesy not to call again. Well, I simply could not believe my ears! I said to you, didn't I, Esmond darling – " rounding upon her fiancé, expression one of wounded indignation – "I said to you I could scarce believe I was hearing aright?"

"Mm," agreed Esmond laconically. He indicated the pot. "More tea?"

Algie could not decide whether this was a request or a query; but obviously Laura knew which, for she took up the rose-patterned china pot from its cork stand and reached across for her brother's cup and saucer.

"Would you care for a drop more, Mr Langton-Smythe?" she asked demurely when she'd finished pouring.

"Oh – yes, yes, please." If she'd invited him to a jug of hemlock he'd have accepted with equal enthusiasm for the sake of receiving it from such an endearingly sweet creature.

Taking advantage of Jessie's temporary silence, he ventured on boldly, "If I may make a suggestion, Miss Moore, it strikes me you won't be satisfied until you've spoken to Mrs Enderby personally, so why not come along and have a private word with her at the Electric Picture Theatre?"

"Oh, but I'd already decided to do so," came the somewhat tart reply. "It's merely a matter of choosing the right time and opportunity."

"Well, she won't be there this evening, I'm afraid. We're only showing an educational programme – the new labour exchanges, that sort of thing, no musical accompaniment. Tomorrow . . . " He paused for a moment, thinking. "Yes, tomorrow there's a matinée performance of *Jane Eyre*. Now you'd enjoy that, Miss Moore. An excellent production, very dramatic."

It was on the tip of his tongue to persuade her to bring Laura, too, but that would hardly be feasible in the circumstances. Instead, he went on in as casual a way as he could contrive, "I can always get complimentary tickets, you know, if there's ever a programme any of you would care to see."

"Can you now?" Esmond Bates, for the first time, showed some slight sign of interest in the conversation. "That's extremely good of you. I may well take you up on that invitation when the Crippen trial opens at the Old Bailey next month. As a solicitor, you'll understand I'm following the case with very close interest. I dare say the news-reels will report it fully?"

"Oh, indeed, yes," Algie assured him. There had been a great deal of publicity given to Dr Crippen and his mistress Ethel Le Neve at the time of their attempted flight to Canada on the S.S. *Montrose* in July, and the news-reel films had been full of pictures of Scotland Yard's Inspector Dew bringing the fugitives ashore at Liverpool following their arrest by means of wireless telegraphy. The whole thing had captured the national interest. There were even popular songs to be heard about it everywhere just now.

"If you'd like, sir," the young man went on helpfully, "I'll keep a look-out for any items coming on to the 'reels and let you know about it in good time."

"That's very decent of you. I live out at Weatherfield, you see, and it's quite a way to come into Lewes. Having advance notice would be of the greatest help." Esmond smiled his thanks; then, draining his cup of tea, he pushed back his chair and addressed himself to his fiancée.

"It's almost four o'clock, my dear. I really must be making a start soon or I'll be running myself late for the meeting at Tonbridge tonight. You'll excuse me, won't you, Mr Langton-Smythe? It's a society debate on certain points of law, and I'm expected to speak."

60

Algie rose with him and held out his hand. "It's been pleasant to make your acquaintance, Mr Bates. If you'd let me know where I might be in touch with you with news on the trial?"

"Ah, yes. Of course. You can reach me at my address." The other leaned across to remove his Homburg hat from the wall-peg behind him. "The Holloway, Weatherfield."

He pushed his chair tidily away under the table and reached to assist Jessie, who was just getting to her feet.

"Do you care to walk with me to the High Street, dearest? I must call in to see Stephen at the office before catching my train. I'm sure Mr Langton-Smythe won't think we're deserting him if we leave him behind in Laura's company to finish his tea."

"No, not at all, sir!" Algie came in with alacrity, forestalling any slight chance of being denied this opportunity. He was almost tempted to add that he could imagine no desertion more agreeable.

"Jessie? Oh, she lives with her parents still, in the High Street beyond Westgate," Laura Bates answered shyly, in answer to the enquiry about her future sister-in-law. "Not very far, I believe, from Mrs Garland's – I mean, Mrs Enderby's." There was a nervous little laugh at the mistake, and she went on hesitantly, "Do you know Southwood Place at all? Have you been there?"

"Not actually inside the house, no. But I've accompanied Mrs – Dinah to her front door many a night when we've been late coming away from the Picture Theatre. The streets can be a little unsafe for ladies at that hour."

He wished he were able to impress Laura with an account of some heroic deed whereby he'd protected his female companion from assault by a violent ruffian – three or four violent ruffians – fighting them off single-handed till they turned and fled like rats into the darkness. But alas, there had never been anything more perilous than the occasional maudlin drunk to be avoided by the simple expedience of crossing the street.

"And you yourself live in Spences Lane, you say, Miss Bates?" he pressed on, anxious at all costs to keep the

61

conversation flowing for fear she might make a few seconds' silence her cue to depart.

She nodded.

"You've been there long, have you?"

"Twenty-three years."

"Now that's what I'd call a precise answer!"

"Well . . . you see, I was born there."

"Ah."

There was a slight pause; and then Algie rushed in again, "Do you live together with your parents still? Like Miss Moore?"

A shake of the head. "Only my father. Mother died when I was just a baby. We have a step-mother, Esmond and I. And of course there's our dear governess – Megwynn Evans – she's with us still." The tone, which had hitherto been soft, almost reserved, suddenly warmed with unguarded affection. "She's an angel, the best and truest of friends. I simply couldn't be without her."

Algie made a mental note that when he met this governess he must remember to treat her with the greatest deference: obviously she would be a most useful ally.

"What an unusual name," he remarked keenly. "D'you know, I can't recall having heard it before."

"Megwynn? It's very pretty, don't you think."

"Oh, yes. Rather! Doesn't sound quite English, somehow."

"She's from Wales," Laura volunteered readily, shyness for the moment overcome by enthusiasm. "From a village in the Forest of Clun. I tease her sometimes because she still has her accent, and when she's vexed she says things like *Duw* and *dyna gawl*. I'm afraid when I was small I used to repeat her and fancied how very grown-up I sounded – "

She came to an abrupt halt and a sudden furious blush spread over her face, beginning at her chin and fading into the hairline at her temples.

"Oh, do go on!" Algie urged. "Please?"

But the only response was a slight compression of the lips as the girl ducked her head and gave it a little shake.

It was almost like watching a flower close up for the night, he thought, utterly enchanted. One minute she'd been

62

blossoming forth, and the next had shut herself away again within that shrinking-violet modesty.

"I went to Wales once as a boy," he said hurriedly, seeing he was in danger of having her retire altogether. "To the south. Carmarthenshire. A little place called Pendine. I don't suppose you know it? One of our maids had a sister who ran an inn there with her husband. The Green Bridge, I think it was. I'd had mumps, you see – or whooping cough, I can't remember – and they sent me away there to recuperate. They said the sea air would be good for me. It was, too. I wanted to go back again the next year, but they packed me off to preparatory school instead."

Laura raised her head slightly. The hand which had half-crept its way towards her gloves on the table beside the empty plate withdrew once more to join its partner in her lap.

Timidly she enquired, "And have you ever been back since?"

"No. But I mean to, one of these days. I shall take a cottage there for the summer and spend my time rambling about the lanes or exploring the sea caves or riding along the sands as far as the river estuary. And when the sun sets, I shall light my oil lamp and read Swinburne or Matthew Arnold."

A wistful, far-away expression stole into the other's eyes, and she said softly, "How pleasant that sounds . . . and oh, how I envy you, able to make such dreams come true . . . "

"'What else be dreams, if not the food of hope?'" Algie quoted in reply. "I can't for the moment recall who wrote that, but he was absolutely right. Unless we have our dreams, what have we got to strive for in life?" A pause. "You enjoy poetry too, do you, Miss Bates?"

She nodded. Then her glance slipped past him to the large moon-faced clock on the wall above the cashier's cubicle, and the wistful expression faded.

"I really do have to go now," she said, her hand re-emerging from her lap to take up the pair of gloves.

"Oh – must you?" There was no disguising the disappointment in his voice. "Won't you stay and share another pot of tea with me? Or perhaps you'd prefer an ice? Or something else?"

"Thank you, but no." Laura rose gracefully to her feet. "I'm expected at home. We have guests to dinner this evening."

"Ah." There was no arguing with that.

He stood up with her and went round to draw the chair away to allow her to leave the table. "If you're walking back to Spences Lane, then may I be allowed to escort you?"

"Oh, no – please, no, there's no need – "

"But I'm going in that direction myself, Miss Bates." Her protest was cut short by what Algie hoped didn't sound too much of a lie. "So it's not in the least out of my way."

Picking up the bill-chit which the sulky-faced waitress had left beneath his saucer, he added, "I won't be a moment. I'll just go and pay this – " and turned away towards the cashier.

Unfortunately, the cashier had just then chosen to start counting out a pile of shilling-pieces into columns, so that it was quite two or three minutes before the young man was attended to, ample time for his companion to draw on her gloves, loop her reticule over her arm, and be out of the tea-room door and several dozen yards away along Station Road.

Finding her gone, Algie promptly hurried off in pursuit, half-running down the street to overtake her.

"Sorry . . . bit of delay back there – " he began upon reaching her side; but got no further, for before he could say another word Laura had thrust out a hand as though to push him away, and looking about in a most fearful manner, said in beseeching tones, "Oh, please, please, don't follow me!"

Mistaking this reaction for timid awkwardness, he responded with a laugh, "It's no inconvenience, Miss Bates – truly."

"That wasn't what I meant." She began to hurry on again.

He followed. "I'm sorry . . . I don't understand. What *do* you mean? Is it that you don't like my company?"

"No, no, not that."

"Then what? Because I play the fiddle in a picture house?"

"No!" She paused in her flight; and again there was that frightened glance around her. "It's – it's my father, Mr Langton-Smythe. Forgive me, but I'm not allowed to encourage the attention of gentlemen . . . especially not in public."

"But you've just spent the past half-hour sharing a table with me at Desatti's," he protested.

"We couldn't be seen there."

"Couldn't be seen? There were people all around, other customers – "

"I mean, *he* couldn't see us." She bit her lip. "Oh please, don't come any further with me. I've so enjoyed meeting you, and thank you for your company. But please, if you wish me no ill, go away now."

"I still don't understand. But . . . very well, if that's what you want, Miss Bates." Algie held out his hand. "Let's not say goodbye, though. Only au revoir."

She gave a hesitant smile, looking up at him for a moment before turning quickly away.

"Better if it's goodbye," she said over her shoulder. "But I won't forget you. Whenever I read Swinburne, I'll remember . . . "

Then she was gone, hurrying away from him down the slope of Station Road; leaving him to stand there watching until her peach-pink figure had disappeared from view, taking with it the line of poetry he'd quoted to her earlier:

"What else be dreams, if not the food of hope?"

6

"Shall I clear away now, ma'am?"

Putting her head in at the open parlour door, the housemaid looked enquiringly across at the fair-haired young woman seated at the upright piano.

"Yes, if you would, Florrie." Without pausing from her playing, Marion Bethway threw a quick smile over her shoulder. "And puppy will need taking out in a moment, please. Angela has been feeding it on chocolate biscuits."

"Only two, Mama," protested the child in pigtails and pinafore who was kneeling on the carpet beside the piano stool, a small brown bundle of squirming fluff cradled tightly in her arms. "Only two!"

The maid came across to pick up the tea tray from the lace-covered table in the window embrasure.

"I'll just take this through to the kitchen, ma'am, then I'll come straight back for little puppy and put it out in the yard for a bit," she said, retracing her steps towards the door.

"But you promise you won't lose him again?" Angela cried, her young mind still full of the memory of yesterday's fright when her birthday pet had somehow managed to wriggle under a loose board in the garden fence to escape into next door's shrubbery.

Her mother took her hands away from the piano keys, and in the sudden stillness the thin high squeaks of the protesting puppy sounded unnaturally loud as it struggled to free itself.

"Of course we won't lose Traddles again, darling. Corporal Jackson is coming tomorrow especially to mend the fence, remember? And in the meantime, Florrie will keep it safely in the yard."

"Traddles is not a 'it'," declared Angela pertly. "He's a 'he'."

This little show of insolence was ignored; and when the puppy had been carried away to be relieved of the effect of

66

too much chocolate biscuit, Marion Bethway lifted her small daughter up on to her lap.

"Now – " she said, reaching forward to turn over the pages of the music book on the stand in front of her. "Which nursery rhyme shall we sing together next? Shall it be 'Hickory, dickory, dock'? Or would you like this – 'Sing a song of sixpence'? It's the one we found in your *Squirrel Nutkin* book, isn't it, when Auntie came this afternoon? Do you remember the picture of the squirrels bringing Old Brown's present?"

Angela nodded in the exaggerated manner of the very young, the rosy-cheeked little face grave with concentration; and wriggling down again from her mother's knee, she ran across to the window seat where earlier she'd been sitting with her aunt Dinah Enderby to look at the new Beatrix Potter storybook brought as a fifth-birthday present.

"Here it is!" she announced, picking up the book and holding open the pages at an illustration of squirrels around a large pie-dish. "Four-and-twenty blackbirds baked in a pie."

"Then we'll sing that together, shall we?"

There was a shake of the head. "No. I already sang it two times with Auntie and Baby."

Putting aside the book, the child returned to her mother, and stretching up on tiptoe began turning over the music until she came to a piece bearing a drawing of Humpty Dumpty. This was her favourite, with its mention of "all the king's horses and all the king's men", a reference she'd associated from earliest age with her father, Captain Bethway, for it had always been a special bedtime treat whenever Angela had been particularly good that he came to the nursery to tell her how he and his soldiers – contrary to the rhyme – had indeed managed to put Humpty Dumpty together again.

"This one," she said, "please." And even before her mother's fingers touched the keys to start the merry tune, she'd lifted the hem of her smocked pinafore and holding it out in both hands curtsy-fashion, began to dance sedately round and round the room singing the words of the rhyme in a lisping pipe.

Coming at that moment along the garden path from the stables behind the house, Francis Bethway paused to enjoy this charming little scene, mother and child together framed in the wide oblong of the curtained window, their two faces as identical in concentrated expression as they were in the prettiness of feature and colouring, and lent an added enchantment by the mellow autumn sunlight slanting between the lime-trees to rim them both in gold against the shadows of the cosy room.

He stood for a while just beyond the window, watching them through the outline of his own reflection; until Angela, suddenly catching sight of him there, cried out to her mother – and the spell was instantly broken, the magic of the scene extinguished, the moment's prick of conscience stifled.

With a wave of greeting, he continued along the path and through the wicket-gate; and by the time he'd reached the front door, Florrie was already there to take his peaked forage cap, with Angela beside her to greet him.

He swung the child up into his arms and carried her back across the hall to the parlour, smiling at her excited chatter of news; and setting her down again, kissed his wife upon the cheek and said prosaically, "Sorry I'm rather late, dear. Dinah's already gone, has she?"

Marion Bethway nodded. No point in asking the reason for her husband's delay. He would only have fobbed her off with some ready excuse which might or might not be the truth – impossible to know which since Francis was such a plausibly good liar.

"Yes, she had to leave at three – " she began; only to be interrupted by little Angela breaking in impatiently, "Look, Papa, look!" demanding his attention by pulling at the braided sleeve of his uniform. "See what Auntie bringed for my present!"

"*Brought*," he corrected. "*Brought* for my present. And where are your manners, young lady? You must wait your turn when Mama is speaking."

The child's expression fell at this rebuke, and the Beatrix Potter book held up for his admiration was at once withdrawn behind her back as a sign of hurt resentment.

Seeing the down-turned little mouth, Francis gave his

daughter's flaxen pigtails an affectionate tug; and moving across to settle himself in one of the easy chairs by the Dutch-tiled fireplace, patted his knee invitingly.

"Come over here to Papa," he said, "and we'll look at your book while Mama tells me Auntie's news."

Instantly mollified, Angela ran to clamber up into his lap. She had lately started attending a morning kindergarten in Lewes and was at that early stage of reading where even the simplest of words required studied concentration, so that her account of Squirrel Nutkin's adventures owed rather more to the pictures than to the complicated letter-jumbled lines of print opposite.

Encouraging her with the occasional sound of interest as they turned the pages together, Francis glanced over his shoulder at his wife. Marion had now reseated herself at the piano, motionless, her back turned to him, and something in the tense bearing of her slender body prompted him to ask, "You're all right, are you, dear?"

"Yes, of course." She did not look round to answer.

He waited a moment or so; and when it was obvious she would make no further response, asked again, "Well? And how was Dinah this afternoon? Is she finding newly-married life to her taste?"

There was the faintest sketch of a shrug. "Apparently."

"Only apparently? Didn't she say? I'd have thought you women would have talked of little else – yes, poppet, yes – " this to his daughter, protesting against his straying attention. "Yes, there are the nice little squirrels again." Then, looking back towards Marion – "She didn't mention how the pair of them are settling in together at Southwood Place?"

"Not really, no."

"And you didn't ask?"

A shake of the head.

He waited again, pretending to occupy himself with Angela's pictures; until impatience got the better of him, giving a slight edge to his voice as he enquired, "Well what *did* you and Dinah talk about?"

"Oh . . . the children." Marion's fingers played lightly up and down the piano keys. "Angela's birthday party yesterday. Little May's new tooth. That sort of thing."

"That's all? Just that? Nothing else?"

"If you'd bothered to be here at the time you promised your sister, she might have said something of greater interest to us all." She shifted herself on the stool to look round at her husband, not a hint of reproach in her expression despite her words, only that long-suffering, dull-voiced resignation which he'd come to know so well, and weary of so much.

"Damn it, Marion, I wasn't able to be here. Something came up to delay me at camp. You know we start these manoeuvres in Wiltshire next week – "

Sharpness threatened Francis's tone, but was swiftly moderated in order to tell his daughter, "There, sweetheart, now we've looked at your book you go and take it up to the nursery like a good little girl while Papa talks to Mama."

He lifted the child to the floor; and observing the sudden stubborn set of the chin and the threatened frown of resistance between the pale, fine brows, went on more firmly, "Do as you're bid, please, Angela. Take the book to the nursery. Or do you wish to be put to bed early without a story from Papa.?"

This threat at once produced the desired result: the frown disappeared to be replaced by a look of wary appeasement, and without a word the child turned obediently and trotted across the room out through the half-open door.

Her father waited a few moments until he heard the sound of her small double-footfall on the hall stairs; then he threw a glance at his wife, and getting up from the chair said sourly, "Now, Marion, what's all this about? I come home after two days on duty expecting a little comfort and cheer at my own hearthside, and instead I'm met with turned backs and sulks and snapes. Now what is it, eh? What's got into you this time?"

She rose wearily from the piano, and without looking at him moved away towards the window.

"You know what it is, Francis, so why do you bother asking.?"

"What, that I was delayed coming away from camp?"

"Not that, no." A trace of melancholy crept into the low voice. "Don't pretend with me. How long have we been

70

married? Six years? Seven? And how often in that time have you been unfaithful – "

"So that's it," he broke in angrily, guilt fuelling his temper. "That's it, is it. That's what's troubling you. You think I've started having another affaire – "

"I *know* you're having another affaire, Francis."

Marion turned by the window, the sunlight outside silhouetting her figure so that her face was in shadow, hiding the sudden telltale brightness of unshed tears. Quietly she went on, "Don't you think I'm not aware of all the signs by now? Haven't I had enough in the past not to know what they mean – the excuses, the delays, the absences . . . the pretence of affection whenever we're in public, the neglect when we're together alone? I don't need barrack gossip to tell me what's going on. No – ! " seeing he was about to interrupt again and snatching her hands to her ears. "I won't listen to your excuses, Francis. I won't hear your lies. I don't wish to know anything about this woman. All I ask is that you try to behave with a little more discretion this time . . . try not to flaunt your infidelity where people who know us will see . . . "

For a moment she stopped herself, faltering on the edge of tears, the small head with its cloudy mass of honey-pale hair drooping forward on the slender neck.

When she spoke again her words came almost in a whisper. "I hate their pity . . . their sham concern . . . hate the false fronts they put on, as though they think I'm too stupid to know what's happening. Please, Francis . . . promise me – promise me you will try to be discreet?"

He shifted awkwardly, half-turning away, anger tempered by a sudden acute discomfort. Much as he was irritated by his wife's martyr-like sufferance in the face of what to be honest was nothing more than a bit of dalliance on the side, he hated to see how much he wounded her by his selfish behaviour.

Bad conscience prompted him to wonder whether it might not be kinder to deny this new liaison, swear it was ended, that the girl had left Lewes. Or had the rumour-mongers among the officers' wives already laid their wagging tongues to the name of Sissy Desatti? And if so, then how could he

71

give his word to Marion that the new affaire would be as brief as all the rest when he knew in his heart of hearts that this time things were different – this time he'd broken his own strict rules of the game, and against his better judgement allowed himself the dangerous pleasure of falling in love.

There had been no arranged rendezvous following that first meeting together during the summer storm on the Downs. Knowing that if he wanted to start a relationship with Sissy he'd have to take the initiative himself, Francis Bethway had deliberately waited almost a fortnight before trying to see her again. Let her wonder whether she hadn't been forgotten, said the voice of experience: that way she'd be thinking of him constantly.

Their second meeting had been at the tea rooms in Station Road. Normally he had no reason to patronise the place; but it happened that one of his fellow officers, Freddy Seton, had a particularly sweet tooth, and a chance remark made as the two were coming off duty one afternoon had handed Francis his opportunity – quite literally on a plate.

Seizing the chance, he'd suggested casually that he and Freddy go along to Desatti's to sample their new and much-advertised "Comet" speciality – a vanilla ice pudding moulded to resemble a fluted rocket, served with a tail of paper-fine meringue filled with whipped cream and flavoured with liqueur. A light dusting of pounded sugar crystals added a finishing touch to the realism of the effect. Comets were all the rage just now, with the arrival in the skies of Halley's Comet on its 75-year journey through space. It would not be seen again until 1985, a lifetime away, a fact which had prompted commercial enterprise to produce all kinds of weird and wonderful ephemera to commemorate its visit.

Fortune had appeared to favour his gamble, for Sissy herself was assigned to wait on their table; and it amused Francis no end to catch her off-guard and watch the sulky-faced hauteur slip for a moment as she recognised him, her look betraying both interest in seeing him there and admiration for the handsome Army uniform before being quickly masked again by a pretence of indifference.

He and Freddy Seton had done themselves proud on her extra-generous serving of Comet Pudding, and when he came to repay her with an equally generous tip, his fingers had managed to linger caressingly on her smooth wrist before sliding the coin into her palm.

Taking advantage of Freddy's temporary absence from the table, he'd said softly, "What can you recommend me next time?"

The girl hadn't batted so much as an eyelid. "Depends on what you fancy – sir."

"Something . . . nice and tasty."

"Another Desatti special?"

"Yes, that sounds the sort of thing." Then, seeing Freddy starting to weave his way back between the brass-potted plants and check-clothed tables, he'd added quickly, his voice suddenly serious, "Six o'clock. All Souls churchyard. I'll be waiting by the clock tower."

By ten minutes past six, when she had still not arrived, the mood of pleasurable anticipation was beginning to evaporate, and for the first time in his experience Francis Bethway found himself feeling just a little uncertain whether or not a woman would keep an assignation with him. Five minutes later the uncertainty had started turning to annoyance that he'd been stood up in such a casual fashion; and by the time Sissy Desatti's small lithe figure eventually appeared between the table-top tombs at the other side of the disused graveyard, he was no longer in any humour to play the role of suave and charming suitor.

"Oh, you're still waiting, are you?" she'd announced smugly as she neared the angle of the clock tower wall where he was standing.

"Actually, my dear, I was just about to leave."

The coolness of his manner seemed to amuse her. "Well, off you go, then. I wouldn't dream of keeping you. I only came by to tell you not to hang about too long. Your wife might wonder where you've got to."

Tempting as it was to make a dignified retreat from the scene, Francis was damned if he was going to be ordered off by this little madam, as though he were merely another of the callow youths she'd doubtless cut her teeth on in the past.

"Wife?" He lounged back against the wall and treated her to a nonchalant smile, one eyebrow half-raised in a practised look of cynical humour. "What on earth could have led you to think I have a wife?"

Sissy returned the look with equal practice. "For a start, the way you scuttled off to meet me here on the sly. If you'd nothing to hide, why choose a hole-and-corner place like this – unless, of course, you don't want anyone seeing what you're up to?"

He took the shrewdly-landed blow with all the expertise of an old hand at the game; and with hardly a flicker to show she'd scored a point, answered blandly, "My dear girl, when I make love to a woman I don't wish half of Lewes for an audience."

"Oh, don't give me that, Frank Bethway!" She threw back her head and laughed, showing a tip of pink tongue between the scarlet-carmined lips. "I can smell a married man a mile away. You're like a lot of well-fed toms after the cream."

Despite his injured pride at the way she'd kept him waiting, Francis could not help but find something quite fascinating in the girl's impudent boldness.

"Well," he said, beginning to mellow slightly to his earlier humour, "I'm not sure the comparison is entirely flattering. But I want things to be on the level between us, my dear, so just to avoid any misunderstanding, then yes, I'll admit – "

"There's a dear little woman at home," Sissy finished for him in a sarcastically sing-song, heard-it-all-before voice, "but alas, we've nothing in common and she doesn't understand me any more."

That was not how he'd have preferred to phrase the statement, whatever its nub of truth, and he'd answered rather less tolerantly than before, "Sometimes, you know, the cat may get at the cream only to find it too curdled for drinking. A word of advice, Sissy dear. Don't be pert at the expense of my wife."

"Oh?"

"And there's no need to put on that face. You know very

74

well what I mean. She has nothing at all to do with any of this, and I want it kept that way."

"So you're not going to promise you'll give her up for me? Well, that makes a change from the usual old tune, I must say." Suddenly, the pertness was gone and a flash of real anger showed in the girl's Italian-dark eyes.

Francis reached forward and took her by the arms, giving her a little shake.

"Listen, we're going to have some good times together, you and I. That's what I promise. A lot of fun, a lot of pleasure. I'm a generous man, you'll find, and I like to enjoy myself – "

"But no strings attached." Sissy pulled herself away.

"That's right. No strings attached."

She looked him up and down for a moment in an insolent, weighing-up sort of manner; then gave a shrug and said, "I'll have to think about it, won't I?"

And before he'd had time to react, she'd suddenly leaned forward on swift tiptoe and kissed him full on the mouth, her warm moist tongue slipping between his lips; then spun away again out of reach and gone running off along the weed-choked path, laughing as she went.

7

"I wouldn't mind, Mrs Smith," young Marjorie said fretfully, "but they can't seem able to keep their hands to theirselves."

She threw an uncomfortable glance around the kitchen of Southwood Place, then turned her blue, slightly bulbous eyes once more upon Dinah Enderby's housekeeper, busily scraping carrots opposite at the scrubbed-top table as she listened to the maid's tale of woe.

"I mean," Marjorie went on, "it ain't as if this house is their'n, even. They come here the pair o' them, bold as brass, giving orders like they owned the place, or some'at. And them wi' lodgings o' their own an' all, up in Star Street."

"Aye, a pity they can't see fit to stop in Star Street," put in Mrs Smith grimly, wielding her chopping knife to top and tail the carrots as though wishing herself at the throats of Guy and Neville Enderby. "But it ain't what they're used to, is it – so they say. No butlers nor the like to wait on 'em hand and foot. They'd rather be down here scrounging off Miss Dinah's goodwill and belvering to be fed at all hours."

"I don't mind it so much when it's Mr Warwick as gives me the eye." Marjorie took up her lament again, folding pleats in the starched white crispness of her apron to occupy her nervous fingers. "At least it's only a wink now an' then, and there's no harm in that. But them brothers of his – " She gave a little shudder. "D'you know, Mrs Smith, I were at the second bedroom window this morning, bending forward to straighten the nets, when that Mr Guy come creeping behind me and put his hand right up . . . well, where he shouldn't. Ooh, it gi' me such a fright! I didn't know where to put meself for a minute. And what he said to me I dursn't repeat, not even if I'd understood half o' what he meant."

"Disgusting, I call it." Mrs Smith shook her head.

A large, raw-boned woman with greying hair beneath an old-fashioned mob cap and hands red-knuckled from long years in service, she had first come to Southwood Place with her handyman-gardener husband in the days of old Mrs Garland, when Mr Garland was still alive and young Richard just starting his schooling. There had been some changes in that time, but none so much and so lamentable as Mr Richard's widow bringing home a new husband to be master, with two drunken, reprobate brothers who thought they'd a right to move in too, inviting their mopsies down from London and treating the place like some cheap commercial hotel.

Mr Warwick had made matters worse when he'd let them have the lease of his old lodgings in Star Street, so that instead of every weekend, it was every blessed day now they were coming into the house, expecting meals to be cooked whenever they felt like and drinking all Madam's best, going down to the cellar to open whatever they fancied – generally the claret; and some of those bottles, Mrs Smith knew for a fact, had been laid down years before in old Mrs Garland's time.

"Disgusting. There's no other word for it."

She swept the scraped carrots up in her pinafore apron, and getting from her chair went over to the scullery board where a black-enamelled saucepan stood ready-filled with water.

"And that Mr Warwick, he takes not a blind scrap o' notice," she went on, reaching to the shelf for the salt jar. "Lets the pair o' them do whatever they like, he does. I were only saying to Mr Smith t'other night, surely to God you'd think he'd tell 'em to clear off back to London if they can't be troubled to alter their ways."

"It'll be me as clears off if they don't," declared Marjorie, abandoning her pleating to start worrying at a finger nail, a performance which pushed up one side of her mouth to reveal more gap than tooth. "Three years I've been in service here come Christmas, Mrs Smith, but I'm not a-staying on to be poked and pulled at like I were some'at off the streets. If they wants that sort o' creature, let 'em go down Southover barracks, says I. There's plenty there

77

hanging about of a paynight wi' red shoes and no drawers as'd be happy to oblige 'em both in exchange for the colour o' their money."

"Money, you say?" The housekeeper paused as she came by the table, and leaned forward on her fists. "What money? I'd be surprised if they'd got so much as two ha'pence to rub together atween 'em, that pair. As I said to Mr Smith, it's all very well being gentry-born and talking through your nose at folk, but fine words never buttered no parsnips and that's a fact, as I said to him."

She treated the young maid to a knowing look and a nod before moving on again, adding over her shoulder, "They're none o' them too proud-stomached to live off Madam's charity, if the truth be known."

"An' her daft enough to let 'em, an' all," sniffed the other, examining the damage she'd just made to her finger nail.

"Oh, I wouldn't go so far as to say that, Marjorie." Mrs Smith came back with a trug basket filled with large dark-gilled field mushrooms. "No, I wouldn't say that."

Settling herself down to start peeling them, she went on, "Mebbe that's how it do seem, the way Mr Warwick's got her dancing to his every little tune. But you mark my words, he'll try her patience a bit too far one o' these times. There's fire in the flint, cool as it looks. And when that day comes, as I said to Mr Smith, them Enderbys will find they've bitten off a blessed sight more than they can manage to chew."

One of the Reverend Alec Bethway's parishioners – an elderly bachelor with a somewhat dry turn of wit – when asked why he'd never ventured into wedlock, used always to give as answer the same pithy advice. During her childhood at Eastbourne Dinah had heard it repeated often, and as with so many useless little shreds and scraps carried from the past, it had stayed fixed in her memory like a fly in amber:

"They do say as how marriage is not often merry-age, but very commonly mar-age."

Being so young, she'd never quite understood what the old fellow meant, only that it made others smile to hear him; and so she had smiled too, pretending. But such is the often cruel way of the world that now, when she no longer had need of pretence, she wished to heaven it were otherwise, that she'd never had cause to discover the truth of his words.

". . . Very commonly mar-age." Had the new Mrs Enderby known that the bliss of those first few days of marriage would pale and fade so soon, she would have clung to every moment, begrudging it its passing. After the sterile, unloved years of widowhood, Warwick had awakened her body as a man might tune an instrument long unused, skilfully playing upon her senses to bring her to a quivering pitch of pleasure, each nerve, each fibre singing to the soft, sweet pain of fulfilment; and afterwards, lying warm and sated in his arms, drowsy with love's labour, watching the shadow-flicker of gaslight on the ceiling of their hotel room and listening to the muted sounds of London's streets as the August evening thickened into dusk, she had thought she must surely die of happiness.

She saw her home-coming to Lewes as a kind of triumphal entry, a new husband at her side, a new ring upon her finger, a new name to be known by; joy and a wife's contentment shining in her face. And yet within a month, a single month, the first little hair-fine cracks started to show in the bond of their unity, the first little pin-pricks to snag at the fabric of their marriage.

It all started with Guy and Neville. Not that Dinah objected so very much to their arriving on her doorstep each weekend expecting bed, board and entertainment, as she'd been at pains to assure her husband; but was it necessary to bring along a crowd of total strangers as their guests?

And then came one dreadful night in September. Since coming home to Southwood Place as man and wife, she and Warwick had been sleeping in the main bedchamber on the first floor, a handsome spacious room whose three tall windows looked out towards St Luke's Hill. The smaller rear bedchamber, with its peaceful views of the creeper-covered ruins of Lewes Castle, had been the one which Dinah herself had always used, first with Richard during that early, too-brief marriage; and afterwards, alone with the aching fretful sadness of his loss.

During her mother-in-law's lifetime the main front chamber had been the old lady's domain, an oasis of genteel reclusion where the elder Mrs Garland bore her own long widowhood towards a drawn-out dying, and where Dinah had nursed her, read to her, sat with her during those last few months of semi-consciousness, and at the last, helped to lay her out, robing the bird-light body in its linen shroud.

The room had few enough happy memories. But the new Mrs Enderby chose it nonetheless, preferring whatever associations still lingered from its recent past rather than keep to her old room and conjure up the pale, poor ghost of Richard in her bed each time she made love there with his successor. Even so, despite the new feather mattress, new wallpaper, the rearrangement of furniture, there was something which clung to the atmosphere of that front bedchamber, something which lay uneasily on the edge of Dinah's conscience and made her feel a curious sense of betrayal, as though it were telling her she'd no right to bring Warwick Enderby here as master, that he was as much an unwelcome intruder into the Garland family house as the painted little shop-girls his brothers introduced as "party chums".

It was late on the Sunday evening before the last of the self-invited guests had finally departed and the household could retire for the night. Mr and Mrs Smith lived out, so that apart from young Marjorie who slept in the servants' attic, Warwick and Dinah had the place to themselves for the first time that weekend. She had been unable to relax sufficiently among so many noisy strangers to be able to enjoy her husband's attentions, and consequently was all the more ready tonight to make up for her reluctance by showing herself especially responsive.

It was Warwick, however, who seemed less than enthusiastic for once, going through the motions of love-making in a somewhat cold and perfunctory manner. When he was finished, instead of keeping her close in his arms as he usually did, he threw himself away on his back and lay staring up at the ceiling, the pale wash of moonlight in the room silhouetting the tensely sculpted lines of jaw and mouth.

Turning on to her side and reaching towards him, Dinah asked softly, "Warwick? What is it, my darling? What's wrong?"

He gave an exaggerated sigh. "Nothing. I'm tired, that's all."

"You'd rather we go to sleep now?"

No answer.

She waited a few moments; then said tentatively, "I've wondered sometimes, dearest . . . does it matter so very much to you that you were not the first? You know what I mean . . . that I'd been married before?"

Again there was no reply, only a restless movement of the shoulders that might have been a shrug.

Instinct warned Dinah that she'd be wiser to be quiet now and let him get his rest; but the question she wanted to ask would not let itself be silenced, and before she could stop them the words were already out of her mouth, sounding jealous and petty and just a little cheap.

"I know I'm not the first woman you've ever had. You're too good a lover. Who was she? Won't you tell me about her?"

There was a long pause.

"Tell you about who?" he said at last, wearily.

"The other woman."

"What other woman? Can't you shut up and let me sleep? Haven't I satisfied you enough?"

It was too late now to stop. She heard herself saying, "I don't want to know her name, or anything. Only . . . when it was, and where."

Warwick threw himself irritably on to his side, turning his back away. "What makes you think there was only one before you? There may have been others."

"Others?" Such an unwelcome thought had never occurred before. "Oh, were there – others?"

"Perhaps."

"How many? Two? Three?"

The sudden hurt must have sounded in her words, for her husband turned over again.

"Look, Dinah, why on earth are you asking this?"

"Call it . . . curiosity."

"It won't make you happy if I tell you."

"I don't care. How many were there, Warwick.?"

81

He gave another shrug. "Twenty, I suppose. Twenty-five. I can't remember. Men don't, you know."

Dinah felt nothing for a few seconds; unless it was a horrible emptiness. Then shock, disgust, resentment, followed on each other's heels so rapidly as to choke her and she lay there, silent and unmoving, before the choking sensation passed and she could cry out in a thin, protesting voice, "As many as that? No wonder you can't remember!"

"See, you're angry," Warwick told her coolly, shifting his pillow to a more comfortable angle. "You shouldn't have asked if you didn't want the truth. I hope that's satisfied your curiosity. Now can we get some sleep – please?"

The very thought of her husband sharing with a score or more other women all the loving intimate things he shared with her sickened Dinah to the core. The following day, when Warwick attempted some affectionate little gesture at breakfast, she pushed him away and an argument – the first of their marriage – flared up between them.

Not so much as a word was said of the previous night's painful disclosure, but there was no doubt it was this which goaded Dinah to such a pitch of animosity: had she paused to analyse her emotions that morning, she might have discovered disillusionment as well as deeply hurt pride at the root of her ill-feeling. A sense of injury, too, honed to sharpness by humiliation, for how could she possibly now enjoy the utter abandonment of body and senses in aroused response to her husband's caress, knowing that he'd similarly caressed and aroused a whole line of female partners before her? One or two – even three – she could understand and forgive; but twenty-five? It was more than she could bear.

The disagreement started on a petty note. Warwick had so far failed to pay back the loan she'd made him – and which her bank had stipulated should be a repayable one – and Dinah, irritably, picked on this as an outlet for her grievance.

"Oh, don't start on that again," he complained peevishly, following her through into the drawing room to look for his cigarettes. "I've told you – you'll get the money back when everything's sorted out. You know darned well my allowance has been delayed this month while the family trustees consider what increase they should make now I'm married."

"And in the meantime, I'm expected to provide for your keep out of my own pocket, is that it?"

"Now don't take that tone, Dinah. I would have repaid you weeks ago, I swear I would, but the new motor's cost me just about every last penny in the kitty."

"There was nothing wrong with the Torpedo. You could easily have waited a while longer before spending so much on another machine – "

"What, and run the risk of losing an absolute bargain?" A note of aggrievement crept into Warwick's voice. "Be fair, old girl. You said yourself what a draughty crate the Torpedo was."

"Oh, do stop making excuses for everything!" She swung round on him. "And for heaven's sake what are you doing, rummaging around behind the coal scuttle?"

"I'm looking for my cigarettes. You haven't seen them, have you?"

Dinah closed her eyes and took a deep breath. "No."

"Odd . . . I thought I left them somewhere here last night. Yes, that's right, I had one just before we retired."

"Warwick – " She looked at him again, struggling against a strong desire to lose her temper. "Can we please keep to the subject? I'm trying to discuss the household expenditure and what, if anything, you propose to do about it."

"But I've already explained my position. I mean, what *can* I do about it?"

"For a start,you might ask your brothers not to use my house as some private venue for every tom, dick or harry they care to invite. If I am expected to feed and lodge their friends each weekend, then I certainly think it's only fair they should pay towards the cost."

"Pay towards the cost?" Her husband paused dramatically in his search. "If I may say so, my dear Dinah, that's a remarkably tight-fisted attitude to adopt towards members of our own family. Are you suggesting Neville and Guy ought actually to reimburse you for the privilege of being guests in this house?"

83

"It would show a little good manners if they at least offered something in exchange for all the trouble and expense of entertaining half a dozen of their friends at my table."

"*Your* table? It's my table now, remember. Just as the house is mine, and the – "

"No. No. Oh, no." Dinah felt herself possessed by a sudden wave of fury as her self-control snapped under this final straw. "If you think that, Warwick, then you're very much in error. Southwood Place remains *my* property. And make no mistake, I've no intention of surrendering my independence by signing away its ownership – especially while you're so patently incapable of providing for me as your wife."

"Oh, do talk some sense! I *will* be able to provide for you once this business of my allowance is settled. It's only a matter of a few weeks more at the most."

His tone was matched by the coldly reproachful look he gave as he went across to the sofa in the window embrasure and began hunting about behind the cushions.

"Dash it all, Dinah, you don't give a fellow much chance, do you? Here we are, hardly married above five minutes, and you're already going back on all those promises you made to share everything you have with me."

"I meant my love . . . my life . . . my self . . . my future." Her face had grown suddenly as chalky white as the marble of the fireplace behind her, its paleness emphasised quite startlingly by the vibrant auburn flame of her up-swept hair. "I never meant my property or my personal possessions. I'd have thought that would be perfectly understood by a gentleman of any breeding."

Warwick threw down the cushion he was holding.

"Now look here," he began in blustering retaliation. "I'm growing just a little tired of this ridiculous women's suffrage pie-in-the-sky attitude of yours. It's I that's master here now, don't forget. And no amount of female equality twaddle is going to change that. Now let's have no more of your nonsense about money, Dinah. What's yours belongs to me by right of marriage."

"By God, it does not! You own precisely what you

brought into this house, Warwick Enderby. Three cases of clothing, and nothing more."

"Aren't you overlooking something?"

"Oh, you mean the motor carriage blocking my driveway?" Her voice became heavy with sarcasm. "I believe that was purchased with part of the three hundred pounds I lent to you. Which, in default of repayment, makes it mine."

"The devil it does!" For the first time in their exchange, something approaching the honest emotion of anger showed for a moment in Warwick's handsome face. "I'll have you know that machine was mainly paid for with the proceeds from the sale of my Torpedo. If you're so anxious to know what became of your blasted money – ask the manager of The Strand Palace Hotel."

It took several seconds for the full import of this barb to sink in; then dawning comprehension gripped Dinah in a sort of paralysis, robbing her of her power of immediate response, so that all she could do was to stand there, staring at him, shaking her head in awful disbelief.

"Yes, that's right," he jeered. "It was you who paid for our honeymoon, Dinah dear. The bridal suite, the champagne, the flowers – oh, and a new suit of clothing for me, of course. Tailor-made. I could hardly go to my wedding in something off the peg, could I?"

Somehow she managed to find her tongue again. "But in heavens name – *why*? Why weren't you able to pay for anything yourself?"

For answer, her husband made the eloquent gesture of pulling out the empty pockets of his grey-striped flannel trousers.

A pinched look appeared about Dinah's mouth. "Are you saying . . . you have no financial means of your own? No capital? No funds to draw upon? Nothing, apart from your allowance?"

"That's about it, old girl. Nothing. Not a bean." He paused and then went on cheerfully, "Oh, come on, now there's no need to look as though you've lost a fortune and found a farthing! Things aren't as bad as that." He treated her to one of his boyishly winsome smiles as he moved away from the sofa towards her, his manner changing to a playful

85

cajolery which she found somehow rather sickening in the circumstances.

"I'll admit I'm a bit of a wastrel," he went on disarmingly. "Always have been. But then, life's an expensive business, you know, and one has certain standards to maintain as a gentleman." He laughed. "Perhaps if sovereigns were made square and not round they wouldn't roll away so easily, what?"

"But you must have *something* of your own, surely? Something saved?"

He shook his head. "Money and I don't seem able to stick together for long. Let's face it, if a chap's in the habit of giving it all to the gaming table and race track, there's not likely to be a lot left over for saving, is there?"

There was a long silence.

Then, in a small, suddenly weary voice, Dinah said, "So that's it. Now we have the truth. You're a gambler, are you, Warwick? Is that what you're admitting?"

He gave a light shrug.

"And the reason you've no money is that you fling it all away on horses and cards? That's where you've been off to on those afternoons and evenings of 'family matters' and 'personal business'? Gambling? And I believed you – dear Lord, I believed you! Admired you, even – felt proud of you for being a man of acumen and enterprise. And all the time, you've been going behind my back, nothing better than a spendthrift, a – "

"I prefer the term gentleman of fortune, myself."

"You're a gambler," she repeated, anger blazing up again as the full enormity of what she'd just discovered about this husband of hers struck home. "And you married me to keep you in funds, is that it? You married me as an ever-open purse, a credit account, a convenient source of ready cash to pay your losses. Oh God – "

She flung herself away, hands clutched to her face as though the very sight of him there was more than she could stomach.

"Oh God, Warwick, how could you . . . how *could* you deceive me so? Saying you loved me, that I was more than life to you, that you couldn't bear to be apart from me . . . oh, how could you lie like that?"

"Now don't take on so, Dinah, there's a good girl," he protested, his self-composure just a little shaken by the drama of her reaction. "I *do* love you. You know I do. Don't I prove it often enough? Now stop being silly and come here, let me show you – "

He made to take her into his arms, but she pushed him forcibly away, crying, "Don't touch me!" her head averted so that he would not see the wretchedness and hurt betrayed by the sudden welling tears.

8

Some fifty years or so earlier, in the middle nineteenth century, a visitor to Weatherfield would have found a small rural community isolated among the wooded valleys of the rolling Wealden countryside, linked to neighbouring villages by the threads of cart tracks, droveways and narrow high-hedged lanes, its field and parish boundaries virtually unchanged since medieval days and its families descended from father to son in generations which reached back even further.

At the heart of the village stood its church, St Anne's, in whose graveyard many of those generations lay; and opposite, its green, where the dead in life had disported themselves according to the customs of their day: mystery plays and wassails, mummers and Morris dancing and May Day revelry, summer fêtes and cricket matches.

At the broadest end of this open space had been the village pump and duckpond, fed by a stream which flowed the length of the high street behind a line of railings acting as its boundary; while at the other end it narrowed to a spit of land dividing the road from Buckfield into two encircling arms.

The main arm, the high street, ran away downhill towards the hamlets of Troy Town and Shatterford and was bordered by cottage rows whose plots of garden stretched behind to meet the fields, with a general store, an inn, a smithy and a dame school to serve the small community. The secondary arm proceeded past rectory and church before disappearing again into the countryside on its way towards Spring Hill and the Kentish border.

A rural scene typical of its kind and reflecting the type of life which in later years, when it had all but vanished, would be looked upon with a sad nostalgia by those to whom the march of progress meant the ruination of unspoilt pastoral harmony and country tradition.

Here in Weatherfield, progress came in the unlovely form of statistics: better medical care, diet and hygiene resulting in a rising percentage of live births per family, and so leading to a greater demand upon the community's resources – more housing (which brought in the building contractors), more services (which attracted the commercial developers), more work (which meant small manufactories, yards and the like encroaching upon the surrounding farmland).

By 1910 the metamorphosis of the village was complete, and from rural isolation it had been transformed into a thriving little market town of neat red-brick terraces, its hamlets swallowed up to become mere districts within its urban area. Where there had once been woods and rills and pasture, there now ran streets whose very names were alien to the Sussex landscape: Inkerman and Alma, Mafeking, Kimberley and Ladysmith.

Even the old rough track, which in time past had led ploughmen and shepherds to the refuge of the alehouse outside the village, had been elevated grandiosely to The Holloway, with some half a dozen houses on either side of its former gorse-banked slopes. As for the alehouse itself, a visitor who had known it in the old days would have been hard put now to recognise it as the same place, with its modern façade and enamelled tin advertising signs, and its stables converted to a motor garage with a globe-topped petrol pump standing on the road outside.

Seemingly in an effort to remove itself as far as possible from the ugly contagion of so much progress, the last house at the top of The Holloway was set well back from its neighbours within the privacy of an acre of walled garden and shrubberies, with a curving tree-lined driveway giving it an almost rustic approach. It was this very seclusion which had prompted young Esmond Bates to buy the property some two years earlier when he'd moved away from the family house in Lewes to work as solicitor in what had by now become known as Old Weatherfield, the original village area around the church and green.

His engagement to Jessie Moore the previous spring had

brought a further change: having been with the same legal firm for the past six years, he had lately decided the time was ripe to advance his career, and in the autumn of 1910 he'd gone into partnership with his future brother-in-law Stephen, practising as Bates, Moore & Co., Solicitors, Notaries and Commissioners for Oaths, from chambers in Old Weatherfield high street.

There was an additional attraction about putting down roots in this particular spot, for Esmond's grandfather had been rector of St Anne's church over half a century earlier, and it gave the young man a great sense of pride and continuity whenever he read the name of Esmond Jezrahel Bates among the roll of ministers on the porch board, or looked across the green from the window of his chambers to see the handsome memorial to his forebear standing so prominently above the churchyard wall.

For Stephen Moore, as well, this move to Weatherfield represented something of a home-coming. His mother had been a Pelham-Martin born at Shatterford House – now, alas, demolished to make way for the new railway tunnel – and Jessie and he had spent many a happy childhood holiday here before old Tatton Pelham-Martin's death, when the family had fallen out over the division of spoils and the estate lands been sold off piecemeal (albeit profitably so) to developers.

Like Esmond, too, Stephen had an eye to the future, and welcomed the opportunity of establishing himself in independent practice. As so often had been his complaint, he'd spent quite enough of his years ploughing the same rather dreary furrow in Lewes, drawing up Wills, preparing conveyances and dealing with the minor offences of its citizens, while the senior partners of the firm treated themselves to the plums of the profession.

It had not occurred to him – or if it had, he would never admit it – that the real spur behind his acceptance of Esmond's offer of partnership had been Dinah Garland's marriage to Warwick Enderby.

"I'd no idea you'd left Lewes. They told me when I happened to call at your office last week."

Dinah took the chair placed out for her, smiling her thanks as Stephen went to hang her fur-trimmed coat on the stand by the door before seating himself opposite at his desk.

"You're looking very well," she went on brightly. "The change has obviously suited you."

He gave a brief nod. "I wonder you didn't learn from Jessie that I'd moved out here to Weatherfield."

"Oh – well . . ." The expression faded and she looked away through the rain-smeared window. "I haven't seen much of Jessie lately. You know how it is."

"Mm." He shifted some papers, tidying them together. "But you're still on speaking terms."

"We would be, if we ever met to speak. But since that awful scene . . . you heard all about it, of course? That day she called at the house and gave Warwick a piece of her mind?"

Stephen allowed himself a small smile. "I heard about it. A piece of my sister's mind can be quite a lot for any man to stomach at one serving. I'm not surprised your husband lost his temper."

"But Jessie was quite right to say what she did! It was unforgivable of him to send that silly, spiteful telegram . . . " Dinah bent her head and began pulling awkwardly at the kid-leather gloves lying in her lap. "I've come here to apologise, Stephen. It's a little late, I know. I should have written, perhaps, or tried to see you sooner just to say how deeply, deeply sorry I am. I hope you weren't too hurt by it."

"Hurt? No, not hurt. Annoyed, certainly."

He looked across at her, the pleasant open features marred by a slight frown between the level brows.

"But look here, Dinah, if anyone has to apologise it should be your husband, not you. It was he who sent the wretched telegram, after all. Why make yourself his errand boy?"

She coloured up at that. "Actually, he doesn't know I'm here. And besides, Warwick would be the last person on earth to say he was sorry for anything."

There was a pause while she resumed fidgeting with her gloves; then she went on, "I've come to apologise for myself

91

as much as anything. You see, you were right – you and Jessie. And I was wrong. And I feel . . . guilty. Yes, that's the word. Guilty. Not only because I dismissed your judgement as jealousy, closed my ears to your advice and took no notice when you tried to warn me, but also because of Richard . . . "

"Richard?" The frown deepened. Stephen's eyes never left her face. "Why accuse yourself over Richard?"

"I feel that I've failed him . . . let him down terribly. I feel I've been disloyal to everything we shared together. All those memories I had of him . . . all those – "

The breath seemed to catch suddenly in her throat, and it was with an obvious effort that she struggled to keep her composure.

"Oh dear, I promised myself that I wouldn't cry today. Excuse me – "

Reaching down into the hand-bag on the floor beside her, she took out a handkerchief and gave her nose a good blow.

"I'm sorry . . . I seem to be very weepy just lately. My nerves, I suppose . . . the slightest little thing makes me burst into tears."

Stephen got up and came round towards her, re-seating himself on the edge of his desk by her chair, arms folded, expression one of concern.

"Come now, this isn't like you, Dinah. What's happened? Won't you tell me? You know that anything you say here will be treated in strictest confidence."

She managed a weak smile, and shook her head. "It's a long story, and not very edifying, I'm afraid."

"Well, I'm used to long stories in my profession, and I don't suppose yours is any worse or more dramatic than others I've heard. After all, people don't come seeking advice from solicitors until they've met with trouble of one kind or another. So let's start at the beginning, shall we? Take your time, there's no need to hurry. Tell me what it is that's making you so unhappy."

The kindness in his voice brought Dinah almost to the edge of tears again, and he waited in patient silence while she collected herself, his observant gaze taking in everything about her, from the damp-draggled hem of her brown tweed skirt where she'd walked through the rain from Weatherfield station, to the high-necked cream lace blouse setting off that lovely face above, thinner and paler than when he'd seen her last and its assured confidence replaced by a haunted, melancholy look in the grey-green eyes.

"It's Warwick . . . my husband . . ." she began at last, hesitantly. "I've discovered that he's a gambler."

Her head was bowed, as though she were ashamed of such an admission.

"That comes as no surprise to me," Stephen said grimly. "I'm afraid, my dear, I suspected as much. But please – go on."

Now that she'd taken the first difficult step, she seemed to gain in confidence.

"Sometimes he's lucky and manages to win, and for a day or so we're really quite happy together. He buys me presents – silly things, really, the kind of little gift one would buy a child. Or perhaps he'll take me for a drive in the motor car, down to the coast, or somewhere on the Downs. But it never lasts long. Usually all his winnings have been gambled away again within a week, and we're back to the arguments and the sulks and the demands. And then he disappears for several days at a time, and refuses to say where he's been."

"So you're left in the house alone quite regularly?"

"Oh, not alone, no. Warwick has two brothers. They took his former lodgings in Star Street a month or so ago, but most of the time they prefer to live at Southwood Place. Free of charge, of course."

"I see. I take it, then, that they're both fully aware of the domestic situation between you and your husband?"

Dinah gave a short laugh. "Even the servants are aware of that! Warwick can be very – unrestrained, let's say, when thwarted of something he wants. Which is usually another twenty pounds to spend at Brighton racecourse. I didn't tell you, did I, that I'm expected to finance this little hobby of his?"

"But what about his family?" Stephen's tone was calmly professional now. "What about his noble connections? There must be money there, surely?"

"If there is, I've never seen a penny-piece of it. He receives some sort of monthly allowance from his late mother's estate, but how much I've no idea. It's gambled away almost as soon as he gets it."

"So he makes no provision of any kind for the household, nothing towards the servants' wages, for instance?"

"Good heavens, no. I see to that still. Though things haven't been quite as easy since I forfeited my army widow's pension, of course. All I have left of my own to live on now is my income from the Garland estate and those investments you made on my behalf some years ago. I thought perhaps I might be able to shame Warwick into making some regular contribution by threatening to return to the Electric Picture Theatre – you know, to the job I had as piano accompanist. No man likes to see his wife going out to work, I thought. But I was wrong. Warwick thought it an excellent suggestion. He even offered to come and meet me in the motor car at the end of evening performances."

She paused in her narration, and shook her head as though hardly able to believe the story herself.

"He was fully expecting me to give him whatever the theatre paid me – as pocket money to buy his petrol. Can you imagine! Well, there was a most fearful argument between us, and in the end I told him I *would* go back to playing the piano, if only to escape from his brothers and their awful lady-friends turning my drawing room blue with their smoke and their language every evening. You can't imagine, Stephen, what it's been like for me at times, trapped in my own home. I was starting to feel a prisoner, almost . . ."

There was another pause. She looked down again at her hands, and began twisting her wedding ring round and round. The sound of the rain beating outside at the window added a plaintive, dismal note to the scene.

Her listener rose to his feet and without a word went across to the hearthplace to turn up the gas-fire burning there on a low blue flame. Coming back, he stopped for a moment by Dinah's chair and in a simple gesture of understanding, pressed a hand gently on her shoulder.

Returning to his chair, he leant forward and rested his elbows on the desk top in front of him.

"Jessie told me you'd gone back to playing at the Picture Theatre. Now I can appreciate why. May I ask, by the way, have you revealed any of this to your parents?"

"No. No, I haven't."

"Don't you think they ought to know?"

"Not yet. To tell the truth, Stephen, things have been a little strained between us since the wedding. They were naturally upset that I should've married in a registry office – as far as my brother Kit's concerned, it was tantamount to being licensed to live in sin. Mother's the only one who'd take my side, but she's so devotedly loyal to Father she wouldn't do anything to go against his wishes. And any way, even if I were to tell them of the situation, what could they do? Haul Warwick over the coals for his behaviour? A lot of notice he'd take of that, I'm sure! No, I'd much rather keep them in ignorance and spare them the worry of being anxious on my behalf."

"Well, that's a very unselfish attitude, and shows greatly to your credit. I'm bound to say that you're quite right – there is nothing your father could do to remedy this situation. The Law takes rather a dim view of parents interfering in the domestic disputes of married children."

Stephen laced his fingers together and tapped them thoughtfully against his lip.

"If memory serves me right," he went on after a moment, "your husband's own father is living still, is he not? Have you attempted to confide in him at all?"

"I don't even know where he lives," Dinah answered frankly, "except that it's somewhere in Surrey. Each time I've suggested to Warwick we ought to go and visit him, he's made some excuse to put me off – Mr Enderby's travelling abroad, or else he's indisposed, or has the house decorators in, or some such tale."

"You couldn't write to him, I suppose?"

She shook her head. "I've tried asking Neville and Guy for the address, but they pretend to mishear me, or else promptly change the subject. There seems no point in creating a scene about it."

"You know, don't you, that you could get an injunction to

remove those two brothers-in-law from your property if they were causing you sufficient nuisance?"

"Yes, I did wonder about that. It seems rather a drastic way of showing them to the door, though, doesn't it. I think I'd prefer to wait and see what happens before resorting to the courts."

"As you wish. But the procedure is there if ever you need to make use of it – "

He was about to add something further when he was interrupted by the sonorous chimes of St Anne's clock sounding across the green, and from unconscious force of habit paused to take his watch from its waistcoat pocket to check the time.

"Is that four o'clock already?" Dinah exclaimed, reaching down for her hand-bag. "Goodness, I shall have to hurry. My train leaves in ten minutes."

She got to her feet, stretching herself to relieve the slight stiffness brought on by sitting after being chilled through by the dank October weather.

Stephen went to help her on with her coat.

"Thank you for coming here today and confiding in me," he said gravely. "I only wish there were something I could do to help you."

"But you have helped me. You've listened to me."

She finished fastening her buttons, and turning to face him went on, "We've been friends for such a long while, Stephen. Promise me please you won't abandon me now? I'm going to need a shoulder to cry on from time to time . . ."

He reached out and drew her towards him, holding her there for a moment as he struggled to contain the powerful emotions that suddenly welled up within him. Then, leaning forward and kissing her lightly on the forehead, he said, "Trust me, my dear. I shall always be here if you need me. I give you my word."

"Whatever happens?"

"Whatever happens."

It was still raining when Dinah left the station at Lewes, a thin, mean drizzle blurring the yellow halo of gas-lamps in

96

the streets and draining the light from an ashen evening sky.

By the time she had walked up Station Road and along the length of the high street, the fur-trimmed hem of her coat was sodden and muddied and her buttoned boots were wet through from treading in puddles on the uneven pavements.

Once home at Southwood Place, and the coat and boots removed by young Marjorie to dry by the kitchen fire, Dinah went upstairs to change for dinner. She'd been wearing an amethyst brooch at the neck of her blouse, and it was while she was unfastening the pin to put it away in her jewellery box that she happened to notice the box itself was not in its usual place, on the top of the satinwood cabinet between the windows.

She turned quickly to look around her. She had certainly not shifted it herself before leaving – she could remember locking the lid after taking out the brooch – and there was no reason for Marjorie to move it out of the way to do her dusting.

Concerned, she was about to ring for Mrs Smith, the housekeeper, to come up when her glance fell upon the cabinet cupboard door, which had a tendency to swing open a little if not properly fastened. Seeing it an inch or so ajar, she moved across to look inside.

There on the top shelf stood the missing box, its mother-of-pearl lock cover broken and its woodwork grooved with scratches.

With an angry exclamation, Dinah pulled it out and set it down to open it, hastily checking the velvet-lined compartments. At first sight nothing appeared to have been taken: glass ear-drops, bead necklaces, brooches, bracelets, several rings including her old wedding band – they were all there still, untouched.

Except one thing. The single strand of matched pearls which Richard had given her as his gift on the day of their marriage . . . that was missing.

9

The girl lay helpless, bound hand and foot to the metal tracks, her lovely young face wrung with terror as she struggled to release herself.

Suddenly in the midst of her exertions she was seen to pause, head raised as though listening; and across the foot of the theatre screen appeared the legend:

The whistle of an approaching train!

Algie Langton-Smythe checked his music score by the light of the little gas-jet in the wall overhead. Any moment now the hero would appear, leaping valiantly on to the railway track to sever his dear one's bonds and snatch her away to safety in his arms just as the engine came hurtling round the bend.

He gave a sideways glance at Dinah, pounding away at her piano keys as the approaching climax demanded a sustained *fortissimo* to bring the audience to the edge of their seats. Then, when the grainy screen above had made a flicker-quick change to show heroine gazing adoringly into the eyes of her gallant rescuer, and the piano notes faded away on a diminishing trickle of sound, he put his violin to his chin and began a soft, sweet, sentimental piece to accompany the final legend:

Never to be parted more!

Algie wished that pretty Laura Bates would look at him like that. He shifted himself round for a moment to see over the top of his sawing bow into the body of the theatre. The rosy dimness of the wall lights showed the usual half-full house for a matinée performance, mainly female, and several with young children who were starting to make their noisy presence known now that the final credits had begun rolling up against a background of silhouetted palms (though what palm-trees had to do with it was anybody's guess, since the story had been set among the Rocky Mountains).

Drawing a last long sobbing note from his violin, he waited until the screen had gone blank and the overhead lights started coming up, then lowered the instrument to his side and executed his customary little half-bow to the house. There was a spatter of applause, quickly drowned out by the surge of conversation, coughing, banging back of seats and scraping of heels as the audience prepared itself for departure.

The young man turned away to put his violin into its case, and as he fastened the clips, threw an anxious glance across his shoulder towards the centre aisle seats in the second row. Seeing the younger of two ladies there getting to her feet, he waved a quick farewell to Dinah, busy still at the piano, and nipped smartly under the barrier into the gangway.

Laura Bates paused from drawing on her gloves and leaned down to say something to her companion. Then, as Algie approached them both, his hand out in greeting, she moved hesitantly forward, at the same time responding with a sweet, shy smile from behind the black spotted veil of her brimless toque hat.

"I really am most awfully glad you could come," he exclaimed with enthusiasm. "I hope you enjoyed the matinée?"

"Thank you, yes. Very much. It was most kind of you to send the complimentary tickets." Her voice was soft, and she did not look up as she released herself from his clasp, but kept her eyes modestly lowered. "I trust you didn't mind . . . that Megwynn – that Miss Evans should accompany me, and not my brother?"

"Mind? Not a bit of it! I'm delighted Miss Evans was able to take his place."

He offered his hand again, determined to make as good a first impression as he could upon Laura's chaperone and former governess.

"How d'you do, ma'am."

In return he found himself being examined by a pair of sharp eyes, set in features whose matronly plumpness wore a deceptively ageless look; and not until Megwynn Evans smiled, crinkling the plumpness into a crow's-feet pattern of lines, did her early middle-age betray itself.

Responding to his handshake, she got up from her seat.

"Pleased to make your acquaintance," she said, the lilt of the Welsh Marches in her speech still, even after so many years living here in Lewes. "I thought you played the fiddle lovely, Mr Langton-Smythe."

"Oh – very good of you to say so, ma'am."

"I had an uncle once, liked to play he did. Beautiful music. Made you cry just to listen to him."

"I'm afraid you won't hear many virtuoso performances here. My repertoire's rather limited – " Algie stood aside and invited the two women with a courteous gesture to precede him up the aisle. "'Hearts and Flowers' mostly, and the odd snatch of gipsy music."

He followed behind, violin case under his arm, his eyes drinking in the sight of Laura's small slender figure so becomingly dressed in a toffee-coloured costume coat to match the toque hat.

Passing through the double doors at the back of the theatre, the three of them emerged into the foyer, a well-lit area decorated throughout in red plush to give an impression of comfort and elegance to those coming in from the drab, cheerless streets. Spaced around the walls, large bevelled mirrors reflected the tastefully gilded plaster mouldings on ceiling and staircase, and the framed picture portraits of "screen" celebrities such as Dora de Winton, Percy Moran, Alec Worcester, Blanche Forsythe and the highly popular Gladys Sylvani.

Noting Laura's obvious interest in these, and anxious to rise in her esteem by airing his knowledge, Algie offered to give a conducted tour while they were waiting for Megwynn Evans to return from the ladies' cloakroom down below.

"Of course, the best drama at the moment is being produced by Sir Herbert Tree's London Company," he informed her loftily as they walked along the rows of hand-coloured photograph portraits. "Violet Vanbrugh and Arthur Bourchier – that's Miss Vanbrugh there – they're two who appear regularly in kinematographic roles under his direction. Although on artistic merit, I know some purists prefer F. R. Benson's Shakespeare productions, which are filmed entirely on stage at Stratford-upon-Avon. As a matter of fact, we'll be showing Benson's *Taming of the Shrew* early next year, just a few weeks after Sir Herbert's *Henry VIII*, so it will be interesting to judge between the two."

Laura paused to admire Gladys Sylvani.

"Don't you think she has the most beautiful features," she ventured to put in before they moved again. "Such expressive eyes. And oh – look – here's Warwick Buckland! He played a role in the very first motion picture Esmond took me to see. I must confess . . . I was a little in love with him for weeks afterwards."

Her cheeks coloured at the memory.

Algie had been about to declare that Miss Sylvani's much admired "English Rose" beauty paled to nothing when compared with Laura's own loveliness; but the thought of her throwing away her affections upon some celluloid matinée idol vexed him so considerably that he restricted his comment to a terse, "Cecil Hepworth's company, both of them," casting the debonair Mr Buckland a narrowed glance as he turned his companion's attention elsewhere.

Contriving to change the conversation just as Megwynn Evans rejoined them again, he went on casually, "Oh, by the way, before I forget – I was wondering whether it might possibly interest you at all to visit a production studio? There are several along the coast here – I'd be very pleased to arrange for you both to be shown around one."

Seeing Laura hesitate, he pressed on, "You see, I happen to know the chap who's just recently formed the Brighton and County Film Company. Speer's his name. W. H. Speer. Used to be proprietor of the Queen's Theatre. His place is only a hop and a skip from here – half an hour at the most by omnibus. Or there's the Harry Furniss studios at Hastings. They've been longer established, but they're further off, of course, and I'm not acquainted with Mr Furniss personally."

He paused, a hopeful expression on his young face, waiting for the grateful response which wishfulness had lured him to expect.

There was none.

He waited a few moments, then said a little lamely, "Well?"

"Well – " Megwynn Evans smiled in a way that was kind

and yet had an arm's-length firmness about it. "There's good of you to offer such a treat. But it's Mr Bates you should be asking, really. He'd need to give his permission, see."

"Ah. Mr Bates. Yes . . . yes, of course."

Crestfallen, he looked again at Laura. The prospect of approaching her father filled him with an awful trepidation: by repute apparently, the Inspector of Schools for Lewes was a figure of stern authority and a stickler for discipline, and had already assumed in Algie's imagination the form of a hidebound old bigot who'd sooner see off his daughter's suitors with a shot-gun than allow them to set one foot over his doorstep.

She returned the look with one of smiling encouragement – at least, it might have been smiling encouragement, though behind the black-spotted veil it was rather hard to tell.

The glance was sufficient to put fresh heart into the young man, however, and reminding himself that Laura was well worth the risk of being peppered alive with buckshot, he continued, "Let's suppose, then, that your father is agreeable – you'd like to see around a film studio, wouldn't you, Miss Bates?"

She transferred her look towards her chaperone, as though seeking guidance, and for a moment he thought she must refuse.

Then, apparently making up her mind for herself, she gave a sudden quick nod. "Yes, I should like that a great deal."

Algie very nearly hugged her.

Spirits soaring again, he conducted the two ladies across the foyer to the theatre tea-room, announcing brightly as they went, "If we're lucky, we may even find they're doing some shooting that day – "

"*Duw*, I hope not!" exclaimed Miss Evans, pulling up short.

"No, no, I mean filming a scene. 'Shooting' is the technical term they use when they're aiming a camera, ma'am."

Once settled at a corner table and a large pot of tea and plate of almond spice biscuits ordered, the young man continued enthusiastically, "Who knows, it's just possible the studio might've engaged some well known actor or other in the leading role."

This idea obviously appealed at once to Laura, for her eyes

lit up in wonderment as she asked, "Oh – do you really think so?"

"Well . . . there's a chance. But mustn't raise your hopes too high."

The caution fell upon deafened ears. A smile that would not have shamed an angel wreathed her lips, and clasping her small hands to her breast, she breathed in awe-struck tones, "What a simply divine notion . . . just imagine, Megwynn. Why, I may actually even meet Mr Warwick Buckland himself – in person!"

At the northern end of Lewes, between the River Ouse and the parish boundary of Malling, there ran a sedate, tree-lined road which had started its life as a bridleway hugging the edge of the river marshes. In time it had developed into a convenient detour for heavy-laden horse traffic, avoiding the periously steep descent of Malling Hill; and by the 1880s, having passed through the transitionary stages of Malling Fields and Spences Fields, it had finally settled on the urban map as Spences Lane, and its once wild river borders tamed to gardens, paddocks and orchard plots.

On either side at respectable intervals the slated roofs and red-brick chimneys of large family villas rose above the treeline, approached by sweeping gravelled drives which in early summer blazed with the gaudy-bright colour of rhododendron flowers, and in winter lay mantled in the gloomy green shadows of tangled laurel.

The Bates family had occupied one of these villas since 1882, in which year Ellis Bates purchased the property upon his marriage to his first wife, Sophia. Tragically, she had died seven years later, leaving two small infants, Esmond and Laura, to his care; and though he made every effort to be a good parent, he found the burden of fatherhood an onerous one and had delegated their upbringing to a succession of governesses.

It was not until the arrival of Megwynn Evans in 1890 that the children had known much of affection or warmth in their isolated nursery world. Certainly, they received no spoiling from their father's second wife, Dorothy, a quiet, pale woman who bore them a sickly half-brother in 1893, and after his

103

death seemed almost to shun the two young siblings as though their health and vigour were too painful a reminder of her own failure.

There were no more children of the marriage; and for Laura and Esmond life at Spences Lane settled into the domestic pattern of a middle-class, middle-aged household, dictated by discipline, education and supervised leisure occupation. Their only release from the rigidity of the system was the holidays spent twice a year with Miss Evans at Bonningale, home of their Grandmother Bashford. Here in the rolling downland countryside they were given freedom to enjoy themselves unfettered by their father's regulations, for their grandmother took a perverse delight in ignoring the dictates of her eldest son – posthumous issue of her first marriage, to the Reverend Esmond Bates of Weatherfield – and allowed his children to run colt-wild with their numerous Bashford cousins in the lanes and fields and upland larchwoods around the Bonningale estate.

For Laura and Esmond as they grew towards maturity, this would always remain a time of enchantment: days of golden summer when the sun-warmed skies above the ripening corn were filled with the sweetness of larksong, and frost-sharp days of winter when icicles spangled the hedges and sunsets fired the snows of the Downs with flame-quick colour.

But all too soon the happy weeks would pass and the time draw near again for parting, and they would take home with them both to Lewes small mementos for remembrance – field flowers pressed to paper thinness, glowing leather "conkers", mossy nests of hedge sparrows, feathers of every hue, even once a fossil shell impressed inside a pebble.

As the years went by, leaving schooldays behind, these holidays grew fewer, for Laura and Esmond were now expected to accompany their step-mother to Margate or Broadstairs. It was not until 1905, when Esmond came of age and might consider himself his own master at last, that anything like the old pattern could be re-established; but by then Grandmother Rachael Bashford was dead and there was no longer the same feeling of warmth and welcome since her son George became head of the household. Occasionally brother and sister visited the Arundel area to stay with one or other of the cousins; but the old days had gone, and would never come again.

Once Esmond had moved away from Spences Lane to live at Weatherfield, the conditions governing Laura's life at home grew even stricter, and there were times when she felt she was being treated as a prisoner, almost, denied the liberty to lead a normal social existence. Her father had always been a sternly austere parent, the type of man whose nature leads him to regard firmness as a sign of affection, and the teaching of manners, self-command and discipline as among the most necessary virtues to instil in a growing child – an attitude which had stood him in admirable stead during his years as Inspector of Schools for Lewes, but was hardly conducive of much warmth or spontaneity within his own house.

As Laura blossomed into womanhood, this attitude had been exacerbated by a possessiveness which took the form of over-zealous protection, and had it not been for the companionship of Megwynn Evans she would have found herself completely isolated. The only occasions on which she was permitted to accept any invitation were when either Miss Evans or Esmond was able to accompany her as chaperone; and even this small pleasure was severely limited, for fear she might see more of any one particular person than was considered acceptable.

Contrary to all her hopes, this state of affairs had not been improved by the very generous bequest from a great-aunt's estate which Laura received on her coming-of-age in 1908: instead of liberating her from the chains of her father's authority, the inheritance had but served to shackle her further, for now Mr Bates suspected every new acquaintance of being a fortune-hunting opportunist, and his daughter's social purdah grew, if anything, worse than before.

Had Algie Langton-Smythe known what a lion's den he was entering that day in mid-November when he came to Spences Lane seeking permission to take Laura to Brighton, he might well have been tempted to reconsider the wisdom of his intentions before proceeding a single step further.

Ellis Bates took the card which the maid had presented on a silver tray and held it away from him at arm's length, as though to bring it too close might risk contamination.

105

"Ah. Mr Langton-Smythe," he said frostily, dropping the card back on to the tray and glancing over the top of his pince-nez spectacles at Algie, standing awkwardly at the other end of the entrance hall, his cap clutched in his hands. "You have an appointment with me, I believe, sir? Ten o'clock sharp?"

The Inspector of Schools for Lewes shot a look at the moon-phase dial of the mahogany longcase clock over against the wall. "Two minutes early, sir!"

He retired back into his study; then, once the clock had begun its ponderously resonant chime to mark the hour, reappeared again at the open door.

"Thank you, Annie. You may show Mr Langton-Smythe in."

This pantomime of punctuality had the effect – as was intended – of increasing Algie's state of apprehension, and having handed his cap and muffler to the maid, he promptly ruined a good quarter-hour's combing in front of his dressing mirror by thrusting his fingers through his hair as he entered Mr Bates's study, causing it to stick up in brilliantined ginger spikes.

The lean, stoop-shouldered inspector seated himself at his desk and surveyed his young visitor in silence. Behind him on the wall above the ornate marble fireplace hung a large portrait in oils of a pinch-faced gentleman in the clerical garb of the previous century, whose features bore something of the same cold emotionless stamp as the man below.

Anxious to find favour with the courtesy of a compliment, Algie indicated the painting and said rather too earnestly, with a smile which trembled at the edges with nervousness, "That's a very handsome portrait, sir. Wonderful quality of dignity and – er – and character. An ancestor, surely?"

"My father," came the short reply.

"Ah, yes. Of course. Yes, the resemblance is quite marked, if I may say so, sir –"

"Mr Langton-Smythe," interrupted the other on a note of some impatience, "I should be greatly obliged if we might reach the point of this interview. It concerns my daughter Laura, I believe."

"Laura. Yes, sir." Algie gulped, then added hastily, "That is, I mean Miss Bates, sir."

There was a moment's awkward hesitation.

The inspector began a slow tattoo with his fingers on the edge of his desk. "Well – ?"

"Well, sir – " another gulp – "I should like your permission to take Miss Bates to Brighton one day, to show her around a motion picture studio there. The Brighton and County Film Company, sir."

A further pause.

"I'm sure she would find it all most instructive, sir."

The tattoo quickened slightly. "My answer is no, Mr Langton-Smythe."

"No? Oh – oh, but sir –"

"I said, no."

Ellis Bates leaned back in his leather armchair and eyed the visitor with acute dislike. For a moment Algie was reminded of his own schooldays, when he used to be brought up before his headmaster charged with some misdemeanour or other, to receive a verbal reprimand before feeling the cut of the cane across his cringing flesh.

"What makes you suppose, sir, that my daughter is the type of young woman who would wish to see a place of that kind?" This was said as though a film studio were rather worse than the most depraved sink of iniquity.

"Well . . . I imagined that it might interest her, don't you know. The novelty, and all that . . . " The new starched collar put on for this interview was starting to feel uncomfortably tight, and Algie ran a finger round inside to ease it. "I suppose it's just that Miss Bates semed rather keen on motion pictures and I thought – "

"It is not given you to think, Mr Langton-Smythe," came the acid interruption. "Nor to suppose, nor yet to imagine. You are, as I understand, an employee of the Electric Picture Theatre. A musical accompanist. A violin-player."

Again, that inflexion of tone hinting at a somehow rather different interpretation, as though a player of the violin were only slightly superior to the very dregs of society.

"You are paid to perform, sir, not to think or to suppose or to imagine. What would the world come to if every member of a pit band so far forgot himself as to hob-nob as an equal with those who provide him with a living? The standard of public behaviour is slipping quite low enough nowadays without persons of your type being encouraged to get above themselves."

Stung to self-defence by the coldly insulting manner in which these remarks were delivered, Algie forgot himself for a second.

"I may work in the pit of a picture house, Mr Bates, but with respect, you ought not to infer from such employment that my background is unacceptable or my class of society in any way inferior to your own."

"I was not aware, sir," rejoined the other cuttingly, "that playing the violin in a 'picture house' qualified one to be such an arbiter of class. You will next be asking me to believe, I suppose, that your father was a fellow of excellent breeding because he could grind an organ in the streets."

Such open and arrogant rudeness demanded instant rebuttal and Algie – burning his boats – had no choice but to give it.

"That is an unwarranted attack upon the honour of my family, Mr Bates," he said with some dignity, "and shows a regrettable lack of civility in a man of your station. As it happens, my father is a member of one of the oldest titled families in England – "

"This interview is at an end, sir." Ellis Bates got to his feet and went over to the bell-pull by the fireplace. "I have nothing more to say to you."

"I am a graduate in English and History of the University of Oxford," went on Algie doggedly. "I also have qualifications in – "

"Plainly you did not hear me," the other rapped out sharply, his back still turned upon his visitor. "I have *nothing* more to say to you, sir."

"And I may not take Miss Bates to Brighton?"

There was no reply. Only the noise of the maid opening the study door, and the order – "Mr Langton-Smythe is leaving, Annie. Kindly show him out. And he is not to be admitted to this house again."

10

"I see they're calling another general election for next month," said Corporal Walter Jackson, folding back the pages of *The Daily Graphic* newspaper and addressing himself to his betrothed, Florrie Cox, housemaid to Captain and Mrs Francis Bethway. "That's the second one this year. They must think we've nothing better to do wi' our time than traipse along to bloomin' polling booths."

Florrie licked a forefinger and dabbed it expertly at the face of the heavy flat-iron she'd just lifted off the hob of the kitchen range. Satisfied that it was hot enough, she took a firm grip on the flannel binder protecting its handle and began smoothing it over the linen bedsheet spread across the board in front of her.

"About time they gi' us females some say in the matter," she remarked, working the iron up and down in slow sweeps. The warmth of her labours and the heat from the fire had brought a fine pearling of perspiration to her brow, and she paused for a moment to wipe it away with the back of a hand before continuing, "Never seemed fair to me, it hasn't, us women not being allowed the vote. We've got rights, just the same as you men – I've heard 'em say so, them ladies that come to gi' speeches at public meetings."

"Ah, you don't want to listen to them, our Florrie," the batman told her, looking across the top of his newspaper. "Fill your pretty head wi' a lot o' nonsense, they do. When you're my missus you won't be wanting to be distracted wi' all that sort o' thing."

They smiled at one another in the affectionate manner of two people who had grown to know each other very well and were comfortably at ease together, with none of that artificial veneer put on for top show before marriage.

The young woman lifted the flat-iron back on to the hob to heat again, and glanced down over her artilleryman's shoulder. A headline caught her eye and she bent forward to read the piece below, mouthing the words slowly to herself; then, frowning, straightened up and said, "Read that bit out to me, will you, there's a duck, while I get on wi' pressing these few sheets?"

"What – this bit here about Crippen?" Wally indicated the article with his head.

"Aye. I'll have Mrs Bethway ringing down for nursery tea in half an hour and I want to get this lot finished out o' the way first."

Returning to the pressing board, she lifted one end of the bedsheet and folded it over, then over again, and carried it across to the wooden clothes-horse to air.

"When's he to be hanged, does it say?" she wanted to know, coming back with another sheet from the pile in the laundry basket.

Wally glanced quickly down the lines of closely-typed print. "Twenty-third, I think. That's next Wednesday, is it? Aye, next Wednesday. Four more days, and then – " He drew a forefinger in a sudden snatched gesture across his throat. "It's down the hatch for Dr Crippen."

"Ooh, don't!" Florrie shivered in mock horror. "I know he's deserved it, poisoning his poor wife and cutting her up into collops as he did. But the thought o' swinging on the end of a rope . . . " She shivered again and picked up her flat-iron. "I wonder they let that Miss Le Neve off scot-free. If you ask me, she was in it wi' him right up to her – "

She was about to say up to her neck, but deciding that wasn't quite the expression to use in such circumstances, finished her sentence with a jerk of the head and an expressive roll of the eyes.

Wally made a non-committal sound and continued his perusal of the *Daily Graphic* article.

"There's not much here," he said after a moment. "Crippen's old father's gone and died, that's all. Out in America. Something about 'penniless through lack of remittances from doctor, his only support'."

"Oh?" There was a pause while the young housemaid leaned across to a bowl of water on the kitchen table, and dabbling her fingers in its surface began flicking drops over the bedsheet to dampen the creases in the linen.

110

Then – "Well? Read what it says there, won't you? About the old man a-dying."

Wally cleared his throat; and without pause for punctuation, rattled off the entire first paragraph on a single breath.

"'Los Angeles November eighteenth Myron H. Crippen aged 88 years father of Dr Hawley H. Crippen under sentence of death in London for the murder of his wife died today in this city friendless and penniless his death due to the infirmities of age was hastened by grief over his son's crime – '"

"Here, slow down a bit!" cried Florrie, interrupting. "You'll catch the London train at that rate." Another pause, another flick of water. "Would you like some more tea if I put the kettle on?"

"Oh, aye, that 'ld be nice. Shall I go on?"

A nod. "But not so blessed fast, mind."

While she went into the scullery to fill the kettle at the brownstone sink, Wally resumed his reading, raising his voice so that she could hear him above the running water.

"'Death occurred in a rooming house, and the only person at the aged man's bedside was the woman who managed the place. Dr Crippen was the sole support of his aged father. No remittance had come since the son's flight from London with Ethel Le Neve and his arrest in Canada some months ago. Facing actual starvation he was helped by a few persons whom he had come to know during his residence in Los Angeles.'"

The newspaper was closed up.

"Is that all?" Florrie asked, setting the kettle on the hob beside her flat-iron, which she picked up in turn to resume her pressing.

"Aye, that's all. There's nothing else about it. Which makes a change." Wally folded the paper and cast a quick look over the sports news on the back page. "We've had scant else but bloomin' Crippen all year, strikes me."

"That's two poor souls he's killed wi' his misdeedious ways. First his wife, and now his father." The iron sizzled as she sprinkled more water over the sheet. "I don't know what the world's coming to, I'm sure, such wickedness as there is in it. I tell you some'at, Wally – " leaning forward towards him across the board, her voice lowered – "I oft-times think

111

to myself that's what'll happen here, some'at like that, the way *he*'s been a-carrying on upstairs."

"Who, Dr Crippen?"

"No, you great lummock – Captain Bethway!"

"What, you think the Captain'll bump his missus off and bury her in the coal cellar?" The batman gave a laugh. "You've been reading too many newspapers, my girl."

"I don't know so much." Her voice was lowered still further. "He's got hisself another woman again, and Mrs Bethway's in a right old taking about it. Ever since the battalion come back from exercises, them two have been at it hammer and tongs up there, night after blessed night. It's not like her to make such a fuss about a thing – she's usually such a quiet, timorous soul, put up wi' anything from him, she will. But not this. Not this time."

There was a pause. The kettle had begun to sing quietly on the hob, and Florrie went across to pour off some water into the brown-glazed teapot, swirling it round to warm it before going to empty it down the scullery sink. Coming back, she spooned in some tea from the tin caddy on the table and when the kettle had boiled, filled up the pot and set it down beside Wally.

"There you are, my duck. Help yourself."

He nodded his thanks.

"*You* know who it is, don't you?" she went on, returning with the last of the bedsheets. "You must've seen her round the camp, surely?"

"Who's that, then?" He gave his attention to putting milk and sugar into the mug at his elbow.

"This new woman he's started taking up with."

"Now, Florrie, you should know better than go asking me a thing like that. The Captain's my superior officer, remember. He's a good soldier, always treats his men right, and I've got a lot o' respect for him. What he does wi' his private life is no business o' mine, so I keep my nose out of it."

Florrie pulled a face.

"The Major's wife seen 'em out together," she started again after a moment or two. "Their maid Daisy heard her saying so. Saw the pair o' them a-coming off the Downs wi' her up on the back of his horse, bold as brass. Black-haired creature like a

112

gipsy, Daisy said the Major's wife described her. All flounced out in red, just like some'at off the halls."

Wally stirred his tea without comment, knocking the spoon on the rim of his mug before laying it down on the oil-cloth table cover.

Seeing that he wasn't going to be drawn into giving information, and knowing well enough that to press him would only provoke a stubborn silence, Florrie decided to let the matter drop. Folding the final sheet and draping it with the others over the clothes-horse, she tidied away, and then went out to the scullery pump to wash her hands before starting to prepare afternoon tea for the nursery.

"You know what I think, though, our Wally," she said over her shoulder, pausing from taking a loaf out of the crock, "the way things are going in this house, it wouldn't surprise me in the least one o' these days to see the Captain's name in black print in the newspapers – just like that Dr Crippen's."

It was a very cosy, domestic little scene. The greyness of the dank November day outside the nursery window had been banished by the cheery warmth within; the low moan of the wind in the chimney cowl muted by the rustle of flames in the hearth and the comfortable homely tick of the mantelpiece clock. On the rag-work rug in front of the fireguard, Traddles the birthday puppy (growing into a sensible young animal who liked his creature comforts) lay tucked in sleep with his nose beneath a forepaw, twitching in dreams. And watching from the shelves around the posy-patterned walls, an assortment of dolls with china heads and flaxen curls, stiff little arms held out in empty embrace, the firelight casting their shadows against the corners of the quiet room.

He ought to be happy, Francis Bethway told himself. Happy. Yes, a happy man, full of domestic pride and contentment, sitting snug in the comfort of his own home, his baby daughter on his knee, money enough in the bank, good health, good career, not a cloud to darken the horizon of his future . . .

Yet here he was, tormented in mind and body, unable to get his rest, damning himself and all around him – and for what reason? All because one stubborn, headstrong little bitch had

113

got him eating out of her hand with unfulfilled lust – love – longing – whatever it was, so that now he was reduced to such a state of frustration that his life had become a hell upon earth and his masculine pride been wounded to the very quick.

He should give her up, he knew that. Commonsense shouted it at him day and night. He should give her up, stop trying to see her, send no more letters pleading for another meeting, another chance to hold her in his arms and kiss that teasing, mocking carmine mouth. He should try to forget her, forget his hunger for the body she refused to give him, tell himself she wasn't worth it, all this misery and anger and constant dramatics.

If he'd known that Cecilia Desatti was going to lead him such a merry dance, he'd never have bothered himself with her. One moment she'd be all over him, rousing him to such a pitch with her knowing little hands that she had him almost on his knees to her, begging for more; and the next instant she'd become the outraged virgin protecting her virtue and ready to scream rape if he so much as laid a finger on her; or else some spiteful hussy indulging in open ridicule of his behaviour, pouring scorn on his ability to please her, laughing at his love, making him feel like some beardless youth who'd never fumbled at a woman's skirts before.

All hell had been raised in some of the arguments they'd had between them – usually out on the Downs, where the wind whipped the words from their mouths and only sheep were witness to the violence of their quarrels. Several times Francis had returned to camp with the red marks of her fingers across his cheek, to be bathed with iced water by his batman, Corporal Jackson, before he dared show his face at home to Marion. In return, he'd given Sissy a shake or two to think about; and she'd gone running off, screaming her hatred, swearing he should never go near her again. But a few days later, a week, he'd see her there outside the camp, waiting.

They were like two moths, battering themselves to shreds upon the flame of their own desires . . . if only she would give in to him, let him possess that tantalizing body, in a month or less the whole affair would be over and they could

114

go their separate ways in peace. But no. Not Sissy. Whether it was her Italian family background, her strong Catholic upbringing or her own proud obstinacy, she'd sworn to go to her marriage bed virtually as pure as the driven snow. The fact that Francis, and quite a few before him, had already trampled their footprints here and there seemed to worry her not in the least: as long as there was nothing to show for it, a man might kiss and caress her as much as he pleased – but only so far, and no further. No matter how abandoned her behaviour (and there were times when she could be very abandoned indeed) there was always a point in their love-making when Sissy said no. And meant it.

Francis Bethway found the whole thing intensely frustrating.

"Damn her!" he said suddenly, out loud. "*Damn* her!"

His voice shattered the quiet of the room. The dog on the hearth and the child in his arms both started at the sound, one looking up in a searching manner before yawning nervously and subsiding again; the other, roused from the edge of sleep, giving a complaining wail and rubbing dimpled little fists into her eyes.

"Oh, there, my sweet heart – did your Papa make you jump?" he hastened to apologise, adopting a half-crooning tone of voice. "There, then . . . there, there, then . . . you're not going to cry, are you?"

Little May gave every appearance of being about to do exactly that.

Seeing the baby blue eyes disappearing into the plump rosy cheeks as the infant screwed up her face for the first yell, her father took prompt action, and swinging her up in the air, set her down upon his crossed legs, ride-a-cock-horse fashion. This was a game May adored, and the threatened outburst of tears faded as if by magic, to be replaced by a beautiful smile revealing four pearly teeth in the pink gums.

Holding his daughter by the hands, Francis began bouncing her gently up and down, at the same time reciting in rhythm:

"This is the way the gentlemen ride,
A gallop a trot, a gallop a trot,
This is the way the gentlemen ride,
A gallop, a gallop a trot."

May squealed with delight, her noise encouraging Traddles to join in the merriment with high-pitched little yelps of excitement as he jumped up against Francis's chair.

"This is the way the ladies ride – "

"Heavens above, what a rumpus in here!" The nursery door had at that moment opened, and glancing over his shoulder, Francis saw Marion was there, a hand upon the knob, young Angela just behind her. "I could hear it all the way from the stairs."

"We're playing a game, aren't we, May?" he responded cheerfully; and jigging the baby up and down again – "Oh, this is the way the ladies ride – "

"Now, Francis, don't excite her too much," he was admonished as his wife came over towards the fire. "She'll be sick on your uniform, and then you'll blame me. Angela, take Traddles down to Florrie, will you, darling, and ask her to let him out into the yard for a while."

"But Mama – "

"Do as you're bid, there's a good child."

"But Mama, it's raining," Angela insisted. "He'll get wet, poor little thing."

"So will the hearth rug if puppy doesn't go out soon." Then, seeing the lower lip begin to pout rebelliously, there was added by way of inducement – "And you may ask Florrie for a chocolate biscuit for yourself from the tin."

The child's expression lightened at once. Squatting down, she held out her hands to the puppy, who ran towards her, wriggling with enthusiastic affection, and obediently allowed himself to be led away by the collar with only a roll of the eye to signify his preference to stay here in the warmth of the nursery.

"Has she been good while I've been out?" Marion asked, lifting May into her arms.

"Good as gold." Francis looked up at her. "You don't seem very surprised to see me here."

"Ought I to be?"

"Well, I wasn't expected, was I? I hadn't sent you word from camp that I'd be home this afternoon."

His wife made no answer, occupying herself with little

116

May, kissing the small fingers and stroking back the fluff of curls from the infant's forehead.

"You might say you're pleased to see me," he went on, straightening the creases in his blue uniform trousers as he got to his feet.

She glanced at him over the baby's head. "I *am* pleased to see you, Francis. It's quite a change to have you home twice in one week."

Something in the coolness of her tone warned him that she was not in the most receptive of moods, and treading carefully to avoid the aggravation which of late had led to several bitter scenes between them both, he said mildly, "I wanted to see how May was. She seemed fretful the last time I was here . . . Monday, was it? Did you send for the doctor to look at her?"

Marion shook her head. "It was only teething pains. I rubbed her gums with a little honey and that seemed to ease them. Francis – "

She paused; then drew in a deep breath and after a moment went on, not looking at him, "Actually, Francis, I've just now come from Dr Marshall's."

"Oh? About Baby?"

"No. No, about myself."

"There's something wrong with you?"

She bent her head and pressed a cheek against little May's soft curls. In the glow of the firelight she looked very lovely standing there, and he felt a sudden warm tenderness towards her.

"No, there's nothing wrong." she answered at length in a low voice. "It's simply that I'm pregnant again."

"Pregnant – ? What – another child?"

She looked back up at him, and he saw that there were tears shining in her eyes.

"Yes. I'm sorry . . . "

"Sorry? Good Lord above, why sorry? Marion – " he reached out and put a hand on her shoulder, feeling its soft curve beneath the wool blouse. "What's the matter? Aren't you glad we're to have another child?"

"Oh, how can you ask me that? I'd be more than glad to

117

bear this baby if only I could be sure its father wanted it. But in the present situation – "

" I *do* want it." He stared at her. Despite everything, the two of them still shared the marriage bed together, and in the dark anonymity of the night their relationship as husband and wife had continued its natural course. "It's ours – yours and mine – and a son, please God. *You* want it, don't you?"

"Yes," she replied simply, and the tears spilled over in slow drops and ran unheeded down her saddened face.

"Well, then – "

"Listen to me. If you wish me to carry this baby, Francis, you must alter your ways . . . I mean, give up this woman you're seeing . . . stop being unfaithful. If things go on as they have been between us these past few months, I shall become ill. No – hear me out, please. Dr Marshall says my health cannot take the strain of what I am being put through by your behaviour. I was perfectly candid with him today . . . and he is ready to see you himself if necessary, to make it clear that unless I have peace of mind I may be in danger of losing this child."

Her mouth trembled a little, and she bit her lower lip; then, in control of herself once more, went on more calmly, "The choice is yours, Francis. It is entirely up to you whether to save our unborn child . . . perhaps the son you've always wanted. Or whether to sacrifice both him and me for some passing lovesick fancy for a creature of no importance."

There was a long silence.

Then suddenly, unexpectedly, the Captain began to laugh. It was true he wanted a son – more than anything, more than Sissy Desatti even. A son to bear his name, a son in whom he might see himself reflected as a man. The choice was his, was it? Well, a pity about Sissy, but she'd had her chance . . .

The decision, it seemed, had already been made.

11

"Dinah – darling! I wondered whether I'd see you here. Warwick's let you out for the afternoon, has he?"

Dinah Enderby recognised the voice without turning.

"Hello, Jessie," she responded coolly, stung by that little shaft of sarcasm.

"Come to join the affray, like me?" Jessie Moore appeared beside her, and she could smell the faint scent of Guerlain's *Après L'Ondée* on the other's skin as she leaned forward to brush cheeks and kiss the air in greeting.

From all around the small hall came the noisy chatter of some three dozen or so people engaged in conversation as they waited for the arrival of the platform party; and glancing about her to wave to one or two of the ladies she knew, Jessie went on, "A pity they decided to cancel the band and the banners. There's nothing like a march through the streets to rouse the hackles of the opposition."

She took her friend by the arm.

"You think we may have trouble during the meeting?" Dinah asked, allowing herself to be led through the knots of people towards the front of the hall, and marvelling at the way in which Jessie always managed to take immediate control of the situation, no matter what.

"Oh, bound to! I mean, The Women's Social and Political Union, *here*, at The British Workmen's Institute – it's like a red rag to a bull. Look, why don't we sit at the end of the row by the platform, and then if it seems to be getting too unpleasant we can nip out smartly through the side-door."

"But won't we be right in the line of fire if they start throwing things from the back row?"

"Don't worry – I've brought my brolly along. Frightfully handy for parrying the odd egg or whatever."

Jessie brandished her black silk umbrella and laughed;

then, seating herself, patted the neighbouring chair, her gesture more one of command than invitation.

"Now, you elusive creature, tell me – how are you these days? Do you realise, it's been *ages* since we last exchanged any kind of conversation. We shall soon be reduced to passing each other by with distant bows from either side of the street, Stephen says, like two elderly rivals for the vicar's affection – "

"How is Stephen?" Dinah put in as she sat down on the dealwood chair.

"Oh, much the same as ever. He joined us with Esmond for luncheon last Sunday, and bestirred himself sufficiently to ask me to spy out the camp and let him know how things were with you."

"Did he tell you I'd called on him in Weatherfield recently?"

"Why, no. But then, if it was a professional visit, he wouldn't. The very soul of discretion, that's Stephen. I suppose you went to consult him about that awful Warwick whatever-his-name you married?"

"Supposing I did?"

There was something in the off-hand manner in which Dinah responded to this barbed little shot in the dark that made Jessie pause a moment and give her friend a sharp sideways look. Then, with a shrug of the shoulder, she went on, "Well, I can't say I'm much surprised. Lord knows, it's plain enough that things aren't exactly tickety-boo between the pair of you. But it's none of my business. I'm keeping out of it."

"Really?" Now it was Dinah's turn to show some sarcasm. "What about the dreadful row you caused when you came to the house all those weeks ago?"

"Well – the fellow needed putting in his place! Anyway, he knows my opinion of him."

"He should. You've aired it often enough in the past."

"Oh, darling, don't let's quarrel." The other tugged irritably at the fashionable fox-fur stole worn draped round the neck of her coat. "The fellow's caused quite enough trouble between us already. I'd hate to give him the satisfaction of ruining our friendship entirely."

There was another tug, bringing the fox head close to Dinah's arm, its leather snout wrinkled in a snarl and its dull glass eyes glaring up at her in a most malevolent fashion.

"On the other hand," Jessie added, with one of her sudden bright smiles, "perhaps he's not completely the villain I paint him – I mean, he *has* let you out to attend this meeting."

"Actually, he's gone away on one of his mystery jaunts," Dinah replied, without much enthusiasm. "I've no idea what day he's back again."

"Ah?" Her friend gave another of her quick sideways looks. Then, starting up – "Oh, here's Miss Bradman – " as a stout lady encased in a tweed golfing costume appeared on the steps at the side of the platform. "Looks as though they're starting at last."

Miss Bradman made purposefully for the table at the centre, and positioning herself behind it, clapped her hands several times to gain the hall's attention.

"Would you kindly all take your seats now," she called above the chatter of conversation; and when it had started subsiding, repeated herself, adding, "There are plenty of chairs down here at the front. Come along, may we have more people near the platform, please?" An exhortation which few seemed inclined to follow until one or two brave souls began edging their way forward along the aisle, bringing a dozen or so more in their wake.

There was a burst of ragged applause when finally the platform party appeared, with Miss Bradman, in her role of chairman, showing the way. Dinah knew the main speaker by name as well as by repute: she had been a member of the original Kensington Ladies' Discussion Society which had supported the radical politician John Stuart Mill in his efforts to promote women's suffrage by moving an amendment to the Reform Bill. The other speaker, a Mrs Hannah Gold, she had heard several times before at local meetings of The Women's Social and Political Union, a firebrand orator whose passion for the cause invariably attracted notice wherever she appeared in public.

"I see the *Sussex Express* is here," Jessie leaned across to whisper, with a motion of the head towards a young man

121

standing against the wall, notebook at the ready. She was about to comment further when Miss Bradman called the meeting to order, and so fell quiet and settled herself back in her seat.

After the chairman's opening words of greeting and introduction, the first speaker rose to her feet to begin an address on the life and works of John Stuart Mill, that doughty champion of the suffragist movement. It was a speech which the elderly lady had delivered many times in many other halls in other towns, and despite the eloquence of her delivery, constant repetition had dulled its vigour, robbing her words of freshness so that she sounded rather as though she were reading aloud from someone else's notes.

Keen as her interest was in the subject, Dinah could not help but find her thoughts after a time drifting away to one perpetual theme which of late had occupied her mind to the virtual exclusion of all else: her husband Warwick Enderby.

As soon as she had discovered the string of pearls missing from her jewellery box she had suspected Warwick of taking them. He had denied it, of course, heatedly – in fact, had gone so far as to accuse the young housemaid, Marjorie, of being the culprit, trying to pin guilt on the fact that the girl had only this last week handed in her notice and was going into service elsewhere in the town.

All in all, it was quite a performance; but Dinah knew her husband rather too well by now to believe either his denial or his accusation, and acting upon a strong suspicion, she had gone first thing next morning to the pawnbroker's on the corner of Southgate Street.

There was her cherished string of pearls, pawned the previous afternoon for a paltry five guineas. And yes, a gentleman answering to Warwick Enderby's description had brought them in (no mistake, he was a regular customer) but alas, sorry, many apologies, it wasn't possible to let Madam have them back without the ticket.

What was its number? The pawnbroker consulted his book and told her. She had returned home, and feeling very like a criminal had waited her chance to search the pockets of her husband's suits in his dressing-room wardrobe. There, among a motley collection of unredeemed pawn tickets

122

issued by brokers not only in Lewes but also in Brighton, London and Hastings, she had found one which tallied with the number she'd been looking for.

Her pearls – no, dear dead Richard's pearls, since they'd been his wedding gift – were saved; but her marriage from that moment was irreversibly in ruins.

That evening when he came in from his club, she had confronted Warwick with the proof of his deceit, and listened with scorn as he tried to defend himself behind the contrived theatricality of wounded pride, contrition, self-defence, explanation, pledges to reform . . . the same words, the same gestures, the same excuses which she'd come to know so well from so many other scenes like this.

At the end of it all, when he'd drunk himself into a state of maudlin bravado, she had told him firmly that she no longer wished to share the same bed, and that very night had moved herself back once more into the rear bedroom, shutting her ears to Warwick's half-hearted assault upon her locked door.

A prolonged round of applause from the audience in the hall brought Dinah out of her gloomy reverie and back to the present. Beside her, Jessie Moore was clapping as warmly as the rest, fox-head nodding up and down on her arm in glassy-eyed agreement; and looking towards the platform, Dinah saw that the guest had come to the end of her talk on John Stuart Mill and was taking her seat again, and Miss Bradman rising to interject a few words before giving the floor to the next speaker.

"Now we're in for some fun!" Jessie murmured out of the corner of her mouth as Mrs Hannah Gold got to her feet. "Watch out for the opposition."

Sure enough, no sooner had Mrs Gold started her address to the meeting than there came a hostile shout from the back of the hall, a man's voice bawling out something unintelligible. His interruption was countered at once by loud hisses and calls for silence; and when it was restored, Mrs Gold resumed speaking again, her words crisp and clear and sharp as she quickly got into the stride of her argument.

Her main bone of contention was the duplicity of the

Liberal Prime Minister, Mr Asquith, in his treatment of the so-called Conciliation Committee which had been set up earlier in the year under the chairmanship of Lord Lytton. This committee had drafted a bill acceptable to all sections of suffragist opinion, whose second reading had been carried in the House by a majority of one hundred and ten votes. But Mr Asquith had thereupon refused further facilities for its passage through Parliament, effectively killing the hopes of thousands of women stone dead.

"Defeat snatched from the jaws of victory!" cried Mrs Gold furiously, her handsome features working as she brought her clenched fist down upon the table top to stress her disgust at this betrayal.

"The rape of justice by a Liberal dictatorship!" she added for good measure, while the other members of the platform party smiled in grim agreement from their seats behind her.

"Sisters, we must take to the streets again to redress our wrongs – "

"Good idea," came another interruption from the back. "On the streets is where women like you belong."

This was ignored. "We must take to the streets again – not peaceably with banners and marching bands as we did before, but this time with the weapons of violent resistance. They will not dare to stand against us, those gentlemen of dishonour who taint the fair name of democracy, when they see what a whirlwind they have unleashed against themselves by their failure to recognise the justness of our cause – "

"Why don't you get back to the kitchen?" called another, different voice. "If you put as much hot air into your cooking as you did into your ranting, your old man 'ld be a bloomin' sight happier for it."

There was some raucous laughter at this; and turning to glance over her shoulder, Dinah saw a small group of men ranged against the back seats who had obviously entered the hall after the meeting had started. That was the problem with these suffragist gatherings, she thought vexedly, they tended to attract unemployed trouble-makers from the nearby public houses, and fire regulations meant that the doors could not be locked to keep them out.

As the heckling continued, Mrs Gold rose to the challenge.

"There – " she cried, pointing above the heads of her audience, "there is a perfect example of reactionary prejudice exercising its brute intolerance of free speech! Sisters, can we but wonder that our beloved country has such a discreditable Government when we see the type of citizen who elected it into power. Well may they laugh now as we rail against the injustice of the present system – well may they point the finger of derision at those brave young suffragettes who have carried our war-cry throughout the length and breadth of this land. When the day of our emancipation dawns, I promise you there shall be no more laughter heard from them as liberated womankind flocks to the polls to change the face of British politics – no more pointed fingers of derision as their bastions of bigotry are toppled and women take their rightful place within the corridors of the Mother of Parliaments!"

She paused, a look upon her flushed, defiant face such as must have inspired the followers of Joan of Arc; and then, throwing out her arms dramatically, tossed back her head and cried out, "Votes for women!"

"Votes for women!" echoed her audience with ringing enthusiasm.

"Votes for dogs!" came a caustic shout from the back. "Why should bitches get all the support? Votes for dogs!"

This created something of a hubbub, with Mrs Gold's supporters seeking to make their indignation heard, the opposition lobbing jeers and cat-calls back at them, and Miss Bradman from the platform calling out in vain for quiet please in the hall.

The continuing disturbance appeared to act as a stimulant upon the speaker's powers of oratory, for she now commenced a tongue-lashing of her detractors which was sufficiently impassioned to crush them into silence. Not for long, however. Within a short time the more rowdily vociferous of the group had started heckling the platform again, and as Miss Bradman rose to remonstrate, a solitary missile came flying over the heads of the audience to smash in a pulpy red wetness against a leg of the table.

"Tomatoes!" exclaimed Jessie, shying back to avoid the spatter. "Time for the old brolly, I think."

125

So saying, she reached beneath her chair and extracted the black silk umbrella, holding it in readiness before her.

"Makes a change from eggs, I suppose," she added, as cries from the rows behind indicated that several more shots had found a mark amongst the ranks. "Do you remember Tunbridge Wells – " ducking as something else winged past towards the platform – "the awful smell of all those rotten eggs, like sulphur?"

"I think it's time we took our leave, don't you," Dinah said hastily, collecting her things from beside her chair and needing to speak up rather to make herself heard above the general racket which was now breaking out within the small hall.

The other gave a nod; and raising her umbrella, held it open over their heads while they got up together and began pushing their way along towards the side-door.

There appeared to be some confusion starting on the platform as a furious Mrs Hannah Gold strove to continue her diatribe above the hubbub, while the rest of the party huddled like startled sheep behind the bulky defence of Miss Bradman's generous figure. It was quite obvious that chaos was about to descend upon the proceedings, and those in the audience not staying to hold their own against their assailants were already making for the main entrance door leading into Little East Street, bags, hats, books, even chairs held up in self-protection from the missiles.

Jessie deftly succeeded in fending off several over-ripe tomatoes as she and Dinah made their hasty retreat behind the shield of the open brolly. The pair of them, fashionably attired complete with fox-fur, must have made a curious sight, for the *Sussex Express* reporter standing by the side-door was grinning from ear to ear with amusement as he leaned across to swing it open for them.

"Never mind," Jessie declared once they were both safely into the alley outside and she was shaking off the worst of the damage to the black silk, "let him smirk as much as he likes. At least we've managed this time to get out in one piece – which is more than we did at Tunbridge Wells."

She pulled a face, recalling that previous incident in the

spring, when several suffragist supporters had been physically assailed by a drunken crowd of rough-heads and Jessie herself, her *crêpe de chine* outfit flecked with stains from the eggs that were thrown, only narrowly avoided being pushed headlong down a flight of stairs.

"What a lark, though! I do so love a good rumpus. Come on, let's go round to the front, shall we? The police should be arriving any moment and we don't want to miss all the fun."

Tucking her arm through Dinah's, she made off towards the mouth of the alley to join the crowd already gathering on the pavement outside The British Workmen's Institute. To her vexation, however, there were to be no arrests, for by the time the police van appeared upon the scene the troublemakers inside the hall had vanished, leaving only the debris of empty paper bags, upturned chairs and spattered walls as evidence of their recent activity.

After a while, seeing the crowd starting to drift away, murmuring their disappointment at being cheated of a good bit of drama to end the afternoon, she uttered a loud sigh and said, "Hey ho, what a bore. No point in staying, I suppose. We may as well go home." Then, brightening – "I know! Why not invite me back for tea at Southwood Place? Oh, do, Dinah, do – it will be quite like old times again. And since Master's away, it's safe to invite me in without incurring his displeasure."

"There's no need for your sarcasm," responded the other tolerantly. "As a matter of fact, I was just about to ask you anyway."

Their arms linked, the two young women started off together along Little East Street through the gathering dusk of the November day. Above the rooftops some light still lingered in the western sky where the sun's last rays tipped the clouds with saffron; but by the time the pair reached St Luke's Hill a purple twilight had fallen in the streets, and since the gas-lamps had not yet been lit, they were almost at the drive gate before Jessie remarked suddenly, "What's that in the road? A handcart?"

Dinah peered ahead. "Yes . . . yes, it is."

"Someone's moving furniture, by the look of things."

"Oh, that must be Marjorie. She's leaving us, you know."

"I can't say I'm surprised."

They were beside the cart now, and as they passed Dinah slowed her step to look in over the side. What she saw there in the half-light made her stop abruptly, a hand to her mouth.

"No – !"

"What is it? What's wrong?" Jessie was instantly all concern.

For a moment the other was hardly able to speak, so great was the sudden violence of anger which replaced her initial astonishment.

Then, finding her voice again, she said in a curiously flat tone, "He's home again," and gestured towards the cart. "That's none of Marjorie's stuff. That's mine."

It was rather more than a single strand of pearls this time: it was a set of four Regency ebonised dining chairs, an ormolu clock and a pretty little inlaid rosewood workbox which had belonged to Richard's mother.

12

"Well? What did you do?"

In the comfortable glow of the parlour firelight, Isabelle Bethway's expression was a conflicting study of disbelief, amazement and concern as she looked across at her daughter.

Dinah had come home to Eastbourne to spend the few days of Christmas at her father's vicarage, unable to tolerate even the thought of passing the festive season at Southwood Place. She had informed Warwick bluntly that she wanted him and his brothers out of her house while she was away, and after a good deal of acrimony the three of them had slunk off to London to amuse themselves after their own fashion in the less selective clubs and gaiety halls of the West End.

"What did you do when you discovered your furniture there at the side of the road?" Isabelle repeated.

Dinah looked down at her hands, unable to meet her mother's troubled eyes. It had been awful to spoil their Christmas-tide in this way, but she'd had no choice. Far better to be truthful than hide behind excuses; and once one part of the sorry tale was told, then of course her parents had wanted to know the rest of it. All of it. From start to finish.

"I didn't do much at all, I'm afraid," she answered at last. "It was Jessie. You know, I don't think Warwick knew quite where to put himself when she went marching into the house . . ."

Despite the pain, a faint smile lifted the corners of her mouth at the memory.

"She was wonderful. Like a very refined Billingsgate fish-wife. For a good five minutes she gave him the length of her tongue without a pause to draw breath, and I don't believe she repeated herself once."

"But did it do any good?" Isabelle queried doubtfully. "I

wouldn't have thought him the type to be intimidated easily."

"Oh, but he is, Mother. At heart he's a coward, like all shallow men. I can just imagine him as a child, running home crying with his fist in his eye because someone wouldn't play with him. And telling tales to teacher to get his own back. He hates – scenes, as he calls them. Hates anything not going the way he thinks it should. Life must be arranged to inconvenience him as little as possible . . . if not, he becomes petty and sulky and behaves as though it's all everyone else's fault but his own."

"You're very disillusioned, aren't you, my dear," her mother said sadly.

Dinah bit her lip, and after a moment nodded.

"What a pity it is you had to marry in such haste – "

"Oh, don't, Mother, don't!" The anguish in that cry seemed to ring through the cosy quietness of the room. "The mistake is all mine – mine – and I must bear its consequences. But please, don't *you* reproach me. I have enough to burden me already, without that."

She raised her eyes; and seeing the hurt reflected in them, Isabelle reached out her hands across the hearth.

"My darling, I am not reproaching you," she said softly. "The pain is yours alone, but the grief is shared by us all. The good Lord knows, we are fallible creatures, and our lives are threaded through with past mistakes. Our only consolation is that we have much to learn from them, for as your dear father has very often said, it is in our weakness that we find our greatest strength."

Again, Dinah's face was lightened a little by a smile. "I seem to hear the echo of a sermon there."

"Well, there's a great deal of truth in what he preaches," her mother answered loyally. "His Christmas Day message of yesterday was full of hope for those who despair of the darkness in their lives."

"Hope, yes. But no answers."

"How do you mean?"

"I don't believe that prayer is any answer, as Father says it is. What is the use of prayer inside a cage? Will it lift the bars

130

and let me free? Will it undo the vows of my marriage to Warwick?"

"My dear, you must continue to put your trust in God," Isabelle said very quietly. "Remember, no prayer is ever wasted. He never says no to us . . . it's just that occasionally, for His own loving purpose and the good of our souls, it takes Him a little while to say yes. And often, when our prayers at last are granted, it's in a way which we least expected."

Dinah looked down at her hands again.

After a time she said, rather awkwardly, "When Father and I were here alone together last evening, he said something about God never giving us a cross to carry heavier than He knows we can bear. He said it, I thought, as though he meant his own particular cross was me. Well, Francis and me. He'd just been speaking of Francis, you see. What sorrow it was to him that the family should be so divided."

"Indeed, it has been a sorrow to us both. But here, you see, is an instance of God's mercy at work." In the gentle flicker of firelight her mother's face softened with happiness. "Marion is expecting another child, and she seems certain that this time it will be a son. I received a letter from her on Christmas Eve and she has never sounded more content. She says Francis is so concerned for the health of her pregnancy and a safe delivery that he has become quite the reformed character, even to ending his relationship with some young woman or other in Lewes – an affaire which poor Marion says has caused her untold heartache these past months."

"Yes, but will it last, Mother? I seem to recall he's made these promises of his before. In fact, he and Warwick are two for a pair – both very good at turning over new leaves and swearing hand on heart to behave themselves in future. And neither meaning a single word of it."

Dinah twisted her wedding band back and forth on her finger, an unconscious gesture which was becoming something of a habit with her.

"Having known my brother Francis all these years," she went on bitterly, "the wonder is that I could have let myself

131

be quite so blind to the same selfishness and guile in Warwick!"

"Love can be very cruel to those caught in its spell," Isabelle said with great sympathy. "It has a way of blinkering us to reality . . . a way of twisting our vision so that the person on whom we fix our affections becomes an image, an ideal, of what we want them to be. I know. I speak from experience, my dear. There was once an occasion, when I was very young and very naive,that I felt love's cruelness for myself."

"I never knew that." Her daughter raised her head to cast a look at the trim, slight figure sitting opposite whose face and form and vivid auburn colouring – though fading now – so nearly reflected her own that but for the disparity in age, she might have been looking into a mirror. "You didn't tell me there was ever another you loved. I've always thought Father was the only one."

"Oh, it was such a long time ago now. Such a long, long time ago."

"But who was he? May I know?"

Isabelle Bethway hesitated before answering; then gave a shrug and a little, careless laugh. "His name was Harry Weldrake. Your Uncle Frank's brother-in-law."

"Harry Weldrake? Oh, I remember him! He died when I was quite young, didn't he?"

There was a nod. "Of drink, dissipation and self-neglect."

"You said that as though you hated him."

"God forgive me if I did. He was a very . . . callous man, as I discovered to my cost."

"Then what was it that attracted you to him?"

The older woman shrugged again. "Appearances."

"He was handsome?"

"Oh, indeed! But with the sort of arrogant good looks which cover a multitude of defects. Harry Weldrake was like – well, how can I put it – like one of those Christmas gifts which comes beautifully wrapped, but once opened is found to contain something rather cheap and mean and shoddy."

"He sounds remarkably similar to Warwick," Dinah commented, the edge of bitterness returning to her voice.

"That is judging your husband too harshly." Getting up

132

from her chair, her mother stooped forward to take the brass-handled poker from the fender and began prodding at the logs burning in the hearth-grate. They fell inward upon themselves in an incandescent pile of wood ash, causing Isabelle Bethway to shield her face from the sudden fierce heat as flames and sparks went shooting up into the chimney mouth.

"Put on a few logs more from the basket, will you, dear?" she asked, rising to re-seat herself. "Kit ought to be arriving quite soon now – I want the place nice and cosy for him. It's biting cold out tonight and those railway carriages can be terribly draughty."

Then, once her daughter had finished her task, she went on again, taking up the thread of their conversation – "To say that Warwick Enderby is anything like Mr Weldrake is being just a little uncharitable. Some resemblance is there, I agree, but only superficially. And your relationship has at least one advantage which mine didn't, Dinah – that of kindness."

"Kindness?"

An emphatic nod. "Your husband is not an unkind man, whatever else he may be. And you must learn to use that kindness, my dear, if you wish to save your marriage. You must learn to appeal to his better side – "

"Does he have a better side?"

"Oh, I think so. When I met him that time you brought him here to be introduced, he did not strike me as a villain. In fact, I rather liked him. A good deal of false charm, yes – but underneath it, an amiable enough nature. He is not a vicious man, as Harry Weldrake was . . . only a weak one. And with a greedy appetite for money."

"You seem to believe there's some hope for our marriage."

"I do."

There was a pause. Dinah raised her eyebrows a fraction and drew in a breath in preparation for the blow she was about to deliver.

"Well, then, I ought to tell you, Mother – I am seriously considering the possibility of a legal separation."

The piercingly bitter east wind had dropped a little overnight, and for a while next morning the sullen clouds thinned enough to let a lemon-pale winter sun break through to give some semblance of warmth to the view from the vicarage windows.

Tempted outside together for a stroll after breakfast, Dinah and her brother Kit – his starched clerical collar abandoned in favour of a warm red woollen muffler – walked down through The Meads towards the seafront promenade. It was a direction taken countless times since the days of childhood, when Dinah could remember walking beside the nursery-maid with Kit perched in his baby carriage and Francis as usual showing disobedience by running on ahead without permission.

For a while the two of them talked of those days, recalling memories of bygone youth spent here, as they took their way through the narrow streets of this hilly part of Eastbourne, descending to the sea past knapped-flint garden walls where last night's frost still clung between the stones and sparkled like diamonds in the sunlight.

By the time they'd emerged on to the front at the western end of the promenade and turned into The Parade, their conversation had progressed from past to present: to Kit's parish of Christ Church in Tunbridge Wells, and the hurly-burly of its Christmas season, with sermons to be written and services conducted, charity meals to be organised, gifts delivered, the old and the sick to be visited – and all this between innumerable social invitations from the more affluent parishioners to celebrate Advent in a proper festive spirit.

"I'm not surprised you're putting on so much weight," Dinah remarked, casting a critical glance at her brother's tight-buttoned overcoat. "All that eating and drinking – "

"Nonsense! I manage one good meal a day, that's all."

"Yes, generally starting at eight of an evening and ending at twelve, with courses enough to sink the table and bottles of wine by the dozen. Oh, you need not deny it – " as the Reverend Kit Bethway opened his mouth to protest – "you should read your own letters! Full of shining good deeds, yet somehow always ending with a dish by dish account of the last dinner you were invited to attend in the parish. Such attention to detail smacks of gluttony, Kit. And gluttony, as you know, is a deadly sin."

"Ho, you're a fine one to speak of sin," came the slightly aggrieved retort as the blow struck home. "What about imprudence, eh? And self-indulgence. And lack of judgement. Not to mention breaking the fourth Commandment and ignoring the seventh Sacrament of the Church. Which, if I may remind you, is the Sacrament of Christian Marriage."

"I know. You told me that last night. Several times." Dinah looked away, across the promenade towards the dull, flat sea. "*Must* we have another sermon about it?"

"No. I've made my opinion plain enough on the matter. I don't intend to waste more breath by repeating myself."

"Good. Then don't."

In silence, the two of them walked on together. Down below on the shingle a boy was playing with a small brown dog, throwing pebbles for it to chase along the water's edge, and the sound of its excited yapping echoed between the massive wooden bulwarks of the breakwaters.

"There's one thing I simply fail to understand, though," Kit said suddenly when they'd gone on some way further, "Why in heaven's name were you in quite so much haste to re-marry? And in a London registry office, of all places?"

His sister sketched an exaggerated shrug; and when it seemed that was the only response he would get to his question, he went on testily, "You know, you can't brush the whole thing aside as though it's no longer relevant. We both realise that you've trapped yourself into something you very much wish now you hadn't. What I'm asking, Dinah, is – why? Why, after ten years of respectable widowhood, suddenly rush blindfold into a marriage for which you were so ill-prepared?"

She slowed her step. They had reached the bandstand now, and in the shelter of its raised platform and shuttered wooden sides they were out of the cold wind whipping in from the Channel.

She sat down on one of the slatted benches and hunched her shoulders forward, tucking her mittened hands deep into the pockets of her coat.

"Why, Kit? The answer to that is simple. I was in love. And needed very much to be loved in return."

He seated himself beside her. "Would a few months more have made so very much difference? It would have looked better, you know, if you'd quietly announced a formal engagement – "

"Looked better? Better for whom?"

"Well, for you . . . for the family. Dash it all, Dinah, people of our sort don't go charging off to registry offices! They do things the decent way. Betrothal – banns – church wedding. All the proper trimmings."

"But I didn't want the trimmings. I simply wanted to be married to Warwick Enderby as soon as possible. And at the time it seemed so . . . romantic, I suppose, like an elopement almost, to do it the way we did and surprise everyone afterwards."

"Surprise is the word! My goodness me, you certainly succeeded in that." Kit blew out his cheeks. "I presume it never occurred to you that the whole thing might look – well, a bit underhand? To be perfectly honest, Dinah, my immediate reaction was to think you'd landed yourself in a rather compromising situation and needed to cover your lapse from grace as expediently as you could."

"You thought I was pregnant, you mean."

He nodded, awkwardly.

"As a matter of fact," she said in a level voice, "I think I may be barren. For which I am profoundly grateful."

For a moment her candour rather left her brother lost for words, and to cover his embarrassment she went on, "Just imagine how much worse my position would be if I were expecting Warwick's child."

"But you've only been married for – what, five months?" Kit found his composure again. "How do you know . . . I mean, what makes you think you might be barren?"

"Oh, call it one of those mysterious feminine intuitions." She gave a half-smile, tinged just slightly with sadness. "It's odd, wouldn't you agree, how life has a way of twisting round on us. When Richard died, almost the greatest part of my grief was that I had no child to remember him by. Yet here I am a second time, losing a husband, and heartily

136

thankful I've nothing more for my memories than his name."

"Oh, come now, you're hardly losing Warwick Enderby. As I said last night – well, as Mother and I both said – you really must try to be a little more patient, a little more tolerant. All marriages have their teething troubles. It's a matter of compromise, of talking things over between you both and seeing where the difficulties lie."

"I *know* where the difficulties lie!" There was a sudden note of anger in Dinah's voice. "Do I need to give you the list again? The deceit, the irresponsibility, the lies, the evasion . . . stealing my belongings for a pawnbroker's ticket to get money for his gambling . . . coming back drunk and out of pocket, smelling of cheap perfume from his brothers' little shop-girls and expecting me to fall into bed with him and thank him for the privilege? You talk to me about patience, Kit! You talk to me about tolerance!"

She turned on him, her lovely face pinched white with emotion.

"It's too late for all that – much too late. For compromise . . . for everything. As things stand now between Warwick and me there's only one solution to our marriage – and that's a separation."

Her brother returned her look with one of tight-strained resignation. "Why must you be so obstinate, Dinah? Don't you ever listen? I've told you, there's not a solicitor in the land would agree to take your case. You simply haven't the grounds."

"Oh, haven't I!"

"No. A judicial separation can only be obtained as a result of misconduct such as desertion, adultery or cruelty continuing for two years or more. Two *years*. Not two months. You ought to realise that what you're contemplating is a very serious step, and with grave social implications, and shouldn't be used as a threat each time tempers run high. A marriage is not a china cup to be smashed in anger."

"Stephen Moore will help me," she said stubbornly.

"I doubt it. Whatever his personal fondness for you as a friend, he's as bound by the Law as any other in his profession. But go and consult him by all means – "

137

"Thank you for the permission!"

Kit sighed loudly. "I was going to say, he can advise you far better than Father or I on this business of Warwick pawning your property – which I must admit is a despicable way for a husband to behave."

"Well, I'm glad we see eye to eye upon something at least."

Dinah huddled further inside her coat and stared aggressively ahead of her.

For a while neither of them spoke again, and in the stillness the thin keening of the wind in the shuttered bandstand seemed to reflect the bleakness of their separate thoughts, echoed by the lonely mew of seagulls wheeling overhead in the emptiness of a misty winter sky.

Then Kit said at last, "Come on. I'll buy you a cup of coffee in The Devonshire Rooms. Things will look rosier on a warm stomach," and, putting an arm around his sister, gave the hunched shoulders a squeeze. "Try not to worry too much, Dinah old girl. After all, you know what they say – when you think you've reached rock bottom, the only way to go is up again."

She managed a wan smile. "Is that what they say?"

He nodded. "And remember, if things ever get so bad that not even crying helps – well, brothers have their uses, and Lewes isn't far from Tunbridge Wells."

13

In the incense-scented dimness of the church, the glow of so many little flames cast a soft golden sheen as the congregation filed slowly one after another along the centre aisle, their votive candles shielded in cupped hands from the draughts seeping in from the blustery, sleet-driven February streets outside.

As they approached the gleaming brass communion rail before the steps of the High Altar, each one genuflected in turn before moving away to the left to continue the procession down the side aisle towards the doors at the back, their voices echoing in ragged unison as they repeated the words of the antiphon *Adorna thalamum tuum, Sion* after the priest leading ahead.

It was the second of February, 1911, the Feast of the Purification – Candlemas – and Cecilia Desatti, her mother and two sisters and youngest brother were among the few dozen or so of the faithful who had gathered at St Pancras's in Lewes to observe this feast-day, the Church's commemoration of the Blessed Virgin's presentation of her infant son in the Temple forty days after his birth at Bethlehem.

But for the fact that it also happened to be her mother's anniversary, Sissy wouldn't have bothered coming: being a Thursday, she could have gone instead to London with her older brother Giacomo and wandered round the Knightsbridge stores while he saw to business at Covent Garden and Billingsgate, ordering his stock of supplies for the coming week. If he was in a good mood, he would sometimes treat her to luncheon at the recently opened Selfridges' emporium where there was the grand novelty of a roof garden; but usually they made do with a plate of pasta and a glass of rough red wine at some little *ristorante* near Charing Cross.

The priest ascended the steps of the altar and raised his

arms. "*In nomine Patris et Filii et Spiritus Sancti . . .* " He crossed himself, the light catching the silk embroidered panels of his white chasuble.

"Amen," muttered Sissy gracelessly, in response to a nudge in the ribs from her sister Benedetta. The ritual of the procession concluded, the congregation had returned to their pews now and were kneeling for the start of Mass, faces rimmed by the glow of candles, the black lace mantillas of the women shadowed against the glossy darkness of their hair. Benedetta already had her rosary beads in her hand, head bent, eyes closed, lips moving soundlessly in the *Ave Maria*.

Pious little madam, Sissy thought scornfully. She twisted her neck to see along the pews past their mother. Her other sister, fifteen-year-old Carlotta, was likewise engaged in saying her beads, but her head was raised and her eyes fixed raptly on the altar, not out of reverence, as might appear, but out of the first raw pangs of calf-love for the young server, a gangling youth in a lace-trimmed cotta who was chanting the responses in run-together Latin.

She ought to be praying too, Sissy told herself. That was what she'd come here for, wasn't it? Surely they couldn't all be deaf as well as dead, those saints in heaven whose names she'd invoked in private litany since childhood.

She clasped her hands tightly against her breast. Mary, Mother of God, pray for my mother, especially today, she thought. St Cecilia, my blessed patron, pray for me. St Francis of Assisi, pray for Frank Bethway and intercede on my behalf . . .

It wouldn't work, of course. What she was asking was a sin. She could hardly blame the holy saints if they totally ignored her petitions, since they weren't in the business of influencing the hearts and minds of men towards infidelity.

But I'm not asking for Frank to leave his wife, she argued silently. All I want is that he should love me more than her . . . all I want is to have him back again, and for everything to be the same as before between the two of us. We had such good times together. If you let him return, I'll say a novena . . . I'll come to Mass every day for a month. Well, a week, anyway. And I promise I'll put a notice in the newspaper to

140

thank you if you grant my request. Pray for me, please. Pray that Frank will change his mind and want me back again.

She lifted her head. In the cobweb thickness of the air, the smoke from the incense burner hung like layers of blue mist above the altar before slowly drifting away towards the shadowed ceiling.

"*Confiteor Deo omnipotenti* . . ." The server began the general confession on behalf of the congregation, striking his chest three times at the *mea culpa* as he took the blame for his sinfulness upon himself. Young Carlotta sighed dramatically, her dark eyes aglow with the yearning fervour of devotion, until a sharp glance from her mother made her drop her gaze hurriedly to her tangled rosary beads, cheeks blushing scarlet at having been caught out in such unspiritual ecstasy.

Sissy had not been to confession for some time, and she wondered idly whether her soul was in any imminent danger of being damned because of it. On the last occasion, not wanting her own parish priest to learn of her relations with Frank Bethway, she had taken herself into Brighton, to one of the priests there, to unburden her conscience of the sin of leading another into temptation, as well as her usual dirty-washing list of impure thoughts, words and actions, lack of chastity, disobedience, vanity, and other venial offences.

Her confessor had advised her to make haste and be married, for she was a prey to lustful and lascivious inclinations, he said, and a husband might well be the cure of them. She had said her prayers of penance on the omnibus back to Lewes, looking out from the top deck window across the dead winter landscape and feeling something of its bleakness creep inside her as the daylight faded to an ashen dusk among the empty fields. What was the use of a husband . . . It was not marriage she wanted, but Frank; and if she couldn't have him she wanted nobody else.

Life could be so unfair, such a cheat. When she'd had him twisted round her little finger, it had all been a game, something to feed her vanity and keep her amused, like having a dog to pet or punish according to whim. She had had no end of men after her – he was just another, dancing around hoping she might be as bad as her looks promised.

141

She'd despised the lot of them, even while enjoying the attention and the compliments and gifts, despised them in the way she'd always felt for anything weak and ridiculous and stupid. They didn't mind being made to look fools, so long as they thought she might give them a glimpse by and by of something more than her ankle; and for that she had teased them all with cruel contempt, encouraging them by a yard only to slap them down when they tried to take more than an inch.

That was the way it had been with Captain Bethway, too. Already she'd noticed the first signs of boredom appearing and wondered whether it wasn't time to end it all between them. But then, suddenly out of the blue, he'd done what no other man before had ever dared to do to her: *he* had been the one to end things first, and say goodbye.

Not just goodbye, either; but good riddance.

It had been the first week in December. A Saturday. They hadn't seen one another for almost a fortnight, not since their last argument, and Sissy had been in half a mind to ignore the message sent asking her to meet him.

The weather had decided her: a fine, crisp, sunny afternoon, and a chance for a breath of fresh air after the heat and steam and rush of the tea-room kitchen. To show the Captain that she was still considerably vexed with him, she'd deliberately arrived twenty minutes late at their rendezvous in All Souls churchyard; but for once there was no sign of him anywhere, and the thought that he might not have bothered to wait provoked her into real annoyance. What was she to do now? Should she go, or should she stay? Unable to make up her mind, she'd looked this way and that; then, feeling the chill from standing out here in the open, she'd begun walking slowly away from the clock tower along the brick-edged path leading through the disused part of the churchyard. If he'd still not arrived by the time she'd reached the gate into Pinwell Lane, she told herself, then she would go – and be damned to him.

She'd got perhaps halfway along the path, where it wound beneath a bare-branched screen of overhanging trees, when a sudden holloa from behind made her pause and look round over her shoulder. There was Frank Bethway now by the tower, not waving to her as he usually did, but standing with his hands in his jacket pockets and obviously expecting her to start walking back again.

For a moment Sissy thought of ignoring him and going on, so that he'd have to run to follow and catch up with her. Then she decided it would suit her better if she stayed here where she was, and so in a dumb-show of stubbornness went and seated herself on a leaf-strewn bench at the side of the path.

"Oh, you've decided to show your face, then, have you?" she greeted him caustically a few minutes later at his approach. "I've got nothing better to do with myself than wait about here in the cold for you to turn up, I suppose?"

"You should have had the manners to be punctual for a change."

Something in the tightness of his tone made her look him sharply in the face as he bent forward – not to kiss her on the cheek, as she thought he'd intended, but to brush away the leaves from the bench before seating himself at her side.

"You're a fine one to talk about manners, Frank Bethway. Keeping me here since three o'clock – "

"Don't exaggerate. You haven't been waiting that long. I saw you crossing the road as I came down, and that was hardly above five minutes ago."

She tossed her head; then, putting on a display of petulance, said, "Where've you been to, anyway?"

"That's my business."

"All right, no need to bite my nose off! You're in a funny mood today, aren't you?"

He hadn't looked at her, nor even tried to touch her; only bowed his head and leaned forward to rest his elbows on his knees, hands clasped between them.

"Frank? Did you hear me?"

There was a long pause before he bothered to answer, and in the clearness of the sharp winter air the background noise of the streets carried distinctly, the staccato clip of hooves and rattle of iron cart-tyres drowned now and then by the rough throaty rumble of a motor engine.

"I don't suppose what I've come to say will matter to you

much," he'd said at last, as though he were talking to himself. "After all, you've never really cared."

"Cared?" Sissy did her best to sound indifferent. "Cared for what?"

"For me . . . for us."

"I don't know what you're on about."

"Yes, you do." Still, he hadn't looked at her but kept his eyes fixed upon his gloved hands.

Somewhere close by a bird began a melancholy piping, its song answered by another across the churchyard, like the echo of a lament among the silence of the leafless trees.

"How long is it we've known each other, Sissy?" he began again after a moment or so. "Can you remember? Have you kept count of the months since we met?"

She shrugged. "I don't know. July, wasn't it? Something like that. Why?"

"It seems a bit of a waste of time now, don't you think. I mean, we've hardly got very far, have we."

She eyed him suspiciously, wondering where this was leading; and seeing her hesitate, he went on, "Let's be honest, my dear, you don't seem to have developed much of an affection for me."

"What, just because I won't go off and spend a hole-in-a-corner weekend at some hotel at Worthing?" A sudden loud note of indignation fuelled her reaction. "I was wondering what all this was about. The usual thing, is it? Why won't I give you a bite at the whole cherry instead of a nibble here and there? Well, you know what the answer is – "

"I'm not talking about that," he interrupted tersely. "The word I used was *affection*, my dear. Affection. A certain warmth of feeling. Fondness. Enjoyment of another's company. Let's leave aside for the moment any discussion of the physical aspect of our relationship."

"Oh, that makes a change, I must say. Normally it's all you can ever think of – the 'physical' aspect. I'd have thought by now – "

"What *I* think by now," he interrupted again, "is that I'm getting a pretty poor exchange for my trouble and money – yes, and my affection, to use that word again. I promised you at the start that we'd have some good times together.

144

And so we have. But a man does expect something more from a friendship of this sort than being led a merry dance by a female whose attitude seems to be all take and no give."

"There's gratitude! You've had my company, haven't you? You've had my attention?" Sissy gave another toss of the head. "You married men – you want it all. Well I'm sorry, Frank, but if you think I'm going to sit here and listen to you telling me yet again what's what between us – you've got another think coming."

She made to get up, but hardly was she on her feet before the other's hand came out and caught her by the wrist, dragging her down.

"Let go of me! What d'you think you're doing – "

"I'll let go of you when I've finished. I'm not in a mood for any of your tantrums today, my girl, so sit down and shut up."

"I'll do no such thing!"

Again she tried to rise, and this time he was quite rough with her, hauling her by the waist backwards across the bench. In the struggle, his army great-coat which had been draped casually about his shoulders over the civilian suit, fell to the ground behind; but he let it lie there among the drifts of withered leaves while he concentrated on restraining Sissy from kicking and hitting out at him.

"Keep still, you little wildcat! By God, I'll box your damned ears in a minute."

"You do – " she spat back at him, "and I'll scream this place down, see if I don't. Now take your hands off me. You're hurting."

He pushed her away from him, almost contemptuously. "Oh, go to the devil, then. I'm sick of you."

"Not half as sick as I am of you, Frank Bethway."

Released from his grasp, the young woman jumped up and began straightening her wide-brimmed hat. "I don't know why I bothered coming to meet you. I meant what I said last time – I'm finished with you. You hear? Finished! I don't want ever to set eyes on you again."

"Good." The Captain leaned over to pick up his coat and rose to face her. "Because that's exactly what I came here to say to you, my dear. This relationship is at an end. I'm glad we agree upon that, at least."

There was a long pause, during which the expression on Sissy's face altered perceptibly, shifting from anger to a kind of puzzled annoyance. The carmine bow of her lips parted; but for a moment, mistrusting the evidence of her own ears, she seemed at a loss for words.

Then she said uncertainly, stupidly almost, "What d'you mean – we agree? Agree about what?"

"The wisdom of terminating our relationship." Francis Bethway gave his coat a shake to brush off the leaves. "You're quite right, my dear. It's high time this business was over and done with between us. There's really no point in carrying on as we are . . . the whole thing's becoming something of a bore."

He threw an indifferent glance in her direction.

"Well, why look surprised? It's what you wanted, isn't it?"

His behaviour, so different from usual, threw her into awkward confusion. Normally whenever they'd had one of their rows and she'd told him to clear off and not go near her again, he would treat the quarrel as a storm in a teacup and make a joke of it, chivvying her out of her temper by saying it was all in play, and they shouldn't let a few high words spoil the fun of their friendship.

In return, she would sulk and pout and refuse to speak to him until he'd made amends for his behaviour and won her back again with apologies and gifts of money to buy herself something nice.

"Well – isn't it?" The Captain repeated himself, and there was an icy calmness about his manner now. "It's what you want."

She'd hesitated; and had given an uncomfortable little laugh before answering with a shrug, "Yes – I suppose so."

"Then there's nothing more to be said." He threw the great-coat over his shoulder and turned away.

"Goodbye, Sissy."

And that was all. Before she'd had time to react, to speak, to raise a hand to stop him, he was gone . . . walking off along the path, moving with that long purposeful stride, head up, back straight, that she'd always secretly admired as one of the attractive things about Frank Bethway that made him stand out from all the rest.

146

She remained rooted where she was, frozen in disbelief, staring blankly after him and waiting for him to pause and turn back again; but without so much as a single glance behind him as he reached the end of the path, he had disappeared from sight past All Souls clock tower and so never saw her reach out – too late now – towards him, nor heard the low cry of his name escape her lips.

Behind among the winter-bare branches the bird started up its dreary, cheerless song again, and in the sudden emptiness of the day it seemed one of the most hateful sounds she had ever heard.

The sanctuary bell was rung three times, its brassy clangour piercing the heavy stillness of the church.

Sissy raised her head slowly from her hands and looked towards the altar. The priest had just risen from genuflecting, and was holding up the consecrated wafer of the Sacred Host above his head for the adoration of the faithful, the sleeves of his linen alb falling back to show the worn frayed cuffs of his black jacket.

He replaced the Host reverently in the silver paten before him on the altar and genuflected again, then took up the chalice to begin the consecration of water and wine.

"Simili modo postquam cenatum est . . ."

The young server, kneeling to one side, rang the sanctuary bell three times more to signify the completion of the sacred mystery, and the congregation bowed their heads over missals and rosary beads in silent veneration, their faces shrouded by the shadow of candlelight.

Sissy made an effort to marshal her prayers, but her mind refused to concentrate and her thoughts went wandering off again beyond the confines of the church into the sleet and cold of the streets, carrying her away across the town to the gates of the barracks at Southover.

Ever since Francis Bethway had walked out of her life that afternoon two months ago, she had heard not a word from him, and her own fierce independent pride had held her back from being the first to attempt any reconciliation. The nearest she'd got to it was just before Christmas, when his friend Freddy Seton – the one with the sweet tooth who

147

liked Comet Pudding – had come into the tea rooms. While serving his table, they'd fallen into conversation and she'd asked off-handedly after the Captain, saying she hadn't seen him about the town for some time and wondered how he was.

But if Lieutenant Seton had mentioned her enquiry back at camp, clearly it had fallen on stony ears for the silence remained unbroken.

In the weeks since then Sissy had felt herself lapse into a curious state of mind, as though anger, rejection and longing had wound themselves round and round inside her into a tangle of tight knots. That was bad enough; but even worse was the constant sensation of being trapped – of being caught in a no-man's-land of conscience, torn two ways between the bonds of her belief, and the self-willed demands of her nature: on the one hand full well aware that what she wanted was wickedly wrong, yet on the other, not caring a damn how wrong it was so long as she got her own way in the end, at whatever the cost. For an unmarried woman to lose her virginity was an irrevocable act, and left the everlasting stain of mortal sin upon her soul.

Her knees were beginning to ache and she shifted uncomfortably on the coarse wool-worked hassock, earning herself another nudge in the ribs from Benedetta beside her.

Well, though it might indeed imperil her immortal soul, she meant to get Frank Bethway back, she told herself defiantly, shooting her sister a look and pulling a face when the other put a finger to her lips and nodded towards the altar.

By fair means or foul, she'd get him back. She swore it. And this time, she'd make very sure she kept him.

14

"No, no, *no*. Cut the camera! Cut!"

The small man with the large megaphone came bustling forward into the fierce glare of the studio arc lamps.

"He's supposed to be dying, darling. Dying. Not taking forty winks. I thought we'd rehearsed this scene."

He gestured impatiently towards the bandage-swathed figure in the hospital bed, who was taking quick advantage of the interruption by having a few puffs at a cigarette passed to him by one of the crew.

"When you turn him over to change the dressing, do it *gently*. All right, darling? He's got to survive to the end of the second reel, and he won't do that being dragged about like a bolster pillow."

The pretty young actress in the nurse's uniform received this criticism with a sugared smile which failed to reach her eyes.

"But he's too heavy for me, that's the trouble," she said sweetly. "It might help if he'd turn over by himself."

"How can I do that when I'm lying here unconscious?" her patient demanded from the bed, his voice a little muffled by the cigarette between his lips. "It's meant to be realistic, isn't it? You want to go and do some homework in a real hospital, Daisy old dear. You won't find nurses there pulling their patients half out of bed and complaining they won't shift for themselves – "

"That's enough of that, now. We'll take the scene from the beginning." The small man turned on his heel and disappeared back again into the darkness beyond the circle of studio lights. "And let's try and do it properly this time, can we, darling."

His leading lady shot a narrowed glance in his direction, then, with a tug at the starched white bib of her apron, moved away. Behind her, the scenery flats showed the pale grey walls of a hospital ward, with tall verandah windows opening on to a painted view of a sunny, flower-filled terrace. In contrast to this artificially-created impression of warmth and light, beyond the glare of the lamps stretched the darkened vast expanse of the disused warehouse which had become the studios of The Brighton and County Film Company.

"Right. Quiet on the set, everyone, please. Lights . . . camera . . . scene five, take three. And – action!"

The small man, who was the proprietor of this enterprise, called out his directions through the megaphone. The clapperboard opened and closed in front of the camera lens, and Miss Daisy White took up her position centre stage on the studio floor.

An immediate transformation came over her as she paused there for a long moment, eyes turned now in a look of ineffable pity upon her patient (whose cigarette had been hurriedly disposed of) before she moved off in a kind of glide towards the cupboard at his bedside.

This being a silent motion picture, it hardly mattered how she spoke her lines; but Miss White acted out her part to the hilt, and in a voice full of tender concern, she cooed to the bandaged form, "Major . . . oh, Major Howard . . . I fear I must disturb you. It is time to change your dressing . . . " at the same time fluttering her hands towards the cupboard door.

Sitting against the wall at the back of the studio, Algie Langton-Smythe grinned to himself at such exaggerated theatricality, and cast a look at his companion, Laura Bates, to see her reaction. Despite having watched this particular scene twice already, she appeared utterly spellbound, leaning forward on the edge of her seat, hands clasped tightly in her lap, eyes wide in captivated wonderment, lips slightly parted. Beyond her, her chaperone and erstwhile governess, Megwynn Evans, sat equally attentively and plainly enjoying the drama, both real and contrived, being played out on the studio floor.

Algie had a great deal for which to thank her; and he acknowledged as much now as his gaze returned to feast itself upon Laura's lovely profile, for it had been Miss Evans who had acted as go-between after he'd been so unceremoniously shown the door by Laura's father. Her first little deed of clandestine kindness had been to smuggle out a letter from Laura apologising for Mr Bates's incivility – a letter to which Algie had promptly responded in tones of the most charitable sentiment via the same messenger.

In the weeks which followed he had seen Laura only at a distance, deeming it prudent that they should not be observed in company together; but the correspondence between them flourished, thanks to the connivance of Miss Evans who was clearly in sympathy with the young pair, and already a kind of courtship at second-hand was beginning to develop. That Laura ran the very real risk of discovery was an ever-present threat – and a serious one – yet the thrill of danger served only to add a touch of knife-edged excitement to the whole enterprise.

Their one meeting – at the Electric Picture Theatre, when Esmond Bates brought his sister and fiancée Jessie Moore to see *East Lynne* – had given the impression that the two of them had no more than a slight social acquaintance with each other: a piece of play-acting which had amused them both vastly in the privacy of subsequent letters.

"You won't forget, will you," Laura had written early in the New Year, "your promise to take Megwynn and me to Brighton to visit a motion picture studio? I should like that so much, Algie dear, and am sure we could contrive some excuse to make to them at home."

It had proved easier than they'd thought: Miss Evans had a friend who lived near the coast at Rottingdean, and what more natural than that she should take Laura with her when she went for the day. Mr Bates had granted his permission with hardly a hesitation; but just in case, should he ever enquire of the friend (in the unlikely chance of their meeting) Megwynn Evans had arranged that she and Laura go into Rottingdean for tea after leaving the studio.

"Good! Stop the film there."

The small man with the megaphone was back on the floor of the set, and this time his rubicund face was wreathed in smiles of satisfaction.

151

"That was wonderful, darling, wonderful. We'll print that take."

He consulted his pocket watch and nodded over his shoulder to his crew. Then, turning again to his actors – "All right, let's run through a quick rehearsal of the next scene, where Captain Browning comes in from the terrace and sees – "

"Mr Speer, *dear* Mr Speer, can't we leave that now till tomorrow?" his leading lady interrupted in tones of entreaty, giving him her most appealing look. "It's so hot under these lights my make-up will need a change before we do any more, and that's going to take fifteen minutes. May be longer."

"Oh, longer – definitely longer," came the laconic comment from her stage patient, now sufficiently recovered from near-death to sit up and enjoy another cigarette. "The time it takes for Daisy's face to be scraped off and trowelled on again cannot be measured in mere minutes."

His snidely humorous spite provoked instant response.

"At least it's never taken me the entire morning to get rid of last night's hangover and stop shaking enough to walk straight!" Miss Daisy White threw back pettishly. "At least it's never taken me the entire morning to learn a few lines and repeat them on cue!"

"Are you by chance suggesting something about me, darling?" the other enquired, smiling at her blandly through a lazy cloud of smoke.

"Yes – I'm suggesting you're an incapable half-soaked old lushington, and the only reason you were cast for this picture is your ability to lie on your back and look like a tailor's dummy."

"And the only reason *you* were cast for this picture, Daisy dear heart, is your ability to lie on your back. Full stop."

This bit of theatrical cattiness evidently touched too near a nerve, for the reaction was a loud scream and an indignant appeal to the world at large – "Oh! Did you hear that! Did you hear what the awful old ham just said? Implying I share the same gutter-level morals as him! Of all the damn' cheek! How dare you . . . how dare you, you – you – "

The actress gestured wildly, momentarily at a loss for the most stinging epithet to hurl at her traducer. "You – "

"I rather think it's time we were leaving," said Algie Langton-Smythe, getting up from his seat at the back.

"Oh, no – please." Laura's eyes were shining. "Not yet, Algie. Do let's see what happens."

"I'll tell you what happens. The fur is about to fly."

"Honestly – ?"

The young man smiled at her eagerness.

"Well, don't say I didn't warn you," he cautioned, sitting himself down again. "This next scene is a piece of real twopenny-coloured drama, in which Miss Daisy White will show her scarlet claws and generally behave like the temperamental female she really is."

"How do you know?"

"What?"

"That she's temperamental."

"They all are, all actresses. You see – "

He indicated the floor of the studio set where Miss White, still holding centre stage, had entirely cast aside her role of Florence Nightingale for that of Untamed Shrew and was breathing fire and fury upon her fellow artist in unmistakable terms, against a background chorus of placatory noises from the proprietor and his crew.

"I've seen it all before," he went on airily. "It's part and parcel of the mystique, you know, this exhibitionism."

"It is?"

A nod. "They're expected to behave like that – and so they do."

Megwynn Evans shifted herself on her chair to lean forward.

"If you ask my opinion," she came in with just a touch of amusement, "it's an act they put on for their own self-importance. They crave attention, see. It's like food and drink to them it is, to be noticed. The trouble is with their kind, they don't know where reality finishes and fantasy begins."

This was quite a long speech from the usually short-worded Welshwoman, and Algie looked at her in some interest.

"You're acquainted with the acting profession, are you, Miss Evans?"

She smiled obliquely, and tapped the side of her nose.

"Let us say I'm acquainted with human nature. It amounts to much the same thing. All stars and rockets."

"Ah."

He waited expectantly for some elucidation; and when none was forthcoming, turned his attention again to the young woman at his side.

"Well, if you really don't wish to leave yet awhile, I'll show you over the studio sets, if you'd like, Laura. There's time enough, isn't there, before you must catch your 'bus to Rottingdean?"

"Yes, I think so." She turned back the cuff of her coat sleeve to consult her watch, one of the new ladies' models designed to be worn upon the wrist on a black silk band, which her brother Esmond had given her at Christmas. "There *is* time, isn't there, Megwynn?"

The other glanced up at the large wall-clock above the dressing-room doors. "That depends upon how long Mr Langton-Smythe intends to keep you, *cariad*."

"Oh, not long," he hastened to reassure her. "They seem to be done here now, anyway – "

With a nod he directed attention again to the scene on the set, reaching its finale beneath the pitiless glare of the arc lamps. The bed-bound "Major Howard", apparently unperturbed by the slanderous aspersions cast upon his sobriety, had risen to his feet and was unswathing himself Egyptian mummy-fashion of his bandages, while Miss Daisy White, having exhausted her repertoire of hysterics, was leaning upon the neck of little Mr Speer and weeping very prettily as she allowed herself to be led away towards her dressing room.

Several other actors, who had had nothing to do during this entire performance but stand around the walls and look on with the indifference of those who had seen it all before, commenced a languid applause at her departure before taking themselves off, their scripts beneath their arms, into the darkness beyond the scenery flats.

"Would you care to join us on the tour, Miss Evans?" Algie invited, holding out an elbow.

She shook her head. "Thank you, no. I can see all I want

154

from here, and you young folk will get around best without me."

"Are you sure? I mean, you won't feel lonely?"

"*Duw* – go on with you!"

Smiling, she shooed at him with her hand; and for some while after he'd moved away with Laura on his arm, the smile remained there still, warming her plump, pleasant face as her eyes followed the two of them together.

She had had charge of Laura since the other was a motherless little girl of four, and loved her more even than if she'd been her own flesh and blood. Nothing was too good for her; and if her father was over-protective, then Miss Evans was even more so – not as a disciplinarian, but as zealous guardian of Laura's happiness.

Her reasons for this close and careful cherishing went beyond mere bonds of affection to something of a deeply private nature, something which the Welshwoman had been at pains throughout her life to keep a secret. And with good cause. There had been a time, years before when she'd first come to Lewes as governess to Mr Bates's children, that she'd become friendly with a handsome young man; and having no one to guide or advise her, had fallen headlong in love with him. That he was considerably her junior and a student still had mattered not at all: the ardour of his adolescent passion swept commonsense from her normally sensible judgement, and within a few months of their meeting she'd found herself pregnant with his child.

That, of course, had served to put a very different complexion upon their relationship. The ardour cooled as rapidly as first it had blazed, and far from showing sympathy, the young man showed instead a clean pair of heels as he hurried to decamp from her life. But for the merciful fortune of an early miscarriage, Megwynn Evans might have found herself that most stigmatised of creatures, an unmarried mother; as it was, however, Fate had dealt with her kindly on this occasion, and shy of tempting it twice, she'd resolved from that time forward to forswear the company of men and devote herself entirely to the care of her two small charges.

It was a lesson painfully learned, and had the effect of

155

colouring the Welshwoman's attitude adversely towards romantically inclined gentlemen of a footloose nature, determining her that no such similar experience of an unhappy love-affaire should ever be allowed to wound her Laura's tender heart. Without appearing to put restraint upon the other's already strictly limited social life, she kept diligent watch of every young man who came near, and if Laura seemed to look on him with any favour, would nip the attraction swiftly in the bud with a few quiet words of faintly damning praise.

Such was her influence that the younger woman always paid heed to the older one's counsel: small wonder, therefore, that any would-be suitor lost heart so quickly, for even were he not deterred by Laura's sudden lack of interest, the chilly disapproval of her governess-companion (and the ogre's shadow of her father in the background) invariably proved a most intimidating obstacle to the pursuit of his amorous intentions.

There had been nothing about young Algie Langton-Smythe, when first he came to her notice, that made Miss Evans suppose he might be any different from the rest – indeed, the fact that Laura spoke of him so warmly was quite enough to condemn him in the other's eyes as someone who should be firmly discouraged from further approach. Having once made his acquaintance at the Picture Theatre, however, she was forced to admit even to herself that there was little about him one could actually dislike, while instinct told her there was a good deal more of breeding there than appearances might suppose.

Nor was her instinct proved wrong, as she discovered from Laura's father after Algie had been to see him at Spences Lane that day in mid-November.

Repeating his emphatic instruction that the young man was not to be admitted to the house again, Mr Bates had made some disparaging comment about the other's social standing, dismissing as "all tinsel and paste" his claim to belong to one of the oldest titled families in the country. This was the first time Megwynn Evans had heard anything of Algie's background, and "tinsel and paste" or not, that inherent snobbery peculiar to the servant class was sufficiently aroused in her to make enquiries of her own at the Lewes Lending Library.

There, contained in the pages of Burke's and Debrett, was information enough to ensure that Algernon Edward Victor Langton-Smythe became her chosen one for Laura.

"You've brothers of your own, have you?" Miss Evans had asked him quite innocently one afternoon after the matinée programme was finished and the theatre auditorium emptied of its audience, leaving them alone together.

The question had been put in response to his enquiry whether any of her family lived here in Lewes; to which she'd answered no, they were all at Bettws-y-Crwyn still, those who were left, and she hadn't seen them in over twenty years.

She watched him take his striped blazer jacket from the back of his chair and throw it casually across one shoulder. "You've brothers of your own, have you, Algie?"

There had been the slightest little hesitation.

"One, ma'am."

"Only one?"

A nod.

"And is he younger than you?"

"No. Older." He bent to pick up his violin case from beside the music stand.

"So there's only the two of you, is there?"

"Three, actually." He straightened himself again. "We have a sister."

"A sister. There's nice. She lives at home still, does she?" Miss Evans was watching his face very carefully. It was evident from his manner that he was less than comfortable with these questions about his family. Perhaps it was natural diffidence; but why should he go to such trouble to keep his background dark even from Laura? It was something the Welshwoman meant to find out.

"Georgiana? Oh, yes, she's still at home," he'd replied after a moment, looking about the auditorium as though his mind were preoccupied with other things.

"I don't suppose you see much of her, though, do you? No visits and that, you always so busy here six days a week – and

157

there's your job at the hospital, too." She knew from Laura that besides playing as an accompanist, he also worked from seven each morning until one o'clock as a clerk in the records office of the Victoria Hospital in Nevill Road.

"Well, it is a bit awkward, yes . . . visiting." The young man gave a little laugh that sounded like embarrassment. "I mean, there's my work, as you say, Miss Evans. And I'm a member of the Alexandra Cycling Club, you know, which takes care of my day off on Sundays."

Somehow, it all sounded rather too much of an excuse to justify his estrangement from the family circle.

"But you could travel by bicycle home of a Sunday, surely?" she'd persisted. "It isn't far."

"Oh, I don't know. We never seem to ride much in that direction."

"What, not up through Buckfield? It's lovely, is the countryside round there. We used many a time to take the pony and trap when Laura and her brother were little. Drive out for a picnic, we did."

Algie had smiled and looked at her, but made no comment.

"See, where it is now your people live? Laura did say. Near Tunbridge Wells somewhere, isn't it?"

Megwynn Evans knew the address exactly: Bells Yew Abbey, the manorhouse of a medieval estate which had passed into Algie's family at the time of Henry the Eighth's dissolution of the monasteries, and was regarded as one of the most exquisite gems of English architecture in the southern counties. She'd read all about its history at the library.

"Yes. Quite near Tunbridge Wells," he'd replied, appearing to give his attention once more to the deserted auditorium.

Then, almost apologetically, as though realising how evasive his answers must seem, he'd continued after a moment, "Actually, ma'am, my people and I don't see much of each other from choice. It was expected I'd go directly into the family business, so to speak, after leaving Oxford. But to be honest, I rather wanted to do other things first – see something of life and the world before knuckling down to estate management."

He paused, and glanced at her again.

"Estate management?" echoed Miss Evans, scenting progress at last. "But that's interesting work, look you. Better than playing in some old picture house."

"Oh, I don't know so much. It's jolly good fun, working here. And I meet all sorts of people. See all sorts of things. It's an experience I wouldn't have missed for anything. My mother's being really very understanding . . . but I'm afraid the Pater's washed his hands of me, he says, till I come to my senses. I'm letting the side down, and all that. Being a bit of a Bohemian."

"A Bohemian? Is that what he calls you?"

"Among other things."

Suddenly he'd smiled, and held out an arm to her. "Come along, Miss Evans, I'm forgetting my manners and that will never do. Now that you've played postman by bringing Laura's letter, the least I can do in return is offer you tea in the foyer."

It was a tactful way of saying that he'd had enough of questions, and she gave him full marks for the courteous manner in which he'd managed to deal with her persistence.

Watching him now, as he introduced Laura to Mr Speer beneath the bright lights of the studio set, the governess-companion allowed herself a smile of satisfaction. Yes, Algie would do very well. The only remaining fly in her ointment was Laura's father, Ellis Bates. Knowing what she did, however, of a certain incident in that gentleman's past, she had no doubt that a little subtle blackmail applied at the right time might prove very persuasive . . . very persuasive indeed.

15

"Yes, sir? Can I help you?"

The young housemaid looked nervously out through the door, anxious to try and remember what she'd been told about answering the bell. It was her first week in service at Southwood Place, and her first employment since leaving school at Christmas.

"Hello – you're new, aren't you?" The gentleman standing on the porch step smiled at her, a friendly warm smile that made her duck her frill-capped head and blush awkwardly.

"Yes, sir."

"And what's your name? May I know?"

"Jane, sir."

"Well, Jane, I'd best tell you my business, hadn't I, or I can see I shall be kept here on the step. It's Mr Stephen Moore, to see your mistress."

The blush deepened in Jane's plump, round cheeks. There was something which she had or hadn't done in answering the door like this which was not what she'd been told to do . . . or may be not how to do it; but for the life of her she couldn't remember what.

To show willing, however, she dropped a quick curtsy and opened the door wider.

"Yes, sir. Will you come inside, please sir?"

"Thank you."

"And can I take your hat and coat, please, sir?"

Stephen Moore smiled at her again as he removed his brown felt trilby and handed it over together with his gloves before unbuttoning his Raglan overcoat.

"Is your mistress alone?" he asked.

"Yes, sir. I think so, sir." Jane took the damp garment and draped it clumsily over one arm, as she'd been shown, while trying to hold hat and gloves in her free hand. "She's in the morning room, sir."

"Then don't bother to announce me. I can see my own way."

"Yes, sir." The housemaid bobbed another curtsy and paused uncertainly, before edging herself away down the entrance hall, the hem of the overcoat dragging behind her on the crimson Turkey carpet.

Stephen watched her progress for a moment; but as his mind returned to the purpose of this visit the smile faded from his face. Seeing him standing there still, Jane called back over her shoulder, "It's the second door along the passage, sir" jerking her head vigorously since both hands were already occupied.

He nodded and signalled a gesture that he knew his way; then took himself off along the hall past the foot of the sweeping flight of stairs, and on down the panelled corridor towards the rear of the house.

"Stephen!" Dinah Enderby stood up to greet him as he knocked at the morning-room door and entered. "How lovely to see you. How are you? And how was Manchester? Was your visit successful?"

He came across the room and took her outstretched hands.

"I'm fine. And yes, Manchester was worth the long journey." He leaned to kiss her cheek, smelling the scent of freesias on her smooth skin. "My client has appointed a new supervisor for the orphanage, at my suggestion, and there's to be a full enquiry into the past management of the place."

"So you won. I'm pleased." Dinah released him. "Sit down, won't you – no, here, here by the fire. What a miserable day it is. I've never known the weather be as cold and wet as this for so long. Have you driven down?"

"No. I came in from Weatherfield yesterday and stayed the night at my parents'. You're to be matron of honour at Jessie's wedding, I understand."

"Yes." She re-seated herself opposite him, the reflection from the cheerful blaze upon the hearth warming her face. "It sounds very grand, doesn't it. Matron of honour. I'd have preferred chief bride's maid, but Jessie says that's out of fashion now, and besides I'm too old to be a maid. For which I thanked her."

They both laughed.

"And how have you been keeping, yourself?" Stephen asked, settling back in his chair and giving her one of his long, perceptive glances. She had lost more weight – he'd noticed that as soon as he came in the room – and the lemon silk costume she was wearing seemed to hang from her slender shoulders, accentuating the sudden fragility.

"Oh . . . I'm well enough, I suppose. Better, anyway, now that Guy and Neville have moved away."

"Ah, they've gone at last, have they?"

She nodded. "Back to London. New Year's Eve. The day after they'd received your letter. That threat of court action obviously proved the final straw – though you know, I think Jessie had done a lot to wear down their resistance, the way she bullied and badgered them. How I wish I'd had her courage sometimes! Think of the trouble I might have been spared."

Stephen continued to look at her, and his expression grew sombre at the thought of what fresh trouble he was about to inflict upon her. The information he had, though, would not sweeten with keeping, and it was best that she should hear the truth from him, who cared for her, than learn it at some later date from a less sympathetic source.

He sat forward suddenly in his chair and leaned his elbows on his knees, hands clasped so that the knuckles showed white. Something in the tension of this attitude seemed to warn Dinah, for she returned his gaze with a look of quick enquiry as she waited to hear what it was he was about to say.

He cleared his throat.

"When I left Manchester last week," he began quietly, "I decided to break my train journey south at Wolverhampton. The business which had taken me to that part of the country presented an opportunity to kill two birds with one stone, as it were – collate evidence for this defence case I'm handling, and at the same time make some private enquiries on your behalf, Dinah."

The expression of her face sharpened into a small frown, and she opened her mouth.

He forestalled the interruption by holding up a hand. "No, just a moment, my dear, before you start asking questions. Hear me out first. You'll remember you told me some time last summer, before your marriage, that your husband is related on his mother's side to a Lord Claverley. And that the family seat is a place called Whitmore Reans, in Staffordshire?"

"Yes . . . I remember."

"Well, merely from curiosity to know how far back the title went, I happened to look up Lord Claverley's reference – this was after you came to consult me in October. I must tell you now – and it's kinder if I'm blunt – I found no trace or mention of his title anywhere. Not in the usual annuals and almanacs, nor in the lists of British nobility, nor in any of the genealogies such as Burke's. I'm sorry to have to say this, my dear, but the fact is – Lord Claverley does not appear to exist."

Stephen paused. Dinah's face had gone suddenly very pale, and stamped upon it was such disbelief that he hated himself for the pain this lovely woman must needs suffer from the wounding truth of his disclosure.

After a moment he forced himself to continue.

"There is, however, a *place* called Claverley – just a few miles over the Staffordshire county border from Wolver-hampton. And by rather suspicious coincidence, as I discovered from my gazetteer, Whitmore Reans lies within the municipal area of that same town. Wolverhampton. Which is the reason I broke my journey there returning from the north."

"And . . . what did you find?" Dinah asked apprehensively, her voice very low.

"That Whitmore Reans is not the country seat of any make-believe Lord Claverley, but a suburban working-class district of several dozen terraced streets, in which the only building of any note is a large brewery."

"How can you be so certain? I mean . . . perhaps you made a mistake and looked in the wrong place?"

He shook his head. "No mistake. I checked both the electoral register and town hall records. I'm sorry, Dinah, but it rather looks as though Warwick Enderby was spinning a tale and a half when he painted you such a true-blue picture of his pedigree."

"He was so . . . plausible!"

"Yes. I'm afraid gentlemen of his type generally are. They wouldn't make a living otherwise."

"But the cuff-links, the monogrammed cigarette case – "

"Simply part of the trappings. He could have bought them anywhere. At a guess I'd say they came from one of the pawn shops he uses as business premises."

Distress mounted upon disbelief. "And his two brothers – oh, Stephen, do you suppose they were all in this together . . . this deception?"

"Unfortunately, I'm sure they were," he said gently. "They had to be, else how could they profit from your marriage?"

Keeping a careful watch on Dinah, he leaned back to make himself more comfortable, resting one leg on the knee of the other; then, by way of reflection, added thoughtfully, "What a world of difference there is between him and someone like young Algie."

"Algie? Algie Langton-Smythe?" Dinah's tone registered a note of confusion. "What has he to do with this?"

"Oh, nothing really. It's interesting to draw a comparison, that's all, between the genuine article and the clever fake. Opposite facets of human nature, I suppose one might say. Our friend Algie keeps his light so closely hidden under a bushel of modesty, I mean, to look at him, an unassuming young chap playing violin in a theatre pit, who could possibly believe he's the thoroughbred he is?"

He paused again.

"Of course, you're probably not aware, are you, my dear. That the Honourable Algie is younger brother of Lord Burrswode, and second son of Viscount Monchelsea."

"No, no, I didn't know that . . . not the details. He never says much."

"Precisely. He never says much. Unlike that husband of yours, who airs his non-existent noble connections for everyone to hear. Together, the pair of them make a most fascinating study in contrasts – "

"Stephen – what about Warwick's parents," Dinah broke in distractedly, far more concerned just now with the need to consider her own situation rather than anyone else's. "He

164

claims his father was an actor. That he took leading roles in Shakespeare. Was that all part of the lie, too, do you suppose?"

"I don't know. It may be. The Enderby name doesn't ring any theatrical bells. But there's obviously some acting ability in the family, to judge by your husband's performance. He certainly excels at carrying off – "

A sudden loud knock at the morning-room door interrupted whatever it was he was going to say. He looked across at Dinah.

"Yes?" she called, raising her voice a little.

There was some fumbling at the handle before eventually it was turned and the door pushed open to reveal the new housemaid, awkwardly balancing a laden tray against one hip.

"Jane? What do you think you're doing?" Her mistress rose to her feet, clearly annoyed. "I thought I gave orders I was not to be disturbed while Mr Moore was here."

"Beg pardon, ma'am, I'm sorry for the bother, I'm sure. But it's the Master – it's him as told me to serve him wi' his coffee here." Poor Jane turned bright red, not knowing where to look; and in an effort to redeem herself, hurried on at a gabble, "He's just this minute got up, Mrs Enderby, ma'am, and he rang down to the kitchen for me to bring him a tray in the morning room. I said you said as how you wasn't to be disturbed, wi' a gentleman visitor calling to see you, and he says what gentleman visitor. And then he says never mind no visitor, I want coffee serving me in the morning room, and see it's there ready piping hot when I come down."

The coffee pot was in imminent danger of sliding into a collision with the cream jug during this monologue, and Jane righted the balance of the tray only just in time.

"Please inform Mr Enderby that I'm occupied here, and that he must take his refreshment elsewhere," Dinah said shortly. "I shall ring for you when Mr Moore is leaving."

"I trust he won't delay his departure," interrupted a voice from outside in the hallway, "if his presence prevents my orders being followed. Jane, be a good girl and go and put the tray over on the table."

The door was pushed further back, and Warwick Enderby came in. Though it was almost eleven o'clock, he had not bothered to dress yet and was wearing a crimson quilted bed-robe over his pyjama trousers. His moustache had not been trimmed, nor had he shaved, for there was a dark growth of stubble shadowing his jaw and throat. As he came across to the fire, he scratched at the bristles and yawned, then pushed his fingers through his rumpled hair, shoving it untidily back from his forehead.

"Morning, Dinah," he said carelessly, moving past her to throw himself down in a chair, slippered feet thrust out upon the hearth-rail. Then, yawning again without troubling to put a hand to his mouth – "Where's that coffee, Jane? Isn't it poured yet?"

The young housemaid looked anxiously towards her mistress. Dinah's face had taken on a tight, stony expression; but she gave the girl a quick nod of permission before turning away.

"Beg pardon, sir, how d'you want it serving?" Jane enquired nervously.

"Oh – two sugar lumps and plenty of cream." Warwick raised his arms above his head and stretched himself with a grunt. "Anything for me in the post this morning?"

"Yes, sir. I left your letters on the tray in the hall, sir."

"Go and fetch 'em, there's a good girl. And then take yourself off out of the way and tell Mrs Smith I shan't be wanting any lunch."

Only when he had coffee cup and morning post at his elbow did he deign to glance across in Stephen Moore's direction.

"Still here, are you?" he commented rudely, ignoring the fact that the other had risen to his feet and had been standing not two yards from him for the past five minutes. "Am I keeping you waiting?"

"My business happens to be with your wife," Stephen responded levelly, refusing to let himself be baited.

"Oh, really?" Warwick yawned once more, and reached for his cup. "Well, any business of my wife's is business of mine. So what is it this time?"

There was a pause. Stephen gave Dinah a querying look, his eyebrows raised.

"You may as well tell him," she said, quite tonelessly.

"Tell me what?" Warwick glanced suspiciously from one to the other as he took a sip of coffee and put the cup back down again. "You've been cooking something up, have you?"

"On the contrary, Mr Enderby, it is *you* who've been doing the cooking."

"Is that so, now." He reached into his bed-robe pocket and produced his silver cigarette case. Taking out a yellow Turkish Abdullah, he rapped its tip smartly on the lid to compress the tobacco, and without removing his eyes from Stephen Moore, placed the cigarette to his lips and lit it with a match.

"I must ask you to justify that remark," he said, blowing out the flame and tossing the spent match-end towards the fire.

"Certainly." This little show of bravado did nothing to impress Stephen: he knew it for what it was, a breathing-space in which to play for time to think. "Allow me to refresh your memory, Mr Enderby. You claim your deceased mother to have been a cousin of the present Lord Claverley, whose principal residence, as I understand, is Whitmore Reans in the county of Stafford."

Warwick's eyes narrowed slightly as he inhaled upon his cigarette.

"Are these facts correct?" Stephen challenged.

The smoke was exhaled again from an out-thrust lower lip. "You must know they're not, I suppose, or you wouldn't be asking."

"Then you admit that you lied to your wife when you described yourself as being related to the aristocracy?"

"Oh, no." A crooked smile played upon Warwick's handsome face. "I'm blue-blooded, right enough. But the wrong side of the blanket, that's all. A bit of a bastard, you might say. Not the sort of thing one goes around admitting in public – and certainly not to ladies of quality like Dinah."

He transferred the smile across to her.

"Though had I known at the time that her own dear

167

mother was born without benefit of clergy, I might not have been so quick to spin her the line about Lord Claverley."

Two small red spots appeared in Dinah's pale cheeks.

"Whatever the circumstances of my mother's birth, there has never been any attempt at deception," she hit back in a low, yet furiously vehement tone. "And the fact that her father died before he could give her his name is no slur upon her honour. How dare you rake up such an intimate confidence as justification for your own tawdry imposture!"

She was so angry – so hurt – that she would have struck the smile from his face had Stephen not been present. She had revealed to Warwick the history of her mother's past just a few days before their marriage, not wishing to keep anything concealed from the man with whom she was so very much in love. She had told him the facts in trust, as a kind of confession; and now to have them thrown back at her, and in front of a witness who also happened to be a personal friend, was more shaming than she could bear.

Sudden tears welled in her eyes, and she quickly averted her head so that neither man should see her humiliation.

"Come, come, old girl – there's no need to get up on your high horse," she heard Warwick say. "None of it matters now, anyway, so let's not fall out over a little illegitimacy in the family. You want the truth? Very well, you shall have it."

He inhaled on his cigarette again, flicking the ash negligently into the hearth.

"My mother was the result of an evening's frolic at the Cremorne Gardens on Boat Race day between a milliner's assistant and a peer of the realm. My father – though he aspired to Shakespeare – spent his career treading the boards of third-rate music halls entertaining the vulgar masses with songs like 'Burlington Bertie'. My brothers and I were raised in that pearl of the Midland counties, Wolverhampton, by our paternal grandmother – a lady who claimed she'd been brought down in the world by ignorant men, though the exact nature of her complaint was never made clear. Perhaps fortunately."

"Has it never occurred to you, Mr Enderby," Stephen said, "that you might have spared your wife a great deal of pain and distress had you been quite as honest in the beginning?"

There was a shrug. "First impressions are what sell a man, dear chap. My father always said that to be a successful salesman one needed the following requirements: good looks, good health, good temper, good voice, good manners – and a good story."

"And what was it you were hoping to sell *me*?" Dinah demanded, swinging round on him again, the tell-tale tears dashed from her cheek with the back of a hand. "Tell me, Warwick!"

He gazed across at her with that irritating little smile and raised his cigarette to his lips.

"Why . . . Prince Charming, of course."

There was a pause while the cruelty of those words sank in.

"And that was what I bought." She shook her head, as though she could not believe it herself. "A sham, a pretence – an actor, as well as a gambler and thief!"

"At the time, you seemed to think you had quite a bargain."

"At the time, I'd fallen very much in love. It was not until after our marriage that I woke to discover what an utter blind fool I'd been – "

"A discovery urged upon you, I don't doubt, by our friend here Mr Moore, whose zeal in ferreting into my affairs is matched only by his pique at being pipped by me at the post."

He shifted his gaze to Stephen, watching for the reaction.

It was not slow in coming.

"Can you adduce one cogent piece of evidence for that offensive remark, sir?" the other asked, his voice coldly polite.

Warwick let out a laugh and leaned forward to toss the cigarette end into the fire.

"My dear fellow, we're not in some starchy courtroom here. In words of plain English, you've been fancying Dinah for years but never had the nerve to tell her. So don't pretend it didn't put your nose out of joint when *I* appeared on the scene."

He leaned back again in his chair, hands behind his head, his smile more crooked than ever.

"Oh, come now, you can't deny it. You're too much of a gentleman."

169

"A title to which you, Mr Enderby, have patently forfeited all claim." Stephen's usually open, pleasant features were marred by the deep groove of a frown, the only sign of his anger. "My friendship with your wife extends over many years, and it ill becomes you or anyone to misconstrue its nature by suggesting that it's any other than a warm affection based upon mutual respect."

As he said this, he directed his glance at Dinah. Her face was masked by an oddly shut-in expression, with only the slightest quiver of the chin betraying how near she was to crying. He found himself longing suddenly to hold her, to assure her that all would be well in the end, that she mustn't give way too much to despair; but instead, he said quietly, "I think I should leave now, my dear. There seems no point in prolonging this conversation."

He did not trust himself to speak again to Warwick Enderby. It would be a mistake to give the fellow the satisfaction of knowing how close he had come to the truth.

16

The angel in the churchyard was no longer the pearly-pure vision it once had been. The passing seasons had taken their toll of its alabaster whiteness, discolouring the outspread wings and marking the upturned face with rainwater streaks so that from a distance it looked as though the eyes were weeping grimy tears. Between the folds of the flowing garment, a slime of green moss was beginning to coat the stonework and the naked feet were crusted with patches of yellow lichen.

"The whole thing could do with a thorough good clean," grumbled Esmond Bates, using a stick to poke aside the withered spears of wild daffodils obscuring the inscription at the base of his grandfather's memorial. "I ought really to have done something before now, I suppose, the state it's getting into."

His fiancée Jessie Moore, one hand linked with the arm of her friend Dinah Enderby, the other holding firmly on to her wide-brimmed hat in the blustery April breeze, leaned forward to see past his shoulder to read the chiselled words. The two young women had come up together to spend a day here in Weatherfield with the particular intention of visiting St Anne's parish church, where Jessie and Esmond were to be married on June the third. Never one to conform to traditional social practice, Jessie had made up her mind to wed here in her fiancé's parish rather than her own, in view of the close associations between the Bates family and St Anne's, where Esmond's grandfather had once been rector.

It was the memorial to this same grandfather which the three of them were now examining so critically before meeting the present incumbent, the Reverend Wilfred Nesbit, inside the church.

"'The souls of the righteous are in the hand of God, and

171

there shall no torment touch them'," Jessie read out, pulling a face at such prim Victorian piety. "'Sacred to the memory of Esmond Jezrahel Bates, rector of this parish, who laid down his life on the sixth of September, 1852: this memorial was erected by his only child, Ellis Kember Bates. *Cineri gloria sera est.*'"

She straightened herself.

"You're the scholar, Esmond, darling. Translate that, please."

"What, that last bit d'you mean? It's one of Martial's epigrams. Martial the Latin poet. He was famous for them, you know."

"But of course. We're frightfully well acquainted with Mr Martial and his epigrams, aren't we, Dinah?" She rolled her eyes at her friend with a look of drollery. "But what does it *mean?*"

"Ah . . . let me think. I should know. Oh, yes – 'Glory paid to ashes comes too late.'" It pleased Esmond that he'd remembered correctly. "A loose translation of that would be – if you wish to honour a man, honour him while he lives."

"You're so clever!" His fiancée released Dinah's arm to stretch up and plant a kiss on his cheek. "Is it any wonder I love you as I do?"

Esmond grinned.

"Come along, now," he said, throwing the stick down among the fading daffodils, "it's eleven o'clock. We don't want to keep Mr Nesbit waiting, or he may refuse to marry us."

"As if he'd dare!" Jessie cried. "Are you coming as well, Dinah?"

The other shook her head. "Not just yet. Not while you're discussing wedding banns and hymns and things. I'll stay out here and pay my respects to the family."

"As you like. Esmond will come and fetch you if we need your advice."

Taking his elbow, and still clutching her hat, Jessie led her fiancé off towards the lychgate path. For a few moments Dinah watched them; and then, as the deep-throated chimes of St Anne's clock began tolling the hour, she moved slowly in the opposite direction, picking her way between memorials and grassy grave-mounds towards the wall at the far side of the churchyard.

Here, shadowed by the overhanging branches of a thicket of hazel and alder, three plain headstones stood together in a plot of turfed earth, marking the last resting place of her grandfather, grandmother and uncle.

What a tale of human tragedy lay buried in this spot, she reflected sombrely, standing at the edge of the plot and letting her eyes wander from the mute grey stones to the sweet-smelling border of rosemary bushes which her mother had planted for remembrance years before.

She glanced again towards the name on the left.

FRANCIS MORGAN 1820–1852 R.I.P.

He had been a stallion leader by trade, taking his great black Shire from farm to farm around the country to cover the mares for breeding. The son of a gipsy, he had earned himself a reputation, so the story went, for being nearly as virile as the horse he led, fathering a number of bastard babies around the isolated farming communities of the Weald. Among them had been Dinah's mother and uncle.

Her gaze shifted to the middle stone.

DINAH FLYNN 1831–1871 R.I.P.

She had never known this grandmother after whom she was named; but she'd been told she closely resembled her, and it was a curious sensation to stand here and imagine that other, dead all these years, once being a handsome young red-haired woman living at Weatherfield alehouse and raising the two small children she'd borne her faithless stallion man. He was going to marry her – so the story went again – but had died in the same accident which killed Esmond Bates's grandfather, when both men were trampled by Frank Morgan's horse.

Dinah's gaze moved to rest on the final headstone.

FRANCIS PATRICK FLYNN 1849-1872
Lord, have mercy.

173

This was her uncle Frank, acclaimed as one of the best bare-knuckle prize fighters in the southern counties, and the very image, they said, of her brother Francis Bethway. Thank God his mother had died the year before him, for had she lived to see his finish it would have broken her heart in two. He'd been a handsome fellow, but arrogant and hot-tempered and the very devil when drunk. Marrying into wealth, to a woman for whom he cared nothing, he had killed his mistress's husband in a fight, and after being found guilty of manslaughter, ended his young life by his own hand in Maidstone Gaol.

They were a family which seemed always to have courted trouble, Dinah thought despondently. In one way or another, ill fortune had cast its shadow on them all, blighting each generation with the taint of illegitimacy, violence, hardship, or some other attendant adversity. Even she herself had not escaped the malign influence of whatever star these forebears of hers had lived their lives beneath: in her case, it would seem that destiny had fated her to know nothing but unhappiness in marriage, first through the too-early loss of one husband, and now through the self-seeking duplicity of another.

"Hello, Dinah. I hoped I'd find you here."

The suddenness of the voice so close behind in the midst of her sober thoughts made her jump. She turned quickly, a hand going to her breast; and then, relaxing again as she saw who it was, she made the effort to smile and said, "Oh, it's you, Stephen. You're early, aren't you?"

He returned the smile, his deep-set brown eyes full of warmth. "I've had enough of the office for one morning. I saw you with Jessie and Esmond across the green from my window and decided I couldn't wait till twelve-thirty before meeting you. You haven't forgotten we're having luncheon together?"

She shook her head. It had been arranged that the four of them should go for a meal at The Man in the Moon, the renovated hostelry which had formerly been the old ale-house at the foot of The Holloway, and after that, to spend a few hours of the afternoon at Esmond Bates's house so that Jessie could make up her mind what redecoration needed to be done before she moved in after the wedding.

"You don't mind my joining you here, do you?" Stephen asked.

"Of course not. I was just . . . visiting some of my relatives." Dinah indicated the simple little grave-plot behind. "And thinking to myself that if the dead could speak, what tales they'd have to tell us."

Her companion studied the names engraved upon the three headstones.

"It's a nice place to be buried, here by the trees," he observed after a moment, tactfully, knowing a thing or two of the Flynn family history from living and working in Weatherfield, where memories were long and tongues sometimes longer. "I hope I'll be laid to rest in a spot like this when my turn comes."

"Don't be so cheerful!"

"No, I mean it. I'd hate to be shovelled away under some dreary old memorial like Esmond's grandfather's over there." He turned to give a nod towards the soaring angel figure spreading its discoloured wings in the fitful sunlight at the other side of the churchyard.

"Esmond's very proud of that memorial," reproved Dinah. "So you'd best not let him hear you criticising it."

"Oh, but I'm not criticising, my dear. Merely expressing an opinion. Let's change the subject . . ." There was another pause. "How have things been in Lewes since our last rather unfortunate meeting?"

"You mean, how is the situation with Warwick?"

"Yes. Has there been any improvement? I'm afraid I've been rather out of touch with events these past few weeks with all the travelling back and forth to Manchester for the orphanage inquiry."

Dinah allowed herself a small, joyless smile. "Things have been easier since he packed his bags and departed – "

"Oh? he's gone, has he?" There was an eager note in the hasty interruption.

"Not for good, alas. Just for the time being. He'll be back again at the end of the month. Some business to see to somewhere – which usually means gambling."

She looked down at her wedding ring, twisting it to and fro on her finger, and then went on inconsequentially, "I

175

wish I'd brought some flowers for the graves. Is there a florist's barrow in the high street, would you know?"

Stephen shook his head. "But there's a violet-seller often about this way," he offered helpfully. "Would you like me to go back across the green and look?"

"No, no. It doesn't matter. It was only a thought."

"Are you sure? I mean, it would be no trouble." He cast a glance at her lowered profile, softly framed by waves of auburn hair drawn away from a centre parting into a loosely twisted bun at the nape of the slender neck. On top, perched at a becoming angle and secured by a pearl-headed hat pin, she was wearing a little velvet beret in place of the full-brimmed "Merry Widow" style of hat she generally favoured.

As though aware that she was being admired, Dinah looked up quickly.

"I really must remember to plant some bulbs here this autumn," she said, for a moment meeting her companion's eyes and then glancing away again. "The rosemary's nice, but it doesn't bloom long. Perhaps a few small rose bushes inside the border would add a splash of colour – what do you think?"

"I think it would make this corner of the churchyard most attractive. Cut flowers are all very well, but they don't last. And there's nothing looks worse, to my mind, than dead blossom on a grave."

Stephen was about to add something more when the sound of a voice calling out from across by the church distracted his attention, and both he and Dinah turned to see who it was.

"Ah, I think the presence of the matron of honour is required," he said, raising a hand in response to Esmond Bates's wave. "Come along, my dear. Let's leave the dead to their well-deserved rest, or we'll have sister Jessie out here to disturb the peace and quiet, wanting to know what the pair of us are up to."

By midday, when the four of them came out from St Anne's, the last of the cloud cover had scudded away before the breeze, and the dull sky cleared to a spring-fresh blue.

Full of enthusiasm for their morning's meeting with the Reverend Nesbit and his helpful guidance in the choice of nuptial hymns and readings for the order of service, Jessie was in one of her most exuberant moods, and, declaring that the sunshine was too lovely to be wasted, insisted that they should walk the couple of miles or so to lunch at The Man in the Moon.

This did not please Esmond, who had recently acquired his first motor car and was anxious to show it off at every opportunity; but as usual, his fiancée had her way and they all set out on foot across the green, Jessie on Esmond's arm and Dinah upon Stephen's.

Their route led them down through Old Weatherfield village, whose antique origins were still discernible in the number of Georgian and Queen Anne buildings lining the high street behind the façade of shopfronts; and once past the crossroads, out along what had earlier been a country lane to Troy Town but was now an urban street of terraced houses and allotment patches.

"There used to be nothing but fields and woodland around here when my mother was a child," Dinah said reminiscently, looking about her at the slate-roofed townscape as they went along. "I can't imagine it, can you – all that countryside submerged beneath bricks and mortar."

"It's called progress," answered Jessie over her shoulder from ahead. "D'you know, I read somewhere that by the year two thousand and fifty there'll be standing room only for us all. Can you conceive of such a thing! So many people that we'll each be reduced to occupying a little five-foot patch of earth."

"Oh, it will never come to that," Esmond told her dismissively, pausing to re-light his pipe which had gone out. "You really mustn't believe everything you read, dearest."

"How do you know it'll never come to that?" she challenged.

"Because there will always be war and pestilence to keep down the population."

"We haven't had a war in Europe since Waterloo – "

"What about the Franco-Prussian conflict in 1870?"

"But *we* weren't dragged into that, were we?"

"Don't speak too soon, Jessie," her brother put in. "The signs are, this country is bound to be drawn into some sort of dispute before very much longer, to judge from the Kaiser's sabre-rattling."

"Oh, pooh. Who takes any notice of him? He just likes playing soldiers, that's all."

"Yes. Real-life soldiers. We lost enough good men during the South African campaign. God knows, a European war would wreak a far more terrible carnage."

"You're in a very gloomy humour today," Dinah told him, giving his arm a little shake of reproval. "What's brought this on?"

"Oh, disregard him, do!" cried Jessie. "He spends far too much of his time reading the fate of the world in a few dismal newspaper articles. And then getting himself thoroughly down in the dumps about it. Now you can't say that's not true, Stephen – " as he went to interrupt her. "Look how depressed you let yourself get over that colliery disaster they had last winter up at Bolton."

"I admit I was depressed. I happened to be there in the area, don't forget, and saw what it did, to lose three hundred and forty-four men from one pit. There wasn't a single family who weren't robbed of a husband or father, or son or brother. The suffering was beyond description . . . not only the physical pain of bereavement, but the burden of financial hardship laid upon those families for years to come."

"Now if you're going to make a speech, Stephen dear, Esmond and I will walk a little faster," his sister said plaintively, hating to have her good mood spoilt. "Besides, look, we're almost at 'The Man' so do let's change the topic of conversation. I dare say their beef will be quite salt enough without us sitting there weeping over it."

She thrust her arm more firmly through her fiancé's and hugged herself possessively against him, going up on tiptoe as they went along and whispering something in his ear.

"You know, Stephen, you ought to consider entering politics," Dinah commented, half-seriously. "You'd really be rather good at it."

He looked down at her with the beginning of a smile. "Actually, my dear, I'll let you into a secret. I do have

178

ambitions in that direction. Government needs a social conscience, and it's up to ordinary fellows like me to see that the so-called labouring class is fairly represented."

Dinah loosed his arm to applaud, adding gravely, "You will, of course, fight for the introduction of women's suffrage?"

"But of course."

She placed her hand upon her heart. "Then I promise, when it comes, you shall have my vote."

By now, the four of them had arrived at their destination, and after some discussion it was decided to take luncheon out in the garden at the rear of the building. It was sheltered here from the breeze, and the April sun was warm enough to make an *al fresco* meal seem most inviting.

"The dining room's pleasant enough," said Esmond, holding open the side-door for the two ladies, "don't think I'm finding fault with it. But one does notice the occasional smell of fumes coming in through the window from the garage there – "

He indicated a single-storey wood-fronted structure at the side of the road, formerly the old alehouse stables and now converted to cater for the passing charabanc trade, with a sign above advertising "Motor Carriage Accommodation" and a solitary pump topped by a white glass globe bearing the name "Benzole".

Parked outside, somewhat incongruously, was a farm wagon loaded with turnips.

"The last time we were here, Esmond and I," said Jessie as she went in through the door, "there was the most heavenly machine standing there in the road. Gleaming black coachwork, morocco leather seats, walnut and chromium-plating – oh, it was a dream! I wanted Esmond to buy the same model – "

"Not at that price," he cut in firmly, ushering her down the passage towards the garden door at the other end. "Not on my income. Now the pair of you go and find us a table outside while Stephen and I investigate the bill of fare in the bar."

"Yes, and while you're ordering drinks for yourselves, you might send out something for us," came the answer back. "Two half-pints of cider, I think, since we're both emancipated enough to be seen drinking in public."

Leaving their companions, Jessie and Dinah went through into the large walled garden and after looking round chose a spot away from the path, screened by a wooden trellis. Its covering of rambler roses had not yet come into bud, but the tender green shoots formed an attractive arbour above the benches, and there were clumps of violets, cowslips and primroses along the grassy borders between spears of early-opening bluebells.

The view from the garden had lost much of its pastoral prettiness with the growth of the town encroaching upon it from several sides; but there was still a vista of unspoilt countryside in one direction, looking out towards the Kentish Weald, and in the clear sunlit air it was possible to see the smudge of smoke from a train travelling along the line to Hastings between fields of fresh spring corn.

"Didn't I hear it was some distant relation of your mother's who owns this place?" Jessie asked chattily when their cider had been brought out on a tray by a snub-nosed girl.

"Yes, that's right." Dinah took a long sip from her glass.

"What's his name – Adams, isn't it?"

"Mm."

It was Joel Adams, and he was her mother's half-brother, one of old stallion man Morgan's numerous issue by different women in the district.

She took another sip. "We hardly know him, though. There's very little contact with that side of the family." She had never mentioned to Jessie anything of the illegitimacy which stained her background: it was hardly something of which she was proud.

"Oh, look – !" The other jumped to her feet and waved. "Here they are already. Heavens, that was quick. Who's the fellow with them, I wonder?"

Dinah leaned forward to see round the trellis.

"Good God, it's Warwick!" Some of the cider spilled over the rim of her glass as she hastily put it down. "But what on earth – "

"Look who's just come into the public bar," called out

180

Esmond, making a half-hearted attempt at a laugh as the men approached across the grass. "Small world, isn't it."

"Hello, Dinah old girl." Her husband's manner was completely casual, as though he found nothing extraordinary in the coincidence of their meeting here. "Surprised to see me, eh? I though you might be. I was motoring through on my way back to Lewes and needed to pull in for some fuel."

He gave her one of his boyish grins and perched himself on the edge of the table.

"You don't mind if I join you and your friends in a bite to eat, do you?"

All the sunlight seemed suddenly to go out of her day. Mutely, she looked towards Stephen.

"Mr Enderby has kindly offered to pay for the meal," he said, his manner coolly professional. "It would seem that the business which took him from home has been concluded earlier than he thought. And with some measure of success."

"You mean he's made a kill at gambling." Dinah found her voice again. "Well, congratulations, Warwick. Thank you for such generosity."

Picking up her glass, she raised it as though to toast him, and then quite deliberately poured the cider away on the ground.

"You know, we really should be drinking champagne. I'm sure they'll find a bottle if you ask. After all, we have something to celebrate – and it's not every day beggars can be choosers."

She had no need to add who she thought was the beggar.

"Who does he think he is, I wonder," Jessie said indignantly, "throwing his money about like that."

"His ill-gotten gains, don't you mean," commented Esmond, emptying his glass.

"Yes – his ill-gotten gains!"

The luncheon had proved a most awkward meal, and only Warwick Enderby appeared to enjoy it. He and Dinah had made their goodbyes and left now, returning to Lewes together in his motor car despite Jessie's protestations that she and her friend had already arranged to travel back by train later in the afternoon.

181

"What on earth you two were thinking of, to let him pay for everything – " She warmed to her grievance. "It almost choked me, having to sit at the same table and watch him behave for all the world as though he expected us to be *grateful*! You should have ignored him, the pair of you, when you noticed him there in the public bar – "

"We did – "

"You should have acted as though you hadn't seen him, and come straight out."

"Jessie, we *did*." Esmond was tempted to shake his fiancée hard, much as he loved her. "Unfortunately, he saw us first, and came across to speak. What were we to do? Pretend we didn't know him?"

"I would!"

"The fellow was obviously intent upon thrusting his company on us," intervened Stephen, "so there was little point in cutting him." It rankled sorely that what should have been a happy day for the four of them had ended in so abrupt and embarrassing a manner; and the sight of Warwick Enderby lounging at the table over several bottles of inferior wine – which was all the bar could provide at short notice – and treating Dinah in such an exaggeratedly over-familiar fashion, had been almost more than he could stomach.

"A man like that has no sense of decorum," he added sourly.

"What I can't understand is why Dinah's let herself be dragged off home by him," Jessie complained. "She could have sent him on to Lewes by himself and stayed to spend the rest of the day here with us as we'd planned." She waved irritably at a bluebottle which had alighted on the table, drawn by the smell of wine in Dinah's untouched glass. "It's not like her to give in so meekly."

"That wasn't meekness," said Stephen. "That was diplomacy. She had no choice but to leave with him if she wanted to avoid a scene. It was quite obvious her husband had drunk enough to be unpleasant if she'd said no."

"Odious man."

There was a pause. In the distance, a plume of smoke showed the Hastings train making its return journey through the springing countryside.

182

"It's a curious thing, you know," said Esmond reflectively after a moment, taking a turn at waving off the persistent bluebottle. "Despite the way he behaves, he does appear quite genuinely to care for her. One can see that from his expression occasionally."

"Well of course he cares for her, darling! She keeps him. The trouble is, *she* doesn't care for *him* – and can anyone blame her? She should make it impossible for him to continue living under her roof."

"The trouble is, of course, that Dinah's hands are tied," came in Stephen quietly. "Tied by the laws governing matrimony. It's one thing to threaten a civil action against sponging brothers-in-law, but it's quite another to attempt to eject a husband. She has very little grounds to go on – "

"What are you talking about," his sister interrupted him. "Very little grounds, indeed! The man's a cheat and a liar. He deserts her for days on end. He refuses to support her."

"None of that would hold much water if presented as evidence," Stephen came back smartly. "He's a cheat and a liar, agreed. But that's a defect of character, and it would be hard to prove to the satisfaction of a court that Dinah has suffered either physically or materially as a result. He deserts her. Agreed. But the Law would say that since he invariably returns, desertion as such is not intended. He refuses to support her. Does he? What about his winnings from gambling? She shares some of that, I believe? And what about her own behaviour? Can't it be argued that by withholding conjugal rights, Dinah herself is acting in a manner prejudicial to the welfare of her marriage?"

"Now that's hardly for us to judge," interjected Esmond, giving the other a hard look as though to warn him to have a care what he said in front of Jessie.

"Oh, don't be stuffy, darling," she told him. "We all know what's going on there. Dinah's made no secret of the life the pair of them lead together at Southwood Place. In fact, she told me recently she heartily wished he'd find himself some other female and have an affaire, so that she could divorce him for adultery. And why not? Why shouldn't she? She's her own woman, when all's said and done, and modern enough in her views not to care overmuch what society may think of such action."

"The difficulty with adultery, though," said Esmond, not very cheerfully, "is proving it."

"She's considered that, too. She said she was thinking of engaging the services of a private agency – "

"What? Oh, but surely, she doesn't want to get herself involved in a sordid business of that nature," Stephen broke in. "Modern woman or not, there are some things best left for others to deal with. Besides, this is the first I've heard on the subject, and I am, after all, acting as her legal adviser. Why hasn't she consulted me?"

"Why indeed?" Jessie examined her fingernails, a habit she had when trying not to show her annoyance. "Perhaps because she knows all she'll get for her time is a long lecture, and very little else. Do I have to remind you, brother dear, how practised you are at dragging your feet where poor Dinah's concerned?"

He gave her a sharp look. "And may I ask what precisely you mean by that?"

There was another shrug. "All this is your fault, you know. If anyone's to blame for Dinah's miserable plight, it's you. Oh yes, it is, so there's no need to glare quite so fiercely! If you'd made up your mind a little sooner to marry her yourself, as I kept telling you, she'd never have grown weary of waiting and fallen into the arms of the first smooth-tongued adventurer to come along and pay court to her."

In the long silence which followed, the buzz of the hapless bluebottle drowning in the glass of wine went entirely unheeded.

17

Dearest Frank,
    I am sorry we parted on such bad terms. What a pity,
seeing as how our friendship meant a lot. I don't believe
you ever really cared for me like you said, or you wouldn't
have made me so miserable.
    I miss you. There, now you know. Do you miss me at
all? I don't suppose you do. I hate you sometimes, but I
never stop thinking about you and remembering the good
time we had together.
    You said I was proud. Well, it's made me eat my
pride to write this letter. You said I was cold and
unfeeling. If only you'd give us another chance, I'd make
you so happy, Frank, you'd see I would, I promise.

The note was signed "Sissy" with three crosses beneath for
kisses. It had been slipped into the hand of Corporal Walter
Jackson when he went on duty one morning a few weeks
ago, and now, much creased with reading and re-reading,
lay folded away in the inside pocket of Captain Francis
Bethway's tweed jacket, hanging on the back of a hotel
bedroom chair.

The westering sun streaming in through the window
bathed the room in light, burnishing the polished mahogany
furniture blood-red and gilding the mirrors and glassware. It
was an expensive room, the best which The Fordhouse at
Buckfield was able to offer.

Francis lolled idly in a brocaded tub chair which provided
ample room for him to swing one leg over its arm and smoke
his cheroot in comfort as he watched Sissy Desatti. She was
like a child, he thought to himself, a satisfied smile curving
his lips beneath the trim military moustache. The way she
was moving about the room, touching things, examining,
admiring, her dark eyes going from one object to another

. . . and back again repeatedly to the bevelled-glass mirrors to preen herself in the new *crêpe de chine* dress he'd bought for her.

He reached down an arm over the side of the chair and picked up his glass from the tray on the dusk-pink carpet.

"Come and have another drink," he said.

There was something enjoyably decadent – exotic almost – about drinking gin and Indian tonic water on a pink carpet at five o'clock in the afternoon, with the sunlight warm on one's skin and the prospect of a whole night's love-making beckoning from the spacious double-bed.

"You're trying to get me tippled, aren't you." Sissy walked slowly over, her bare toes curling into the deep plush pile underfoot, hips moving provocatively beneath the soft material clinging to her limbs.

She leaned forward and rested her hands on his shoulders so that her body was caught between his legs. "You're trying to get me pie-eyed."

"Not before dinner."

He grinned up at her, and pursed his lips for a kiss. Now that she'd decided to stop being such a flighty little madam, he was delighted by the change he'd found when he agreed to resume their relationship. In the last few weeks she'd shown him all the ways she knew to please a man, with none of that leading him on only to spurn him game she'd played before; and now tonight was going to be his turn to be the teacher, to take her over the threshold of experience and show her what pleasures there were to be had from the lessons of love.

That note from her had reached him just at the right moment. Marion's pregnancy was well advanced and for the last couple of months she'd refused to let him touch her for fear of harming the baby. True to his promise, he'd stayed a faithful husband, but it was a frustrating business for a man who needed a woman as often as Francis Bethway. Besides, he was still more than a little in love with Sissy, and her invitation had been an irresistible bit of flattery.

"What time are we going down, then?" she asked, wrinkling her nose at the smoke from the cheroot as she drew her mouth away from his.

"Going down where, my darling?"

"To the dining room, of course. It's generally where you eat in a hotel, isn't it?"

"Ah, but we're not eating in the dining room." He smiled up into those Italian-dark eyes, seeing them widen a little at his next words. "I've ordered dinner to be served for us here."

"What – here? Here in the bedroom, d'you mean?"

"It's not a bedroom, Sissy dearest. It's a suite. And yes, I mean here."

He pinched her cheek affectionately.

"Now have another drink with me, eh?"

"All right . . ."

Running the fingers of one hand through his hair, she straightened up. "I'll say this for you, Frank. You know how to treat a girl to the best, and no mistake."

She blew him another kiss and winked, then moved away towards the window humming a few lines from a popular song of the moment.

"Let's eat here in the window bay, shall we?" she said over her shoulder, picking up her empty glass from the table. "It's a nice view. I like it. And we'll get them to fetch us some candles – then when the sun's gone down we needn't put the lights on."

"That sounds wonderfully romantic," Francis announced, getting to his feet with his own glass and going over to the mahogany dumb waiter to replenish its contents from among the bottles there. It was on the tip of his tongue to add that dinner by candlelight had cost more young women their virtue than the serpent's apple; but on second thoughts Sissy might take that amiss, and the mood of the moment be spoilt.

"In fact, it sounds the perfect way to start a love affaire," he went on instead.

"Frank – you don't think they've guessed we're not married, do you?" she asked when he'd brought her drink across to her. "The clerk at the desk eyed me up and down a bit sharpish, I thought, while you were signing the register."

"You've got a suspicious mind. He was admiring you, that's all. Thinking to himself what a ripping little corker you looked."

187

He put an arm round her shoulder, hugging her against him.

"And you do."

Then, taking a long sip from his glass – "I'll tell you how they know the ones who aren't married. They're the couples who come along and sign themselves 'Mr and Mrs J. Smith' and look at one another all the time and smile a lot. Now, a genuine Mr and Mrs wouldn't do that, you see. The ones who've been married a few years hardly ever bother looking at each other – why should they when they're so used to what's there – and they certainly don't smile and carry on like a pair of turtle doves, not in public, anyway."

He gave her another hug and kissed the top of her head.

"No, you did very well, Sissy my darling. And you didn't flash that ring about, which is another tell-tale sign of unmarried bliss."

"It is?" She raised her left hand and studied the engraved gold band on her wedding finger. Francis had given it to her earlier this afternoon, when they'd met at Buckfield station. It was a memento, he said; he'd had it a long time, ever since South Africa. (Actually, he had bought it the previous week at a second-hand shop, but the other story sounded more the thing that women liked being told.)

"You see how crafty you have to be in these places," he went on casually, leaning forward to stub out his cheroot in the ashtray on the table. "I mean, what wife draws attention to the fact she's wearing a wedding band? It'd look odd, don't you think – especially a new one that'd had no wear."

"You seem to know a lot about these things." Sissy's comment was not made with any rancour; merely as a statement of fact. "I suppose you've had the practice."

"You don't really want an answer to that, do you?"

She tilted her glass and swallowed a mouthful of gin. This afternoon was the first time she'd tried the stuff – the family always had wine at home – and she wasn't sure if she liked it or not, but Frank insisted it was the smart thing to drink these days.

"Do you?" he asked again, teasing.

Instead of replying, she rested her head back against his shoulder and made a little sound half of protest, half of

188

contentment. The reflection of the sun's rays on the window dazzled her eyes and she closed them, feeling suddenly almost too languid to move, as though she could just sink down on to the thick plush carpet and go to sleep.

"Do you love me, Frank?" she murmured. "Really love me?"

"Of course I do."

"You won't stop, will you . . . after tonight?"

"After tonight I'll love you more than ever, I promise. You don't need to worry, my darling. Mr Morgan's going to take good care of you."

Sissy smiled. Morgan was the name in which he'd signed the hotel register, and when she asked why, he'd told her Frank Morgan had been his grandfather, a man for whose memory he had the fondest regard and affection.

"And you're not going to go off and leave me again?"

"Not if you're a good girl and do as you're told. This has got to be our secret, remember. We don't want it spoiled by others finding out about it, do we?"

Certainly not her family, she thought drowsily. If ever they discovered what she'd been up to, there'd be the very devil to pay for ruining her chances of a good Catholic wedding. Not that there was much worry of them learning anything, though. She'd laid her plans too well, telling her mother she was going to spend the night with her friend Marie McGrath – a story which Marie had been persuaded to support by the bribe of Sissy's best bit of jewellery.

She half-opened her eyes again. There was a dovecote below in the hotel garden and one of the birds had started a soft throaty crooning as it strutted about on the roof. After a moment it was joined by another, and in a sudden flurry of white feathers both took wing together, rising against the light towards the trees.

"I wish we could do that, don't you, Frank," she whispered dreamily. "Just fly away . . . "

By half past seven, when dinner was served in their suite, an evening haze was beginning to fall on the countryside and the view from their window was full of rose-pink streamers of cloud sweeping across the sky towards the deeper corals

189

of sunset. The doves had returned to roost now, and the only other sound from the garden was the birdsong of a thrush rising sweetly above the occasional muted noise of activity from the public rooms of The Fordhouse.

Against the darkening mirror of the windowpanes, the flicker of candles reflected softly in the sheen of silverplate and glassware on the table, hollowing out an alcove of light among the gathering shadows of the room; and such was the magic this setting created that even the single early rose their waiter had put by Sissy's place seemed to hold a velvet flame in its petals.

"I asked them to pick it especially for you," said Francis, watching her bend her small dark head to smell its perfume. "I noticed it earlier growing below in the garden. The first rose of summer."

"Now who's being romantic." Sissy laughed and brushed the flower with her lips before putting it back in its silver *epergne* and turning her attention to the plate of clear soup before her.

"I hope they give us a lot to eat," she went on eagerly, applying herself to a bread roll. "I'm famished. D'you realise, I've had nothing to eat since I bought myself a bun at Lewes station."

"You'll get more than enough to satisfy you tonight, I promise, sweet heart."

"Oh, I'm sure I will, Frank . . . but it was food I meant."

"So did I."

They exchanged looks across the table, smiling into each other's eyes at their intimate little joke.

"Have some wine," he invited, taking the chilled bottle from the ice-bucket stand beside his chair.

"D'you think I should, on top of all that gin?"

"Of course you should. It's good for the digestion. Besides, a good wine is the most civilised drink in the world."

He filled both their glasses, and then raised his own in salutation.

"To us, my darling."

"To us," she responded, almost defiantly, tossing back the heavy blue-black waves of hair from her shoulders. "Mr and Mrs Frank Morgan!"

When the soup had been cleared away by the silent waiter, there was more wine to follow with the dish of buttered prawns served with sippets of toasted bread; and then a bottle of smooth-bodied red to accompany the main course of cutlets *à la Duchesse*. It was a leisurely meal. After refreshing their palates with rose geranium water-ice (a speciality of the house) the two of them ended dinner with a glass each of spicy sweet muscatel to complement the dessert of *vol-au-vent* of fruit with stoned cream.

Sissy's slender figure gave the lie to her healthy young appetite: she'd been used all her life to eating good food, and without over-indulging herself she managed to do full justice to the excellent fare served this evening. Any slight feeling of nervous anticipation there may have been earlier very quickly disappeared as the wine began taking effect, and before long she was talking excitedly and laughing a great deal and treating everything her companion said as though it were wonderfully clever and witty.

By the time the remains of the meal were cleared away and their waiter had departed, pocketing a handsome tip from Francis, she was feeling utterly, deliciously relaxed and quite extraordinarily happy.

"Oh Frank, I do love you so," she sighed, smiling, not looking at him but at their candle-lit reflection mirrored in the darkened window. "I never thought I could feel like this about anybody, ever."

He made no answer, but got to his feet, pushing back his chair and going across to get himself another cheroot.

After a while she went on softly, as though talking to herself, "I wish today never had to end. If only we could wake up tomorrow and find it was this morning all over again . . . oh, if only we could. It's not fair, the way the best times always go so fast, as if they can't wait for you to enjoy them . . . and when you're in a hurry and wanting something to happen, it seems to take so long . . . ages and ages. I wonder why life has to be like that?"

She propped her elbows on the table and rested her chin in her hand, staring into the yellow candle flame; then reached out and took the rose and began twisting its stem to and fro between her slender fingers.

191

"I think we should draw the curtains," Francis said, watching this dumb-show through the smoke of his cheroot and recognising signs of wine's melancholia beginning to creep into Sissy's euphoric mood.

"Oh – must we?" she murmured to the rose. "Can't we leave them open so we can lie in bed and watch the dawn come up?"

He smiled indulgently. "Somehow, my darling, I don't think either of us will very much know or care enough to notice when it does."

Leaving the cheroot to burn away in the ashtray, he took off his jacket and hung it on the back of a chair; then, loosening his tie as he came across the room to the window, he pulled the heavy curtains shut to close out the night.

"Sissy?"

The shadowed outline of the rose against the candle flame seemed to be fascinating her.

Francis leaned down and kissed her hungrily on the nape of the neck, brushing aside the loose tendrils of hair.

"I love you," he said.

Then, with the practised ease of experience, he began slowly to undo each of the little pearl buttons which fastened the back of her dress.

There was something about the broad-shouldered figure in tweed jacket and cap which caught Mrs Ernest Thompson's attention. It wasn't often she was here in Buckfield, but her widowed sister-in-law (whom she seldom visited) had been inconsiderate enough to fall off a chair and break her hip and require several weeks in a nursing home, which of course put Mrs Ernest Thompson under an obligation to visit the tiresome creature.

She paused by a milliner's shop window, pretending to study the display, and looked cautiously back towards the hotel entrance along the high street. There was a large signboard outside, saying The Fordhouse, and underneath, still standing where she'd first noticed him, the man in the tweed outfit. He had a woman with him now, a young woman with very dark hair done up on top of her head under a red-feathered hat, clinging on to his arm in a rather forward manner, Mrs Ernest Thompson thought.

192

Oh, it was really too, too aggravating, not being able to put a name to the face, and she was certain she'd seen it before. At the golf club, perhaps. No, no. Not there. She moved a little way up the pavement to the next window, offering surgical appliances, and looked back again.

Horse traffic obscured her view for a few moments; and when she could once more see across the street she observed the gentleman briefly removing his cap to smooth down his hair, before he bent to pick up the small port-manteau at his feet. It was only the merest glimpse of uncovered head, but quite enough to jog Mrs Ernest Thompson's memory.

Of course!

Good heavens.

Just wait until she told Ernest.

She gave her divided attention to the bronchial inhalers and dropped arch supports; and as soon as the pair had boarded the hansom cab for which they'd been waiting, directed her eager steps across to The Fordhouse.

So sorry to seem a nuisance, she enthused to the young desk clerk, but the lady and gentleman who'd just now left from the hotel steps – acquaintances of hers . . .

Mr and Mrs Morgan, did madam mean?

Why, yes. That was their name. Mr and Mrs Morgan. So silly of her, but she'd neglected to ask them how long they were staying in Buckfield.

Only the one night? Really, how too, too disappointing. Though not to worry, she'd be seeing them again before long, no doubt, in Lewes.

After all, Mr Morgan and the Ernest Thompsons' married daughter were next-door neighbours but one.

18

It had all started five months ago with the incident which the newspaper headlines described as "The Battle of Sidney Street".

In the early weeks of January, police investigation had flushed out a nest of foreign anarchists in the Whitechapel district of London. Evading arrest, the group had barricaded itself inside a house in Sidney Street and engaged in a running gun-fight with the forces of law and order; whereupon troops were called in to besiege the area, and the Press gave prominent display to a photograph of the Home Secretary, Mr Winston Churchill, in top hat and muffler, peering cautiously from cover past the snouts of Army rifles.

Gun battles with armed revolutionaries in the streets of the capital were hardly a common occurrence, and public alarm had been fuelled by lurid newspaper descriptions of bearded Russian anarchists with smoking bombs lurking in the shadows of Parliament, ready to plunge the country into chaos. Insurgents, spies and double agents became the talk of the day, and taking their cue from the Press, film studios were not slow to exploit this national preoccupation, producing numerous short "two-reelers" of cloak-and-dagger melodrama.

They proved immensely popular, not least because of their endings, in which the villain perished to great applause from the audience, either shot in a hot-air balloon duel, crushed beneath the wheels of an express train, or blown to smithereens by his own bomb.

One of these motion pictures, made by the Harry Furniss studios at Hastings using locations on the South Downs and finishing with a spectacular climax on the rim of Beachy Head, attracted great attention locally; and in the weeks before it came to the picture house in Lewes, *The Red Hand*

Brigade was being advertised all over town on bill-boards and hoardings and the backs of sandwich men.

It opened at the end of May with a Saturday matinée performance, showing to a packed house; and though the "sold out" sign at the box office window may have had the manager rubbing his hands, the sight of all those crowded seats and craning necks was rather less than welcome to young Algie Langton-Smythe, who'd arranged to meet his sweetheart Laura Bates directly after the picture show.

Had their rendezvous been somewhere in town he wouldn't have minded so much being held up and made a few minutes late, but having borrowed a motor bicycle and side-carriage for the afternoon, he was meant to be collecting Laura at exactly half past four from the end of the Bates' drive in Spences Lane.

"It's cutting things dashed fine as it is," he complained to Dinah Enderby while the two were in the theatre pit before the performance sorting their music into order. "Laura's managing to sneak out from the house while her step-mother's at some charity fête or other, but the trouble is, the Governor's expected home at half past five, so we've less than an hour for our spin across the Downs."

He picked up the sheets of overture music to Herold's *Zampa* and began flicking through them; then went on despondently, "It's a pretty poor show when a chap and his girl have to ration their meetings like this. No wonder the darling feels like a bird in a cage, kept shut away as she is. If it weren't for dear old Miss Evans, she'd never have any sort of freedom of her own."

"I don't know why you must always refer to Miss Evans as old," observed Dinah, playing a one-handed scale up and down the piano keys to test the loud pedal for the dramatic scenes. "It makes her sound as though she's half-way to being an antique, and she can't be more than forty if she's a day."

"Fifty, don't you mean." Algie tucked his violin beneath his chin and joined in with a few notes of his own.

"Hardly that! Don't forget, I've known the Bateses all my life, so I can remember Miss Evans the year she first came to them as governess. I must have mentioned this already, surely – about my mother being a godchild of Laura's grandmother, Mrs Bashford – "

She finished the scale and took her hand from the keys, flexing the slight stiffness from her fingers – "and the visits we used to make to Bonningale in the summer when the Bates children were there with Miss Evans on holiday."

She did not add that there'd been something of a scandal in the family when the new governess became the object of her young brother Francis's fledgling attentions. Dinah had been far too naive at the time to guess what had gone on between the pair, but her mother told her much later: Miss Evans had behaved foolishly and there'd been a child on the way, mercifully miscarried early in the pregnancy before anyone knew. Certainly, Ellis Bates had never suspected his children's governess of conducting herself improperly with a boy almost five years her junior, or she would not have remained in his employment a moment longer than it took to throw her bags out into the street.

"And when was that?" Algie enquired, trying to divide his attention between Dinah and his violin. "The year she first joined them, I mean."

"Oh – " She had to think for a second. "1890 . . . 1891."

"She hasn't worn very well."

"Perhaps life hasn't treated her very kindly."

He started tuning his instrument, the discordant sounds adding to the general noisy racket filling the auditorium.

"I hope they start the first reel on time," he began again after a while, fretfully glancing up across the jam-packed rows of seats towards the back projection box.

"They should, with the extra one."

"Extra one? What extra one?"

"I thought you knew? This picture's a three-reeler."

"Oh, Lord, no – not really, is it?" Algie's boyish features crumpled in dismay. "That's torn it. I thought it was only two. Now I'm bound to be late – damn!"

He threw himself down on his chair, violin across his knees, his head in his hands; then, thrusting back the hair from his eyes – "Oh, well, there's no helping it, I suppose. I'll just have to turn up as soon as I can and tell Laura the spin's off."

"Look, if it would help at all," offered Dinah hurriedly, seeing the manager about to make his way down to announce the start of the programme, "I'm sure I'd be able to get through the last bit without you. I'll give them *Zampa* again – they won't notice in all the excitement. Plenty of loud pedal. And if I run short, they can have *The Entrance of the Gladiators* for good measure."

"Dinah, you're a brick!" Hope rekindled itself in Algie's face. "What's the final piece of music before the second interval?"

She checked hastily down her pencilled list. "*Aïda.*"

"Right, I'll slip away after that while the reel's being changed. With any luck I should be over at Spences Lane with time to spare."

Luck, however, was not on Algie's side: his exit caught the observant eye of the manager, and he was ordered back to the pit for the final reel, miserably sawing his way to "The End" through a celluloid mayhem of anarchists' plots and explosions.

Thus it was that when he finally left to keep his rendezvous with Laura he was a good half-hour late; and such is the way of things once they start going wrong, her father had been able to conclude his business in town half an hour early, so that the two of them happened to arrive in Spences Lane within minutes of each other.

The metallic throb of the motor bicycle alarmed Mr Bates's pony considerably as the machine sped past on the leafy road, causing it to side-step in nervous fright and all but drag the trap over the kerb. Bringing the animal under control and cursing below his breath at young hot-heads who must needs pollute the peace of the day with the noise and stink of their infernal machinery, the Inspector of Schools for Lewes continued his way homeward; and on rounding the bend of the road a short while later, was further incensed to find the same motor bicycle now drawn to a halt outside his own drive entrance – and who but his daughter Laura in the very act of seating herself in its side-carriage.

"I say – I say there!" cried Mr Bates indignantly, rising from his seat and addressing his anger to the driver of the

197

machine, a young fellow attired in striped blazer jacket, a pair of goggles and a leather cap worn back to front, like a coal heaver's.

His next words were choked off abruptly as he was thrown back again into the trap, for no sooner had the pair caught sight of him than the engine was urged again into roaring life and a moment later was propelling them both away down the road in a noxious cloud of exhaust smoke, sending his pony bucking and kicking between the shafts.

"I demand a truthful answer, ma'am!" barked an irate Ellis Bates, scarcely before his study door had opened half-way to admit the frightened face of a maid and the short, plump figure of his daughter's governess-companion. "And I will have one – by God I will!"

"It is an apoplexy you will have, look you, sir, unless you compose yourself," Megwynn Evans answered calmly, turning to see that the maid had shut the door properly behind her. "Indeed, there is nothing to cause such agitation – "

"Oh, but indeed, ma'am, there is! I would have you know that I have just this moment witnessed my daughter Laura blatantly flaunt my authority and without my permission – without my prior knowledge, even – allow herself to be taken away in some contraption or other by a person entirely unknown to me."

"I beg leave to differ, sir. The young gentleman *has* been introduced to you, and in this very house."

Mr Bates's mottled features, normally so chalky pale, became flushed with colour, a most alarming indication of the depth of his ill temper. In all the years she'd been in his employment, Miss Evans had only once before seen him in such a rage, when a schoolteacher bearing a grudge for unfair dismissal had forced his way in and under the influence of drink violently accosted the inspector here in his own study.

"The *gentleman* has been introduced to me, d'you say?" he threw back with sneering emphasis. "Then, ma'am, I must note your prejudice in his favour by giving him rank. Had you said scoundrel, or ne'er-do-well, or rogue, I might

198

have understood you to mean that young idler Langton-Smythe who had the effrontery some while ago to push his way into my house under the pretext of being a *gentleman*."

Miss Evans regarded her employer with impassive self-restraint. She had known that this interview must be faced one day – the friendship between Algie and Laura could not go undiscovered for ever – and was well prepared for its confrontation. It was a stroke of good fortune that the step-mother was absent from the house just now, for it meant she could speak her mind openly without the hindrance of a witness to curb her words.

"With respect, sir, you know very well it is Algie Langton-Smythe whom you saw with your daughter outside. And it is no prejudice on my part to call him a gentleman, since his rank is very much superior to my own."

"I need no reminder of his rank from you, ma'am."

"Indeed, but you do, sir – "

"And again, indeed I do not. D'you think I would allow any tom, dick or harry to come here prating to me of rank as an excuse to pester my daughter, and not wish to protect her from such an upstart by availing myself of the truth?"

"Then you will know who he is, sir."

"I know *what* he is! A malcontent who has been ejected by his family into the gutter to shift for himself as best he can. Let me tell you, inherited nobility is little indication of a man's character – younger sons of peers make ten-a-penny bankrupts in the courts. An aristocratic title may have turned your head, Miss Evans, but be assured, without breeding and good manners it is merely a paper crown to impress the servant class."

"There is nothing at all wrong with Mr Langton-Smythe's breeding or his manners," Megwynn Evans answered mildly, choosing to ignore that barb of scorn for her own position in society. "You have said that you wished for the truth, Mr Bates. Very well, you shall have it. If I may be seated, please – ?"

Her request was met with a surly response, a gesture of the hand towards an upright chair against the wall, and she was forced to go across and fetch it for herself – an additional discourtesy on Ellis Bates's part, since there were several more comfortable seats in the room.

He swung his own winged-back armchair round so that it faced across his desk, and sat himself down without waiting.

"Well?"

"Well, sir. It's like this – if anyone is to blame for what has happened this afternoon, it is me and not Laura. I knew all about their meeting, see. The motor bicycle and everything. I helped to arrange it between them."

"Did you now." There was the quality of cold steel in those words.

"Indeed, sir. And if you will be so kind as to let me finish before you begin venting your displeasure, I will tell you what else it is I have been doing. Since you allow your daughter no liberty to enjoy herself as any other young creature of her age, I have encouraged her to show some independence and break the rules you try to force upon her. She is not a child now, and she is not a simpleton to be shut away in the hope that what she does not know of life she will not miss. She is a woman, look you, Mr Bates, wanting a future for herself that is not confined to the four walls of this house. She is also in love, with a young man of the right background who loves her in return and would do anything to make her happy – "

"Now that is enough!" Ellis Bates brought his clenched fist down with a crash upon the desk as he came to his feet again. "My God, woman, I have nursed a viper in my bosom all these years – "

"A Welsh dragon, perhaps, but not I think a viper."

"Be silent, I say. You have abused your position sufficiently as it is without adding the insult of levity to the damage you have done in this house. To think that I regarded you as a person of honour – to think that I gave you my trust and respect for so long, valuing your service to my family – you, who now stand condemned out of your own mouth as the seducer of my daughter's morals."

"Stuff!" Miss Evans was not having that. "I have let a little light and air into her life, that is all. And you will thank me for it, too, when you come to your senses. *I* am not frightened of you, Mr Bates, even if the rest of your household are."

"A healthy fear of one's betters is a sign of a dutiful and unassuming nature, ma'am, so it does not surprise me to learn it is lacking in you, who have demonstrably shown yourself conniving, deceitful and insolent. You are not frightened of me, you say. Very well, we shall see about that. You will not be quite so bold, I think, when you are put out on to the street without a reference, to take your turn among the queue of unemployed at the doors of the labour exchange."

"Again, sir, I beg your leave to differ." The other's tone remained bland and she returned Ellis Bates's rancorous glare without so much as a tremor of the eyelid. "If I am dismissed from your service, Laura shall come with me –"

"The devil she shall!"

"Oh, yes – she has sworn as much already. She is over twenty-one, old enough to be her own mistress, and quite able to support herself. What is more, she has the Law on her side, look you, so you cannot prevent her from leaving this house if she wishes to make a home for herself elsewhere."

A small, tight smile appeared suddenly on the plump face. "But do not let it worry you, Mr Bates. It will not come to that. You would never dismiss me, I'm sure."

"Oh, would I not, indeed!" Her employer was almost choking on his own fury. He leaned forward, resting the knuckles of his fists on the desk top. "If you think that, ma'am, then let me tell you, you are greatly in error. I am giving you notice this moment that you shall be out of my house before this next week's end. As for my daughter – I shall deal with her immediately she returns, and we shall see then whether or not *I* choose her to remain beneath this roof, or whether she shall be sent away for her own safety to a place beyond the sphere of your pernicious influence."

"What a bully you are," Miss Evans said levelly. "And what an evil temper you have when crossed. *Duw*, but I can quite believe it that you killed that poor woman all those years ago."

Ellis Bates's mouth had already opened to deliver a

caustic reply before the full import of what had just been said struck home. The ugly mottled colour paled from his thin cheeks, leaving them a sickly hue. He closed his mouth again, and a most extraordinary expression flickered across his face – too quick to catch, but enough to tell the Welshwoman that her shaft had found its mark.

There was a sudden silence in the room, a tense, accusing silence, and in the stillness the tick of the mantelpiece clock seemed to be keeping pace with the harsh sound of his breathing.

"I think . . . you had best explain yourself," he said at last, his voice as soft and cold and needle-thin as she had ever heard it. "What . . . 'poor woman' do you mean?"

For a moment she felt herself gripped by a spasm of panic and her resolution wavered; but she had come too far, and too much was at stake, for her nerve to fail her now.

She swallowed hard and looked him steadily in the face. "I believe her name was Louisa Linton."

"Louisa Linton."

"Yes."

Ellis Bates sat down and drew his chair towards the desk, resting his hands together on its edge. "I have never heard of a Louisa Linton."

That was his first mistake, and he knew it even as he spoke the words.

" – I should say, I cannot recall a person of that name."

He should not have said that either: it sounded too much of an evasion, and where there was evasion, there was something to conceal.

Megwynn Evans permitted herself the small smile again. "Then perhaps I can help you to remember, sir. 1891, it was. Out at Weatherfield. The lady was a doctor's wife, an invalid, confined to a wheeled chair."

She paused. There was a grey, pinched look to the other's features now, and the hooded eyes watched her in unblinking, careful scrutiny.

"Shall I go on, sir?"

Another pause; and then the toneless answer, "If you will. I find all this . . . most interesting."

"I thought perhaps you might. So did the police and the

202

newspaper men. The circumstances of her death caused a lot of speculation, see. Found dead, she was, alone in the house with a broken neck on the May Day holiday. And they never did find the gentleman they were looking for, the one who'd been seen hanging about by the gate."

She waited again, but this time there was no response, only a further tightening of the bloodless lips.

"The newspapers were full of it. 'Unknown Witness Mystery.' 'Police Seek Identity of Caller.' That sort of thing. I heard you discussing it once after dinner – a red herring, you said, and everyone agreed with you. Everyone, that is, but Dr Linton. You remember now, sir? That day he came here? Very suspicious, he was. And you showed him the letters his wife had been sending you – "

"How did you know about those letters?"

Ellis Bates could not stop himself. It was said in a moment, before he had time to think.

He hesitated; then gave a shrug, realising too late that he had just damned himself out of his own mouth, and went on viciously, "The devil take you, woman, you are twisting the facts."

"Indeed not, sir. I saw those letters for myself, before you destroyed them."

"My God – ! And you read them, too, I suppose."

"Yes. I read them. That's what set me thinking, see. The day Dr Linton came to this house, you asked me to tell him a lie should he wish to enquire where you'd been that May Day afternoon. You asked me to say that you had gone with the children and me to hear the band of the Rifle Volunteers on the castle green. Now why should you need an alibi like that if you'd nothing to hide? It never occurred to me at the time that perhaps you'd been in Weatherfield yourself – "

"That would be very hard to prove, I think."

"But damaging to your reputation, Mr Bates, if the story got about that you'd solicited the family governess to falsify the truth."

"No one would believe you!"

"There's some that might. The newspapers, for instance."

"Damn you, madam, don't you dare to threaten me – "

"Oh, indeed but I am not threatening you. I am making an

observation as an accessory after the fact. Supposing they were to learn about those letters of Mrs Linton's . . . and her husband's suspicions . . . and the way you made me lie for you. Why, they might put two and two together, look you, and make a very interesting little tit-bit for their readers."

Ellis Bates dropped his gaze and appeared to study the blurred pen strokes on the leather-bound blotting pad beside his right elbow.

Several long moments went by.

Then he said suddenly, harshly, "Very well. I agree I was in Weatherfield. But the woman was already dead when I called at that house. It was obvious to me she had fallen from her chair down a flight of stairs and thereby sustained the injury which killed her. What point was there in my staying at the scene? It was not the sort of business in which a gentleman of my standing would wish to have his name embroiled. I came away at once."

He might have been bluffing, but Megwynn Evans thought not. The story sounded plausible enough: the public reputation of His Majesty's Inspector of Schools for Lewes must be kept inviolate, at whatever cost to his conscience. Moreover, she knew him for the type of man heartless enough to shun personal involvement in anything of ill-consequence, having seen him drive on and leave a dog writhing in a yelping bloodied heap in the road where he'd run it down in his trap, rather than trouble himself to halt and do whatever was humanely possible to help the poor creature.

She folded her hands in her lap and examined her employer calmly. A single bead of perspiration glistened on the high, pale forehead and his fingers trembled slightly as he reached to brush it away.

"If that were so, Mr Bates," she told him smoothly, "if Mrs Linton were indeed dead when you found her and you did not report it, think what a dim light would be cast upon your character were the newspapers to put it in their columns that you had run away from your duty as a citizen."

There was a further long silence while he digested this possibility. Then he pushed back his chair and stood up, thumbs tucked inside his black waistcoat pockets in an empty gesture of bravado.

"Let us make an end of this," he snapped. "What is it that you want of me in return for your . . . discretion. Money?"

"No, sir. Not money." Megwynn Evans followed him to her feet.

"No?" Her answer seemed to cause him some surprise. "What, then? Blackmail must have a price, surely."

Once again, that tight little smile appeared. "Blackmail, Mr Bates? There's an ugly word. I would prefer to call it a bargain struck between the two of us. My silence in exchange for – " she paused, savouring the moment – "in exchange for Laura's future."

This time Ellis Bates said nothing, only stood looking at her, thin lips parted slightly, his pallid features contorted into what might almost have been a snarl.

"No one shall ever hear a single word more pass my lips on the subject of Louisa Linton," she continued blandly. "And in return, you will please give permission for your daughter to meet with Mr Langton-Smythe wherever and whenever she wishes. No, sir, do not interrupt. If you want me to keep my side of the bargain, you must agree to keep yours – and *Duw*, I shall hold you to it to see that you do, look you!"

Miss Evans picked up her chair and returned it to its place against the wall, then moved across to the study door.

There she paused, her hand on the porcelain knob.

"Oh, might I suggest that you make a beginning today, Mr Bates, when Laura comes in. She'll be expecting the worst, see. Show her what a kind Papa she has, and tell her she may invite her young man here to tea with the family next Sunday."

19

Of all the days in the week, Thursday was the one which the Reverend Christopher Bethway enjoyed most. Sunday – well, Sunday was work, and if he were honest (which he hoped he was) he'd have to admit that he was always relieved to reach the end of Evensong and put behind him for a while the duties of church service. Not the worship, of course – not that! Prayer and praise were the bread-and-butter of spiritual life. But the congregation of Christ Church, Tunbridge Wells, were inclined to shy away from innovation, preferring the tried and trusted, the safe, accustomed boundaries of Anglican tradition, and they did not take kindly to being roused from their Sunday torpor in the pews by a sermon crackling at the edges with fire and brimstone.

Kit Bethway enjoyed writing sermons. As a student at Durham he had found their challenge a stimulus to theological argument, and relished the cut and thrust of words to give biting edge to his homilies. It had galled him, therefore, to have to curb the excessive zeal of his evangelism and serve up in its place lukewarm, bland, diluted platitudes so as not to offend the sensibilities of the more self-righteous souls of the parish.

The choice, however, had been between their acceptance and their frosty tolerance; and since the former meant frequent invitations out to dine, he had soon learned to temper the fiery rhetoric of his student days and swallow some pride along with the salmon and sirloin and rich suet puddings.

All of which, socially and spiritually, took care of six days out of the seven. Thursday, though, was different. Thursday was his to do with as he wished, his time off from labouring in the parochial vineyard. Thursday was the day on which he might exchange his black serge jacket for a grey flannel suit and indulge himself in pursuit of the pleasures of croquet, or archery, or bicycling, or art – or if the weather were inclement, his 'cello practice, stamp collection or *Jane's Fighting Ships*.

On this particular Thursday, half-way through June, the choice of pastime had been decided for him the moment he opened his curtains on an early morning world of cloudless summer sky and birdsong.

By seven o'clock he had breakfasted on gammon and eggs washed down with strong sweet tea, and taken himself along the high street and across the London Road on to the Common. This was one of the most attractive features of the town, Kit had always thought: countryside on the doorstep, as it were, acres of wooded heathland surrounded by the urban arms of the two main roads into Sussex, a place of almost deceptive peace and quiet, for out of earshot of the traffic one might easily believe oneself to be in some rural landscape.

His paints, brushes and sketch-pad in a bag slung over his shoulder and his easel under his arm, he made his way along the leafy paths to an open area of heath beside the cricket ground, where there was an outcrop of sandstone known as the Wellington Rocks. It was still too early in the day for many people to be about here: apart from himself, there was only a woman alone on a bench with her laundry basket beside her, on her way to work at the Mount Ephraim Hotel, and at the edge of the cricket ground, two men standing in conversation while their dogs raced up and down in the early sunlight.

Hoisting up his easel, Kit clambered among the rocks to a flat-topped shelf which some local wag had christened "the Pulpit". From here he could see across the valley of the Wells to St Mark's church spire on the ridge of Broadwater Down, and beyond that, the thick-massed treetops of Broadwater Forest rising like green hills against the pale blue horizon.

Now that he had got back his breath (not that the climb had been hard, but his appetite for good food showed in a certain corpulence of girth) he began sizing up the scene to decide what feature should be the focus of his painting, joining forefingers to thumbs to form a square and holding them up at eye level to act as a frame. He could remember from childhood watching his mother do this when Francis, Dinah and he were taken out in the governess cart on excursions into the Downland countryside: landscapes had always been Isabelle Bethway's favourite form of art, and it showed in her work, giving her pictures texture and light and sinew, very far removed from his own "pretty daubs" as Dinah irreverently called them.

Thinking of his sister recalled the young curate's thoughts to the meeting they'd had just a week ago. He had been summoned down to Eastbourne last Thursday to attend what their father had referred to in his letter as a family conference at the vicarage, to decide what must be done for the salvation of Dinah's marriage.

In Kit's own opinion, the entire Enderby affair had been a most fearful mistake, one for which his sister was paying dearly with her peace of mind; and privately he was now inclined to agree with her that the best course of action was the legal separation she'd decided upon. Unfortunately, however, this could not by law be proceeded with until the marriage had been in existence for at least two years, and in the meanwhile Warwick Enderby was perfectly entitled to remain at Southwood Place and insist upon his conjugal rights.

Kit took out his sketch-pad and leaned back against the rock. In an hour or so the sandstone would have soaked up some heat from the sun, but for the moment it still retained the chill of night and he could feel its coolness through the thin flannel of his jacket. He began to draw, roughing out the lines of his picture in pencil strokes. The washerwoman had moved from her bench now, but he sketched in the stout little figure with its wicker basket to give some human interest to the scene.

It was very quiet. Just the birds, and the occasional faint background noise from the road beyond the trees as a motor vehicle drove past towards the town centre.

The family conference had proved rather a dramatic experience, with the four of them putting their cases for and against the marriage like counsel in court. Their mother, naturally, had opened her argument with a defence of Dinah's wishes, appearing to take her daughter's side for much of the morning's discussion; but she was too loyal a wife not to support her husband's views, and in the end it had been the Reverend Alec Bethway's opinion which prevailed: that for the sake of the family's good name, Dinah should attempt to reconcile her differences with Mr Enderby and give their marriage the chance to succeed.

She had argued against it furiously, even tearfully, reproaching her father for such a cautious and unsympathetic attitude. Was he so concerned to avoid the stigma of divorce, she had cried, that he could sacrifice his own daughter's happiness for the sake of respectability? And if she did proceed to disencumber herself of her husband as she intended, would he then forbid her to enter the family home again, as he had with her brother Francis?

The mention of Francis Bethway's name – so long taboo – caused some hot words to be spoken, and some hasty accusations thrown, and the scene had ended on an acrimonious note with Dinah rushing in tears from the room.

After luncheon, however, some of the wind seemed to have blown out of everyone's sails. Whatever it was Isabelle Bethway had said to her daughter privately had obviously borne fruit, for Dinah seemed suddenly much quieter, resigned almost, Kit thought, and had finally conceded with an ill grace to her father's insistence that she and her husband should make some attempt to iron out their personal disagreements.

It was a Pyrrhic victory. She confided to Kit afterwards that she'd agreed only with the greatest reluctance, out of respect for her parents' wishes. It would make not a jot of difference to the outcome, she said: whatever happened, she was still determined to apply for a separation in fourteen months' time, on her second wedding anniversary in August 1912.

The young curate gave an unconscious sigh as he gazed out over the cricket ground. Well, they'd all done what they could, he thought. He held out his pencil sketch at arm's length and compared the view with his own interpretation of it. Hmm, not bad. If he were quick now, he might just be in time to capture the way the sunlight gilded the trunks of that avenue of lime trees.

Whistling a tune to himself, he set up his easel and started preparing his paints. Poor old Dinah. What a pickle. Never mind, though. What was it that Dr Samuel Johnson had said of marriage – the triumph of hope over expectation?

Yes, there was always hope. One never knew what was waiting round the corner.

The Thursday following, June the twenty-second, was a national public holiday to celebrate the coronation of King George the Fifth.

In Lewes as elsewhere all over the country, the streets were festooned with bunting and Union flags and loyal messages of felicitation and homage, and there were open-air tea parties for the children to enjoy in the afternoon.

With Marion Bethway's pregnancy so near its term, making it unwise for her to venture out at all, she had written to ask her sister-in-law if she would mind taking young Angela to the party being held in a local school playground, to avoid disappointing the child. Dinah was not working at the Picture Theatre that afternoon; which was just as well, as things proved, for when she arrived at the Bethway house to collect her niece she found the front door ajar and the little girl sitting alone on the hall floor, loudly demanding to be allowed up into her mother's bedroom to see the new baby.

"What, has it arrived?" Dinah exclaimed in some surprise.

"Of course it has. The man's got it in his black bag. I saw it." Angela's eyes were as round as marbles. "It was the same bag that he bringed my sister in."

"Oh, Miss – " Florrie the housemaid came running back from her errand to the kitchen. "Thank the Lord you're here! The doctor hasn't long come, and I'm being driven to distraction wi' this child under my feet."

"Is it true what Angela says, that the baby's already born?"

Florrie shook her head and the perspiring features

210

screwed themselves into the lop-sided grimace of an exaggerated wink; but before she could reply, young Angela was piping up from the floor in her self-important little way, "Yes, it was borned at the hospital, and the man's bringed it in his black bag to put inside Mama's bed to keep it warm."

"*Brought*," her aunt reminded her, distractedly, stooping to take her beneath the arms and stand her on her feet. "He's *brought* it, not bringed. Remember?"

"But he hasn't *brought* it, Auntie Dinah, 'cause if he'd *brought* it, then it costed some money, and that can't be so 'cause my Papa told me new babies were given free to good homes."

Dinah looked at Florrie.

"Now, Miss Angela, run along, do, and fetch your bonnet and gloves," the maid admonished sharply. "And don't let me catch you a-going upstairs again, either."

The child pulled a sulky face, hunching her shoulders as she twisted away from her aunt's hand and took a few reluctant steps along the hall, scuffing the toes of her shoes behind her on the drugget carpet.

Then she turned suddenly, brightening. "Can we take Traddles to the party, Auntie Dinah? Please?"

"Oh, but are dogs allowed, do you think?"

There was an emphatic nod of the beribboned flaxen curls.

"Are you quite sure, now?"

Another nod. "Anyway, my friend Cynthia is taking *her* dog. She told me so. She asked her Mama, and her Mama said yes."

Dinah gave it her consideration. "Well . . . if you promise to be a good girl, and look after Traddles properly to see he doesn't make a nuisance of himself – "

"I will! I will! I promise!"

Without waiting for further answer, Angela went skipping off down the hall, deaf to Florrie's loud shushes for her to go quietly and not disturb the house with her noise.

"I've scarce this minute got little May off to sleep," she told Dinah vexedly. "Behopes the mite stays quiet there in the nursery till the midwife's come, or I'll just have to leave her a-crying."

211

"How long do you expect it will be before the baby arrives?"

"Oh, I couldn't say, Miss, I'm sure. My sister now, she had her babies quick as shelling peas, but Mrs Bethway's been a day at a time wi' both confinements, poor duck."

Dinah's expression showed some sympathy. "When did the pains begin?"

"First thing this morning, soon as ever she woke. I had to leave her for a short while while I ran out to ask at number forty-five if they'd use their telephone to send for Dr Marshall. When I come back, her waters had broke, so I put her to bed again and stayed wi' her till doctor got here in his motor car. I haven't had chance to send word to the barracks."

"You mean Captain Bethway doesn't know his wife's in labour?"

"No, Miss. He wasn't here last night at all." A prim note crept into Florrie's voice. "He's been keeping hisself very . . . occupied o' late."

She looked hard at Dinah. At the same moment there was a sound from somewhere overhead, an involuntary cry of anguish, swiftly stifled, and both women turned their heads sharply towards the landing door at the top of the stairs.

"I'd best go on up in case I'm needed," the maid said, moving away.

"Is there anything I can do to help?" the other enquired of her anxiously.

She paused at the bottom step. "Well . . . could you go down to the barracks, d'you think, Miss, and ask them to tell the Captain?"

"Yes, of course. I'll take Angela with me. The walk will do us good. I can leave a message with the duty sergeant at the guardroom."

Dinah held out her hands as her young niece came running back again along the hall, Traddles on a leash at her heels and her bonnet ribbons hanging unfastened.

"Careful – !"

"Please may Traddles have a slice of cake if he's good at the party?" the child asked, fidgeting from one foot to another while the ribbons were tied.

"*If* he's good. Hold still a moment. There. Now say goodbye to Florrie."

There was a dutiful little wave of the white cotton gloves.

"And please may I see the new baby if *I'm* good?"

"We shall have to think about that when we come home again."

Angela accepted this without demur. "Do you know, Auntie Dinah," she said, looking up gravely, "Mama has promised a little brother for May and me. She's ordered him 'specially, with black hair and brown eyes. And she says that when he grows up, why, he will be just like our Papa."

There was a loud snort. Florrie had paused half-way up the stairs.

"Behopes not – " was the comment she threw down over the banister rail. "The Lord knows, one's already more'n sufficient trouble as it is!"

The duty sergeant at the regimental barracks made a note of Dinah's message, casting an appreciative backwards glance through the guardroom door at the fetchingly attractive red-haired woman making her way with the small child and dog along the sunlit road towards the sentry gate.

Ten minutes later, an orderly had handed the note to Captain Francis Bethway in the Officers' Mess; and ten minutes after that, Francis was spurring his bay gelding Trojan into a canter across the parade ground.

At half past five, while the country was still in the throes of celebration and innumerable children at innumerable street parties up and down the land waved paper flags and toasted their King in lemonade from coronation mugs, Marion was safely delivered of her third baby.

It was the son and heir that Francis had always wanted; and in honour of the day, the jubilant father named him George. George Francis Morgan Bethway.

20

"My dear, it was heaven – absolute heaven!"

The new Mrs Esmond Bates leaned back in the garden hammock and raised her arms languorously above her head.

"The most perfectly lovely place you could imagine, like a medieval painting come to life."

She half-closed her eyes and twined her fingers together, watching the way the dim shafts of sunlight through the overhanging leaves glimmered on the heavy gold of her wedding ring. Then she shifted her head slightly to look down towards Dinah Enderby, seated close by on a rug beneath the willow tree.

"Do you know it at all?"

"Lavenham?" Dinah leaned forward to examine a ladybird which had just alighted on the page of the book propped open against her knees. "No. No, actually I've never been to that part of the country."

"Oh, you *must* go. You'd love East Anglia. It's unbelievably picturesque. And Lavenham itself – how can I describe it?"

"A medieval painting come to life, you said."

"Mm." The bride of a month smiled to herself among the hammock cushions, remembering moments of her honeymoon with Esmond. "Only much, much more romantic. Don't you agree it was wonderfully clever of the darling boy to decide upon it for our wedding tour? He couldn't have found a more divine spot. And the hotel – oh, my dear! Full of oak beams and mullioned windows and winding stairways, and even a little courtyard garden with a fountain."

Dinah blew gently upon the ladybird and watched it spread its scarlet wingcase and take flight across the daisy-covered lawn. "How did Esmond happen to know of it? You never told me."

"What, The Swan, d'you mean?"

214

"Well . . . Lavenham itself."

"Oh, now this will interest you." Jessie half-raised herself on one elbow. "He's been doing some digging about in the family history. Parish registers, property deeds, that kind of thing. It seems his grandfather – the one who was rector – came originally from St Albans, where *his* father had been a schoolmaster. And his father before him – Esmond's great-great-grandfather, Oliver Bates – well, he'd been born at a little place called Kettlebaston in Suffolk. And when Esmond went over there to see what other bits of the family tree he could find, he discovered Bateses going back for generations all around the Lavenham area."

Dinah looked suitably impressed.

"What's more, my dear, he showed me some of them, too. Or at least, their gravestones. They seem to have been a prosperous lot – wool merchants and country magistrates and the like."

"How very respectable."

"Ah, not entirely. There was one who was hanged for murder in sixteen something-or-other."

Jessie lay back again in the hammock. "But we aren't to mention him, of course. Father-in-law won't have it. He got quite waxy when Esmond began discussing the subject at luncheon on Sunday."

"Really? Why? There's always one black sheep in any family." Dinah could certainly think of several in her own; and in particular one who was presently rather too near home for comfort – her husband Warwick Enderby. In obedience to her parents' wishes that she try to patch up her domestic differences, she had made a conscious effort to be slightly more agreeable to Warwick; and he had reciprocated by behaving more arrogantly than ever, appearing to regard her reluctant olive-bearing attempts at reconciliation as evidence that her intransigence was at last beginning to weaken. For one whole week there had been a strained peace at Southwood Place, and then the shoddy fabric hiding the cracks had split apart under the stress of such an unnatural calm, and after a violent argument their married life had resumed its usual course again.

She waved away a wasp from the glass of barley water on

the rug beside her; and reluctant to spoil the day and mar her friend's newly-wed happiness by voicing such dark thoughts aloud, instead added lightly, "But perhaps it offends your father-in-law to admit there's a flaw in his family. He has his pride, does Mr Bates."

"Pride, and something else," Jessie responded. "He's being altogether a little odd at the moment."

"Take no notice, that's just his way."

"No, I think it's something more. Do you know, my dear, he's deliberately refusing to speak to what's-her-name, Laura's old governess . . . Miss Evans. There's an awful atmosphere in the house, too, as though the most ghastly row is simmering. Esmond thinks it's to do with your friend Algie."

"What – poor Algie again? All he's done is to fall in love, and it's being treated as a major crime!"

Dinah closed her book with a snap and threw it aside. "Anyway, I thought Mr Bates had decided to give them both his blessing?"

"His blessing?" Jessie let out a laugh. "Good Lord, I'd hardly call it that. He allows Laura and young Algie to 'consort together socially' as Stepmother-in-law puts it, but if anyone so much as dare mention the fact to Father-in-law's face – why, my dear, it's tantamount to committing lese-majesty! The name of Algernon Langton-Smythe is *not* to be spoken at Spences Lane."

"Oh, but how ridiculous . . ." The other made a sound of scornful disbelief. "You mean, Algie and Laura are permitted to meet, but it mustn't be discussed in front of Mr Bates?"

Jessie nodded; then, deciding that she'd had enough of the hammock for a while, sat herself up and swung her white-stockinged legs over the side.

"Between you and me, Dinah dearest, there's a slight whiff of fish about the whole business."

"Fish – ?"

"Mm." She glanced about her in a furtive manner – a needlessly dramatic bit of play-acting, since there was no one but themselves out here in the sunlit garden – and lowering her voice a little, went on, "As you know, Esmond has always been extremely fond of Miss Evans. Now, whether she's hinted something to him I really couldn't say, but he admits there's more than mere coincidence between his sister's sudden release from the Dolorous Tower and Miss Evans's fall from favour."

"Of course there is – she's been chaperoning Laura's clandestine affaire with Algie, and Mr Bates has discovered the fact."

"Oh, no, no. There's far more to it than that. Far more."

Jessie got down from her perch and went to help herself to a fresh glass of barley water from the table. In the distance, the sound of someone whistling "Let me call you Sweetheart" carried from the street above the muted noise of town traffic, but here in the garden of Southwood Place a drowsy stillness seemed to linger among the scented beds of flowers in the heat of the July afternoon.

She replaced the muslin cover over the jug and took her replenished glass across to her friend, seating herself down beside her on the rug, her back against the ridged grey bark of the willow.

"Do you happen to remember Dr Linton who lived out at Weatherfield when you were a child?"

"Linton?" Dinah thought a moment. "Linton. Oh . . . yes, didn't he have a practice somewhere in Church Lane?"

"That's the one." Jessie took a long sip. "His wife was one of those pretty, fluffy little women – you know the type, all ribbons and bows and artifice. Cats in kittens' clothing. She enjoyed ill-health, as they say, but appears to have kept herself busy with doing Good Works for St Anne's church – " a pause for another sip – "which is how she and Esmond's father made one another's acquaintance."

Dinah had to think again. "When he was a benefactor of the parish, do you mean?"

A nod. "Esmond thinks she must have been on the committee at the time the memorial to his grandfather was erected. She died about 1872. Rather suddenly. And rather unexpectedly, I gather. But not before she and Father-in-law had struck up quite a lively correspondence."

There was a further pause.

"Well? And is that all to the story?"

"Now don't be so impatient! I shan't tell you if you

217

interrupt." Jessie administered a light tap. "I've only just begun. According to one of the Bashford cousins, apparently these letters to each other were – oh, what was the expression I heard the other day – *hot stuff*. You know. Passionate. Not the kind of thing at all one would expect of Father-in-law. Of course, he was a widower still at the time, so I suppose he was entitled to feel a little warmth – but surely not towards a respectably married woman."

"It seems hardly credible, I agree."

"Indeed. Well, to cut corners, my dear, Esmond happened to fall into conversation some months ago with a person who'd been in service with the Lintons. He did tell me the woman's name, but I forget now. She works at The Rising Sun in Weatherfield high street – he used occasionally to go there for luncheon, it being so conveniently placed for his chambers. Though now that we're married, of course, he comes home for all his meals – "

Another pause. "Now I've lost the thread of what I was telling you."

"Someone who'd been in service with the Lintons," Dinah reminded her patiently.

"Ah, yes. That's right. Well, you know how people love to tattle about other people's business – "

Her friend allowed herself a smile, but forbore to comment.

" – apparently this woman had learned he was Mr Bates's son, and a little impertinently I though but then what can you expect these days, she began telling him about Mrs Linton and the friendliness there'd been between her and Father-in-law. Esmond couldn't resist asking whether she knew anything about the letters, and she said oh yes, Mrs Linton used to keep them in a box beneath her pillow, and the ones she wrote in return to Lewes she'd send out to be posted after the doctor had left the house on his morning rounds."

Jessie stopped to sip once more from her glass.

"*Very* curious, wouldn't you say?" And without waiting for an answer, continued on the same breath – "But there's more! The day after we returned from Lavenham, Esmond called by at Spences Lane and happened to overhear the most frightful row going on in the study between his father and Miss Evans. He didn't know it was her, of course, until she came out, and even then he wasn't much surprised because Father-in-law has a habit of losing his temper quite regularly. But what *did* make his ears prick up, he says, was hearing his father mention something about 'those d--- Linton letters' and Miss Evans reply 'you should have burnt them sooner', or words to that effect."

Jessie paused for air.

"And – ?" Dinah prompted, fascinated by this rattling of family skeletons.

There was a shrug. "Then the maid knocked at the study door to announce Esmond was there, and everything went very quiet. And as far as we know, that was the last time Father-in-law has deigned to address himself to the woman."

"So . . . what do you suppose lies behind it all?"

"Who can say? So many tantalising clues, my dear! Plainly, Miss Evans knows something – "

"And whatever it is, you believe it's the reason Mr Bates has had to consent to Laura seeing young Algie?"

An emphatic nod.

"But what does Esmond think?"

Jessie shrugged again. "I don't know. That's what's so perfectly maddening. Esmond does *not* think. Esmond has gone suddenly very silent on the whole subject. When I asked him on Sunday evening whether Miss Evans had perhaps mentioned anything to him, his only answer was to start lighting his beastly pipe – you know, the way he always does when he's being obstinate. And when I threatened to sulk if he didn't tell me, all he'd say was that we'd be wise to let sleeping dogs lie."

She tilted her head and finished the last drop of barley water, delicately wiping the corners of her mouth with a forefinger.

"But I'm not sure I should leave it there, my dear. Do you? It's all very well the family closing ranks, if that's what they're doing – *I'm* a Bates now, which gives me every right to know what this business is about!"

Algie had taken off his striped blazer jacket and left it folded over a handle of the motor bicycle, together with Laura's kerseymere dust-coat which her step-mother had insisted she must wear. The front stud of his turned-down collar was unfastened, and his Old School tie pulled casually loose, revealing the fine golden hairs at the base of his throat. Somewhat incongruously, he was still wearing the leather motoring cap turned peak-to-aft – a style copied from watching Percy Moran in the popular "Lieutenant Daring" adventure series.

The poem he was reading aloud was scarcely in keeping with such attire, especially the red trouser braces, but Laura's thoughts were evidently far removed from anything as mundane as appearances, for the sidelong glance resting upon her companion was full of melting admiration as she listened to the glorious pagan imagery of Swinburne's *Atalanta in Calydon*.

Above them both, the cloudless summer sky stretched from the rim of their gorse-filled hollow to the distant sparkling horizon of the sea, and in the luminous afternoon stillness which held them like an enchantment, the only sounds were the carol of larks and the far-off bleat of a Downland flock.

> "And time remember'd is grief forgotten,
> And frosts are slain and flowers begotten,
> And in green underwood and cover
> Blossom by blossom the spring begins . . ."

Algie read confidently and with feeling, attuned in sympathy to his hero-poet's lines, letting his voice linger, or quicken, or fade so as to give his listener the impression of word-pictures forming from sound.

Reaching the end of *Atalanta*'s "Chorus" he paused and looked from his book; and propping himself up by his elbows on the close-cropped turf, said, "You're not bored yet, are you?"

"Bored?" Laura smiled at him shyly. "Of course not."

"That's good." He smiled back. "I'll read you some more later, if you like. *Ave atque Vale*, perhaps."

Then, seeing a look of puzzlement shadow her brow, he explained, "'Hail and Farewell' – written in memory of the poet Baudelaire."

"Oh . . . " The young girl's head drooped a little, her tawny brown hair falling forward in a loose wave. "You must think me very ignorant not to know about these things."

"Now you're not to say that. I won't have it, d'you hear?"

Algie sat up, reaching forward to take her by the hand. "If anyone's the duffer, it's me. I mean, what good am I except for spouting Swinburne or playing the fiddle in a picture house?"

She glanced at him from beneath lowered lashes. "But you *know* so much. About literature, and art, and composers – and – oh, and motor engines, and air balloons – "

"And shoes and ships and sealing-wax, not to mention cabbages and kings," he finished for her, the smile broadening into a grin. "D'you know what the Pater said to me when I saw him this weekend? He said I'd be very good as a gentleman's valet but a pretty poor show as a valet's gentleman. By which I understood him to mean that my head's stuffed with all the wrong facts. The sort that qualify me to be cock of the walk, if you like, but not king of the castle."

"It's better to know a little about everything, surely," Laura said in loyal defence; and then – "You didn't tell me you were going to visit your parents, Algie."

"No, I only decided at the last moment. I wanted to tell the Pater of my decision."

He paused for a moment.

"You see, dearest – " squeezing her hand – "I think it's time I gave up my work at the Picture Theatre and the hospital and got down to something slightly more respectable."

She raised her face to his, and again there was that little look of puzzlement. "Give up your work? But I thought you enjoyed it so much?"

"Oh, I do! The problem is, though, there's no future in it for me. As Mama said, I can't go on earning three pounds and ten shillings a week for the rest of my life. Well . . . I know what she means. One of these days I've got to face up to the fact that I do have a duty to the family name. And somehow, you know, Laura, it's not so much fun kicking over the traces any more. Not since I've met you."

He placed his volume of Swinburne's poems aside on the

grass and pulling off the leather cap, tossed it behind him towards the motor bicycle, then wiped his perspiring forehead with the back of his hand.

"You're not too warm here, are you?" he asked anxiously.

Laura shook her head. She could feel the sun beginning to burn her shoulders through the thin material of her pleated blouse, but was reluctant to admit as much for fear Algie should decide they'd leave the Downs and drive back into town: it was so beautifully peaceful here in the hollow, and so far away from the everyday world, and the angry silent hostility of Spences Lane.

Instead she said tactfully, "Though if you're feeling the heat, Algie, perhaps we might move into the shade?"

"A good idea. It *is* pretty sweltering out here."

He got to his feet, bending to help his companion up by the hands, and moved with her a few yards away into the coolness of a spreading gorse bush whose shadow covered one end of the hollow. The buttery fragrance of its yellow flowers scented the still air with a smell of summer, and before seating herself again she reached out to break off a spray.

"Here, let me." The young man forestalled her. "Those spikes can be sharp."

Heedless of his own caution, he pulled down a long sprig and succeeded in pricking himself quite deeply in the thumb.

"Ouch!"

"Oh, what have you done? Let me see – "

Laura seized the offending gorse and tossed it away, kneeling to inspect its damage. "Dear, you're bleeding! Hold still a moment and I'll bind it with my handkerchief."

Taking a square of embroidered linen from her skirt pocket, she pulled him down to face her and began attending to her task, lips slightly parted in concentration to show the tip of her tongue between small even teeth.

Algie watched her tenderly.

When she had finished she glanced up at him again and smiled, about to say something; but before she could speak, he had taken her face between his hands and heard himself blurting out, "Laura . . . oh, Laura . . . I do love you so."

It was not at all how he had rehearsed the scene. Almost

since that first meeting of a year ago, he'd gone to sleep each night imagining Laura was in his arms and he was saying something terribly sophisticated, rather in the fashion of Stewart Rome or Alec Worcester: something like, "Oh my darling, you look so dashed attractive in this moonlight. Don't you know what you've done to me, damn it? You have stolen my heart away."

Now that the dream had come true for him, such matinée idol words sounded silly and artificial; and all he could do was repeat himself awkwardly, feeling a flush of embarrassment reddening his ears.

"I love you, dearest . . . I love you, truly I do."

Laura's cheeks had coloured up in turn; but instead of trying to push him away as he'd feared, she placed her small hands over his and in the ghost of a whisper replied, "I'm glad . . . I love you, too, Algie."

"You do?"

"Yes."

"Gosh!"

He gazed into her eyes for several long moments, his heart hammering loud enough, he thought, to be heard right down in Lewes and his throat so dry with nervousness that he had to clear it several times before he was able to speak again.

"Would you – would you mind awfully if I asked you – well, you know, if I asked you to marry me? Oh, darlingest Laura, please say yes. I simply can't live without you. In a few years' time, I promise, I'll be perfectly able to support you as my wife. The Pater wants to put me in charge of managing the family estates, you see – only I'd have to go back to college first to learn all the ropes. If we were to get engaged, we'd belong to one another, wouldn't we, so it wouldn't seem so awfully bad being apart for a while. And we'd be married in two or three years – not long to wait. Oh, do say yes, my darling, won't you?"

Laura's lips curved into a soft smile. "And what if I were to say . . . no?"

"I'd kill myself."

"Honestly?"

"Honestly!"

"Heavens, how drastic. Then I suppose it had better be

223

yes. And . . . thank you for asking me."

"Not a bit. I'm jolly glad I did."

He returned the smile; then his young face grew suddenly serious once more. Bending his head, he kissed her a little clumsily on the mouth.

"Sorry, I don't seem to be much good at this," he mumbled as he drew away, his hands still cupping her burning cheeks. "Haven't had a lot of practice . . ."

And pulling her against him, his arms going tightly around her slender body, he kissed her again.

21

Cecilia Desatti's naked shoulders gleamed palely in the dim shafts of sunlight which filtered down between the rafters from the bright day outside, casting a shadowy luminosity within the interior of the barn. Up here in the loft the air was intimately close and warm, with a lingering faint aroma of tobacco smoke and leather masking the dusty smell of summer hay from harvests past.

Sissy lay on her back, her head pillowed against Francis Bethway's flat-muscled abdomen, her scarlet silk petticoat thrown across her hips. It amused him that she always had this need to cover herself after they'd been making love: a little touch of the prude in her still, he thought, requiring her for modesty's sake to veil the loveliness which shortly before had been offered in such total and abandoned giving.

He had never known a woman as ardent as this one, so eagerly ready to please a man. Taking her that first night, at The Fordhouse at Buckfield, had been a revelation beyond his wildest dreams or expectations, for having made up her mind to become his mistress she had given herself with a generosity that was completely without restraint, matching him as an equal in the sharing and bestowing of sensual fulfilment. He had known that a love affaire with Sissy would be an excitingly original experience, but how exciting – and exactly how original – he could never have guessed in a hundred years.

The Captain smiled to himself, and unclasping his hands from behind his head, reached down to touch her face, tracing a finger lightly from the sweat-pearled hairline, across her forehead to the small, high bridge of her nose and slowly down over the parted lips and softly rounded chin to the creamy smoothness of her throat.

She made a little sound of pleasure and turned her head to kiss his hand, pressing her mouth against its soldier's calloused palm.

"Again," she murmured.

His smile widened. "No."

"Yes . . ."

"Greedy."

"I don't care. Again."

She rolled over, her long loose hair tickling his bare skin, and began stroking her fingertips up and down along the inside of his thigh.

"Mmm?"

"No!"

"You can't?"

"I won't."

"Liar, I don't believe you. You can't, you can't."

This teasing was all part of the erotic game they liked to play together, a game in which Sissy's light mockery would gradually turn to cajolery and then to pleading, and her lover's refusals end in the sudden play of a mock-violent assault.

"You can't," she repeated, raising herself up slightly so that her full, firm breasts brushed against his nakedness. She leaned forward, laughing, and began moving herself sinuously, the silk petticoat sliding from her hips, her dark eyes half-closed like a cat's.

"You can't – "

Francis started to laugh with her; then, abruptly, cutting short the game with an unexpected roughness, he gripped her shoulders and threw her over on to her back, pinning her beneath him against the hay-strewn floor.

"Oh, can't I," he said softly, teeth bared in a wolverine grin of pleasure. "We must see about that, my beauty."

The shafts of hazy light dimmed within the loft as a cloud passed over the brassy face of the sun; but neither noticed. One or two hens scratched about below on the barn floor, and the Captain's horse, tethered outside, rubbed its neck against the doorpost; but neither heard anything. For a while they were blind and deaf to everything except each other.

When they had finished making love again, they lay a long time without speaking, side by side, feeling the pounding throb of their bodies slowly quieten and the sob of their laboured breathing ease into stillness.

At length, it was Sissy who was first to break the silence. Stirring a little, she wiped the trickles of sweat from her temples; and without opening her eyes, said drowsily, "I wrote you a letter, you know, Frank."

He made no answer, only grunted and shifted himself on the wooden boards, one arm across his forehead.

Several more minutes went by before she spoke again, her voice still a murmur, as though what she had to say was hardly worth the effort.

"I wrote that if you wanted to finish with me, I'd understand."

There was a sound that might have been a snort of amusement. "Finish with you? What's this, Sissy – second thoughts?"

"No."

Francis stretched himself and yawned; then, levering himself up on an elbow, looked down at her. "What, then?"

She opened her eyes. "You've got a son now. Doesn't it make some difference . . . to you and me, I mean?"

He gave this his consideration. "Should it?"

"I don't know. I thought perhaps it might. You wanted a son so much."

"True. And now, thank God, I've got one. But I'm not intending to forfeit you on that account, my pet. You're too important to me."

He bent his head and kissed her lingeringly on the lips, not like the hard, demanding kisses of his love-making, but gently and with real affection.

"What did it say, this letter of yours?"

"Oh, just – 'dear Frank, don't feel you're obliged to carry on seeing me if you don't want to.' Something like that."

"Nothing else?"

"Well . . . I said perhaps your first duty was to your wife now. After all, she is the boy's mother."

"I don't need you to tell me my duty, Sissy – "

"I'm sorry. Don't get angry with me. I know we agreed not to talk about your family and your home, and that."

"I'm not getting angry with you!" He kissed her again; then, sitting up, reached behind him for his jacket thrown on top of his clothes across a hay bale, and took his cigar case from an inside pocket.

227

"If you're worried that my behaviour might be criticised," he went on, lighting a cheroot and shaking out the match carefully, "don't be. No one can say I haven't conducted myself as a gentleman these past months. I've been completely faithful to you and to Marion both. It'd be a different matter if I'd continued to have liaisons with other women, but I haven't – I've shown myself to be a good husband and a caring father. So far as society's concerned, the fact that I now have a son is neither here nor there. What matters is that my family aren't being neglected as a consequence of my keeping a mistress. So you see, our situation is perfectly respectable, my darling."

"But your wife doesn't know that you're back with me, does she." Sissy's voice sounded suddenly a little flat. Sitting up in turn, she took the scarlet silk petticoat and hugged it against herself, her arms across her breasts and her legs drawn up.

"Why have you never owned up and told her, Frank, if what we're doing is so respectable?"

He drew heavily on the cheroot. "She's had a difficult pregnancy. It might have upset her. Look – I don't really wish to discuss this now."

"It's got to be discussed some time." Sissy rested her head against her knees and looked at him sideways, her dark hair spilling in untidy waves. "*Will* you tell her?"

"No."

"Why not? You aren't ashamed of me – you said as much a moment ago."

"It's not the sort of thing a fellow does, baldly informing his wife that he has a mistress. Either she knows or she doesn't, it's as simple as that."

"You mean, somebody else has to tell her."

Francis shrugged. "It happens."

"Don't you think that's being a bit two-faced?"

"Conducting an affaire, my sweet, is a two-faced business. A man has to divide himself down the middle and become two halves of the same whole – one half belonging to his wife and children, the other to his mistress. Provided he manages the situation with tact and decorum and thoughtfulness for all concerned, his position is no more inconvenient than if he were to spend his time, say, between his country address and his London club."

"No wonder they call this a man's world." Sissy gave a tight little laugh. "Just suppose for argument's sake it was the women behaving themselves like that – having a cosy husband keeping the sheets warm at home, and some handsome young piece for a bit of slap and tickle on the side? Who'd bring up the children then, or run the house, or keep the family together?"

"You're becoming very moral all of a sudden, my dear. What's brought this about?"

She looked down at her feet, and pulled a face. "Conscience, I suppose."

"You've been spending too much time at that church of yours again. I've told you before, you're a guilt-ridden lot, you Catholics."

"That's a cheap thing to say, Frank."

He smiled. "*Mea culpa*. Isn't that the response?"

"Yes, but there's no need to mock."

"I wasn't mocking. Now who's the one getting angry."

There was a silence. Sissy picked at a frill on her petticoat. Francis studied the smoke from his cheroot, watching the way it spiralled lazily up in the shafts of sunlight.

After a time he said, "So this is what your letter was really about. Not 'dear Frank, you're under no obligation to continue seeing me,' but 'dear Frank, I've had an attack of conscience and think we ought to part.'"

"That's not true!" She glanced at him again, sharply. "Why are you trying to twist my own words against me? All it was was giving you a chance to do the decent thing and save your face, if that was what you wanted."

"Save my face? Oh, you mean withdraw from our relationship in an orderly manner, all flags flying?"

"You know what I mean. And don't be so flippin' sarcastic."

"Temper, temper!"

Sissy bit her lip and turned her face away. Sudden tears pricked behind her eyes and she had to swallow hard to get rid of the lump that was filling her throat. Why did it always have to end this way between them just lately – the passion,

229

the intimacy of love-making, and then for no reason this feeling of resentment she had that made her so on edge every time.

She heard Francis shifting, getting up to start dressing himself; and with her forehead still pressed against her knees, said abruptly, "I think my mother knows about us."

He stopped and looked down, his shirt only half pulled on over one shoulder. "What was that?"

"My mother. She knows about us." A pause. "Well . . . not for sure, perhaps. But she suspects something."

"Has she – said so?"

The girl gave a shrug, followed by a quick shake; then pushing herself to her feet, her back turned on her lover, began to drag the petticoat over her head, saying tonelessly, "She knows I'm not spending my nights away with Marie McGrath."

"I see." Francis finished buttoning his shirt. "And how did she discover that?"

"Marie and me had an argument. She wanted me to give her a little gold crucifix my grandparents had sent me from Italy for my First Communion. I said I wouldn't – she's had enough of my jewellery as it is – "

"Bribery in aid of corruption." He came over and put his hands on her small, slender shoulders. "You should have offered her money as I suggested. I'd have done the paying."

"I told you, Frank, it didn't seem right."

"Yes, I remember. You said it made you feel like a second-hand whore – "

"Like a whore at second-hand, I said!"

"Ah, so you did." He turned her round to face him, his eyes beneath the straight dark brows half serious, half amused.

"It isn't funny, Frank," she said defensively. "Marie went and told her sister I'd been offering her things to keep her mouth shut about where I was spending my nights away from home. And her sister must've let something drop to their mother – "

"Who goes to church with your mother," he finished for her.

Sissy nodded. "And you know what a lot of old nabble-traps they are at that place. Mass every day, and nothing else

230

to do after but sit drinking cups of tea and minding other folk's business."

"The human nature doesn't change. I seem to recall it was much the same in my father's parish at Eastbourne," Francis commented drily. "Wherever there's women, there's gossip, and wherever there's gossip, there's a certain amount of malicious claw-sharpening."

"Yes, well I'd prefer it if they didn't sharpen their claws at my expense."

"I don't think you've any need to worry, my pet." Moving a hand to the small of her back, he pressed her half-clothed body against him. "If your mother knew about it, she'd have confronted you with it by now."

"I don't know so much. And don't start that again, Frank – "

He nuzzled at her neck. "Why not?"

"Because I'm talking to you."

"I'm listening."

"No you're not. Look – stop it, will you!"

She slapped his hands away.

"This is serious, Frank. I wish you'd pay some proper attention."

"Isn't that what I'm doing?"

"Oh, you know what I mean – "

He silenced her protest with a long kiss. Then, turning aside, took up his shirt collar and lifted his chin to start fastening the studs.

Sissy watched him out of the corner of her eye.

Suddenly she said – somewhat irrelevantly – wrinkling her nose, "I can smell burning. You haven't gone and set the place alight, have you?"

"No, it's all right." He leaned across to pick up his cheroot, left smouldering on the edge of his cigar case while he dressed himself.

Doing up the buttons of his trousers with one hand, he raised the cheroot to his lips and drew in a mouthful of smoke, expelling it again in a slow trickle; then said casually, "There's something you haven't told me yet, isn't there."

"About what's going on at home, you mean?"

"Yes."

The girl bent her head, pretending to occupy herself with tying the laces in the bodice of her petticoat.

After a moment or so she answered reluctantly, "It was something my sister Carlotta heard . . . she'd slipped out into the alley behind our yard the other night to meet this boy she likes. She's not supposed to see him. He's an altar server at St Pancras's and his people want him to be a priest."

"Poor young devil."

"What?"

"Nothing. Go on. She'd met him in the alley, and – ?"

"Well, when she came back into the yard, the kitchen windows had been left open and she could hear my parents talking. She had to wait there in the dark for a bit till they'd gone, because there's only the one door."

Sissy paused. Biting her lip, she stooped to pick up her flounced cotton skirt and began to pull it on.

"And – ?" Francis prompted her again.

"And she caught something Mama was saying to my father. About me."

There was a hesitation.

"I didn't want to tell you this, Frank."

"Well, you've started now, so we may as well know the rest of it."

Another hesitation while she fastened the little pearl side-buttons on her waistband.

"It was about sending me away. To my uncle. In New York."

"New York – ?"

He stared at her.

"*New York*?"

"Yes."

The Captain looked around the loft, aimlessly, in the manner of someone unable quite to comprehend what they've just been told.

"My uncle emigrated there from Italy, years ago – before I was born," Sissy rushed on, anxious to fill the sudden silence. "He opened an ice-cream parlour in a place called Brooklyn, and now he owns six or seven, all called Desatti's like our tea-room – "

232

"Damn what they're called!" Francis recovered himself again. Throwing his cheroot to the floor, he ground it savagely underfoot. "D'you think I'm going to let them send you away from me half-way across the other side of the world?"

"I don't see how you can stop them. I'm their daughter."

"You're also my woman. The woman I'm in love with. God in heaven, Sissy, why didn't you tell me of this before?"

"I didn't know myself till yesterday. Our Lottie never mentioned it. She was frightened I'd get her into trouble for meeting that boy. She only came out with it when I swore I wouldn't say anything to Mama."

Sissy put on her white blouse, tossing her hair free of the collar.

"Besides, my father's head of the family," she went on sullenly, buttoning up the cuffs. "If he decides it's best for me to go and live with Uncle Giuseppe, I've no choice but to obey him."

She flashed a quick sideways glance. "Things might be different if you were free to marry me – but you're not."

"No, I'm not," Francis echoed tonelessly.

He finished putting on his own clothes in silence. What had been the perfect afternoon for them both had suddenly turned sour and depressing. He felt trapped, caught in a corner, and it angered him to be rendered so incapable of breaking free of it. From whichever point of view he looked, the answer was still the same. He couldn't leave Marion and the children – especially not his little son – it would be more than his conscience and his Army commission were worth. But neither could he give up Sissy Desatti. He realised now just how much she meant to him.

Straightening the knot in his tie, he said aloud, "We shall just have to wait and see what happens, I suppose. And in the meanwhile, it's probably wise to be as discreet as we can about meeting again."

"No more Mr and Mrs Morgan?"

"No more Mr and Mrs Morgan. At least, for a month or two."

Sissy's mouth turned down. She looked at the wedding ring he'd given her, that first night at The Fordhouse, and which she always wore to these trysts of theirs.

Not for the first time in their relationship, she said with some feeling, "You married men . . . you're all alike."

"Oh, for heaven's sake, don't start that again!" Francis glanced at her in quick exasperation. This was the beginning of a conversation they'd had before, and of late more frequently. "You know what the situation is, sweet heart. There's nothing I can do to change it."

"Your wife could divorce you – "

"She won't. She won't, and that's flat. Now I don't wish to discuss it any more, d'you understand?"

The girl set her hands on her hips and raised her chin defiantly.

"All right – stay married to her. See if I care! But I'll tell you this, Frank. You're going to miss me. When I've sailed away from you across that ocean to New York, you're going to wish you'd fought a bit harder before you let me go."

Mrs Ernest Thompson had not been idle. Much to her invalid sister-in-law's bemusement, she visited her at the nursing home in Buckfield assiduously every week, never failing to stop on the way from the station to buy flowers or fruit from the high street greengrocer just a few doors from The Fordhouse – "such lovely fresh things he has, my dear!"

On one occasion only had the purpose of her charity been rewarded, when the reception desk clerk responded to her enquiry with information that her friends the Morgans had booked in for the night on the previous evening, but had left again immediately after breakfast.

Oh, *what* a pity to have missed them both a second time. But never mind, they'd be sure to come again. Wouldn't they?

A tale never loses in the telling. In the weeks since she'd first uncovered "Mr Morgan's" shady secret, Mrs Ernest Thompson had embroidered upon it wonderfully to her husband, her sister, and of course, her married daughter (not to mention several ladies at the golf club) spreading her juicy bit of gossip like little drops of poison.

In time, the poison worked its way through the system, seeping from the golf club to the Officers' Mess, and from the
Mess to the officers' wives, growing a detail or two more tainted with each re-telling.

Slander may be sport to tale-bearers, but it is a kind of death to those whom they abuse. When eventually the toxin of Mrs Ernest Thompson's tittle-tattle reached Marion Bethway, its effect was more damaging than any of them could possibly have foreseen.

22

"Talk about laugh! I thought I'd ha' died, the way he kept a-looking in at that window and seeing 'em all on their backs wi' their legs in the air."

Florrie Cox shook her head in happy remembrance. It was her day off, and she and her fiancé, Corporal Walter Jackson, had been to The Electric Picture Theatre to see a comedy called *Father's Saturday Afternoon*.

"And what about when he shut the door and them blessed shelves fell off the wall," she went on, starting to laugh again.

Wally grinned, squinting into the sun to see if it was safe for them to cross the road.

"Aye, it was comic, was that."

He steered Florrie round behind the wheels of a passing horse-drawn van, gallantly removing his peaked forage cap to keep the dust from her face. It had been a long dry summer and the streets were white with a fine layer of powdery chalk blown from the Downs. Usually the water-carts kept the worst of it down until the autumn storms washed it away into the drains, but in the meantime it flew everywhere, getting into folks' eyes and clothes and settling indoors all over the polished furniture.

"The news-reel pictures they showed after the interval – " he put his cap on again and changed sides so that his companion was on his left arm, away from the gutter – "I thought it was proper interesting, all that about the Prince o' Wales's investiture."

"Ooh, yes!" Florrie mouthed the word 'investiture' to herself several times, to remember it for the future; then added aloud, "It's a big castle they've got there in Wales, isn't it. I wouldn't fancy much going there myself for holidays, mind, not wi' all the ruins. You'd think they'd ha' repaired it a bit."

"It's meant to be a ruin, is Caernarvon," Wally explained patiently. "Nobody lives there. It's a national monument, or some'at. The reason they held the investiture there and not Buckingham Palace was on account o' the first Prince o' Wales being born in the castle, centuries back."

"Don't you know a lot!" Florrie gazed up at her artilleryman with pride in her eyes. "Is that why Prince Edward had to wear such clothes as he did?"

"How d'you mean?"

"Well, you know – long white stockings and pantaloon drawers, and that fur cape. Was that how the first prince used to dress hisself, d'you reckon?"

"Search me." They turned the corner into Warren Street. "I'll tell you some'at, though. There's a chap at our barracks, his sister's married to a guardsman who was on duty for the ceremony. He reckons the Prince would've looked better kitted in naval cadet uniform than in that daft rig-out. Made him look like a dolly-shop on legs, he said."

"Now, Wally – " His fiancée gave his arm a shake of disapproval. "That's the heir to the throne you're a-speaking of."

"It wasn't me said it, love, it was him at the barracks' brother-in-law."

"Then he ought to know better, him a guardsman an' all. I won't have a word spoke against our Royal Family, you know I won't."

It was time to change the subject.

The two of them had reached the side gate to the Bethway house by now, and as he reached to undo the latch, Wally exclaimed with sudden forced liveliness, "Here, I forgot to ask – how's the baby coming on? Doing well, is he?"

Baby George was Florrie's favourite topic of conversation. The July investiture at Caernarvon Castle was forgotten in a moment.

"Oh, he's a little duck, he really is," she responded over her shoulder eagerly, going ahead down the area steps. "You won't hardly know him when you see him again, he's put on that much weight while you've been away on exercise. Mind you – " pausing to unlock the scullery door – "he fair wears me out some days wi' his belvering. Talk about a pair o' lungs! To hear him, you'd think he never got sufficient in his belly."

She turned the knob and went inside; and hanging the key on its hook above the sink, went on again, "Since his mother's milk dried up, there's bottles for everlasting being stood on the range to warm. I told her, she ought to wean him, but she won't hear of it."

Wally removed his forage cap.

"Have you time for a cup o' tea, my love?" Florrie stopped herself to ask, pulling off her gloves to go and fill the kettle.

"Aye."

"Well now, sit yourself down, and I'll cut us some cake to go wi' it."

She moved busily about, setting a corner of the kitchen table with a clean white cloth and putting out cups and saucers and tea plates; all the while keeping up a running conversation with hardly a pause, it seemed, to draw breath between her words.

"Yes, I told her. Mrs Bethway, I says, you ought by rights to wean that child if you want him to thrive. He may be not yet three months old, but he's got an appetite that'd do credit to a child twice that age. But no, she says, no, he's lusty, that's all, it'll develop his lungs to let him cry, she says. I ask you!" Florrie threw up her eyes. "I know what I'd do if he was any babe o' mine. He'd be fed on clear broth morn and night, and sops o' bread and milk to fill his little belly."

"The Captain's very proud of him, to hear him talk o' the boy," Wally managed to get in while the teapot was being filled.

"Proud?" The kettle was placed back on the hob. "Proud ain't the word for it! Anyone 'ld think he were the first man ever to have a son, the way he dotes on that there child. No sooner is he home of a night than he's up them stairs to the nursery – "

Florrie came to a sudden full stop and turned her head sharply.

At the same moment, the door at the top of the scullery steps could be heard opening, and a voice – Marion Bethway's – called, "Are you there?"

238

"Lord a' mercy!" The housemaid snatched a hand to her breast as her mistress's feet appeared in view just below the ceiling level. The sight of her employer coming down in person to the servants' basement instead of ringing as she always did from upstairs was so unexpectedly disconcerting that for several seconds Florrie wondered whether something dreadful might not have happened in the house while she'd been out.

Then, recovering herself, and remembering she was still wearing her hat, she pulled it hastily from the mousy bun of her hair and asked, "Ma'am? Is there anything wrong? Wally and me, we were just a-sitting down for a cup o' tea. We've not long come in from the picture house."

Marion nodded vaguely towards her husband's batman, who had risen smartly to his feet. Her face was very pale. She seemed to hesitate, as though she'd forgotten why it was she had come down here.

"Mrs Bethway – ?" The maid took a step towards her, holding out a hand. "You don't look at all well, ma'am. Don't you think you ought to let me take you up to your room?"

"No, no. Thank you, Florrie. There's no need. I merely came to tell you that Baby is asleep in his perambulator in the garden. You won't disturb him, will you?"

"O' course not, ma'am."

Marion gave the ghost of a smile; then, without another word, turned and went back up the steps, moving slowly and heavily, like an old woman.

Florrie waited until the scullery door had closed above.

"Well I never," she whispered, eyeing her fiancé, "fancy making an appearance down here just to tell me that. Why ever didn't she ring for me to go up?"

Wally re-seated himself. "Belikes she thought it might've disturbed the child."

"What – out in the garden?"

"Well, I don't know." He looked pointedly at the teapot. "I've got to be off in five or ten minutes – "

"I hadn't forgotten."

She poured him a cup; and cutting a slice from the cherry madeira cake, passed it across to his plate, before starting

239

again, "She'd been a-crying. I could see. She had that mopey look about her."

Wally nodded, his mouth already full of cake.

"She knows, you know," his beloved went on. "She heard it from one o' the other officers' wives. About the Captain taking up again wi' that gipsy."

He swilled the cake down with a gulp of tea.

"Eye-talian."

"Eye-talian?"

Another nod. "She's an Eye-talian, not a gipsy. Her father's that ice-cream johnny in Station Road."

"How d'you know that?"

He tapped the side of his nose. "A little bird."

Florrie stirred her tea. "The same little bird, I suppose, that's been a-singing its tune over half the camp."

Her fiancé finished his cup and pushed it forward for a re-fill. "I dunno about that. All I can say is the word's got around that he's seeing this Sissy again, on the sly."

"As if folk haven't got anything better to do than to tattle!"

"Hark who's talking." He took another bite of cake.

"I'll pretend I didn't hear that," said Florrie, aiming a slap at his head. Then, leaning across the corner of the table and lowering her voice again – "I'll tell you some'at, though. There's been ructions here since Missus found out. Seems the Captain had promised her never to have nothing more to do wi' this Eye-talian piece, and now – well, what wi' just having a baby and hearing her husband's up to his old tricks again, she's been in a right taking, has Mrs Bethway."

Wally grunted some comment through a final mouthful of cake.

"You'd think he'd be content wi' a wife and three little 'uns, a man in his position," she went on, emptying her own cup. "I can't understand it, gallivanting about the way he does. There must be some'at wrong wi' him. A dose o' salts is what he needs."

"I've told you before, Florrie my love, it's none of our business."

The artilleryman pushed back his chair, and picking up his

240

forage cap from beside his plate, got to his feet. "Now I'm due on duty at six, so I'll have to go."

He leaned forward and gave his beloved a kiss on the cheek. "The cake wasn't half bad. Will you bake us another for next time?"

"I might. If you behave yourself." She returned his grin with ready affection. Then – "I'll let you out through the garden. It'll be quicker going round by the stables than all along the road. And you can have a quick peep at the baby."

"Won't it wake him up?"

"Not if we don't make a noise."

Leaving their tea things to be tidied later, she led the way down the scullery passage to the door at the end, and through that into the garden behind the house. The September sun was beginning to sink now, its light rimming the tops of the lime trees, and the shadow of their leafy branches stretched across the lawn to the maroon and cream perambulator standing there.

A fine gauze net had been attached from the hood to the handle to keep away flies, as well as deter next-door's cat from jumping up inside on the sleeping infant; and as Florrie and her betrothed approached, she remarked on the fact that one side of the net had come unfastened.

"If I just lift it up a bit, you can see him," she whispered, taking the corner loop to raise it.

Wally dutifully bent forward, with that expression upon his face men generally wear when confronted with other people's babies.

After a moment or so, the expression altered to a slight frown.

"Here, Florrie, does he look alright to you?" he said, very quietly, out of the corner of his mouth.

"How d'you mean?" She leaned forward in turn to look under the net. Then her hand went to her face.

"Oh, my Lor' – "

She pulled the net away completely. Baby George Bethway lay motionless on his side, swaddled lightly in a blanket, his head with its fuzz of fine dark hair turned towards the undersheet so that only the tiny profile showed.

Cautiously, the young woman reached out and touched

241

the rounded cheek. The peach-bloom skin felt unnaturally cold.

She turned to Wally. "I think you'd best go in and fetch Mrs Bethway."

He did not need to ask why. He had seen death before, and even upon the face of one so newly born, there was no mistaking the blue-white waxen pallor of its mark.

The house was quiet again now. Marion had been put to bed under sedation by Dr Marshall. The baby's body had been removed to The Victoria Hospital for examination. The two little girls, May and Angela, had been kept out of the way upstairs in the nursery till both were asleep.

No one had closed the curtains in the drawing room, and the tall, dark rectangles of its windows framed the lawn outside, empty now, and silvered by moonlight between the fingering shadows.

A message sent to Southwood Place had brought Dinah Enderby to do what little she could for her bereaved sister-in-law. Once the sedative had taken effect she'd come downstairs again to sit with Francis here in the drawing room, keeping a silent vigil while her brother drank himself to the point where his pain exchanged the vicious sharpness of its edge for the blunted ache of misery.

It was now half past ten, and she was beginning to wonder whether she ought to stay the night, or walk down to the station and take a hansom cab back to Southwood Place.

She put aside the book she'd been picking through and looked up at the slumped figure in the chair opposite.

"Francis – " she began, hesitantly.

The sudden sound of her voice in the long stillness penetrated the fog of his mind and he raised his head from between his hands.

"Francis, shall I sleep here tonight – in case Marion should need me?"

He squinted across at her.

Several moments went by. She tried again.

"Did you hear what I said?"

This time there was an answer.

"Yes. I heard you."

"Well – ?"

"You may please yourself what you do." He sounded indifferent, but Dinah detected the underlying current of tension in her brother's tone.

"Then I think I'd best stay," she responded practically. "The state you're in, you'd be little use to her if she went into another attack of hysteria, and it isn't fair to expect Florrie to cope alone. She has the children to look after."

Francis grunted.

After a further few seconds of silence, he said abruptly, "Should I write to Eastbourne – to Mother, d'you think? They'd been told, hadn't they, about the baby's birth?"

"Yes, Marion informed them. And yes, I think it only right you should let them know what's happened."

"I suppose there'll be the very deuce to pay because I hadn't had the little chap baptised."

"That wasn't your fault, Francis. You're not to blame. You were going to have the ceremony at the regiment's chapel next month, Marion told me."

He grunted again, and reached for the glass of brandy and soda on the side-table at his elbow. Though he'd drunk almost half a bottle of spirits in the past hour, there was no unsteadiness in his movement, no slur in his voice, nothing to betray its effect but a slight unfocused look about his eyes.

"Where's he gone, d'you think, Dinah?"

"They've removed him to the Victoria, Dr Marshall told you."

"I don't mean that. I mean, where's he gone if he can't be taken up to heaven?"

Dinah glanced down at her hands. The only emotion she had ever previously witnessed in her brother was that of selfish anger, and she found it curiously embarrassing to see sudden tears spring into his eyes as he said this. He had been raised in the tenets of the Anglican Church, yet even so, who would have supposed that the teachings of childhood could have lingered so long in the background of his mind.

"Of course the innocent mite will get into heaven," she said, just a little uncomfortably.

"But he hadn't been christened – "

"Now, Francis, you are not to think about such things.

243

You're upset, dreadfully upset. The whole thing has come as such a harrowing shock. All we can do is to trust in God's mercy that the baby is already in His safe-keeping."

"How like Mother you sound. That's exactly the kind of thing she would have said. Trust in God's mercy!"

He gave a loud, humourless laugh and drained his glass.

"Where was God today, I'd like to know," he went on again, wiping the back of his hand across his mouth. "Where was God when my son's life was being snuffed out like a twopenny candle. Visiting the sins of the fathers, I suppose."

He hauled himself to his feet to go over to the sideboard.

"Join me in another drink?"

"No, I won't, thanks."

He poured more brandy and added a splash of soda. Without turning, he said, "You think it was an accident, don't you . . . what happened here this afternoon."

"But of course it was an accident. Dr Marshall said – "

"I heard what Dr Marshall said, Dinah. The net wasn't properly fixed to the perambulator, he said. Possibly a cat or something might have got in and lain on the baby's face, he said. Smothered the little fellow . . . "

Francis's voice faltered. He took a gulp from his glass.

"It does happen," his sister told him quietly.

"I don't believe it. I don't believe that's the reason my son died." He looked at her across his shoulder. "Oh, he was smothered, all right. But not by any next-door cat."

"Francis, do please stop this! You're only tormenting yourself. We won't have an answer until there's been a proper examination."

"Didn't you hear what I said, Dinah?"

He turned round to face her again. In the pallid light of the ceiling lamp she could see a sudden dull rage in his expression.

"My son was smothered. Deliberately. To pay me back in a way that would hurt me hardest."

"You've had too much to drink – " She made to get up from her chair.

"No. Stay here and listen to me. Don't you see? It was Marion who killed him. I loved that child more than anything in the world, and she knew that. She stifled him with her hand – a pillow – I don't know – because I'd broken my word and gone back to Sissy Desatti."

"My God, you don't know what you're saying!" Almost transfixed with disbelief, Dinah stared at him. "*Marion* killed her own baby – out of revenge? Is that what you think?"

"Yes. She threatened me she'd do it. If I didn't mend my ways, she said. I wasn't a fit father to bring up any son . . . "

Francis Bethway closed his eyes. The muscles in his neck stood out like shadowed cords. For a few moments there was an awful, numbing silence in the room as his anger ebbed away again into grief.

Then he went on, brokenly, "Oh, but she'll pay for it. Our marriage is finished. I've done with her. When she took the life from that child, she forfeited her right to remain my wife."

23

"Well, this is a fine how d'you do," said Warwick
Enderby, folding back the pages of his *Sussex Express*,
"your family getting its name all over the newspapers."

Dinah treated him to a look of her usual polite indifference and carried on arranging a vase of michaelmas daisies
and late-flowering chrysanthemums.

"I'd hardly call a report of a Coroner's inquest being 'all
over the newspapers'."

"It's not the inquest I'm on about, old girl. It's this piece
here – "

He turned the page towards her and indicated a boldly-
printed headline. "'Bereaved father demanded full investigation.' Haven't you seen it?"

"No. And before you start – I don't wish to hear it, thank
you." She picked up another spray and began stripping off
the leaves.

Warwick watched her expressionless face for a moment or
so, then with a shrug flicked the tip of his cigarette against
the ash-tray and went back to reading in silence.

The inquest into baby George's death had taken place at
Francis Bethway's insistence amid circumstances which had
aroused a good deal of local speculation. He had refused to
accept the result of Dr Marshall's post-mortem examination,
which found death to be due to inhibition of the vagus nerve
– a natural malfunction which had caused the infant to cease
breathing – and instead contended most strongly that his
son's untimely demise had been brought about by means of
foul play. He had not gone so far as publicly to name his
wife: he had no need. Those who knew the state of their
marriage were not slow to see for themselves which way the
finger of suspicion appeared to point.

A public enquiry had therefore duly been held, to satisfy
the requirements of the Law where possible doubt existed as
to the precise cause of death.

Captain Bethway being who he was, a commissioned officer holding the Military Cross, the inquest attracted the attention of the local Press, who accorded it an unnecessarily sensational coverage in their columns. After all, nothing much had been happening to exercise their talents since T.W. Burgess swam the English Channel a few weeks earlier.

The judgement of the court, confirming Dr Marshall's opinion that baby George Bethway had died from natural causes, came as something of an anti-climax, and rumour-whetted appetites had had to be satisfied with picking over the scraps in search of something tasty.

Warwick Enderby broke the silence of the morning room again.

"It says here your sister-in-law has left her husband. Taken the two children and gone."

"Where does it say that!" Angrily, Dinah threw down her scissors and came round the table.

"Here. On page four." He held the newspaper out for her. "'Dramatic good-bye at station'."

She snatched the offending paper from his hand.

"Oh, what ridiculous nonsense!" she exclaimed, reading quickly through the report. "Of course little Angela would make a fuss at being parted from her pet dog. I wonder Marion hadn't the sense to see that before letting the child take it on to the platform. As for leaving Francis – "

She tossed the paper aside on the table. "For heaven's sake, all she's done is gone away with the children to visit her family for a while. These past weeks have taxed her terribly. The poor woman needs a long rest, away from all this – this relentless publicity."

Warwick made no comment, merely smiled in a somewhat cynical fashion as he tilted back his head to blow out a cloud of cigarette smoke.

Returning to her flowers, Dinah took up the vase and carried it over to a small gate-legged table in the bay window.

"At least it rather evens things up between us," he said after a pause, watching her.

"What things?" She didn't bother to turn round, but stood there with her back to him, looking out at the sombre autumn scene.

247

"Well – my brothers being detained as guests of His Majesty."

Her gaze followed the flight of a flock of sparrows across the leaf-littered terrace. "I hardly see the connection between that and what's happened here."

"It's the notoriety, old girl. Names in the newspapers. There's nothing sticks as persistently as printer's ink."

"Your brothers received no more than they deserved. Perhaps six months in prison will teach them to respect other people's property."

Her tone was flat and showed not the slightest interest in what she was saying. A month or so earlier, Guy and Neville Enderby had been together found guilty of the fraudulent misuse of a large sum of money entrusted to them for investment by a particularly gullible young woman. Dinah's only comment at the time had been to liken that case to her own: as part of their attempted "reconciliation" Warwick had confessed that the three hundred pounds borrowed at the start of their relationship to tide him over after forfeiting bail for a friend, had been acquired totally under false pretences. The truth of the matter was that the friend – whom he'd described as an officer in the Seaforth Highlanders – was in fact a chicken farmer who had emigrated to South Australia several years before to scratch an honest living on the outskirts of Adelaide.

The revelation had hardly helped to smooth things between the two of them.

"Oh, by the by – " Warwick stubbed out his cigarette and stretched himself languidly before getting to his feet. "I shall be away from Lewes next week. Just thought I'd tell you."

Dinah remained where she was, still looking out across the terrace. "How kind. As long as you're back for Bonfire Night."

"Why, what's happening on Bonfire Night?"

"You have a very short memory." She turned slowly, quite unconscious of the dramatic effect created by the steel-grey light falling upon her from the window.

"It happens to be the one night of the year when the streets of Lewes are not safe for an unaccompanied woman to be out on after dark."

"Oh, come now, old thing – a few high-spirited chaps letting off fireworks?" He laughed dismissively.

"It's rather more than 'a few chaps letting off fireworks', Warwick, and you know it. Not all that long ago someone was burnt to death because of the lighted torches they fling about. I don't want anything similar happening to me. Now, I have to be at the Picture Theatre that evening, and since Algie has given in his notice and won't be here, I'd be much obliged if *you* would trouble yourself to escort me safely home."

He sketched her a mock bow of respectful obedience.

"It shall be as you command, O Dinah dear."

Then, hands thrust deep into his trouser pockets, he turned and sauntered away towards the door, whistling a snatch of song: a man to all appearances without a single care in the world.

" – And you'd better make some arrangement about the dog. Put it into kennels until you can find someone to take it."

Francis Bethway inspected himself in the mirror above the Dutch-tile fireplace. Behind him, across his shoulder, the housemaid's face was reflected as a pale oval of consternation beneath her white lace cap.

"Someone to take it, sir?" she echoed stupidly. "What, take it away, d'you mean?"

"Yes, of course I mean that."

"But sir – Traddles is Miss Angela's dog, sir. It'll break her little heart to come back and find the creature gone – "

"Damn it, Florrie, do you not listen?" The Captain swung about on his heel. "This house is to be closed up for a while. Therefore provision of some kind has to be made – the animal can hardly be left here alone. Besides, Angela will have dogs a-plenty to distract her in Gloucestershire. Her grandfather breeds fox terriers."

The maid bit her lip. In the doorway behind her, the object of this discussion sat forlornly, ears drooping, eyes full of that worried sadness which speaks so eloquently of a dumb beast's anxiety. The plumy brown tail thumped

249

uncertainly as Florrie threw a quick glance round; then faltered and grew still again.

"Well – go along. Take the animal downstairs and shut it in. I don't want to find it wandering about up here." Francis Bethway spoke brusquely, a sign of his impatience.

"And would you serve tea in ten minutes."

Florrie bobbed a dutiful curtsy and moved away; but not before shooting a final sideways look at the young woman who had been sitting all this time in silence at the opposite side of the fireplace.

As she said to her fiancé Corporal Jackson afterwards – what a thing, imagine bringing *her* here; you'd think the Captain would have more sense of what was decent and proper than go flaunting his fancy-piece in front of servants in his own house.

It would probably not have made much difference to Florrie's indignation to learn that Cecilia Desatti had been reluctant to come to Warren Street. All along, she'd known it wasn't right for her to enter the home of a woman whom she'd displaced in her husband's affections; and having allowed herself to be persuaded otherwise, she was now feeling guilty, embarrassed, and rather uncomfortable.

"It doesn't matter about having any tea, Frank," she said, as soon as the drawing room door had closed on Florrie and the disconsolate Traddles. "I'd much rather not bother, not for the moment."

"I've ordered it now."

He moved to the side of her chair and stroked the back of his fingers across her cheek, not looking down but keeping his eyes fixed ahead towards the windows. He had stared so often these past weeks at their view of the garden that he could see its every detail in his mind: the border of flower-beds, the path to the stables, the line of trees and the lawn, lying like an empty stage-set, somehow unreal now that the tragedy was ended and the players departed.

Aloud he said, as though continuing a conversation with himself, "Did she do it here in the house, I wonder? Did she kill him in the nursery and carry his body down to put in the perambulator, as though nothing had happened? Or did she wait until he was asleep out there before she – "

"If you're going to start about that again, I'm off," Sissy told him sharply, jerking away her head and half-rising from the chair. "I've just about had enough of it. Morbid, that's what you are, the way you keep harping on all the while. You heard what was said at the inquest."

"Yes, I heard." Francis seemed to be repeating something he knew by heart. "There was no bruising, no sign of blood in the air passage, no evidence at all to suggest manual suffocation."

"There you are, then." The girl sat back again, sullenly. "I don't know why you can't accept that."

"Marion said – "

"Oh, Marion said! Here we go again. Marion said she'd smother the baby if you didn't stop carrying on with me. And now you think she went and did it, just to show you what for."

"Damn it, Sissy, d'you imagine I *want* to believe she was responsible?"

There was an exaggerated shrug. "Why ask me? It's you that's been kicking up such a song and dance about the whole thing. Anyway, I'm pushing off, Frank. I should never have come here, I know I shouldn't. I feel as though – well, as though everything's looking at me."

This time she got to her feet and stood away from him. Her face had grown thinner in recent weeks, drawing the olive skin tight over the cheek-bones and making her eyes more cat-like than ever.

"I said it was wrong of you to bring me. Your maid thought so as well, I could see that."

"Florrie can mind her own business. She's getting a good enough reference."

"She'd rather stay in service where she is. Do you really have to close the house up?"

He nodded, letting his gaze wander around, at the room where his marriage had not been entirely without its moments of happiness. "There's no point in me staying on when I have quarters at the barracks."

"Isn't she coming back, then – your wife?"

"She said she wouldn't. What with one thing and another. And I certainly don't want to see her here again."

251

Sissy picked up her red velvet tam o'shanter from beside the chair.

"Looks like you're going to be left on your own, then, doesn't it."

"On my own, yes. But not quite alone. I can think of someone who'll still be around to keep me company." Her lover came towards her, with something of the old self-assured smile lifting the corner of his mouth, and made to pull her into his arms.

She resisted, twisting herself away and pretending to tidy her hair in the mirror before putting on her hat, fussing with it to get it at exactly the right angle on the side of her head.

"Then you'd best make the most of me while you can, Frank," she told him off-handedly, eyeing herself.

"Make the most of you? What d'you mean?"

A shrug. "That I shan't be here all that much longer."

There was a moment's long silence; and then, a faint note of impatience back in his tone, he said, "You're not still on about New York, are you? I thought that business had been settled, and you weren't to go."

"I never said that."

"Not in so many words. But you told me nothing more had been mentioned about it at home."

"Well it has been mentioned now." She looked at him through the mirror. "They're packing me off next spring."

"Next spring – ?" He stared back across her shoulder. "Good God . . . but that's less than six months away! You're not really going, are you?"

"Yes."

Roughly he pulled her round to face him, staring down into her dark eyes as though trying to read the truth there. She had a way of saying things in apparent seriousness without meaning them in the least, and this had led more than once to the pair of them being completely at cross purposes with one another. Sissy found it amusing to see him floundering about trying to keep up with her sudden jumps from poker-faced facetiousness to teasing honesty: it was one of her less endearing traits that watching others make uncertain fools of themselves appealed to her sense of the ridiculous in people.

252

"Now what's this about, eh? What's got into you?" Francis gave her a shake. "You don't like being here in this house. Very well, we'll leave and go somewhere else together. Or is it me that you don't like – is that it? Is this sudden put-on act of indifference telling me it's time we ended our relationship for good and went our separate ways?"

He shook her again, harder, almost in desperation. "Come on, let's have the truth from you for once, Cecilia."

His formal use of her real name instead of the pet one by which he always called her halted the show of temper she'd been about to loose on him.

She turned her face away and indulged herself instead in a sullen pout.

"You go on about your wife – about what she might have done. You push her off back to her parents. You tell me your marriage is over and finished. But you never say what *I'll* get out of it, do you – "

She stopped suddenly. There was a knock at the drawing-room door, repeated.

Francis dropped his hands from her shoulders. "Yes!" he called harshly.

The knob turned, and after a moment Florrie came in, pushing open the door with her hip since both hands were occupied with a laden tea-tray. From behind her, faint in the background, a muted howling rose from somewhere in the depths of the house.

"Where shall I put the tray, sir?"

"Oh – down over there." He gestured impatiently.

The maid did as she was bid, then went back towards the door, not looking at either her master or his mistress.

"Will there be anything more, sir?"

"Yes – " came in Sissy, before he could open his mouth to say no. "I'd like my coat, please."

"Your coat, Miss. Very well, Miss."

The door was closed again, shutting out the mournful noise from below.

Guiltily almost, the pair in the room looked at one another in silence, the girl's expression tight and sulky-lipped, her lover's full of troubled resentment.

253

When the coat appeared, it was Francis who came forward to take it, saying, "Thank you, that will be all. I'll see the visitor out myself." And when the door had closed a second time – "Now let's have this clear between the two of us. You are not leaving this house until we've decided exactly where we stand with one another."

He threw the coat over the back of a chair, and reaching forward, plucked the red tam o'shanter from Sissy's head and tossed that in the same direction.

Her response was a loud, exaggerated sigh as she made to snatch it up again. "It's no use. I'm going. I've said all I've got to say."

"Maybe. But I haven't. Now sit down!" The tea-tray with its second-best china stood ignored on the table behind. "It's time we began thinking about our future – if you want to share one with me."

"That's up to you, isn't it, Frank." She swung round on him, the hat clutched in her hand. "I'll tell you something, though. I'm glad I'm being sent away. Yes – *glad*. Because it means I'll find out once and for all whether you want me because you really love me, or whether you've just been making a convenience of me."

"I love you! For God's sake, don't you know that yet? I love you, Sissy. Now please – sit down."

"No, I won't. You still haven't answered my question."

"Which question?" The illogicality of her conversation baffled him.

"The one I was asking when the maid came in just now. What am *I* going to get out of all this?"

"All this? You mean . . . the wreckage of my marriage?"

She nodded sullenly.

"But isn't that obvious, my darling?"

"Not to me, Frank. There's one word you've never used once – and that's divorce."

Its sound hung between them in the silent room like an accusation.

There was a pause before he answered.

"If only things were as simple as that," he said at last, slowly. "I've thought about divorce, of course I have. But I still have two young children to consider."

"Not to mention your Army promotion and your social reputation, I suppose," she came back at him quickly.

"My social reputation can go hang. In fact, it probably already has, thanks to all the mud stirred up by the Press. As for my promotion – " Francis paused again; then after a moment raised his broad shoulders. "Well, since this is a time for telling the truth, I'll be honest with you, sweetheart. My son's death has unsettled me. I don't seem to have the same ambitions for myself anymore. Everything's . . . I don't know – *changed*, somehow, as though I'm looking at my life from a different point of view. The fact is, I'm seriously thinking of buying myself out of Army service and making a completely fresh start with a career in civilian life."

This candid admission took all the heat from Sissy's ill-humour. In the few seconds it took for the words to sink in, her expression had quickened from petulance to a sharp curiosity.

"You've never mentioned this before."

"No. I've only recently begun to consider the possibility."

"But . . . what would you do, if you came out?"

"I don't know yet. It's something I'll have to discuss with you."

"With me?" She laughed suddenly, disbelieving, the curiosity in turn giving way to a pleased bewilderment. "Why with me, Frank?"

"Because any decision I make is bound to affect our future together. And there's no need to look at me in that fashion, as though you think this is more of my double-dealing."

"Isn't it?"

"Not this time. Now do as you're told – come and sit down." He took the tam o'shanter from her and put it aside, then drew her with him on to his lap in the winged armchair.

"Let's stop this silly arguing, shall we – "

She smiled at him out of the corner of her eye.

" – and tell me you love me instead."

Another quarrel was ended. Behind them, quite forgotten now, the tea grew cold in its pot under the daisy-embroidered cosy.

After a while, he leaned back in the chair, his arms still tight about her small waist.

"Now listen, Sissy – " he began; only to be silenced again by another of her kisses.

He tried once more. "Listen – I've had an idea. Only an idea, mind, but I think it may be the answer. I'm strongly tempted to try my luck in America. No, don't interrupt! *Listen*, I said. It seems the place of opportunity for a man like me with experience and training and a sound background. In fact, the more I think about it, the more I'm persuaded it's worth the gamble. So what do you think, my lovely? Would that satisfy you?"

Her face was a picture. "You mean – you mean start a new life, the two of us together, over in New York?"

Despite the half-smile, there was a note of gravity in Francis Bethway's answer.

"Yes. Mr and Mrs Frank Morgan. Why not? We could even sail on the same crossing. Once we were on the other side of the Atlantic, no one would ever know what had become of us."

24

A letter had arrived, addressed to Ellis Bates, Esquire, and couched in that graciously courteous tone which is the hallmark of true nobility. It expressed the wish that Miss Laura Bates might be allowed to stay as weekend guest of the Viscount Monchelsea and his wife the Viscountess, at Bells Yew Abbey. It was understood, naturally, that a chaperone would be in attendance.

Despite his festering resentment at the manner in which he'd been coerced into accepting Algie Langton-Smythe as his daughter's suitor, Ellis Bates had been privately somewhat flattered to receive this invitation. It meant an entrée for Laura into the cream of English society; and whether or not one approved of the misplaced idealism which had driven young Algie into the wider world of lesser mortals, now that he appeared to be stepping back into line again and deferring to his parents' wishes, he was being viewed in a slightly less jaundiced light by H.M. Schools Inspector for Lewes.

The visit to Bells Yew Abbey in September had proved quietly successful. Lord Monchelsea had permitted himself to be captivated by Laura's demure charm, and though his lady wife might murmur at the girl's lack of pedigree, at least she came from good bourgeois stock with the Church and the Law as escutcheons, and her mother's people, the Lovells, could trace their lineage back to the medieval Barons Lovell, one of whom was promoted to the office of Lord Chamberlain by Richard the Third.

Besides, Algie was only a younger son. So long as the girl's father was not in Trade, it hardly disgraced the family that he held no seat in the House of Lords.

The elder son and heir, Lord Burrswode – a more dapper and drawling edition of his brother – had been absent that weekend; but their sister Georgiana was there, and after

257

some initial awkwardness had welcomed Laura as a "chum" much in the manner of Elinor Brent Dyer, whose girls' adventure stories she found "utterly spiffing".

All in all, it had been a satisfactory introduction, as even Her Ladyship allowed at the end of the visit, being graciously pleased to extend a second invitation upon the occasion of her daughter's sixteenth birthday early in October.

Little more than a week after this event, and with his father's permission, Algie presented himself at Spences Lane for the purpose of making a formal proposal for Laura's hand in marriage. Recalling the painful incident of his first interview with Mr Bates, he had dressed himself with impeccable correctness in a flannel single-breasted suit, linen winged collar and coloured silk bow-tie, his rebellious ginger hair parted at the centre and brushed to a lacquered shine with macassar oil. He had wished to be judged upon his own merit; but quite unconsciously, signalled the quality of his background by the gold-headed cane beneath his arm, his hand-sewn white buckskin shoes, and the family-crest intaglio set in the signet ring upon his little finger.

The young man's appearance – so different from that of the threadbare violin-player of first acquaintance – had undoubtedly impressed Ellis Bates; that, and his prompt-to-the-second punctuality. Moreover, the older man would have been less than a middle-class snob had he not acknowledged the honour being paid to his family and felt himself swell a little with the self-importance of being addressed so very humbly and civilly by one who was several degrees his social superior. It had also occurred to him that were anything unforeseen to happen to Lord Burrswode to remove him from his inheritance, the title would devolve upon this young man and his wife; and the prospect of his daughter possibly – just possibly – one day becoming a viscountess was most gratifying to ponder upon.

So it was that when the Honourable Algernon Edward Victor Langton-Smythe formally presented himself as a future son-in-law, he received a frosty but favourable response. Laura was his – though upon one condition: that her companion Megwynn Evans be retired forthwith from further service.

"I must say, that does seem a bit strong!" Mrs Esmond Bates declared. She and her husband, with Algie and Laura and Dinah Enderby, were enjoying a small supper party at Desatti's to celebrate the young couple's engagement.

"Did you agree to it?"

Her question – blunt and to the point as usual – seemed to cause Laura some discomfort, for she cast a quick, nervous look towards her brother.

"Jessie dear, one of these days someone is going to tell you to mind your own business," Esmond said, not unkindly.

"Oh, they have already. Frequently. But it still doesn't stop me being curious."

She tilted her head sideways under its smart little toque and smiled at Algie.

"Well? *Did* you agree to Father-in-law's demand?"

The other opened his mouth to say something; then hesitated, heartily wishing he'd never mentioned the matter.

"You may as well tell her," prompted Dinah from across the table. "You know what she's been like these past weeks about Miss Evans, imagining there's some terrible secret being concealed."

"Actually . . . " Algie cleared his throat. "Actually, as a matter of fact . . . yes, we did agree – "

"There you are, what did I say!" Jessie interrupted triumphantly before he could go a word further; only to be at once interrupted herself by her husband saying, "Oh, do shut up, dearest, and let the fellow finish now that you've nagged him into giving an answer."

She threw up her hands in a gesture of mock-surrender and sat back in her chair.

Keeping a wary eye on her, Algie began again, "If I tell you what's happened, you'll keep it under your hat, won't you. It's not that Laura and I want to deceive her father in any way . . . as I said, we agreed to his condition. Only you see, we simply couldn't discard Miss Evans like an old boot – "

Jessie let out a snort at this description, but resisted the temptation to comment.

"So to play fair all round, what we have done is this." The young man shot a hurried glance towards the neighbouring table and lowered his voice. "Laura has given Miss Evans a month's marching orders, as it were, and in the meanwhile I'm arranging for her to have the tenancy of one of our grace and favour cottages– as a retired employee, you understand."

"That's a neat way of solving the difficulty," observed Dinah, looking up from the menu she was reading.

"Isn't it, though. It was Esmond who thought of it."

"Esmond – ?" Jessie sat forward sharply. "He never told me!"

"And can you wonder," her husband remarked, again without any ill-feeling. "You'd have smelled a rat straight away."

"But what if Mr Bates should discover what you've done?" Dinah asked, ignoring her friend's pretended show of indignation at this signal lack of trust. "Couldn't you be accused of breaking your word of honour, Algie?"

"Oh, no. At least, I hope not! His concern was that Miss Evans mustn't continue in service as Laura's companion. And this way she doesn't. She becomes a private tenant of my father's. I don't see that Mr Bates can quibble about that."

"But *why* should he demand such a condition in the first place?" Jessie came in again, ignoring the menu which her husband was trying to push in front of her. "What is this great and awful mystery that hangs about Miss Evans? The woman's been in service at Spences Lane for years and years. If there were anything unsatisfactory or objectionable, why should Father-in-law wait so long before contriving her dismissal? It's all *most* peculiar. And if you want my opinion – "

"But we don't, Jessie." Esmond spoke for the others. "We have had your opinion upon the subject already. Several times. Now I suggest, my dear, that you give your attention to this excellent bill of fare, knowing what an age you generally take to make up your mind and then change it again."

"Listen to him – isn't he a bully!" His wife took the menu folder from him and made a show of reading through it quickly. "Why on earth I married him, I really cannot think.

Be warned, Laura darling – men are the most deceiving creatures. As bachelors they give entirely the wrong impression, being attentive, courteous, kind and infinitely flattering. But the moment they acquire you as a wife, why, all that flies out of the window! Overnight, they undergo some horrid alteration and you wake to find yourself wed to some crusty, impatient, negligent boor who treats you as though matrimony were a trap you set deliberately to ruin his life. And if you want the perfect example of that, then you've only to take poor Dinah – "

"Jessie dear, if you have one fault, it's that you never know when to be quiet." Esmond's tone had suddenly taken on a note of censure, and the glance which accompanied his words was sufficiently unsmiling to warn his wife that she was in danger of letting her bright chatter spoil their evening's celebration.

She subsided at once, with a little shrug of defiance, and gave herself to examining the choice of supper dishes in studied silence.

Dinah met Laura's eye across the table and gave a smile in return for the other's look of sympathy.

"I'm told you've acquired a dog," said Algie, tactfully quick to change the subject. "In fact, didn't I see you out with one yesterday?"

"Oh, yes. That's Traddles." Dinah's smile widened. "A very athletic young animal. The only way to have any peace in the house is to take him on five-mile walks at frequent intervals."

"What variety of breed is he?" Laura wanted to know, brightening visibly at this chance to talk about something which interested her.

"To be honest, I'm not quite sure. Mostly spaniel, I think, with perhaps a dash of terrier."

"And where did you get him?"

"Well, actually, he belongs to my young niece. I'm taking care of him while the family's away for a while."

This was the truth; though not the whole truth. Dinah had happened to be coming along Lewes high street a week earlier just as her brother's housemaid, Florrie Cox, was approaching from the opposite direction at the end of

Traddles's leash. Naturally, she had paused to exchange a quick word and a pat, and had learned from the young woman that the pair were on their way to the Daisy Bank Home for Dumb Comrades across the river at Cliffe. Upon hearing why (and Florrie had needed no second asking before she'd unburdened herself at length and in detail) Dinah's instant reaction was one of indignation that her brother should dispose of his little daughter's pet in quite such a heartless fashion.

There was no question that Traddles should be abandoned to the unknown – perhaps even to end up as dogsmeat himself – and assuring Florrie that she would deal with the matter personally, Dinah had taken him home to Southwood Place as an orphan from the storm of the Bethways' domestic upheaval.

Having rather more sense than he was credited with, the dog had settled in at once, making immediate allies of Jane and Mrs Smith in the kitchen – who promptly spoilt him – keeping down the rats in the wash-house, seeing off the neighbourhood cats from the vegetable garden, and only so far disgracing himself on one occasion when he'd shown his teeth at the postman.

"We always longed for a dog of our own when we were children, didn't we, Esmond," Laura said wistfully, after a slight pause in the conversation. "For some reason, Papa would never allow us to have one – "

Realising she'd inadvertently strayed back on to the closed subject of her father, she bit her lip and was trying to think of what else to say to disguise the gaffe when Jessie interrupted suddenly with – "Ah, here's Stephen at last!" making an exaggerated waving gesture in the direction of her brother, at that moment entering the dining room from the street.

Divesting himself of coat, hat, scarf and gloves, which one of the staff took from him, he was shown towards their table.

"Sorry to be delayed," he announced as a chair was drawn out for him next to Dinah's, "hope I haven't kept you waiting too long."

"Not at all, old chap," Esmond assured him. "We said eight o'clock, but I knew you'd probably be held up in

262

Weatherfield with that last client, so we haven't ordered yet."

The latecomer greeted the others, leaning across to shake hands with Algie before seating himself and taking the menu offered him by the waiter.

"Well, congratulations are in order, I believe," he said, glancing quickly down the bill of fare then up again at the young couple opposite. "My very warmest wishes to you both. Have you decided yet upon the day?"

"We thought Midsummer Eve," Algie replied for them both. "Though we're not quite sure which year. Either '13 or '14."

"You won't leave it too long, will you." Esmond reached to accept the wine list he'd requested. "I don't wish to sound gloomy, but this business out in the Balkans worries me rather. There may be trouble brewing for us there, and if so I'd feel happier knowing Laura was married and settled in her own home before it blows up into something serious."

This observation was greeted with a dry laugh from his wife beside him.

"Hark to the skeleton at the feast! Really, Esmond, I do hope you're not going to start talking politics again. Not this evening."

"He's right, though." Stephen Moore finished studying his menu and pushed it away. "If the Balkan League move against Turkey, as seems likely, it could very well mean an outbreak of war – "

"So? Turks, Serbs, Greeks, Bulgars – they're always fighting each other over one thing or another. It's a national pastime. Why on earth should *we* be concerned in their backyard squabbles?"

"Because, Jessie dear, we have treaties with these people. If they're attacked, we are bound as allies to go to their assistance."

"How terribly boring." She pretended to yawn. "Well, if you two intend playing soldiers through the meal, Dinah and I will begin our own little discussion of the suffragist movement – and you know how that annoys you."

Esmond ignored this threat entirely.

"I think we'll order now, shall we?" he said, addressing

263

himself to the others. "I can recommend the veal collops, if anyone's interested. I had some here the other week – they were excellent."

While the serious business of the evening got underway, conversation became general and it was not until they'd finished the first course and were starting on the second that Dinah and Stephen began a private exchange between themselves.

Under cover of the surrounding laughter and chatter from the rest of the dining room, he said quietly, "By the way, I was sorry to learn about your brother and his family troubles. It must be difficult for you not to take sides, being so involved."

"Oh, I don't know, Stephen. There's never been much love lost between Francis and me. I've known him too long and too well. It's Marion I feel sorry for. She's done the right thing by leaving him, in my opinion."

"She *has* left him, then?"

"That's what he tells me. In fact, to hear him talk, you'd think the affair was her fault entirely!"

Stephen helped himself to some more potato. "Is the separation permanent, do you suppose?"

"I've no idea. I hope not, for the children's sake. Though for the same reason, I do think it's best they're apart for a while. Francis is behaving quite obnoxiously just now, and it can't be good for little Angela especially to be exposed to all the unpleasantness of it."

Dinah shook her head as she was offered a further serving of vegetables; and applying herself instead to the apple sauce, went on, "Heaven knows, poor Marion needed a month or two away from him. She was on the verge of a nervous collapse after losing her baby in the dreadfully tragic way that she did."

"And nothing that's happened since can have helped her very much." The other finished his wine, and accepting the carafe from Esmond on his left, refilled his companion's glass before attending to his own.

"Incidentally, did you know that one of your brother's little problems is at this moment standing over there, by the cloakroom door?"

He indicated with his head.

264

"What do you mean? That young waitress?" Dinah turned to look over her shoulder across the busy dining room to where a slim dark-haired girl in black dress and white apron was just taking a customer's coat.

"Cecilia Desatti. Otherwise known as Sissy," said Stephen.

"Oh – ! So *that's* Sissy!"

"Yes. I wonder you hadn't noticed her staring at you. Obviously she knows who you are."

"Do you think so?"

A nod. "Someone must have pointed you out to her. Your brother, perhaps. I saw them both together, you know, one day in the summer on Brighton Promenade. Their conduct was – well, shall we say not entirely discreet, and from that and what you'd told me already, I rather gathered this must be the lady-friend."

At that moment Jessie chose to address a question to Stephen, obliging him to break off his conversation in order to give her an answer. The interruption provided Dinah with an opportunity to study the young woman who'd been the cause of so much upset in the Bethway domestic circle, and shifting her chair slightly so that her brief observation was not apparent, she was able to keep a covert watch on Cecilia Desatti.

The other's sultry attractions were obvious even from this distance, and the way she moved, head held proudly on its shapely neck, hips swaying with a natural grace beneath the pleated folds of her skirt, showed Dinah what it was that had drawn her brother Francis like a moth to a flame.

More than once at the house in Warren Street she had heard Marion rail against this unknown Jezebel who had besotted her husband – words which held fear as well as anger, for although Francis had been unfaithful time upon time before, this was the first woman he had openly admitted, in one of their quarrels, being unable to get out of his system by the simple expediency of seduction.

Having seen her now with her own eyes, Dinah could understand a little better why he'd found it so difficult to finish the affaire; though she could still not forgive him for it. Whatever its romantic interpretation, whatever its disguise or its excuse, adultery was adultery, the deliberate breaking

265

of vows; and those who practised it as frequently and casually as Francis put themselves beyond the pale of sympathy.

"Sorry – " Stephen turned back again to take up the thread of their conversation. "Jessie was asking about a cousin of Mother's. A somewhat eccentric old bird."

"The cousin, you mean?"

He laughed. "Yes, the cousin. Though I fear my sister may well be taking after her."

There was a pause while he finished the last of the food on his plate; then he went on again, this time more seriously, "By the way, speaking of lady-friends just now . . . is your husband at home at the moment, may I ask?"

"Not until Friday evening. Why?"

He lowered his voice further. "Then may I call to see you tomorrow? I have some information I'm sure you'll want to hear."

"Oh? What kind of information?" Interest sharpened Dinah's tone. Putting down her wine glass she looked at her companion, and seeing him give a little shake of the head, said quickly, "It concerns Warwick? Tell me."

"No, not here, Dinah. This is hardly the place."

"But it *is* about Warwick?"

There was a hesitation.

"Yes."

"Something serious? Tell me now, Stephen, please. I want to know."

"Well . . . " He leaned sideways, pretending to glance across his shoulder at the crowded tables behind. "I've proof that he's seeing another woman. Sorry, my dear. Rather bad news, I'm afraid. But it means your case for separation is strengthened."

"That's not bad news!"

Dinah took up her glass again as though she would raise it in a toast, and there was a smile upon her lips which could almost be described as one of cheerful elation.

"My husband, seeing another woman? Why, Stephen – that's the best thing I've heard in years!"

25

Virtually ever since 1557 in the reign of "Bloody" Mary, when a number of Lewes townsfolk paid for their Protestant faith upon a pyre of flame in the market square, the celebration of the Fifth of November had been a matter of local honour. In an annual event which had its roots steeped in pagan tradition, fed by the blood of its martyrs and fuelled by anti-Catholic bitterness, the various Bonfire Societies of Lewes came together to turn the narrow streets into scenes more nearly approaching the *autos-da-fé* of medieval Spain.

Once darkness fell, bizarrely-costumed figures formed processions, lighting their way with naphthalene torches and red, blue and green Roman candles as they wound up and down the town, marching to the crash of brass bands behind banners which defiantly proclaimed "No Popery" and "Britons Never Will Be Slaves". The din was further increased by the cheers and shouts of onlookers lining the route, and the flash-bang of squibs and Chinese crackers and fearsome "Lewes Rousers" which split the night with force enough to shatter windows.

Until only recently, blazing tar barrels had been sent rolling down High Street hill to the peril of bystanders and buildings alike, and it was not uncommon for fires to be started accidentally, leaving soot-fogged walls and blistered paintwork. Indeed, even by the turn of the century when the celebrations had grown rather more orderly, it was a wise householder who closed his coal-hole, and a prudent shopkeeper who bolted his cellar trap and covered it over with wet straw.

As the evening wore away and each section of the gaudy, noisy procession passed, the smoking flare of torchlight revealed life-sized effigies borne aloft – grotesque and ridiculous caricatures of Guy Fawkes, and The Pope, and whatever public figure currently happened to be out of favour. At their passage the crowded streets erupted into catcalls and abuse, which later into the night would be changed to cheers as the effigies writhed in the flaming holocausts of bonfires on the waste lands of the town.

This year, the rag-stuffed dummy being chaired along by the Boys was that of the Chancellor, Mr Lloyd George, who had made himself decidedly unpopular with his National Insurance Bill, proposing that each working man should make a compulsory weekly contribution from his wages as a form of social security against illness or invalidity. Pay was poor enough already without the Government dipping its fingers into the pockets of needy folk, and the Bill had attracted a good deal of bitter resentment.

Held up on her way back to the Electric Picture Theatre, Dinah Enderby could get no further than the corner of Market Street while the procession went past; and hedged in by the crush of bodies she could see little above the heads in front. Carried on invisible shoulders, Mr Lloyd George had appeared to float by on a stream of naphthalene flame, his top-hatted head with its large moustache nodding to left and right and the placard bearing his name swinging from the silk lapels of his morning coat.

With fire-crackers exploding all around, pinned back against the wall and half-deafened by the noise, she had been forced to wait until the crowd thinned out, jostling its way along the pavement in the wake of the guy, before she was able to dodge between on-coming band and banner-bearers to cross the road.

There was no evening performance at the picture house tonight. Instead, the management had shown a long matinée programme which had not ended until half-past five. Dinah had stayed behind in the building to let in the piano tuner at six o'clock; but no allowance had been made for the probability of delay, and in fact it was a good three-quarters of an hour later before the man had eventually arrived.

Leaving him to his work, she'd slipped out to find an errand boy to take a message to Southwood Place that Mr Enderby should come to meet her at nine. By then, as the processions converged on the bonfire sites, the streets in this part of the town would have started emptying, making it easier to pass –

but also increasing the risk of an unaccompanied woman being accosted by drunken stragglers whose sport it was to frighten their victims with torches tossed aside and left to burn in the gutters.

She was glad to return to the comparative peace and safety of the Picture Theatre, where the only sound away from the background noise of celebration was the ripple of piano scales filling the emptiness of the dimmed auditorium.

"I've made him a cup o' tea," the box-office lady informed her, jerking a head in the direction of the unseen tuner. "Would you care for one yourself, my duck, afore I leave?"

"No, I don't think so, thanks, Tillie. I'll have one later perhaps."

"Suit yourself, then. When he's done – " another jerk – "let yourselves out by the stage door, will you? I'm locking up here. Don't bother about a key or nothing, just pull the door to behind you as you go, and it'll shut itself."

The woman gave herself an all-over glance of inspection in the foyer mirrors.

"You're sure you'll be all right now, my duck?" she went on, straightening her coat. "I'd stay behind wi' you, but our young Alf's wi' the Commercial Square procession and I want to keep my eye on him afore he starts getting up to anything he hadn't ought."

Assured by Dinah that she was quite happy to remain here by herself until the piano tuner finished and her husband came to collect her, the other went out by the main door, pulling it shut with a bang after her and turning the key in the lock, giving the handle a good rattle to make certain everything was secure.

Her departure let in a draught of night air from outside, carrying with it a reek of smoke and smouldering rag and saltpetre into the foyer. The acrid smell seemed to permeate everywhere, and Dinah noticed that it was particularly strong still as she went down the centre aisle of the auditorium towards the orchestra pit, a fact she commented on to the tuner.

"It's some'at they've put in the rockets this year," he said, peering inside the top lid of the piano to make some adjustment to one of the tuning pins. "Sulphur, I shouldn't

269

wonder. My wife was saying earlier, the way it clings about the place."

He sounded a note, playing it rapidly several times over while listening intently, then adding it to a short scale. Apparently satisfied with the result, he turned his attention to the next key.

Leaving him to get on, Dinah took his empty cup and saucer back up to the small kitchen off the foyer tea-room; and deciding that she would, after all, make herself a pot, sat there for a while looking through a magazine and listening to the ghostly tinkle of the piano below while she drank her tea.

By eight o'clock, judging that he should be nearly finished, she came down again, careful to make sure all the lights were switched off behind her. The reek of burning seemed if anything stronger than before as she came in through the swing-doors at the back, and her immediate thought was to wonder whether something hadn't landed on the roof, as had happened a few years earlier. On that occasion, a rocket had lodged among the eaves and caused some damage to the soffit boarding under a gutterpipe.

Walking down between the rows of seats, however, it seemed to her that the smell began fading after Row L, and by the time she'd reached the front of the auditorium it had gone again altogether.

"You've got a draught coming in from somewhere, that's what it is," the tuner observed, collecting up his pieces into a canvas bag. "I shouldn't let it worry you, ma'am. Belikes it's the smeech o' the bonfires, that's all."

Dinah's comment was that she hoped he was right; but to put her mind quite at rest, when she let him out by the stage door she walked into the street a short way to look up at the old theatre roof. Its outline loomed solid and black against the paler darkness of the night sky, with not so much as a single glimmer of light showing anywhere.

Reassured, she went back again inside.

Now that she was quite alone in the building, after a time she found herself starting to wish she'd asked Warwick to come for her half an hour sooner. The auditorium with its banks of empty seats lit dimly by the "morality" lights along the walls on either side, seemed suddenly just a little eerie and the shadows at the back by the swing-doors played tricks with her eyes if she looked their way too long.

Dinah was not a nervous woman. Normally she paid scant heed to talk about places being haunted; but as she sat there, waiting, she began to think about the old days when the picture house was a theatre hall; and in her imagination she could almost hear an echo of song and music and applause whispering about the silent auditorium. So many people had come here over the years in search of a little pleasure to lift them out of the monotony of their lives, to find laughter and gaiety, and at the evening's end to take away with them the tawdry tinselled glamour of the stage with its cheap, enduring songs . . . so many of them, faceless and forgotten, long dead now; and yet perhaps here still, somewhere in the atmosphere and fabric of the place, so that if one listened hard enough one might hear them in the silence on the very edge of sound, like the sea in a shell.

Dinah felt the hairs begin to rise on the back of her neck. Come, this would never do, she chided herself sharply – the next thing, she'd be thinking she could hear someone singing, as one of the usherettes claimed to have done, scaring the other girls silly with some tale about a ghostly voice coming from where the theatre wings used to be.

Deciding that her nerves could do with some real music to settle them, she got up and went across to sit at the piano, launching almost defiantly into the overture to *Zampa*; but the sudden strident sound in all that vast quietness held a frightening quality of its own, and after no more than a few bars her fingers faltered on the keys and fell still again.

She looked round over her shoulder. Wasn't that some-thing moving up there, at the back of the rows? Oh God, why had she not said half-past eight, instead of nine o'clock? Hardly daring to shift from the piano, she stared across the banks of shadowed seats, the thud of her heart beating in her ears like the muffled tread of footsteps. She never thought she would be so glad to see Warwick Enderby.

When she had learned that night at Desatti's that he'd been witnessed in the company of another woman, her welcome reaction had astonished even herself. Whether or not he was being physically unfaithful was really neither here nor there:

what mattered more was that she was now armed with some solid proof of the failure of her marriage to present as part of her case for legal separation. She had not intended mentioning anything about it to Warwick; but as is the way when tempers run high, something else he'd done recently to annoy her had sparked off hasty words, and before she could stop herself she'd thrown her knowledge in his face.

For once, he had lost his own temper, and quite violently. Several china ornaments which had belonged to old Mrs Garland were sent hurling from mantelpiece to floor before he calmed sufficiently to apologise for their breakage. He was *not* to be spied upon, he said. And if he met Stephen Moore or one of his minions again attempting to do so, he would rather make them wish they'd decided to mind their own business.

Since the beginning of summer, when in obedience to her parents' wishes Dinah had tried to reconcile her differences with the man she'd so imprudently married, the atmosphere at Southwood Place had lost much of its simmering tension. The former intimacy between her and Warwick had never been renewed, and neither had he asked that it should be – in fact, they lived together at a mutually polite distance; and for him to behave in any other way than with a kind of bland, faintly sardonic affability was unusual. This vehement reaction to the discovery of his faithlessness had therefore struck her as suspicious to say the least, suggesting there was something serious in the charge –

Dinah's train of thought broke off abruptly. Out of the corner of her eye she had caught a movement just then, there at the back of the auditorium by the swing-doors. She started up, a hand going to her breast in panic. For a second the light above the piano blinded her, and in her haste to move away she knocked over the chair. The crash of its fall seemed to split the silent air like shattered glass.

Startled, she ran forward into the aisle. Dear Lord in heaven – there *was* something up there. She could see it now, a formless shadow in front of the doors, humping itself grotesquely across the floor towards the first few rows. Her throat tightened, trapping a scream. Whatever it was, it was moving this way, twisting and writhing over the top of the

272

seats; and as it came, the smell of burning which had been worrying her all evening seemed to thicken perceptibly.

Smoke!

That was what it was – smoke! Smoke, pouring in under the doors from somewhere beyond in the foyer.

For a moment Dinah hesitated, looking behind her towards the side exit which led to the stage door and the safety of the street. The instinct for self-preservation urged her to turn and run; but remembering that the fire alarm bell was in the manager's office at the front of the building, she deliberately forced herself instead along the centre aisle, head down against the vaporous tendrils now reaching towards her, fear lending speed to her heels.

There at the back she had to pause, overcome by a fit of coughing, the acrid fumes stinging her lungs and making her eyes water; then, bursting open the doors, she half-fell out into the foyer. The smoke here was too dense to see anything at first, and she had to feel her way forward like a blind woman, hands outstretched, choking, stumbling against programme boards, fighting down the panic inside her, until after what seemed eternity she reached the manager's office.

Its door, of course, was locked. She'd seen Tillie check it earlier before she left. The fire alarm, though, was on the wall just inside the window, and without a second's thought she had pulled off her cloth-topped boot and smashed the glass with the heel.

The sudden strident clangour of the alarm bell was deafening as it leapt into life, reverberating through the silent building. How long before the Fire Brigade should get there, Dinah had no idea. Bonfire Night in Lewes was a busy time.

She dragged her boot on again, not bothering with the buttons, realising that every moment counted now. No use trying to get out by the main foyer doors. They, too, were locked.

Turning back the way she'd come and keeping against the walls where the air felt clearer, she started her retreat towards the auditorium; and now that her streaming eyes were more used to the discomfort, she could see that the smoke was thickest at the entrance to the basement stairwell. If the fire had started down there, it must have gained good hold: apart from the cloakrooms, the basement was used for storage, mostly combustible materials such as paper and paint and old scenery, and reels of film.

As though to confirm the full horror of it all, the smoke clouds pouring up the stairs were suddenly shot through with tongues of dull red flame, and at the same instant there came the *whoomp* of an explosion from somewhere below. The sound galvanised Dinah into flight. Headlong, she threw herself blindly across the foyer and back through the swing-doors, and was almost into the aisle before the density of the fumes seemed to suck the oxygen from her lungs to bring her up short, almost doubled over on her knees.

Ahead of her, beyond the front row of seats, the fascia boarding beneath the screen alcove had caught fire and was burning like tinder, showering blazing fragments into the orchestra pit. Obviously the conflagration in the basement had broken out at this end, too, fed by the old wooden props which had once supported the stage.

Gasping for air, she somehow managed to stagger on down the slope of the aisle. Her only hope now was to reach the side exit before the fire spread that far; but even as she stumbled towards it, a cascade of sparks caught the fringe of the drapes across the alcove and in seconds the whole area was a mass of incandescent flame.

Driven back by the fierce heat, Dinah sought protection between the banks of seats. If she could get to the opposite wall . . . The roar and crackle of the fire was like a living thing pursuing her, the hotness of its breath searing her skin; and she had the sensation of moving in a dream, her limbs weighted by lead as a quicksand of suffocation threatened to drag her down into plummeting darkness.

At the end of the row she collapsed, exhausted, fighting for breath in the choking pall of smoke. By now the exit to the stage door was starting to catch as yellow-tipped tongues licked greedily along its frame, bubbling up the paint into blisters. Sheer desperation spurred her on. Her throat raw from coughing, she staggered again to her feet, a hand against the wall for support, willing herself to reach the exit before it exploded into flame.

That final effort was too much for her.

The last thing she remembered was a voice shouting out something and hands pulling her towards the curtain of fire. Then an almighty crash – and nothing.

When Dinah woke again it was daylight, and she was in her own bedroom. As consciousness returned, her first impressions were a confusion of sound – a dog barking somewhere, voices raised, doors being slammed.

Then she opened her eyes, remembering.

"Oh . . . are you awake, dear?"

Someone whispered close to the pillow. She turned her head, and at the same moment became aware of a terrible pain in her chest, as though her lungs had been skinned raw.

"Now don't try to move."

Jessie Bates's face appeared in front of her, wearing an expression of stern solicitude.

"And don't try to speak, either. Doctor says you must rest your throat."

Dinah wondered why she was whispering. Then a dozen other questions came tumbling into her mind – what had happened at the picture house, who had got her out, had the fire engines reached the building in time –

"You're not to worry, you're quite all right," Jessie went on, patting her hand and tucking it away beneath the coverlet. "A trifle singed round the edges, but nothing serious."

Seeing the relief in the red-rimmed eyes, her voice assumed something of its normal tone.

"You were very lucky, though. Do you realise, you poor darling, you could have been burnt alive. The place went up like a tinder-box, Stephen says. It was all those rolls of film, apparently. There's to be an enquiry why they were kept in such a dangerous condition. The whole theatre's been sitting on a time bomb – imagine! And we've been going there, never realising we might be blown into next week."

A slight exaggeration, but Dinah was in no state to argue. Besides, it was all rather technical. The film on which moving pictures were printed had a cellulose-nitrate base which deteriorated after a certain time. If stored in unsuitable conditions, it had a tendency to become unstable

275

and ignite easily, burning with explosive force. Two years ago, in 1909, the Kinematograph Act controlling the safety and licensing of premises had dealt specifically with this danger: all picture houses must have adequate fire exits and be provided with a damp blanket, two buckets of water and one of dry sand.

At the Electric Picture Theatre in Lewes these had been kept in the manager's office, so as not to inconvenience patrons and spoil the elegant appearance of the foyer.

"Stephen thinks it was a firework," Jessie continued, getting up to look out through the window. "You know – one of those awful Rouser things. There's trouble with them every year. I can't imagine why they're not banned altogether. He says one probably fell down into the basement well and started a blaze among the rubbish there."

She craned her neck, trying to follow something below in the garden.

"He's waiting down there, by the way, pacing back and forth across the terrace. I said he wasn't to come in and sit with you until you'd woken, so he's been engaging himself on your behalf dealing with newspaper reporters. You wouldn't believe how persistent they're being! We had three of them here on the doorstep this morning, and another after lunch – Mrs Smith even found one snooping about in the wash-house just now. I wonder you weren't disturbed by the noise when she set the dog after him. And the questions they ask – my goodness! *Anything* for sensation. Was it true Mrs Enderby had saved the building single-handed, was it true the fire regulations had been broken, was it true that her husband – "

Jessie turned back again suddenly from the window.

"Oh, but of course, you don't know, do you, my darling. About Warwick, I mean – arriving in the very nick of time to rescue you. *Terribly* brave. He's landed himself in hospital with burns and concussion. And now, would you believe, the Press are making him the hero of the hour!"

26

It was three days before Dinah was sufficiently recovered to be able to visit Warwick Enderby in hospital. In that short time the local papers had had a field day with the picture house fire, carrying banner headlines which presented the incident as a thrilling drama for public consumption.

Disappointingly, the hero had refused to give interviews from his hospital bed; but even this was turned to advantage by intrepid reporters refusing to be cheated of their by-lines – "Gallant Husband: 'No Visitors' say Doctors" (inferring that the patient was too badly injured to be disturbed), or else "Official Statement Delayed" (which was true, though misleading).

"I see the police are appealing for witnesses," remarked Isabelle Bethway, scanning the previous evening's edition of the *Argus*. She had arrived from Eastbourne two days ago in response to a telegram from Jessie Bates summoning her to her daughter's bedside, and had been vastly relieved to find Dinah already back on her feet, though still extremely shaken by her ordeal.

"'Foul play not suspected', it says here. I suppose that means they're satisfied the fire was started accidentally."

She looked up from the newspaper. Dinah had been ordered to speak as little as possible, to rest her painfully inflamed throat, and so was limiting her responses to nods or shakes whenever she could.

There was a nod.

Her mother gave an encouraging smile, pleased to see how much better she looked this morning. The weather helped, of course: after a cold snap at the start of the month, they were now enjoying a milder spell of wintry sunshine, and being able to sit out in the fresh air in the garden had obviously had a beneficial effect.

Even so, Isabelle Bethway sounded a note of caution.

"Are you sure it's altogether wise of you to visit the hospital this afternoon?" she asked, folding the newspaper and getting up to put it back on the bamboo whatnot for the maid to tidy away.

Dinah repeated her nod, emphatically.

"It won't tax your strength too much, do you think, dear?"

This time there was a negative shake. Had she voice to speak, the younger woman would have answered that though her feelings of bitter dislike for her husband remained unchanged, it was only right and proper that she should see him, to thank him for his timely action in saving her. At least such braveness of conduct showed that Warwick was not entirely rotten to the core.

"Your father said he would try to get up to the hospital himself," her mother continued, "but he's far too busy at this season of the year, and I told him so, too. There's no point him coming all the way from Eastbourne for the sake of a half-hour's visit."

She seated herself again, stretching out her slender hands to the warmth of the coal fire.

"It's too much to hope that Francis might go to see Warwick, I suppose. The pair are not even acquainted, are they? No, I didn't think so – " this in response to a second shake of Dinah's head. "What a thing, I ask you – his own brother-in-law, too. But there, that's Francis all over. Self first and last, and never a thought to spare elsewhere."

The oval face, so very like her daughter's, showed a fleeting expression of saddened resignation. There had been a letter from Francis some weeks ago, tersely acquainting his parents with the fact that he was relinquishing his Army commission and intended going abroad to the United States of America for a time. He would continue to honour his commitment to his wife and children with a monthly allowance, and trusted that his parents would maintain the close family connection with them during his absence. He would write again in due course.

The letter was received at the Eastbourne vicarage with some hurt and a good deal of indignation; in fact the Reverend Alec Bethway had gone so far in his anger as to declare his hands finally washed of his runagate son, and the fellow might go to the very devil if that was his intent.

Isabelle had wept; but her tears were more for Marion and the two little girls, cast aside, it seemed, on some whim of their father. And all for what? That he might take himself off to a foreign land, abandoning his career, forfeiting his Army pension, uprooting himself from his family? It made no sense. Depend upon it, though, there was a female involved somewhere. Francis's whole life, like his uncle's and his grandfather's before him, was governed by a craving appetite for women; and just as Frank Morgan and Frank Flynn had met violent ends because of it, so Isabelle feared that her son was courting a similar fate.

Well, there was nothing to be done. She could pray for him, though it seemed a wasted exercise to hope anything might come of her intercessions. Francis was a bad seed that had grown into a rotten apple, and except for a miracle, was unlikely to reform himself now.

"Beg pardon, ma'am – "

There was a light tap, and the young housemaid, Jane, put her head in at the door.

"The hansom cab's just this minute turned into the drive, ma'am."

Dinah raised a hand in acknowledgement and got up from where she'd been sitting at the other side of the fire.

"Shall I get your coats and things ready, ma'am?"

"Yes, if you would, thank you, Jane." Isabelle Bethway answered for her daughter. "And tell the driver we'll be out directly."

With a dip of a curtsy, the maid disappeared again about her errand.

Despite the sunny day, a keen November wind had sprung up during the morning and both women had to hold on to their hats as they went out to the cab, the skirts of their coats flapping about their high-laced boots. Fortunately the drive to The Victoria Hospital was a short one, and they were glad to get into the antiseptic warmth of the entrance vestibule.

Warwick Enderby was in the men's surgical ward on the first floor.

"I expect he'll wish to see you alone to begin with,"

Isabelle said tactfully as the pair of them ascended the wide, echoing stone staircase. "I'll wait in the visitors' room at the end of the corridor. No, there's no need for you to come too, dear – " as Dinah made to turn left with her at the head of the stairs. "I shan't get lost. You go along to the ward, and I'll join you there in about fifteen minutes."

Leaving her mother to follow the direction indicated by a pointing hand on the wall, the younger woman made her way to the right to the matron's office. Through the open doors ahead she could see into the aisle of the ward, a well-lit, airy place with a dozen or so screened-off bays on either side.

"Yes? Can I help you?"

The request came from a nursing sister inside the glass-panelled office.

Dinah cleared her throat with painful difficulty. "Mr Enderby?" she asked in a thick whisper.

"What's that?" The other leaned forward, frowning in busy irritation.

Dinah tried again. "Mr Enderby, please?"

"Enderby? Yes, are you a relative?"

She nodded.

The nurse turned away and glanced along the ward through her window. Looking back again she said something; but her words were drowned by the rattle of a trolley going by just then, and Dinah couldn't quite catch the sentence.

"I said you'll find Mr Enderby in the isolation annexe," was repeated briskly in response to her strained look of enquiry. "To the left, at the top. We've had to move him there because of the news reporters. They were upsetting our other patients."

Acknowledging this assistance, Dinah made her way along the ward to the annexe, where she found Warwick the solitary occupant, propped among a starched white mound of pillows, a bandage covering his dark hair.

Seeing who it was approaching from the door, he tossed aside the paper he'd been reading and greeted her off-handedly.

"Well . . . look who's here. Hello, old girl. I didn't expect

280

to be graced with a visit from you. Come to inspect the damage?"

Ignoring the sarcasm, she drew a chair from the wall to sit down and with some effort managed to enquire of him, "How are you?"

There was a shrug followed by a grimace. "Oh, I've suffered worse headaches. And I'm assured the scar will only be a small one. Actually, if you want to know, my main injury's the one inflicted upon me by the local Press – " He waved a hand towards the newspaper he'd just discarded. "I mean all this wretched ballyhoo they're kicking up about me. Making out I'm some sort of knight in shining armour. I wish to God they'd kept my name out of their damn' rag."

Glancing back at his visitor, and seeing that she was having considerable difficulty in trying to speak, he added carelessly, "I suppose I should ask how *you* are. You're not looking particularly chipper. The smoke got into your lungs, didn't it?"

She nodded dumbly.

"Oh, well – " He didn't say that he was sorry; but she didn't expect him to.

There followed a long pause. Warwick looked up at the ceiling in a studiedly bored manner, folding his hands together behind his head.

What an actor you are, Dinah thought bitterly. What a shallow, self-centred fake of a man. How could I have been so blind as to love you as I did. And yet I owe you my life – and with it a debt of gratitude for the one redeeming thing you've ever done for me.

Aloud she said huskily, "I've come . . . to thank you, Warwick."

"Thank me? What for?"

"For rescuing me."

To her surprise he laughed. "You don't want to believe everything the *Argus* and *Express* printed about me, old thing," he said. "Both of 'em publish the most unlikely rubbish if they think it might sell a few more copies."

"I . . . don't understand."

"Don't you? Then I'll tell you. The fact is, it wasn't *me*

281

who rescued you. It just happened by deuced bad luck that I was there on the scene at the time."

Dinah stared at him, a frown of perplexity creasing her pale brow, not certain whether what he was telling her was the truth; and yet hoping desperately that it was, so that the obligation to feel beholden to him was no longer expected of her.

"The trouble is, no one seems inclined to want to hear the real facts," he went on. "They're all too busy trying to turn me into their front-page hero. No use me pointing out that my own skin is infinitely too precious to risk losing in any damn' fire. They don't want to know! Smacks of human weakness – cowardice, if you like. And they can't pin a medal on that."

He threw his listener a look of total indifference.

"To be honest, Dinah dear, if it'd had been left to me that night, I'm afraid you'd have had to have taken your chance alone on getting out alive."

She stared at him, disgust so naked in her face that Warwick had the grace to allow a little self-apology to creep into his voice.

"If you want to know who you should be thanking for your life – well, I'm sorry I can't help. All I can tell you is, I was crossing towards the stage door just as some fellow was hauling you out through the smoke. It happened so quickly. He was no more than a shadow, a voice. That's all I can say. But whoever he was, he deposited you in the gutter, yelled something to me about fetching assistance, and disappeared into the darkness of the street. And that's the last anyone saw of him."

There was another pause. Dinah remained silent, her eyes fixed upon the face of this self-confessed coward who would have left her in that building to die. Misinterpreting her expression, Warwick unclasped his hands from behind his head and indicated the bandage.

"I suppose you're wondering how I managed to come by this. Would you believe it, I tripped over a loose brick in the pavement – " Again he gave a laugh. "My own fault. I was in rather too great a hurry to ensure my motor car wouldn't get damaged. Stubbed my toe on that blasted brick, fell headlong, cracked myself senseless, and came round to find I was on a stretcher being carted off to hospital. Apparently I'd been singed by sparks from the fire while out for the count, and was smouldering somewhat."

Now that he'd begun, he seemed to be finding some private amusement in his story.

"The Press were there, of course. Some young chap or other. Must've overheard my half-conscious mumbling about wife dragged from blaze, and hey presto – the story was already winging its way to the headlines of the morning's paper. It was useless my protesting later that I'd had nothing to do with any damn' rescue. After all, the public mustn't be cheated of a rattling good yarn, especially one with such dramatic trimmings, merely because the hero doesn't wish his valorous gallantry spattered all over the front page of the *Sussex Express*."

The account was ended on another laugh and with a dismissive gesture, as though it meant nothing to its teller.

Dinah could not decide which emotion she was feeling more strongly at this moment – contempt or anger. This man, her husband, had left her lying injured in the street in order to save his precious motor car from the fire!

Not trusting herself to speak, she rose abruptly to her feet; and as she did, saw his eyes slip past her to focus on something behind, and a flicker of what could almost have been alarm register suddenly in their expression.

She looked round. Standing a few feet beyond the doorway into the main ward was a pretty young woman holding a small child by the hand.

Seeing she'd caught Dinah's attention, the woman came forward, smiling a little awkwardly, and said, "Pardon me if I'm intruding, but the nurse said it was all right to come through. To visit Warwick, I mean . . . seeing as how I'm his wife, that is."

Dinah looked at her stupidly. Then, after a slow, numbed moment, turned back towards the man who for the past fifteen months had been calling himself her husband.

Her name was Catherine – Kitty – the young woman said, and she had married Warwick Enderby six years ago at

Hastings. Their son, Warwick junior, had been born in 1908, and would be four next March.

There was no reluctance in the offering of this information. After that mortifying scene in the annexe when this person claiming likewise to be Mrs Enderby had started on about bigamy or something (no one could make out the half of it on account of her voice being so hoarse) Kitty had been perfectly willing to explain her own position.

Now here they were in the hospital visitors' room where they'd been ushered by a scandalised Matron: the two Mrs Enderbys and a Mrs Bethway, who had just finished describing to her the facts of the situation.

"Well, I don't know what to say, I'm sure," said Kitty, embarrassed, not knowing quite where to look. "He's a bad 'un, I always knew that. But I never thought he'd go so far as to try a trick like this."

She pulled at little Warwick's arm to stop him wriggling from the chair at her side.

"I mean, he's been coming back regularly now and then to see us at Hastings, but he's never mentioned a word of anything to me about – " she gestured delicately. "Well, he wouldn't, would he? I'd never have known where he was, even, except somebody told me his name and his picture have been in the newspaper."

Her speech, though uneducated, held the pleasantly broad-vowelled burr of the Sussex countryside.

"I don't know what to say, I'm sure," she repeated herself, glancing at Dinah. "I'm ever so sorry . . . "

She pulled again at her little son, then took him up on to her lap, resting her cheek against his curly dark hair. In an artless, almost naive way, she was possessed of a most appealing charm, and the other woman had seen at once what it was about her that must have attracted Warwick.

Such recognition, though, had been unconscious at the time. All Dinah was able to think of was her own betrayal. This afternoon's entire episode had come as such a shock, such a slap in the face – such an *insult*. And now suddenly to discover that her marriage was a lie, that the man she'd known as husband in the most intimate exchange of physical love was nothing but a cheap-jack imposter, that he'd sullied every precious thing she had . . . She had been numbed by it. And in the face of his guilt, for once he'd said nothing – not a word – merely lain there looking at his son while the woman he'd duped and cheated and ridiculed knew the utter shaming indignity of being made into an object of curiosity and pity in the eyes of the world.

"You had no idea at all what it was he was getting up to?" Isabelle Bethway asked carefully.

Kitty shook her head. "No, I didn't, I swear. He left us when the boy was hardly more'n a year old. Walked out on us, he did."

"Why? May we know the reason?"

"It was money." The answer came with open frankness. "That's all he's ever cared about . . . except mebbe his son. My mother ran a boarding-house in Hastings Old Town, that's where I met him first, when he came to us for a month's lodging. When we married – " Kitty twisted her wedding ring. "When we married we did quite well for a couple o' months, but then his brothers started turning up causing trouble, and not many o' the guests would stay after that. Then when Mam died, Warwick decided we'd sell up and put the money in a motor car business. *That* didn't last long, neither. And then the boy was born, and I couldn't work any more for a bit . . . and as I say, he walked out on us in the end. Said we were millstones round his neck. Parasites."

She paused again, her violet-coloured eyes downcast, her expression one of sad remembrance. Despite it all, she had never once stopped loving him.

"Didn't you approach his family for assistance?" Isabelle prompted.

"Just once, when I went to see his father."

"And was *he* of any help?"

There was another slow shake of the head.

Recalling her own attempts to seek a meeting with this somewhat shadowy figure, Dinah tried a hoarse-voiced question herself.

"What sort of impression did you have?"

"Sorry? I didn't quite catch what you said." Kitty tilted forward.

"Mr Enderby – what was he like?"

"Oh. Well, he talked a lot. About how he'd come down in the world, what wi' folk owing him money an' that. He'd been an actor o' sorts, I believe. But I wouldn't have kept a pig in the place he was living. Filthy dirty, it was, and cluttered wi' empty bottles – you know, brandy and the like, and he smelled to high heaven o' drink. I didn't stop there long. He wasn't a very nice old man. He tried to – "

Again, she made that delicate little gesture.

"And I've never been near him again since."

Dinah exchanged looks with her mother. She'd half-suspected that might be the truth behind Warwick's grandiose representations of his father. An old stager living in drink-fuddled squalor on the make-believe memories of a fame he'd never earned. Little wonder his sons had been so reluctant for her to make his acquaintance!

"You mustn't judge him too harshly, though," Kitty went on. "Warwick, I mean. I know appearances are against him, and he shouldn't have done what he did, going through a wedding ceremony an' that. But he's been real good to the boy and me when he's had the money, coming to see us and bringing us things. Bits o' jewellery, mebbe – "

Yes, mine, thought Dinah.

" – or a nice cut o' meat for the weekend. There've been times I've hated him, I know, but that's the way he is. He likes to play the toff, you see, pretend he's some'at important, swanking about the races or the clubs."

She seemed almost proud of him, this neglectful, unfaithful bigamist husband of hers.

"He certainly does things on a grand scale," Isabelle agreed drily. "The point is, though, my dear, he's committed a serious offence by going through a form of marriage with my daughter. And he may well go to prison for it."

"Oh – don't say that!" Quick fear filled the other's eyes and she pressed her son against her as though to protect him from the sins of his father about to be visited upon his innocent head.

"You won't bring charges, will you?" she appealed to Dinah. "He saved your life, didn't he? It said so in the papers. A hero, it said, risking his own neck to pull you out

286

o' that fire. You wouldn't pay him back by having him up in court, would you?"

"It isn't for Mrs – Garland to decide," Isabelle answered for her daughter.

Mrs Garland.

The unexpected use of her former name hit Dinah with all the sudden breath-taking shock of ice-cold water. Of course! She *was* Mrs Garland still – Mrs Richard Garland. She had never been Dinah Enderby at all. That was just a part of the farce Warwick had played upon her for his own greed-driven ends.

She looked at her mother; and unexpectedly – ridiculously – burst into a flood of tears.

It was the most curious sensation, as though she had been lost to herself for the past year and a half and now was found again. Even the act of removing Warwick Enderby's ring from her wedding finger semed to her a symbolic casting-off of his presence in her life.

She was free – *free*!

Now her only thought was that all trace of him must be cleansed from her house: she couldn't wait to begin, to get back from the hospital to Southwood Place and start ridding the rooms of every last vestige of his occupancy.

Deaf to her mother's pleas that she must have a care for her health, that she ought first to seek legal advice, that she must give herself time to consider her position, the newly-found Mrs Richard Garland descended upon her home like a whirlwind and went through it from attic to cellar. Clothes, shoes, books, shaving tackle, collar studs, pawn tickets . . . all this and more beside was crammed into Warwick's three leather suitcases and delivered to him by cab care of The Victoria Hospital. The few pieces of furniture which were his were put into one of the out-houses, and a note sent to Kitty Enderby at the temporary lodging she'd taken in Spital Street that it would be appreciated if she'd make arrangements with her husband to remove the things as soon as possible.

By nightfall, Southwood Place had been exorcised entirely of its former tenant.

Acting upon her own initiative, Isabelle Bethway had thought it only prudent in the circumstances to obtain prompt legal guidance; and accordingly, in response to her telegram to Weatherfield, Stephen Moore arrived at the house towards midday the following morning.

Beneath the outwardly calm façade of his professional manner, he had never been so furious. Of course Enderby must be prosecuted, he said. There was no question of allowing the fellow to escape scot-free from the consequence of his crime. Bigamy was a felonious offence carrying a punishment of up to seven years' penal servitude – and that was without taking into account the further offences of embezzlement and misappropriation of property. It was one thing for a husband to dispose of his wife's effects without her permission, and avail himself of her personal private income, but when the "husband" was found to be an impostor, then the Law cast a very different eye upon the matter.

Despite all his attempts at argument and persuasion, however, Dinah was adamant: she had washed her hands of Warwick Enderby, and that was that. She wished to expunge his name completely from her mind. And if the three hundred pounds he'd purloined from her was the price she must pay, then it was a cheap enough forfeit to make to be rid of him. She would not bring a prosecution to have her name and privacy dragged through the courts merely for the sake of the Law and its requirements.

Seeing that he was making no headway at all against her obdurate determination, Stephen tried a different tack. Did she not realise she could claim Enderby's property in lieu of legal compensation? He was her debtor, and she had that right. It was a pity she'd acted so hastily in despatching the fellow's things to The Victoria last evening – but he himself would go there straight away and see whether it wasn't possible still to retrieve them from the porter.

Yes, he quite understood why she refused to have the suitcases back at the house: he would remove them for safe-keeping to the left luggage office at the railway station. As for the motor car, still in Market Street where it had been parked on the night of the fire, well, it would not be difficult to dispose of that through a garage.

As always, though, Warwick Enderby was one step ahead of events. When Stephen Moore arrived at the hospital, he was informed that Mr Enderby had already discharged himself, taking all his belongings with him.

And no, he had left no forwarding address.

27

At midday exactly on Wednesday, April the tenth, 1912, the White Star Liner R.M.S. *Titanic* sailed on her maiden voyage from Southampton. On board, occupying separate third-class cabins on F Deck, were Mr Francis Bethway, former commanding officer no. 2 Battery, 1st Home Counties Brigade, and Miss Cecilia Desatti, his mistress.

The ship which was to take them to a new life was the largest and most luxurious sailing vessel ever built. She was as long as four city blocks and as high as an eleven-storey building, and the water-tight construction of her double-bottomed hull was so soundly designed that it was said not even God himself could sink her.

No expense had been spared in fitting out this floating palace: in the first-class areas the light of crystal chandeliers reflected the polished sheen of hand-carved panelling, the glint of cut glass and silver, and the jewel-soft colours of fitted plush carpets. Staterooms were decorated in the Georgian style with moulded plasterwork ceilings and white fluted columns, or else were sumptuous examples of Empire décor. There was a Café Parisien, a Palm Court, a gymnasium, an *à la carte* restaurant, squash racquet courts, Turkish baths, five grand pianos – all and everything which a discerning, moneyed class of passenger might expect.

Lower down the ship, in the steerage accommodation, silver might be replaced by electro-plated nickel and plush carpets by drugget, but there was still an air of solid comfort and quality. And everyone was free to use their own gleaming white-scrubbed promenade deck, where canvas steamer chairs sheltered occupants from the stiff Atlantic breeze behind the wind-breaks of the lifeboat davits – sixteen lifeboats, to serve a total passenger complement of more than two thousand. (A curious discrepancy, perhaps;

but then, of course, the *Titanic* was unsinkable, so what did it matter.)

Francis and Sissy had travelled down to Southampton separately, he alone, she accompanied by her entire family to see her off at the dockside. Their cabin reservations had been made in advance in their own names, so that although the two were segregated in accordance with ship's regulations keeping single sexes apart, at least they were able to be together on the same deck and share the same recreation and dining facilities.

It was a calm, clear day when the *Titanic* sailed; and apart from a slight mishap in harbour when she'd almost collided with the steamer *New York*, the short cross-Channel voyage to Cherbourg to take on more passengers went without incident. By eight-thirty that evening she was underway again, heading this time for Queenstown on the southern tip of Ireland which would be the last port of call before the Atlantic crossing.

Francis found himself sharing a two-berth cabin with a young engineer going out to Colorado to join his brother on a fruit farm at the foot of the Rockies. The young man's enthusiasm for that beautiful wide-open country and its potential as a place where a fellow could make a good living, left a favourable impression on his listener; and several times during the days which followed Francis had discussed with Sissy the idea that he, too, might try his hand at something similar. Having spent so much of his time under the open sky, the notion of an outdoor life in many ways appealed to him.

Whatever private doubts Sissy may have had about it, she kept to herself for the moment: she would have preferred her lover to set his sights on something rather more respectable – the manager of a department store, perhaps, or a property agent – something with a bit of class to show he was going up in the world.

Four days into the voyage, on Sunday the fourteenth, the two of them had spent the evening together as usual among the crowd on the steerage deck, and after supper had watched some of the Irish passengers jigging to the merry tunes of a fiddler in the dance-room. The weather was dry still, though cold, with a fresh wind which cut sharper as the *Titanic* steamed further into mid-Atlantic; but tonight seemed to strike particularly chilly.

Someone said there were icebergs about.

By ten o'clock, Sissy had decided to turn in. She was sharing her cabin with a girl from County Kerry who did nothing but talk about men and pray to St Ann, and she hoped for once to be asleep before the other came in. Left to himself, Francis wandered along to the smoking-room and got into a game of cards with three other men there, standing each of them a whisky by way of credentials.

The game was still in progress when, a little after half-past eleven, one of the players remarked on the increased vibration of the ship and wondered whether she might not have picked up steam. Moments later each of them felt a slight quiver, as though she'd been checked in her headlong speed through the darkened waters, and there was an almost imperceptible roll to port-side.

The four at the table looked at one another, and continued their game; but hardly had a further hand been dealt than they were aware that the engines had suddenly stopped.

Francis left his seat and went to see what had happened. Away from the companionable warmth of the smoking-room the night air outside struck freezing cold, and in the almost velvet blackness of the clear sky, myriads of stars twinkled like glass, so remote and icy in their beauty that it made him shiver just to look at them. Pulling up the collar of his grey knickerbocker suit, he half-ran along the gangway to the starboard well deck, where he could see a small knot of people already gathered.

It was an iceberg, they said, an enormous iceberg perhaps one hundred feet high; it had scraped along the side of the ship and then disappeared into the darkness. Look – bits of it had broken off on to the deck.

Francis had made some quip about taking a piece back to add to his whisky, and returned to the smoking-room. Apparently the ship had been shaved by a 'berg, he reported

292

to his fellow players; nothing to worry about, they might as well have another drink and finish their game.

He was not to know – how could any of them – that for each one of the two thousand, two hundred and eight men, women and children on board that ship, life was about to be forever changed.

By midnight, just twenty minutes after the collision, it was apparent that the *Titanic* had been crippled. A three hundred foot gash had ripped open the first five of her watertight compartments, and she was starting to list badly on the starboard bow. The order was given to uncover the lifeboats – those sixteen lifeboats, considered a mere deck decoration – and to muster the crew and passengers and begin distributing life-jackets.

At a quarter to one, the first boat was lowered away.

There was no panic, only a curious numbed calmness, a dignity which is the hallmark of true courage in the face of insurmountable peril. Husbands and wives embraced and parted, many of them never to meet again, for with so few boats it was a case of women and children alone. There were wives who refused to enter the boats, preferring to stay on board and share the fate of their menfolk; and there were some men who, to their shame, tried to save their own necks, forcing their way through the quiet, patient queues to demand a seat.

Francis, like so many others, had been scouring the ship in search of his loved one; but it was almost two o'clock before he finally came upon Sissy Desatti, among a swarm of people milling around at the foot of the main steerage staircase. Somehow or other the pair of them managed to make their way together up to the Boat Deck, climbing stairs now tilted at a precarious slope, hearing behind them the echoing cries of those cut off from escape.

Boat no. 8 was swinging out ready to be launched. He pushed Sissy forward. For a moment she turned and clung to him – then hands had plucked her away and thrust her over the side. As she half-fell in a tangle of legs and oars and blankets, he called out to her and leaned across the rail to throw something down.

It was his wallet, fastened by an elastic band around his silver cheroot case.

"Remember me!" she thought she heard him cry.

Then the lifeboat was falling, falling, skimming the sides of the ship, hitting the water with a splash that drenched them all. Oars were in rowlocks, orders shouted, and they were moving away yard by faster yard, women two to an oar to pull them from the foundering vessel.

From a quarter of a mile away, the *Titanic* presented a fantastic sight. All her port-holes were ablaze with lights still burning on board, but canted forward at an obscene angle; and over the silent waters drifted the strains of a hymn which the band were playing on the Boat Deck.

Higher and higher the stern rose into the air, its giant propellers glistening in the icy starlight, and at the same time there came a sudden rumbling and crashing as though everything within the stricken ship were sliding in a dreadful chaos towards her plunging bows. For some moments she stood completely upended, like a giant black column against the filmy darkness of the sky, and then began her ghostly dive beneath the Atlantic waters.

There were seven hundred and five survivors. Francis Bethway was not among them.

28

How fast the time had gone. Already another summer was almost over, and its dark green leaves turning to the reds and russets of another autumn. The early morning air was tinged with the melancholy aroma of woodsmoke drifting from garden bonfires; and as daylight faded again to evening, a dank mist brought the first faint touch of winter's sharpening edge.

Looking back, Dinah wondered where the year had gone to. So much had happened, so much changed, and yet she seemed to have been standing aside, a spectator in the wings, watching the days and weeks and months flow by, carrying with them other people's lives but not her own.

She had been ill for a while, perhaps that was the reason for this feeling of detachment – nervous exhaustion, her doctor said. A lengthy rest was advised. Much of the summer she'd spent at her parents' home in Eastbourne, taking long walks into the downland countryside with Traddles as companion, or else roaming the rocky inlets of the coast where the only sound was the cry of gulls across an ebb-tide shore, and the distant hollow whisper of the sea.

There was something about solitude that she found healing to the inner wounds of memory: something about the alone-ness of loneliness that gave her back her strength and peace and self-assurance. She could put away the hurt of Warwick Enderby; she could mourn her brother Francis; she could look back on the recent past and exorcise its pain completely from her mind.

When she returned again to Southwood Place and Lewes at the end of summer, she seemed like the Dinah Garland of the old days, and it was only those who knew her well who remarked the subtle change, the calmness in her face, the quiet repose.

Things had been happening while she'd been away. The

Electric Picture Theatre was rising from its ashes in the smart new guise of a Kinema de Luxe. Algie Langton-Smythe, a student again, was learning the ropes of estate management and considering whether or not to join the Royal Flying Corps after his wedding to Laura next year. Jessie and Esmond Bates were expecting their first child. And Warwick Enderby was believed to have left the country and gone to Australia.

This last news had come in a letter from Kitty, his wife, very belatedly thanking Dinah for letting her have his furniture and personal effects, and apologising once more for all the trouble she'd been put to on his account. By way of a postscript, she thought Dinah might like to know that she'd had word from a place called Malvern, a suburb of Adelaide, saying he intended sending for her and young Warwick as soon as he'd raised the money.

"So that's the end of that," announced Jessie Bates with great finality. "Adieu, and good riddance."

She and Esmond had invited Dinah to spend the weekend with them at their home in Weatherfield, and since the day was a sunny one, they'd all come out to sit in the garden after Sunday luncheon.

"Don't I recall you stating quite clearly that the Enderby subject was closed?" Esmond asked carefully, giving Dinah a look from beneath his brows.

She smiled. "It is. I thought you'd be interested to hear that piece of news, that's all. Now we'll talk about something else."

"Oh, yes – I know what I've been meaning to ask you, dear." Taking her cue, Jessie came in again. "Your sister-in-law. Has she decided yet whether to accept your parents' invitation to live with them at Eastbourne? She was considering it, wasn't she?"

There was a nod. "And I wish she would. She'd be so much happier there. I can't think why she feels it her duty to stay in Gloucestershire – her father's only interest is his hounds and his hunting, and her step-mother simply doesn't see eye to eye with her and would much prefer she left."

"Then you suppose she will?"

"Reading between the lines of her letters, yes. And

Eastbourne would be better for the children, too. Poor little mites, it must be so unsettling for them both, all the ups and downs they've suffered this past year or two. What with the baby dying, and their moving away from Lewes, and then . . . and then losing their father so suddenly."

Only the slightest catch of the voice betrayed how close to the surface still were Dinah's own feelings on her brother Francis's death. Recovering herself quickly, she went on, "Marion would be very wise to accept my parents' invitation. For all their sakes, it's an ideal arrangement."

While she'd been staying with them this summer, Isabelle Bethway had spoken often of her earnest wish that little May and Angela should grow up at the vicarage. They needed the stability of a loving home, she said; and it would give her and Alec the greatest contentment and joy were they able to share their declining years with the children and their mother.

Curiously, Isabelle had borne the loss of her elder son with something almost akin to pride, as though the manner of his death had done much to atone for the thoughtless, arrogant conduct of his life. It was Marion who had taken the news so badly. Considering the mental hurt inflicted by Francis's constant infidelities and bitterly cruel accusations, her distress was quite astonishing.

She had known from his few letters that he was thinking of going abroad for a time; but even so, his last communication, sent from the telegram office at Southampton Docks, had come as a considerable shock. And then to read in the newspapers of the *Titanic* disaster, and be forced to wait several days before the final lists were published, not knowing whether or not he'd survived – it had been one nightmare piled upon another. Not until the official notification that he was "missing, presumed drowned" had she given up all hope, and her grief at his memorial service at the Eastbourne family church had been heart-rending.

Whatever else he was, Francis Bethway had been her husband, the only man she'd ever loved. For that reason if for none other, she would keep true to his memory: the faithful widow of a faithless man.

"Dinah – ?"

297

Jessie's voice startled the other from her reverie.

"Dinah dear, didn't you hear me?"

"Oh – " She recollected herself quickly. "No, sorry, I was miles away for a moment."

"Well, I was saying it's time I went indoors now for my nap. My afternoon siesta, our doctor calls it."

The mother-to-be patted herself proudly. Although baby Bates was not expected until February, its four-month presence was already filling out her slim body.

"You don't mind, do you. I'm sure Stephen won't object to taking care of you till teatime."

There was a wave of the hand towards her brother, who had been sitting all this while in silence, apparently absorbed in his own thoughts though his gaze had seldom strayed very far away from Dinah's face. The two had not seen one another for some months whilst she'd been absent from Lewes, and meeting again, he'd been struck immediately by the change in her: not only the new-found calmness in her lovely features, but the air of repose which seemed to surround her like an aura, giving the impression of a woman utterly at peace with herself.

She was wearing an eau-de-nil linen suit, and with her auburn hair swept back into a chignon he thought he had never seen her looking more beautiful.

"No, of course I won't mind taking care of Dinah," he answered readily. "In fact, I was going to suggest she might like a walk with me. I could do with stretching my legs after that excellent meal."

Dinah turned her head and gave him one of her placid glances. Then her lips curved into a smile. "I was thinking the same thing myself."

"Good. That's that, then," said Jessie, obviously pleased. "Come along, Esmond darling. You can read to me while I'm resting, if you would."

Getting up, her hands pressed against the small of her back to relieve the slight ache there, she added by way of explanation, "It's Matthew Arnold this week. Last week it was Tennyson. Esmond has a theory, you see, that babies are influenced by their mothers' state of mind, and he thinks

298

poetry and music may help me to produce an artistically gifted infant."

"A perfectly feasible concept." Her husband offered her his arm to take. "And what's more, it has the effect of keeping you quiet for a few hours."

"Which is no bad thing," his brother-in-law agreed.

Jessie rolled her eyes in a dumb-show of pretended injury and allowed herself without further ado to be removed from the garden.

Once the two had disappeared inside through the verandah doors, Stephen and Dinah remained seated where they were for a while longer, talking together of this and that, mostly about family news and her brother Kit's advancement to his own small parish not too far distant at Netherton.

"You know, you'll have to consider moving to this area yourself," Stephen said, getting to his feet at last and holding out a hand. "It's where you belong, after all."

"You think so?" She stood up in turn, shaking the creases from her long skirt.

"Of course. Come on, I'll prove it – "

Taking the side path which led them out of the garden by a latch-gate into The Holloway, he walked with her down the slope of the tree-lined road to its junction at the bottom.

Across the way, wrapped in the silence of a Sunday afternoon's early closing, The Man in the Moon public house looked back at them blankly from behind its modern frontage of enamelled wall advertisements.

"Do you know how old that place is?" he asked, shading his eyes against the mellow sunlight slanting between the chimneys.

Dinah shook her head. "Not exactly. Do you?"

"Yes, I've looked up the records. It was built as a farmhouse in 1546, and until the Civil War it was owned by a family called Linton. The name should mean something to you."

"Linton?" She considered for a moment. "The only Linton I can think of was a doctor living at one time in Church Lane. Jessie created some great mystery to do with his wife and Esmond's father – something about an affaire they were supposed to have had."

"Oh, that! There was nothing in the story. Esmond told me himself. The poor woman had written a few hysterical letters to Mr Bates, that's all. No, the Linton I mean lived a generation or so earlier. As a matter of fact, he was your great-grandfather."

"He was? How do you know?"

"One of the parish rectors wrote a paper for the local history society – this is going back a good few years, of course. His particular interest was tracing old established families in the district, and somewhere he'd uncovered the fact that Molly Flynn, spinster, of Weatherfield alehouse, had been the mistress of Daniel Linton, farmer, of Shatterford. And had borne him a child."

"And the child was – ?"

"Your grandmother, Dinah Flynn."

"Well, I never knew about that before." The second Dinah examined the building opposite with greater interest. "So in a roundabout way, the Lintons finally came back into ownership of the original family home. Illegitimately, of course."

"Yes, but not dishonourably. There can't be many local families whose descent doesn't run on both sides of the blanket. Your mother and her brother Frank were the last links in a direct line going all the way back to the original Tudor builder of this place."

Dinah said nothing. For a moment or so she tried to imagine them all – the Lintons and the Flynns – generation after generation reaching away into the long, dead past; and a sudden odd feeling of affinity crept upon her. These people were her forebears, her own bloodline. This house had been home to them for centuries, and this land, buried now beneath concrete and tarmacadam, had been their livelihood.

"I told you I'd prove you belonged here, didn't I?" Stephen said, watching her face. "Come on – " He held out his arm for her to take again. "We haven't finished yet. There's something else."

Compliantly, she allowed herself to be conducted on into

Weatherfield. There was little traffic about and it was a pleasant walk through the quiet Sunday streets where the only sounds were those of children playing on the pavements, while their elders sat outside front doors to take the air and gossip with their neighbours.

As the two strolled along, the conversation moved to Stephen's family and his mother's people, the Pelham-Martins – landowners, magistrates, lawyers and parliamentarians; and from thence to his own hopes of being selected to stand at the next General Election as a socialist candidate against the sitting Tory member for Buckfield.

"You won't forget your promise to support the women's suffrage movement, will you?" Dinah asked him, only half in jest.

He assured her, hand upon heart, that were he elected he would know which way to cast his vote.

By now they had reached Old Weatherfield village, and turning up beside the green, continued their way towards St Anne's and through the lychgate into the churchyard.

Dinah had not been to visit the family graves for well over a year, and was quite expecting to find them looking neglected and overgrown. Rounding the bend of the gravel path, she thought for a moment they'd come to the wrong spot; and then her hands went up to her face in pleasure and astonishment.

"Oh, Stephen – !"

The grave plot had been planted with a border of floribunda roses, and between the three headstones were clumps of heather and wood sorrel, with a few autumn crocuses beginning to show among them here and there. The effect was one of such simple, natural beauty that she was quite overwhelmed by the kindness and thought that had created it.

"You did all this, didn't you." She did not have to look at her companion to know the answer.

"It was better earlier on in the summer," he said, diffidently, "when the roses were out in full bloom."

"I wish I could have seen them."

"You will – next year."

There was a pause; and when he spoke again his voice was quieter and very serious.

"I've missed you, Dinah. Doing this made me feel – well, closer to you, somehow. You're . . . very dear to me, you know."

Uncertain how to respond to this, she stayed silent, looking at the garden he'd made for her – for them all, the other Dinah, the two Franks, and those nameless ones before them.

"We've known each other such a long time," Stephen went on again. "I can remember the first occasion I ever saw you – d'you remember it? At that tea-dance at Lewes when you came with Richard? I think I must have loved you from that very moment, but like a fool I never knew it. Not until – until I realised I'd lost you a second time. It was the day you told Jessie and me that you'd fallen in love with Warwick Enderby and wanted to marry him. D'you remember that, too?"

She shook her head. "I'd rather forget."

"Yes, of course. I'm sorry. I shouldn't have mentioned his name."

"It doesn't matter."

There was another silence between them. The golden sunlight pouring from the west below layers of high, thin cloud bathed the churchyard in its autumn warmth.

"I appreciate it's far too soon to ask," he began again, hesitantly. "But I'm prepared to wait. After twelve years, a few more shouldn't be too hard. You know me, Dinah. You know me better, probably, than I know myself. You know my worth, my prospects, my ambitions, my hopes – everything. If you'll have me, I swear you'll make me the happiest man on earth."

She turned at last to look at him, the slow smile warming her eyes.

"Dearest Stephen, you've always been there, haven't you. Why is it that I've never really noticed until now?"

Between past and future, she reached out her hand to him; and taking it in both his own, he raised it to his lips and kissed it.